The Courage
of a
Butterfly

A personal note from this author to you the reader:

I'm someone who has been to the brink of death and glimpsed into the great beyond. For me, it was a life-changing experience. This book is my story. But before you start reading it, I would like to offer you a thought

My personal belief is that our lives are run by our soul—and, it is done from a higher, unconscious level. I believe there are therefore, no coincidences—

Everything happens for a reason.

With that thought in mind, as you read through this book, ask yourself this question:

Why did my soul place this book into my hands?

There are a couple of pages in the back marked

"NOTES."

Consider using them.

The Courage

of a

Butterfly

by

Edmond E. Frank

Editor: Joyce Mochrie, owner of *One Last Look*
Cover Illustrator: Bobby Daniels Graphics

To the woman herein known as

"Meg"

I loved you then.

I love you now.

I will always love you.

And I believe you loved me the very best you knew how.

For me, our parting was never about love.

True love, once given, can never be taken back.

As often happens when a man meets the Angel of Death,

the dishonesty with which he lives his life vanishes.

If given a reprieve he begins to live his truth.

The consciousness he was then—dies.

For what is death but a change in consciousness?

The constant of the universe is change.

When you do not grow together,

you will always grow apart.

Shakespeare said: "Parting is such sweet sorrow."

Shakespeare lied:

Parting with the one you love is always . . .

fucked up!

On The Road Less Travelled

Ah, "the road less travelled". It's really just the inner journey—the one so few people ever take. You see, being less travelled it is full of potholes, unseen tree roots, and boulders one must get over or around—it's not a road one can take in their limo or even on their all-terrain cycle. Those obstacles, are all composed of the things you have been told about life and believe, but which are not true—lies you cannot see without help.

That help is in knowing life's real truths. Sometimes truth is discovered in your relationship with your significant other, who puts your shit right in your face.

She-eet! That's the real purpose of relationships—love's just the icing. Sad that so few ever partake—most are too busy trying to control one another. Control is *never* love.

Me . . . I got a double whammy of help. Some from my wife, of course. She was very good at rubbing shit. But more so, it came from the Specter of Death. He's the one who showed me what really stunk up my life.

This book, this journey you are about to take, is similar to a book titled ***The Secret*** by Rhonda Byrne. That book gives you an excellent view of life's truth. But there are far more secrets to know. With the Angel of Death offering it all up, my life became ***The Secret*** on steroids. How could it be otherwise?

I've ridden motorcycles most of my life. This book begins in an ICU. That is not the place one would ever want to crash into in life. But it is the place from which I began my journey. Funny thing—it was not my motorcycle that set me on this road less travelled.

Acknowledgments

This book has been a labor of love, on-and-off, for over 25 years. It could be said that it was the school ground for this writer's ability to write. And there have been numerous teachers scattered throughout the various critique groups over the years. It would be great if I could remember and acknowledge them all by name—but I can't.

I will mention the last and most important one: *The Sin City Writers Meet-Up Group.* Many are published and all are excellent writers. They have been the most supportive to me. With the other critique groups, there was always the fact that many of the members were not of this venue: Self-Help, Spirituality, New Age, New Thought. But many of the Sin City group were. Those who weren't were mostly open-minded.

It is not hard to understand that this could be problematic, considering that this venue is about looking at the world from a different perspective than most do. And of course, everyone has an inherent need to be "right." Their whole world would stop spinning were they to see it differently. Therefore, this writer received a lot of flack about the content from some of those other groups. Critiquing is supposed to be about the writing, and that seemed to be a struggle for many. Most liked the story but simply didn't agree with the spiritual which, to this author, is the important part. Without Big D, this story is just a story—everyone has one.

The Sin City Writers Meet-Up Group is run by Toni Pacini. I mention her specifically because she is the driving force behind it. And it has been immensely helpful for me, as has Toni personally. There have also been many beta readers too numerous to try to name.

There is my copy editor and proofreader, Joyce Mochrie, owner of *One Last Look.* She deserves special recognition for the excellence of her work. I thought I'd gone over this writing so thoroughly that it was squeaky clean and was intending to send it to be published. Joyce showed me how untrue that thought was.

And then there is *Bobby Daniels Graphics* who did the cover design. He is a true artist.

Both Bobby's and Joyce's works were very reasonably priced, and I wholeheartedly recommend them to all other authors.

Table of Contents

ABOUT THE AUTHOR

Introduction

Is this book a work of fiction?

> Assuredly! For it is a story that could otherwise never be told.

Is it based on truth?

> Absolutely!

Then are the characters all real people?

> That . . . you must decide for yourself.

Yet, were it so, then all the names would need be changed; the locations, somewhat misplaced; and the people who play a part between these pages might even find themselves playing parts and pieces for others as well. Indeed, should you recognize yourself as one of the characters herein, likely it would not be so.

Or . . . could it be exactly so? This work is based on truth—life's universal truths. If you see yourself herein, it will be because it is the truth of your life also.

It's all about the lessons . . ..
Mostly we ignore them. Some take them to the grave, unacknowledged, unlearned—and unlived. Sometimes it takes the final whispers from Death himself to speak of them in a way we will hear. Only a gifted few then survive long enough to live them.

Redneck Spirituality—Book One

Prologue

Tuesday, October 6th, 1992—1:30 p.m.

"No! Definitely not—not even for that." Doctor Laring's eyes hold a glint of steel, as does his voice. There is no doubting the truth of his next words. "If you do, you might be found dead on the pot. You will stay in bed and use the bedpan."

"How long?" I ask, my voice sounding strangely high and unnatural. "I mean, I don't like this place. It's . . . well . . . look, this place gives me the creeps!"

"Yes, have to admit there is a certain air about these ICUs, Mr. Williams. And if you make it through these next few weeks, we might let you go home. Even so, you'll stay in bed for at least a month. You have a massive pulmonary embolism. That means the major blood vessels from the heart to the lungs are heavily blocked. We have to use clot busting medications and there is a significant danger of bleeding. Also, the fact that not much blood is getting out of the lungs back to your heart causes low blood pressure and makes your heart work harder, increasing the risk of heart failure. Right now, we need to dissolve that blood clot in your leg and just hope no more of it breaks loose and goes to your lungs. You won't survive much more of that."

I swallow, my mouth suddenly dry, as the reality hits. "How will it come?" The words quaver. I pause to clear my throat and take a deep breath before repeating my question—this time, with backbone. "I mean . . . how will it be? You know . . . if I die?"

"Oh, you're not going to die. And if you did, it wouldn't be so bad. There's worse ways to go."

His eyes are avoiding mine and I explode without thinking. "Goddamn you, Doc, don't feed me that fucking horseshit!" Then watch as he snatches up his clipboard and whirls toward the door.

"Wait . . . Doctor Laring!" *God! How it grates to play humble to his arrogance.* "Look, I need to prepare myself. I mean . . . if Death comes . . . if I die? How will it be?"

Now on his way out the door, he pauses and turns back, jaw clenched, hot eyes appraising. "Doc, look, I've got the balls to hear it." Still, he hesitates. "Fuck! Don't you doctors ever have the balls to tell people the truth? What kind of assholes are you?"

In slow-motion deliberateness, he turns to face me directly. "I'm so sick of you redneck Neanderthals! You think you're so tough?" He pauses one long moment, shaking, ducking his head. The hair plugs in his bald spot seem to bristle. "Okay, hotshot, fuck the insurance company and fuck this hospital's policies." He looks up, and something in his eyes gleams almost insanely. "Here it is." The words gush forth, as if some dam inside had been aching to burst. "If another chunk of that clot breaks free—even a small one—it will block the blood supply to your lungs completely. You're almost there now. Most simply lose consciousness and die relatively peacefully, as if in sleep. But you're not a very peaceful person—are you Mr Williams? You'll feel that chunk of curdled blood when it hits. Then as you start to suffocate, and your blood pressure drops, your heart will race. Your lungs will pump, not so much from lack of oxygen—it's not that noticeable when your blood is no longer picking up enough. No, you'll panic. All you bad-asses do." His starched, white smock seems to hiss in deadly punctuation to the words that spill as he stalks back and forth before my bed. "It won't take but a few moments. You'll hemorrhage, and your lungs will fill with blood. First, you'll choke and cough, spraying blood until it covers damn near everything in sight." His right arm, cradling the clipboard, raises upward and outward while the other flails about. "It will last about a minute or two before you pass out from lack of blood pressure. In the end, the blood will merely well out between spasms.

Hemorrhage or asphyxiation—by then, how you die won't really make any difference."

Pausing to look into my face, the anger leaves his eyes. His whole body seems to slump, and in a voice now soft, he continues. "Look, I'm sorry. There's no nice way of telling it. Did you really want to hear it?"

"Yeah," I whisper. "I guess so."

"Hey, just don't move around. Stay in bed and stay calm. You'll beat this." His eyes again are avoiding mine.

"My wife . . . how much of this does Meg know?"

"Well, I spoke to her in the hallway earlier."

"Does she know how serious this is?"

"Look, Mr. Williams, this is the Intensive Care Unit." His shrug seemed to say it all. "Yes, she knows . . . and she's scared, too."

"Did you give her the odds?"

"Yes."

"And?"

"I told your wife that if you got through these first three days, you'd have a fifty-fifty chance."

"So what is it now? The truth, please."

He pauses, his lips pursed, eyes again appraising, and yet, in them I see something that wasn't there before—respect? "Frankly, Mr. Williams, I'm surprised you're still alive."

After he leaves, I lie staring out the window, feeling as if some massive, intangible "something" has changed. It feels like my world has shifted onto its corner, and now everything hangs crooked.

God, this is not some bad movie. This is life in cruel reality, and I am almost out of mine. I remember the ordeal of simply crossing the hundred yards from the car to the hospital. Three times I had to stop, out of breath and light-headed, so weak I could barely stay erect. Clinging desperately, I'd leaned on Meg. Now, thinking about it, there is a numbness, as if I've taken a blow too hard or painful to feel. I might be dead tomorrow. Hell, I might be dead ten minutes from now! Like an all-pervasive dye of unknown color, Death now stains my every sense.

For a time, the questions tumble over one another, imploring to be asked; and asked, the answers burn in the agony of an unfamiliar honesty. Picturing the gravesite, my mind's eye focuses on who will be there to drop the flowers before the dirt clods fall.

My wife and son, of course, but who else? Maybe a half dozen friends—no, wait! Those are more like acquaintances, fellow mechanics. Will any of them even take a day off from work? Would I, for them? I sigh. Nah, most every "friend" in my life is really a friend of Meg's. And yes, a few of them will come, but not for me. Will anyone be there for me, just because they care?

But what about family? Of the hundred or so aunts, uncles, and cousins, I am not sure any will bother making the trip from Utah here to Las Vegas. For a few, the casinos might hold a little attraction, but not openly. Most are staunch Mormons. And me? Well, the doctrines of the church were something I just never swallowed.

Besides, I was adopted. For many, that makes a difference. My "real" parents? She is dead. And he? While he lives only fifty miles away, he has never visited me, nor did he ask me to come the two times I visited him.

Of my adoptive parents? Hell, I'm not sure. Mother has seldom felt well enough for long trips; they've only come visiting but three times over the past twenty-plus years. Will she feel the same about attending my funeral? With a sigh, I realized that as such happenings go, mine is shaping up to be a very minor event.

Fuck them! I don't want anyone looking at my dead corpse anyway. Will they have to sew my lips together just to keep my mouth closed like they did my brother Mike? No! I want to be cremated. That part now settled in my mind; I move on.

So, okay, I haven't accomplished much. I can point to no single "noteworthy" thing about my whole damned forty-five years of living. But what about the people? There must be some whose lives I've affected—changed for the better. If not, then of what use has my life been? What legacy am I leaving?

Goddamn! Every molecule of my being aches to say it all isn't so. My frantic mind now searches the faces in my life for someone—anyone—to whom I can picture and say, "See! See! This person likes and respects, even values me." But in vain, no faces are forthcoming. My beautiful wife's face is not even there, nor even is my own.

Meg! Oh God! Where are you, Meg? Somehow, I expected you'd return after Doctor Laring left. Why aren't you here with me now? How does your massage business mean more to you than me? And you said you had housework. Housework? Is any of that worth missing what little life may be left to me now? I cannot tell you the truth of my fear; you would never respect such weakness in me, yet you know. I know you know the score. I just want to hold you and tell you I love you—now, while I still can! Yet, I know that what it is within you that I most ache to touch is no longer there for me. It looks like I'm dying, and no one cares to see me go.

With tears streaking my face, melting the starched linen of my pillow, I question the God in whom I have long since stopped believing. *Is this it? Is my life all over? God! Please, tell me: what was it all about?* I wait, almost expecting an answer. None comes. *Goddamn You . . . You*—I raise my fists—*You suck!*

Lying with my back to the room, I look out toward the western mountains of Las Vegas. The noises of the hospital, and the traffic around it, suddenly grow non-existent to my senses. In the blur of that silence, I watch the gold of the sun turn amber, then kiss the clouds with ruby just before it fades softly into violet darkness. For the first time in my life, I live a sunset—truly experience it—and somehow know in my heart, I likely will never live it again.

Wednesday, October 7th, 1992—1:15 a.m.

An incessant buzzing intrudes, drawing me from the comfort of my slumber. Then the voice on the speaker in the darkened hallway snaps my eyes wide.

"Code blue! Code blue, ICU 304!"

There comes a rushing of feet and a rattle of equipment. Terse mumbles, words I cannot quite hear, issue from the room next door. Then one voice takes over.

"Charging!"

"Clear!" sings out a second.

Ka-thunk!

"Again! Charging!"

"Clear!"

Ka-thunk!

"Charging! No, wait! Good work, people, we've got him back!"

I stand witness to this, the second such struggle since coming to this ICU two days ago. The first had not fared so well. Perhaps it is in empathy that I feel a growing tightness in my own chest? *No, God no!* It grows tighter! There is no relief.

Like the wringing of a wet towel, all strength seems to drip from me, and with it, I feel something more. It's been here since I first arrived—this presence. So strong is it now, it seems somehow tangible. I'd always laughed when people talked about the Specter of Death, about ghosts and such. I'm not laughing now. I can fairly smell his breath on the antiseptic air, hear his voice in the unsteady beeping of the monitor, see his grin, laughing at me in the confused hash of squiggles across its face. Yes, I know Death's presence hovers near, and he now seems very real.

Whoa! Is it about having accepted him as fact, that I can now see a swirling in the blackness of the night? *Oh God, no!* From somewhere close by, another alarm is buzzing—mine! *Can't they hear it? Why don't they come?* The fist in my chest now clutches hard and steely. I gasp in panic, but somehow the scream refuses to come.

"Just relax. There is nothing to fear. It will all be over before they can respond." Dry and hollow, the voice seems to reverberate as if from the bottom of a 55-gallon drum. Somehow, this answer to the panicky questions on my mind comes without surprise.

"But why?" I whisper. "They . . . next door. Why don't they come?"

"Oh, they will come, and in good time." The voice is calm, so calm, I am incensed by its disinterest. "But it is always so with blood clots like yours. There is nothing they can do but watch and record your passing, and that is always unpleasantly the same. For now, they are busy with one who will live."

"But . . . it's not my—"

"Time? Time now for you doesn't matter. Your time is now mine!"

"Fuck! Who . . . are . . . you?" I gasp, though I know the answer.

"Yes, I am who you think me to be. I'm the angel some call Death"—the voice is calm, and in some surreal way, I find myself increasingly incensed by the don't-give-a-shit tone of it—"and I've come for you."

"Wait! My life's not finished." My whisper is labored; my mouth seems filled with cotton. "Goddammit! Huuumpt-uhhh . . . n-not yet."

"Make it easier on yourself. Just think what you want to say. I will hear you."

Please, Mr. Death. I can't die yet—I won't! I haven't done hardly any of what I wanted to do.

"You have had 45 years. What have you been doing?"

Oh God, Mr. Death. "Hhuh-aaargh!" Again, my involuntary gasp of agony breaks my concentration and the pressure suddenly lightens, almost as if he now has an interest in what I am saying. Encouraged, my thoughts tumble forth. *I've thought about it all day and see it so clearly now: how I've spent my time doing what others expected of me—my parents, my bosses, my wife. But I've done so little of what I truly wanted. My whole life has been wasted in pretending to be who they wanted me to be. You can't take me like this—this fake liar—this person I don't want to be!*

"Why should I give you more time? What are you willing to do for it?"

Anything! Light-headed, clinging to consciousness, I see a blackness swirling around the monitor. The red warning light flickers and becomes two—two glowing eyes now sunk deeply in a skull of ivory. For a long moment, they seem as though they are appraising me.

"Would you learn how to administer the sacrament—but honestly this time?"

What? My mind goes back to my Aaronic priesthood days of blessing and distributing the sacrament to the members of my church, and to the guilt of my secret unworthiness.

"No, no!" the specter chides, chuckling. "Don't get your hemorrhoids in a pucker. You won't have to rejoin the Mormon—or any other—religion. This sacrament is the best and easiest of what I require. In fact, just put it out of your mind. Few who have made me this bargain have ever gotten that far, but you. . . ." The glow in his eye sockets seems suddenly to have warmed. "You don't remember it, but you came to me and made this bargain before you were ever born."

What . . . bargain?

"All you needed to do was ask again and then seal our agreement consciously. I'll accept your refusal to go as being asked." His gaze seems to sharpen like two lasers. "Are you now willing to make it conscious?"

Yes, yes. I'll do it—and anything else you ask. Anything!

"Anything? It may be harder than you think." The calmness of his voice is maddening.

Yes, anything.

"Would you live with courage, stepping through each of the many fears you will face?"

Yes, yes. I will!

"Would you have the courage to follow the joys of your heart—no matter the costs?"

Yes! Absolutely.

"Would you have the courage to take full responsibility for your life, even though it means looking at things about you that you've never yet had the courage to see?"

Yes. Yes, I will!

"Will you follow your destiny with courage and never give up— no matter what?"

Yes, yes!

"Careful now! You don't even know what all this is that I ask." His ivory skull unhinges into a gaping grin. "It is, indeed, harder than it sounds. Have you not heard me say the word 'courage' multiple times? The moment you refuse to face life with honesty and courage, **I will come for you!**" The lights in his eye sockets glow in deadly earnest, then change to a flicker, as if in humor with his next words. "And do yourself a favor and lose this whole 'yes man' attitude. If you say it, say it with intention, not fear."

I'll learn—and I will have the honesty and courage. I say it and am surprised to note the honest intention now behind my words.

"How so? Ha . . ." The flicker is now accompanied by an outright chuckle. "Have you not always regarded yourself a coward?"

The shame burns such that I have no reply.

"I know far more of you than even you can know." His voice is devoid of judgment, almost kindly, as he continues. "I ask far more of you than you can now conceive."

But why? What's in it for you?

"Let's just say this collecting of souls can be a wearing business. Mostly, I'm just a shuttle driver picking up those who have quit on life. I'm so overdue for that special one who requests the limo—and is willing to pay the price."

That's me? Suddenly, I am struck by the absurdity of this conversation. This is the Angel of Death, for Christ's sake! And yet, we are conversing calmly, and I realize I am no longer afraid of him.

"We'll see." He tips his head back and chuckles with satisfaction. "You and I are old friends, and you need not fear me— **ever.**" I find myself suddenly eye-to-eye with the flames within his empty eye sockets. ". . . So long as you keep our bargain."

The price—you said I don't understand it?

"As I said, it's honesty and courage. You don't know it, such as I ask, because you have never experienced it. I call it 'the courage of a butterfly.'"

But you know my secret . . . the shameful truth about me.

"Yes, and it is not as it would seem." I can only gape, not quite comprehending. The grin seems to widen. "Look, when you refused to go, you, in essence, ordered the limo. Only the fare remains to be paid. I cannot give you the courage, but I will give you some time—**if** you will take it and **if** you will learn to live as I ask."

Well . . . uh . . . okay, but how will I know exactly when and what you are asking of me? And "courage of a butterfly" . . . what's that?

"I will be there to tell you. You need only listen for me. And butterflies? Ah, yes, butterflies!" The glowing depths of his sockets regard me somewhat more lightly, though his fist still clutches with a dizzying tightness. "Truth is, evolving in life is the most frightful of all things, even more so than evolving into Death." His voice is fading as I slip into unconsciousness. Do I hear him correctly? "It's a dangerous thing to have the courage of a butterfly, to become more than others are willing to be. Their jealousy often comes with nails and crosses—even stakes and fire."

* * *

"I don't care how well it seems to be working! Get it out of here and check it thoroughly! The readings it was displaying were impossible!"

Squinting in the light, I open my eyes to the parting backs of the charge nurse and a technician rolling some equipment on a tray.

"Mr. Williams, how are you feeling?" The nurse at my side flashes me a sunshine smile.

I take a moment, even pinch myself, then reply; my voice somehow grates like dry gravel. "Okay, I guess. What's going on?"

"Sorry to wake you, but your monitor was acting up and we had to change it." Quickly, she strips the pickups from my chest and side and applies the round, sticky stubs of new ones, then expertly snaps the new wires back on. "There now, get some more sleep. Do you need a pill?

* * *

The sun rises for me the next morning, and for many after that. I do not see Death for nearly half a year, yet I do hear his counsel. Often it comes with a whisper of air where there is no earthly breeze. Always, always, I follow his direction. Always, that is, until now. Now I face the issue of money—and the rage of my wife, Meg, at my spending it.

"No! You're not going to any silly, goddamn, five-hundred-dollar seminar! It's bad enough that you have to act so crazy in front of my friends—skydiving at your age. Jesus Christ!"

"Meg . . ."

"No, I said! Thas's it! I so sick of you sitting around like zombie meditating, and your weird-assed frenz, and you stupeed self-help books and tapes. Now is seminars?" Her Korean accent is becoming more noticeable in the fervor of her now-broken English. "No! You go—I divorce you!"

I can only look, and as my heart reaches for hers in the aching cold of the abyss, my courage lags and I make silent excuses: *Perhaps just this one time, just this one seminar. They have it monthly. I'll find some way to do it next month.* Lying beside her, sleep is a long time coming.

* * *

I awake once more to those baleful glows and the sharp tug of the Angel's fist, once again within my chest.

"Mr. Death . . . no, wait!" I bolt upright, a cold sheen of sweat now flushing my body. "Haven't I done all that you asked?"

"Yes, all but this last thing. Is your life really held so cheaply?"

"Wait! Please, just a minute!" The sweat now streams into my eyes, yet the sting of it is inconsequential with the tightening of his grip. "Look, it's not about the money—"

"Yes, I know. It is the price." The glowering red within his bony sockets are only inches from my eyes. "Our agreement remains—honesty and courage, remember? Still, you do not choose to even learn to understand it. Understood or not, it is the price of your life." The glow now sharpens to scarlet pinpoints. "And you have refused to pay."

"I'll pay it, Mr. Death. Please don't kill me. Whatever it is, I'll pay!"

"Kill you? No. You've got it all wrong. I only collect those who consciously or unconsciously choose to die."

"B-but I'm not choosing to die!"

"You don't think so?" His grin now seems to mock me. "You broke our agreement. I'd say that constitutes a choice."

"Please, Mr. Death, I only thought to put it off for a month. I had every intention. . . ."

"Ah, so you did." He pauses one ominous moment, regarding me closely. "Maybe this will stand to point out just how seriously you need to take our agreement." My breath hisses with an unvoiced shriek as his fist clutches in sudden, fiery agony, then releases. "There is no more of this wiggle room." Abruptly, his gaze changes, seeming somehow to soften. "And incidentally, at ease with the 'Mr. Death' shit.

I am not your master. Believe it or not, I am your greatest advocate—always have been—and I like to be called 'Big D.'"

With that, the blackness of the night returns. All that remains of him is a tight reminder in my chest. As if to further prove his point, the next day, the seminar is gifted to me by a total stranger, a lady who'd bought the ticket but whose husband refused to go.

Still, when Meg hears of it, her reply is terse. "Free? I don't care if they're paying *you*. If you go, I won't be here when you get back!"

Meg does not know about Big D. Somehow, it's clear that there will never be a right time to tell her, nor do I tell her just yet that I am attending the seminar. Instead, I change the subject.

"Meg, I saw Dr. Laring today. It's not as bad, but the clot has come back."

"Course it's back, you silly shit! What'd you expect? They told you never to stop taking the blood thinners." Her glare is cold, as is the surreal implication of her words.

"He wanted me back in the hospital—"

"Now what are we going to do? You lost our insurance when you insisted on changing jobs. Jesus! This will wipe us out."

"It's okay, Meg. I refused—said I'd take it easy a while and get back on my Coumadin. He didn't like it, but then, with no insurance? Well, he took my seventy-five dollars and prescribed the blood thinners."

* * *

The seminar proves to be a turning point. With it, I learn that there are some rules to life, some sort of higher sense to it all. These rules—these "Spiritual Laws"—spell out what is true about life. They remind me of the geodes I once dug from the unremarkable desert clay of a nowhere mountain pass called Dugway, Utah. Simple, veined balls of ugly, gray rock, surprisingly light, yet when opened, they were lined with crystalline magnificence.

And I now see the truth about the many lies we are all taught and everyone takes for granted. And I especially become uncomfortably aware of what our real responsibilities are in life. Pinned like a bug by a hundred pairs of eyes, none so intense as the seminar leader's now facing me down, I provide this particular lesson for the whole seminar.

"Jeff, this is *your* life you are living." He pauses, eyeing me closely. "Well, isn't it?"

"Yes, but they. . . ." I am unwilling to let go of what the now-forgotten thing was *they* were doing to me.

"Are their actions actually physically harmful to you?" His eyes now hold steady, and I find I cannot meet his gaze.

"No, but—"

"Then get this, Jeff." My eyes now involuntarily rise to meet his. "People do what people do. That is about them, not you. Without a physical threat, your only responsibility—your ability to respond—lies in how you *choose* to feel about it." My jaw drops, silently aghast, during the long pause before his last words. "Don't you think you owe it to yourself to *choose* better?"

The lesson about my true responsibilities was harsh. It needed to be for me to stop employing that lie called blame, to cover my own bad choice of feelings. Did the others in that seminar learn from my embarrassing example? I hope so. To that point, I couldn't say my life ever made much difference to anyone. Maybe now it has.

* * *

Over the months, I learn and grow. With Big D's guidance, I dig through the clay of humanity's ancient wisdom and listen to the others, whom I see covered in its dust. One by one, I discover more of those geodes of truth for myself. Funny how most were so simple and always right there, obvious to anyone looking. I see them now and puff out my chest, believing I am immersed in true wisdom. I do not know of the times to come when Big D will place me in the center, alone, but for his light to guide and forbid me to break the geode of my truth. I do not yet see that to which I purposefully have kept myself blind.

Saturday April 9th, 1994—1:30 a.m.

Then, unexpectedly, comes again the ruby gaze of Big D into my night, and his fist once more clutches the insides of my chest. His voice, when he speaks, is insistent, holding the same cutting timbre of my old chainsaw.

"Jeff! You continue to resist the price. Indeed, you remain oblivious to it."

I bolt upright beside my slumbering wife, clutching, choking my body, again ashine in a sweaty chill, and put forth a plea. "Big D! No, wait. Whatever it is, I don't know. Please! Just tell me."

His poised sickle is slowly lowered, and I hear a soft clank as it is leaned against the wall. His grip, too, seems to relax as he settles on the edge of the bed.

"Yes, Jeff. Now is a good time to ask. You have followed my direction, but you have never asked my teaching. This that you must now face, you can never see without it."

Feeling impending doom, I ask, "What? What must I see?"

"Your wife, Jeff." The words hang, deafening in a silence broken only by her gentle snores. He continues, the timbre of his voice now at a low idle. "It's about Meg, about who she is."

"Oh Big D, I know. I've tried to change her . . . tried to make her be who I needed. But I've learned from the Spiritual Laws that I've no right to try to change anyone but myself. It hasn't been easy to change me to accept her, to love her exactly as she is. Yes, I still love her, but somehow, it's not like it used to be. When I look at her now, I no longer feel that same joy, no longer uplifted. Knowing she doesn't feel the same, there is only a longing."

"Yes, and you've loved her well. In fact, that is why I've come—and why the sickle."

"The sickle, Big D?"

"Relax, Jeff, you're safe . . . for now. What with all the time we've spent together, I know you've come to see me as a friend—and I am. That's why the sickle. It's just a prop, but a prop meant to impress upon you the seriousness of this next step."

"What do you mean?"

"I mean, in staying with Meg, are you loving you? Are you following your joy?" His gaze now bores into me as he adds, "That is part of our bargain, you know?"

"I love her! How can I not be following my joy?"

"Jeff! To bridge such an abyss between two hearts always takes the efforts of both. You are stuck at the edge, reaching. Can your joy be found in a heart that is not reaching back? And your destiny, can you truly say you are moving toward it? Do you see how you are again about to break our agreement?"

"Yes . . . but God, Big D! Not my Meg! Oh, how did it all get so fucked up?"

"Fucked up? Yes. It is so, if you insist." His grin gapes luminous in the darkness close before me. I notice his front tooth is chipped very slightly, exactly like my own. "Perhaps it is time you told me how you got so 'fucked up.'"

"What? If I knew that, don't you think I would change it, Big D? Isn't that what I've been trying to do these past eighteen months since we met?"

"Change **it**? S'not what it's about. Try . . . change **you**! This is why you must now tell your story. Write it down. All of it."

"Aw c'mon, Big D! I will because you demand it, but we both know a story is just a story. Everyone's got one. Hell, I've told mine in a thousand ways to as many people over the years. Was a time when no one could talk to me without me boring them with a piece of it. I've no great need to tell it to anyone. And I'm clear that you already know all there is to know about me."

"It's true, you've no need to tell it to others—most of it. Then there was your birth mother and the orphanage she dumped you into . . . and your adoptive mother and the steps of Bingham Canyon . . . and your don't-take-no-shit-offa-nobody adoptive father. . . ." His words trail off. "You've never told a soul about any of **that**, have you?"

"Who would I tell—and why?"

"S'not about **who**." Big D's eyes flicker with his chuckle. "Not even so much about the **why**. Mostly, it's about the journey. You remember your scouting days—about reading maps? Besides the map, all you needed was a compass and two pieces of information." His countenance seems somehow to sharpen with his tone. "What were they?"

"Well, you needed to know where you were and where you wanted to be."

"That's right, Jeff. Now, it's clear you know the 'who' you want to be. But the 'who' you are right now? How did you just describe that person?"

"Well, I . . . uh. . . ."

"Yeah, that's right. That person is some nebulous persona called—how was that again—'fucked up,' did you say?"

"Yeah, I see your point."

"Look, Jeff, you know the 'who' you want to be and the 'who' you started out as. You are going to take a journey. Retrace your steps, and I'll be your compass."

"But . . ."

"As for Meg—" His grip in my chest tightens slightly. "Are you saying you have no more need to live?"

My whispered reply is a long time coming. "But my Meg, Big D." I feel her soft flesh against my leg where she slumbers next to me.

"I don't know if I can live"—his grin is now blurred—"without my Meg."

"Yes. That's been the real issue for some time now, hasn't it?" I feel his fist release the last of its grip and pause just a moment to softly stroke my chin. "Look, you've come far in your understanding of life since our meeting in that hospital. Then was when you first got a look at how you'd given up on life. Don't give up now, Jeff." He pauses to let it sink in. "Look, remember the Spiritual *Law of Balance?*"

"Yes: *'For every sorrow there exists an equal potential for joy: the universe always balances.'* "

"Could it also be said, *'The greater the wounding, the more magnificent can be the healing.'* Like every adult alive, your wounding began in the earliest mists of your memory. It did not begin with Meg. Your healing cries for one last telling of your story, Jeff. Write it down, and we'll talk."

"But Meg . . ."

"Of Meg?" He cocks his head slightly down and to the side. The ruby glow in his eye sockets focuses up, piercingly—like a laser. "You know what you must do."

"But why, why must it be this way?"

"Look, Jeff, look at how you feel about her."

"She is the love of my life."

"True, but you know that in her mind, you are 'fucked up—but she is okay.' Aren't those her sentiments every time you go to the marriage counseling sessions . . . alone? Could that ever be so if you were the love of hers?"

"No, but—"

"All this time, you've had her in your life to love, while lying to yourself that she feels the same love for you? Now you are aware that living this lie—that not living the truth—is the same as giving up on life."

"Well . . . yeah, I guess so."

"Nearly killed you, didn't it? And it may yet, considering that to continue it breaks our agreement."

"But—"

"Ut-tut-tut . . . no more buts! 'Buts' are the same as wiggle room, and you have no more left, y'know." He shakes his head, and I feel something emanating from him. *Disgust?* "Before you make your decision to die for Meg, consider: What is it about for her—the truth?"

"She lives in fear." I grit my teeth, loath to say it, but continue. "I am her security."

"Yes, Jeff, you are the person who enables her to live in that fear, but you know the truth about security."

"Yes." I shake my head sadly. "It is a lie—there is no security in life."

"Ah, so you both have been living a lie." Big D fixes me in the rabid, red flare of his sight, and his jaw unhinges into a wolfish grin. "You both have given up on life? Can you ever be okay with her paying the price?"

"Price? What price?" Even I can hear the panic in my voice, for I know about that price without asking.

"You only know part of her price, Jeff—the part that involves the stroke that may soon kill her." He shakes his head again, and this time the feeling he emits is sadness. "You do not know of the love she may never have the opportunity to feel for someone else—all because you kept her prisoner to her fear."

My mouth is open but nothing comes out. He continues. "Your choice now is will you add your death—the death of her security—to her fears, or will you give her the opportunity to step past her fears?" He chuckles, knowing my answer, then fades into a smoky swirl. Only his words remain, reverberating clearly in that bottom-of-the-barrel tone of his. "Write the book, Jeff. Discover the truth of who you are."

Adults do what adults do . . .
As small children, we often think it is all about us and interpret those events as messages. If we should find ourselves being passed around from one adult to another, and no one seems to want us, we usually decide there must be something wrong with us—that we aren't *good* enough or *worthy* enough. For if we were, wouldn't we be loved, wouldn't we be wanted? The truth is, there's nothing wrong with the child! It is simply that some adults are unwilling to love. Small children have perfect love. They are perfect. God makes them that way, every time! But who they have learned to be by the time they are an adult—yeah, that can be pretty fucked up.

Redneck Spirituality—Book One

Chapter One

Is War Ever Really About the Spoils?

There is nothing so giving, so honest, so loving as the heart of a small child. The hearts of one's parents when at war, however, now that is where love often gets squirrely. Although my innocence is long gone, my memories of it are still surprisingly clear, some few even back to my second and third years of life. They remain stuck like blobs of glue to the fabric of my life.

I was too young to remember much about Ogden, Utah, just that there were lots of snails in the garden—great fun to play with, and tasty, too. But then there were the nights with Mommy ranting at Daddy. I don't remember so much about what, just something about money and about how car parts were not edible. And then there was screaming about his bar tabs and her baby food.

Oh, I didn't really understand it, except for the part about the baby food. From the way they both looked at me then, I knew who was to blame. My three-year-old brain could conceive of no other reason why Mommy took my half brother, Mikey, and left.

Daddy won their war and received the only spoils, namely me—and a lot of hard feelings. He kept the feelings and sent me to live with his mother, Granny Everts.

There's not much in my memory about her, but what there is has also stuck, and is loving. There is her big, round softness hugging me, accompanied by the aroma of flour and baking bread, and her song: "Come, come ye Saints, no toil or labor fear. . . ." Her house was dark and cool, with lots of frilly drapes and dangles on the lampshades. My time with her was short-lived.

Mommy only visited once. It caused a flurry of concern among the uncles and aunts for they, too, turned out for the occasion. I remember it because the words that flew were uncommonly harsh. And they were all about me, about who would keep me—once again, my fault.

Clearly, they didn't trust Mommy, but they must have felt safe letting her take me for a walk. After all, she agreed to leave her purse right there on the dining room table. It must have surprised them all when she swooped me up, sprinted down the street to her car, piled in, and screeched madly away.

I cried. Not because I was afraid or didn't want to go with her, but because in the excitement, I had lost my shoe. I didn't have much, and that shoe was important to me.

Mommy took me to San Francisco where she lived with her friend Lolly, Lolly's husband, Bart, and my big brother, Mikey. He was almost six—two years and eight months older. His father had apparently gone to war and never returned. True story? I was never sure, but this was the one Mikey most often went with. And no one questioned whatever version he told—not more than once.

Bart cursed and hollered at Mikey and me, a lot. When Mommy wasn't around, he slapped us around some, too. I guess he just didn't know that it doesn't pay to piss-off some little kids. Whenever I went into the bathroom to pee, I'd take great pleasure in hosing down the wall. Bart hated it when we missed the toilet.

I was right in the middle of my revenge one day, and really enjoying it, when Mommy opened the door and caught me—sort of wet-handed.

"Jeffy! What are you doing?"

"Oops, I missed!" My reply was accompanied by an embarrassed shrug. Not really a lie; still, at that young age, I thought there was wisdom in such an answer. The next day, Mommy took me to a doctor, who told her how shortening my barrel would improve my aim. He circumcised me. It was a hell of a lesson, but it did make a straight shooter out of me.

Bart didn't seem to like little boys. And even though I no longer hosed down the bathroom walls, his dislike only grew stronger, especially with respect to Mikey. Eventually, Mommy noticed the evidence of Bart's activities. "Where did they get these bruises? What do you mean 'discipline?' How dare you beat my kids!"

A half blink later found us living in our own small studio apartment. It perched on a steep hill and had one of those bay windows so typical of San Francisco, which seemed to hang right over the street. I can remember kneeling for hours on that window seat, watching passersby and waiting for her to come home. Mommy worked days as a waitress and entertained at night—intensively.

Yes, those nights. . . . Although only three, I can remember those nights. Lying with Mikey on our mattress, watching from across the room, I would ask him the questions troubling me.

"Who is that man?"

"Shh . . . he's just one of Mommy's friends."

"But why is she making them noises? Is he hurting Mommy?"

"No . . . shush . . . that's just how grown-ups play. Go to sleep."

"But I don't like it! Make him go away . . . please, Mikey!"

"Shh . . . go to sleep, Jeffy. He'll be gone soon."

Sometimes her boyfriends had their own objections with me. "What about your kids? I don't feel right about them watching."

Mommy's answers were always the same: "Oh, they're just babies. . . . Don't pay them any mind."

* * *

I didn't know if she was doing what she had to do, or just what she wanted. Didn't matter. In the end, it became clear. All Mommy's troubles were because of us. Had to be that we were in her way—Mikey and me.

We soon found ourselves living at a place called Sunny Hills. Situated north of San Francisco near the town of San Anselmo, it was nestled within a little, green valley surrounded by rolling hills covered with oak and eucalyptus forests—a rather pretty setting for such an ugly orphan home.

~ *In the Present with Big D* ~

"Well said!"

Sitting here before the glare of my computer screen, I hear Big D's applause, like an ivory wind chime on a playful breeze. He has come to me often, though not always does he bother to materialize. This time he does. The smoky blackness of his robe hangs in the air beside my chair. He continues. "Jeff, it's been less than three years since our agreement in the hospital. You've learned a lot. You have the knowledge, but you don't yet 'know.'"

Know? "Know what?"

"The Spiritual Laws governing Life, Jeff. You've learned them. Now with the writing of your story, it's time to take that learning to a higher level. Remember our contract?" He chuckles, as if to some private joke, then continues. "Courage and honesty on your part, a little more time and help on mine?"

"Yes."

"We've had that contract much longer than you've been alive, y'know."

"Yeah, you're talking about me ordering the limo, right?"

"Just hang with me here; let's start at the beginning. What is the first and foremost law?"

"*'I am the creator.'*"

"Good, Jeff! What does it mean?"

"It means that *there is nothing in my life that I do not bear a direct responsibility for it being there.*"

"Then how did you, as a child, create adults who didn't want you, and some who even abused you?"

"Well, it's generally accepted that children are the only true victims in life—that with adults, there are never victims, only volunteers."

"True about the adults, not so with a child, Jeff. The law is always the law, remember?"

"Yes, but—"

"And the *Law of the Creator* is primal to them all." He stops for a moment, and the glow emanating from his eye sockets seems to sharpen. "Look, go back to what it means. How did you say that again?"

"*There is nothing in my life that I do not bear a direct responsibility for it being there.*"

"Good, and the key word there is—"

"Look, Big D." I take a deep breath, hold it for a moment, then exhale with a reluctant admission. "I'm confused."

Whack! I feel the sharp crack of his bony knuckles against my forehead. "Ow! Damn, take it easy."

"The key word, Jeff, is 'responsibility'—the ability to respond, something you seem a little short on just now, what with you getting all hung up over 'innocent' little children." With a snort of impatience, he seems to settle and his next words come in a more even tone. "Truth is, your soul has so much more intelligence than this consciousness you know here in life can ever conceive. Yet, even your soul does not really 'know' until you have experienced." He stops to regard me, his gaze now laser bright. "The question remains: How can children be treated so shabbily by adults—and still not be victims?"

"I . . . uhhh . . ."

"Think, Jeff! If you had ultimate intelligence, and you were coming into this world for the purpose of evolving yourself, what would you do?"

"Uh . . . geez, I'm drawing a blank here. Can you help me out without cracking open my skull?"

"Aaargh." His exasperation is clear and I involuntarily duck. "Look, Jeff. Reflecting back at this chapter—and knowing what will be in the ones to come—sure shapes up for one fucked-over little kid. But what was it like being that child back then?"

"Well, it was just life. I took it in stride."

"Good, and I expect you to muster up a little of that now." The glow in his eye sockets holds me and I feel the burn. "Do you remember the *Law of Learning*?"

"Yeah, sure." My face aflame with scarlet humiliation, I continue. "*'Everyone in our lives bears us a gift of learning.'* But I don't see what this has to do—"

"Perhaps it would be easier if you were to couple it with another closely related law which says: *'Everyone participating in our lives is there by prior agreement.'* "

"Wow! Holy shit, it's just like that agreement you and I made in the pre-existence. Why wouldn't we make those kinds of agreements with others before we are born—only makes sense to help one another get our needs met in our personal evolution."

"Exactly! It is exactly so." Again that private chuckle. "But only the more courageous make arrangements with me—as you did."

"Why do you say *more courageous*? I don't see myself as courageous."

"Having courage requires first having fear. You were taught to see yourself as responsible for other people's feelings at a very early age, in particular, for what your parents didn't like—the very people from whom you loved and needed support. That is a scary thing. Walking through your fears is what courage is all about. Why is it so hard to see that you did that very well?"

"Yeah, I suppose." I shrug. "But why does it take courage to make arrangements with you in the pre-existence?"

"C'mon, Jeff, I **am** the Angel of Death, y'know. It's easy to blow right on by those gifts—those opportunities—others are offering you to look at about yourself." His grin seems to widen. "But making that agreement with me requires one to make the same promises you have made. You don't have the freedom to ignore what you will see about yourself—things that will require you to change your whole life." The glow in his empty eye sockets seems to gush with, what? Tears of happiness?

Tears. What does it mean? "Uh . . . I'm not following. And please, just explain without the knuckles this time." I watch closely, ready to duck out of the way.

"The courage of a butterfly—the courage to change—is something that with mankind is most often avoided; not so for butterflies. For you back then as a child, life was just life, and you faced yours with courage. A butterfly faces with eager anticipation, evolving as a chrysalis from a pupa to a butterfly." He pauses, as if in deep reflection, then the glow in his eye sockets twinkle and he continues.

"It's too bad that adults have such a need to teach children that all change is fearful, that changing—evolving like a chrysalis in the cocoon of life—holds the greatest of terrors. It is true, while your souls can have as many reincarnations as needed to evolve, few have the courage. They focus only on the fearful, harsh experiences, never realizing their necessity."

"Necessity?"

"Yes, Jeff, necessity. You can never truly *know* the positive, loving experiences without a comparison. You, of all people, don't see that?"

"Uhhh . . . yeah." I duck my head in guilty embarrassment. "Just never thought about it that way."

"Very few adults do. Most just take the shuttle bus and head for their next life. After enough tries, some will eventually go for the limo ride—those who have stopped *trying* and have the courage to *do*." His gaze now flickers with laughter. "You are the ones who begin choosing to love instead of fear. You are the ones who, in the pre-existence, book a ride with the limo driver. And I much prefer to drive the limo than that damned shuttle bus."

"I'm beginning to feel really happy to oblige you—but just not yet."

"Then meanwhile, be happy that you were such a fucked-over little kid." His chuckles erupt from the bottom of that barrel. "Children have no fear. Until they are contaminated by that of the adults, their lives are filled with wonder." But the truth is that without knowing fear, there is no appreciating the wonder of this gift of life, nor the glory of courage, for there can be no choice made to love. Fear, too, is a necessity. . . ."

Little children are immortal until they discover death. With the knowledge of their mortality comes fear. Life becomes a thing defended as they begin the process of becoming adults. The question then is: What do adults become when they rediscover the fearlessness of their innocence, see how it is still there inside them, and use it to recapture the wonder of life? Do they then become heroes? Or something more?

Redneck Spirituality—Book One

Chapter Two

Who Mourns the Death of an Orphan?

The year was 1950 and the war with Japan, a thing of the past. Many of our country's young men never returned to their sweethearts, and those who did were working them overtime. Possibly that was the reason for the several "single-parent orphans" at the Sunny Hills Orphanage, Mikey and me included. Existing in a space of semi-abandonment, we didn't even rank as real orphans. The others could look forward to being adopted.

The one who named it had a truly sick sense of humor. Sunny Hills was anything but sunny, at least to me. Never was there a kind hand running fingers through my hair, a soft word whispered in my ear, or a loving lap on which to sit. Instead there were cold, distant adults, sharp words, and rigid rules—and lines: children in line, waiting for hand inspections before meals, tables in line, and later, our bunks in line. Our days, our very lives, were lined up on schedules. I became just one in the line.

It being a Presbyterian orphanage and farm, we were constantly being reminded of our debt to God. In fact, all sustenance—or punishment—was dispensed in His name. I did not know what to make of this person called "God," but one thing seemed sure: He certainly didn't care much for orphans.

They kept Mikey and me apart, allowing only half hour weekly visits. But then, Mikey lived in the dorm with the older boys, and they didn't play with the *sissies* in the nursery. I suppose Mikey felt a need to fit in. The weekly visits quickly became monthly, then only as required when Mommy came to visit.

It was the first time I was ever completely alone, separated from everyone I loved. There were bad dreams, and I would wake up screaming. Too often, I suppose, because the people in charge didn't take to my waking the other children, a problem easily solved with socks. The orphanage allowed us only two pairs of socks. The pair I wasn't wearing was washed once a week. By then, they were hard with dried sweat and grit. Mine certainly was that night when the first nightmare happened.

A hand reached out of the night, pinning me to the dorm bunk. In the next instant, another stuffed my mouth with stinking socks. Then came a wide, leather strap cinched tightly over my heaving chest and another over flailing legs. They left me then, in the very darkest of my night—left me in silent, strangled struggle, left me to the *real* nightmare that was Sunny Hills. They left me to the nightmare that was my life. Me, the innocent weapon of war in an adult world of selfish drama; me, in my own dark drama, crying for that mother's self-centered love— now no longer crying, but only trying to stay alive, lying there with a snot-stuffed nose and tear-streaked face, gasping for air around the stinking, gritty lessons of my life. It was then I learned the truth behind one of the great lies of the orphanage: The silent tears of an orphan's life were not because no one answered the cries, and waking up the next morning—that was no longer a sure thing.

Their solution worked. In a month or two, I got the message and stopped—the screaming anyway. Then the unthinkable happened: I took to wetting the bed. Their resolution to this new annoyance began with denial; no breakfast or lunch for me. The oatmeal gruel was not missed. But lunch—the half Graham cracker with a glass of milk—it was *the* meal of our day!

And, too, there was that unshakable shame. It churned with the growling in the empty pit of my stomach alongside the ridicule of the others. "Little Jeffrey can't have any milk and crackers. He's still just a baby, and it makes him pee his bed!"

I was forced to stand before them all in disgrace, to endure the pointing and snickering as they lined up for, and then enjoyed, lunch.

Some made a dramatic production of relishing their food, taunting me as they ate.

Yes, the ridicule set me apart as "not as good as, not as deserving of." I felt a loneliness then, one that has never quite left. How many other orphans, I wonder, were taught just so, to be loners in life? Whenever snubbed, their natural inclination also is to go away—alone?

My only friend in Sunny Hills was another misfit who somehow attached himself to me, a boy almost four, like me. He was lanky, with a black mop of hair, and looked much like Alfalfa in the *Spanky and Our Gang* movies. We spent playtime together and sometimes avoided the work details of our "lesson time" by hiding out in the playhouse in the yard. Oftentimes, he confided in me of his latest escape plan. Once, he made it on a bus all the way to San Francisco. Alfalfa—now there was a *real* orphan!

For Mikey and me, escape was never in the picture. Mommy visited every month or three. We walked the field out front under the shedding eucalyptus trees. Accompanied by the whispering scrape of the long, trailing strips of bark, we listened to her tell us how she'd take us away, always "sometime soon." Usually she brought us candy and once a present—matching six-guns with holsters for Mikey and a crummy coloring book for me.

My fourth birthday passed unnoticed. Much of my playtime I spent with Alfalfa, hanging from our fingers on the old, wedge-patterned, rusty wire fence, staring out at the world. He told me about his dreams—about the cowboy he would become, and how he'd go live in Texas when he busted free.

I was there alone one day, hanging on that fence, when a man wearing a rumpled, gray hat and matching dusty jacket came walking down the road. He stopped to talk to me. Although I'd only been there a couple of months, it was long enough. The attention of any adult was something I knew to be wary about.

"Well hello, little man."

In answer, I twisted my body, wagging it from side to side in silence. It felt uncomfortably odd to be called a man.

"You certainly are a big guy. How old are you?" Distrustful of his praise, I took the easy route and held up four fingers. The man was persistent.

"What's your name?"

"Chef-fwee."

"It's what? I can't hear you."

"Chef-fwee!"

"Jerry? Jerry what?"

"Nue! Chef-fwee! Chef-fwee Ef-forts!"

"Oh . . . Jamie Eforts."

"Nue! Nue! Chef-fwee! Eths Chef-fwee Ef-forts! Chit!" I finished with the word I heard most often whenever Mommy got mad, then stomped off in a purple rage.

Why couldn't adults understand me? Mikey could, but Mikey wasn't around anymore, and I was fast finding it necessary to adjust my vocabulary. Being Mama's little Dutchman and called by charming—though detestable—nicknames like "Dutch" just didn't cut it here. Nobody understood me, nobody found me charming, and nobody cared.

* * *

The day eventually came to make the annual field trip to "do our duty to those orphans before us." Now almost five, I could communicate much better, but this being my first "field trip," I didn't understand the reluctant dread on everyone's face. Not yet.

The entire orphanage gathered up tools—rakes, shovels, and such—for the daylong trek up the canyon. We all lined up on the dirt track behind the orphanage, the bigger children in the front. Some of the older ones were put to the task of watching over us younger, in the back. I wanted Mikey to be my overseer, but again, there was that rule that siblings were to be kept apart. My guardian for the trip turned out to be a mean-spirited, seven-year-old redhead who was covered with big, blotchy freckles. His cohorts called him Spot.

The road ran along the hillside to the right, past the fragrance of the barns and corrals where the older children kept the farm animals: cows, sheep, pigs—even a few rabbits. Sweating freely under the midsummer sun, we hadn't even reached the cooler shade of the oak and eucalyptus forest before Spot foisted his shovel off onto me.

"Here, snotface, you carry this," he said with authority.

I didn't question his authority, him being as old as Mikey. But the other—

"What's 'snotface?'"

"It means you got boogers running outta your nose!" He said it while shoving me on the side of the head and nearly knocking me over.

Now I did question his authority. "I don't either!" I screamed, wiping my face on my sleeve. Then, throwing the shovel down at his feet, I said, "Here, carry this your own self!"

Grabbing me by the shirt front, Spot thrust his face into mine. "You'd better! —if'n ya know what's good for ya."

"No! I won't. Lemme go!" Much bigger than me, he just tightened his grip against my struggles, his mean, little pig eyes boring into mine.

"You know where we're goin'?" He sneered, then went on without waiting for an answer. "We're goin' to the graveyard." His voice trailed off into a menacing pause. "You know what they do here with little kids who don't do what they're told?" Again the pause, his eyes narrowed to a mean glint. "They don't come back!" His scowl turned dramatic. "They just bury 'em and leave 'em." Then, shoving me roughly to the ground, he ordered, "Now, pick up the shovel 'n carry it!"

"N-n-no!" I sobbed, ashamed of the tears now turned gritty by the dust. "I won't! And you can't make me!" I said it, all the while feeling the futility of my lie and wondering if there was truth in his. Spot grabbed the front of my shirt and hauled me to my feet.

"Leave 'im alone, Spot." It was Mikey.

With a jerk, Spot's head swivelled around. Looking past his upraised fist, he stuttered, "Uhh . . . I was only kiddin'.'" His grin was sheepish as he let go, and snagging his shovel, he stumbled backward.

"C'mon, Jeffy." Glaring at Spot, Mikey took my hand.

Head held high, I followed along. Mikey was my big brother—and my hero. Together we finished the hike, arriving at an open spot in the hollow just beneath the head of the canyon. On the far hilltop stood a tall, dazzling-white cross and in the meadow, partially covered by thickets of blackberry brambles, were perhaps twenty or thirty little stone markers fanning out in a semi-circular pattern. Mikey left me sitting in the shade and went off to work with the older boys.

I'd never seen such a place. Eventually, curiosity prevailed, and I wandered over to one of the adults. He was busy issuing orders, and so I tugged at his pants leg.

"Mister! Mister! Is this the graveyard?" I asked, pointing.

The man bent over, his hand enveloping my shoulder, as he replied, "Yep. These are the graves of all the orphans who died here." His eyes regarded me soberly. While his lips pulled back in a smile, somehow it didn't reach his eyes. "We come here every year to pull weeds and make it look nice. It's our duty to those buried here." The blue in his eyes now turned cold. "Now, off you go. Get to work. You do want to pull your weight around here, don't you?"

I nodded, my mind awhirl with questions. *Was the rest of what Spot said also true?* The man pushed me aside as someone else caught his attention. "Hey! You with the rake. . . ." He stepped off to grab the hapless youngster.

Once free of his attention, I ran. Out past the outer line of three plain, white, wooden crosses stuck in soft, bumpy mounds of soil, I hid in the shade behind an oak tree. As I watched the older boys work, again the tears slid from my eyes—tears that defied meaning. I was never given to feeling sorry for myself, nor did I know any of the orphans buried here. How many, I wondered, had died choking on the gritty stink of sweat-hardened socks?

As I sat, I felt a presence and a light touch caress my back. Yet on turning, there was only a slight breeze stirring through my hair, a breeze that didn't seem to reach the leaves on the trees. All around me was silence. Even the constant buzz of unseen insects had fallen silent. Odd? Maybe, but not even near so crazy as the world of Sunny Hills in which I now resided.

* * *

Toward the end of that year, 1951, they told Mommy to make "other arrangements," that my brother was becoming "institutionalized." In other words, his cheese was sliding off his cracker. And perhaps it was the same with my own.

But Mikey was always the tougher one. And although he was never one to admit it, I did not doubt that Mikey also knew the silent tears of an orphan—tears that wet his nights and perhaps, like mine, also lubricated his cracker.

Mommy's mother, Grandma Kathy, lived in Salt Lake City and knew of a couple—distant relatives—who, being childless, were willing to adopt. Their names were Martha and James Williams.

Martha came down to California to get us. That day was bright, and the sweet smell of eucalyptus floated on an unseasonably warm breeze. We walked together with Martha and Mommy in the parking lot beneath those tall trees. The song of birds accompanied the scraping music of the long, trailing bark.

Mommy took Mikey and me aside. After dabbing at her reddened eyes with a handkerchief, she stopped to blow her equally red nose. Then, squatting with an arm around each, and in a voice that cracked, she said, "You guys are getting out of here. Isn't that great!" The forced quality of her smile seemed somehow odd. "And guess what?" Swallowing hard, she continued. "You're going to have a brand new mommy and daddy!"

"No!" Mikey's scream started with that one word, then continued incoherently, piercing the quiet of the morning and drowning out all beauty from the moments before. Except for quick intakes of breath, it did not abate as he was pried loose and dragged off to our new mommy's car. His shoes kicked up bursts of dust and gravel with every foot along the way as he wailed out the horror and outrage that now filled his world.

Me? I just walked along beside them, more confused than disturbed. I was happy to be leaving Sunny Hills, but mainly happy just to have my brother back.

* * *

Only in looking back now have I any concept of the agony he was feeling right down to his soul. It was an agony he kept silent and hidden with the facade of a daredevil for the remainder of his short life. Yes, in those crazy years to come, Mike did every insanely dangerous act he could to prove his courage and worth. And I tried my best to do them with him to prove my loyalty. I wanted to be there for him and maybe even to save his life. He was all I had.

~ *In the Present with Big D* ~

Big D's words come even before the darkening swirl of him encompasses me, rattling the sheets of the notebook in my hand. "Cause and effect, Jeff . . . Others may read your words and see you as quite a victim, your story as a tragedy. But you know that all is not always as it appears—or rather for you, it is only as you choose to regard it."

"I'm not sure I follow. . . ."

"You don't see it as a tragedy, do you?" His form has taken shape, sitting on the rock ledge beside me. His hooded face now looks out over the cool, grassy hillside from our position just above the inactive Lee Canyon ski lift in the Spring Mountains. He seems to share this welcome respite from the brutal summer of Las Vegas.

"No, Big D. Shit happens. It is only now in looking back that I can see how badly my life stunk back then."

"Sunny Hills has affected you. But how was that different from Mike?"

"Mike? Oh, he was angry! He felt betrayed by our birth mother, and those rare times in later life when she would visit, he'd barely speak to her."

"And you?"

"Me? For me, Sunny Hills was a place to fear. Our birth mother didn't seem to factor into it and I held no grudge."

"Anger is only the aggressive side of fear. And betrayal—that is the victim side of it."

"Yes, well for me, it was different. Whereas Mike clearly felt like a victim, his loyalty betrayed, his was a loyalty for which I had no concept. Me? I accepted the new mother almost as if I never had one; just walked away from our birth mother and Sunny Hills and didn't look back."

"Ah, but you did look back!" His head turns as he regards me. The naked bones of his skull gleam white; his jaw is slightly open in a grin. "Where were you just last week?" In the darkness of his eye sockets, an intense fire glows.

"Well, I was visiting my son's family. And yes, I did drop over to Sunny Hills. It is only a few miles from there."

"Tell me."

"Sunny Hills is now a school for troubled teens. I spoke to a couple of the ladies on staff, Judy and Diana. They seemed to know a great deal about Sunny Hills and its history.

"And . . ."

"I told them about some of my experiences. They showed me pictures and gave me a brochure and a copy of my records—yeah, they still had them."

"Then what happened?"

"The folder they gave me to keep them in was covered with a collage of old photos. Glancing at it, I suddenly recognized my childhood face, looking back from one of the pictures."

"And . . ."

"Oh God, Big D! Something . . . I don't know . . . something changed inside. It was like a big piece of my life suddenly went, *Ker-Chunk*!"

"Closures can be weird that way."

"That's not all! There, beside me on the bench in the picture, was Alfalfa."

"And . . ."

"And that was it. I left!"

"And . . ." The glow in his empty sockets seems to flicker with open humor.

"Well, yeah . . . it was a little weird. Driving away, the whiz of traffic all around me on the freeway seemed like light years away—almost as if my reality then as a child, and now, were somehow intertwined. Tears began to flow, and I had no idea why, but it was okay."

"Yes. It was healing for you to mourn. Your childhood died in infancy and is indeed buried there in that graveyard. That was why you felt no loyalty. All you saw in your mother or Sunny Hills was the grave you escaped—and there would be an actual headstone with your name on it, had you not."

"Big D," I whisper, "did Alfalfa, too . . . I mean, did he ever escape?"

"No, not completely."

"What do you mean?"

"Like you, Jeff, Alfalfa was tied and gagged into silence, many times. He, too, learned the silence of the orphan. And he, too, shares your great need to be heard. Like you this day, he has not yet recognized the gift of it all."

"Gift?"

"Yes . . . gift. Again, remember the Spiritual *Law of Balance*—how *'every event of potential sorrow carries the potential of equal joy?'* "

"Yeah, I know that law." Hands held out, empty palms up, I shrug. "But what's the gift?"

"Ah, Jeff." Big D pauses; his eye sockets flicker while he grins wide in amusement. "Alfalfa, too, finds great joy as a writer—a well-known author of westerns."

As a whole, humans spend most of their time unconsciously engaged as actors in a play—usually a drama. We are taught from birth never to reveal our true feelings, our real selves. That to do so makes us vulnerable to those who would use such information to hurt us, especially to hurt our feelings. The truth is, while some may conspire to play those games of power, control, and manipulation, our true friends are not susceptible to such poor integrity, and when being a friend, nor are we. Stepping off the stage is the only way to know your friends. And feelings? We, ourselves, are the only ones who hold the power over our pain. And too often, when seeing who is not a friend, we exercise that power.

Redneck Spirituality—Book One

Chapter Three

New Mommy

I remember well the trip by train to Utah—the way the train rocked and clacked along and the black porters. I'd never before seen a black man and gazed with slack-jawed, wide-eyed wonder when one flashed me a grin. The contrast between the whiteness of his teeth and eyes to the awesome blackness of his face was startling. With the unvarnished innocence of my fascination, the man smiled at me often.

Then there were the tunnels. I especially liked the tunnels, the sudden darkness and escalated din of them. Oh, the wonder of all things new is something somehow only a child can know.

Once through the Sierras and out onto the flat sameness of the Nevada desert, it seemed things began to get a bit boring for Mike. Out of meanness—or with nothing better to do—he started kicking my shin whenever our new mommy wasn't looking. I would retaliate and immediately get caught. After five or six times, she put me over her knee for a thorough spanking.

It was a first for me. Though Bart had slapped me around a time or two—well, maybe a dozen—never before did I feel violated, not like this. While I did not have the vocabulary to express it, I could understand the meanness of an asshole like Bart. But coming from my new mommy—to be held down, helpless, and just beaten—no never! Hopping from foot to foot, I frantically rubbed away at the sting of my burning butt. Then tears streaming, in my agony and outrage, I shouted, "I hate you! I don't want you to be my mommy!" Only in looking back now can I see that the sentiment was mutual.

* * *

It was wintertime at our new home in Bingham Canyon, Utah. With the snow cresting higher than my head, it was quite a change from Sunny Hills. I liked the way it sparkled, and there were lots of hills to slide down. Snow, I decided, was something I loved.

Although still four and a fairly fast learner, one thing I refused to learn was to tie my shoes, even with repeated lessons from Mom. There were several times in that first week that I'd look down the legs of my corduroy pants, making sure the laces flapped free. Then, smiling in delight, I'd tug at her skirt, "Mommy, Mommy, come tie my shoes!"

To her credit, it took all of that first full week before she exploded. Her eyes bulging in rage, she dragged me over to the dresser. "I shoulda had my head examined to take on such a stupid little shit!" Grabbing my suitcase from the closet, she slapped it down before the opened drawer that housed all my meager possessions. "Get your things . . . get out!"

The hallway was dark, and old, and cold in the apartment building in which we lived. Built early in the century, with the unfulfilled dreams of the mines, perhaps that old apartment building knew something of my own life just then, as in the whoosh of warm air, the riches of my new life were shut off with the slamming of the door behind me. At the beginning of the hall, inset within the heavy front door, was a long, narrow glass pane, now decorated with a profusion of ice crystals. But my young eyes now saw none of the splendor. With my old stuffed horse, Red, under one arm, I set my suitcase down to try the latch. The frigid chill of the brass to my hand matched something now inside me, and I was forced to set Red down, too, and reach high with both hands, struggling, finally releasing the frozen mechanism.

Outside, my suitcase thumped as I dragged it down each of the half dozen steps. Shoveled clean, they were dry and white-stained from the rock salt, some of which still crunched underfoot as I sank down to sit on the lowest step. The walkway before me too was dry, though the snow banks on both sides crested half again above my own full height. I sat there looking down that tunnel of snow. It was the only white visible just now in my world of grayness. Above, a dim sun hung in the coal-smudged sky, and all around me was a frigid cold that froze the snot in my nose hairs. With every breath, my nose seemed pinched between the sting of that chill and the acrid scent of burning coal—the source, it seemed, of all warmth in Bingham Canyon. While the taste remained in the back of my throat, the warmth from that coal was now denied me.

I sat there with Red, hugging him to me, seeking in him a warmth from the shivering cold and a compassion no other in my world now possessed. Where will we go? What will we do? Will there ever be another warm bed?

We sat there a long time, just so, wondering together. Then, from the doorway above, Mom called me back inside. Looking up at her, I did not want to go, yet I now knew clearly that she was all that stood between me and a frozen eternity.

Inside, she tried to hold me close as she cried. Leaning back out of her embrace, I watched her, heard her say how she was sorry, heard her swear that she would always be there for me. Yet inside, I knew that was never the way it would ever be between her and me.

* * *

The winter's frigid air changed with spring's muddy chill, when one day my brother, Mike, was carried home in the arms of a stranger who led a crowd of onlookers through our back gate. Mike's blood-splattered face looked like red finger paint gone mad, and the skin on his forehead lay open; his bare skull gleamed white through the carnage. Still unconscious, he was rushed to the doctor and didn't awaken until after they had him stitched up. It was a very traumatic experience, at least for me.

I saw my brother as courageous and capable. Yet, looking at his frail, limp body, I saw a little rag doll with a fragile, porcelain skull, broken and covered with blood and mud as the man laid him gently on our porch. Looking at him then, I learned a healthy respect for the consequences of foolish actions. That was the day I first felt the true essence of Mike's deadly, dangerous life.

They said he was swinging Tarzan style on a rope and fell headfirst onto a rock. The result was a huge scar across his forehead. As if placed there by the Devil's typewriter key was a perfect "Y," dead center from eyebrows to hairline. It marked him for the rest of his life. Being Mike's brother, and the only one in a position to try to keep him alive, meant that for me, too, life's terrible consequences almost always had to be ignored—almost, because I just wasn't the daredevil that he was.

But Mike? Did he ever know my fear? Did the stitched, puckered "Y" above his blackened eyes ever cause him a moment's doubt? No, he seemed to take it in stride, and by summertime, there was only a scar slowly turning white—a scar that, in the chaotic years to follow, would remain vividly white against the red of Mike's anger.

* * *

As the spring muds dried with the summer, Mike and I walked up the steep dirt road behind our apartment building. Located in a tight little mountain valley, Bingham didn't have any roads one could call flat. A typical little brother, I was forever tagging along after Mike and his friends. Like gum on their shoes, they ignored me or scraped me off. There were two of them that day, standing around a cardboard box as Mike and I walked up.

"What's in the box?" Mike asked.

"Water balloons," the larger one with the buck teeth answered. "We're gonna drop 'em on cars down at the train overpass."

"What about you, Gimpy?" Mike asked. "Ain't cha afraid they'll get outta their cars and catch ya?"

"Not a chance!" Gimpy laughed, stretching out the steel polio brace on his leg. "Take 'em 15 minutes just ta get up ta that overpass. We'll be looo-ng gone."

"You comin', Mike?" Bucky asked.

"Me, too," I broke in.

"Yeah, I'm comin'," Mike answered, then rolling his eyes, added, "and you know what to do about Jeffy here." With that, Bucky picked up the box and all three turned and ran, taking different directions. I tried to catch Mike, but he was just too fast. I had to admit, they were getting pretty good at scraping me off. But dang, that sure seemed like fun—the kind of fun a fella just couldn't resist.

The front yard of our apartment house ended at the top of a wall that dropped perhaps ten feet to a very narrow walkway beside the street. Finding a rock as big as I could carry, I hid behind a bush at the edge of the wall. When the first car came along, I heaved. My aim was perfect. The rock sailed right through the center of the windshield—of a police car.

The cop's brakes squealed to a smoky, sideways halt in the roadway. Boiling out of his car, gun in hand, he began waving it at the bush as he screamed, "Put your hands up . . . get 'em up!" It was probably dumb luck that he saw me as I ran away. The rest of the day I spent shivering in the mud under another bush. I watched from its secret confines as the cop talked to Mom and knew that to go home meant I would pay a price.

The price of that windshield was a week of Dad's pay. No pain that I endured could ever be enough to even the bill with Mom— certainly, that spanking was not, nor the scalding of the bath water that followed it.

Perhaps it was merely the difference in the temperatures, what with my having been in the chilly air outside all day. For though I was pre-warmed under the hand of Mom's anger, still, when I was made to sit in that bath water, it burned! I shrieked in agony, crying, begging to be let out. Mom struggled with me for a moment. With her eyes bulging in rage, she slapped me several times across the face, screaming, "Oh, stop being such a baby! It's **not** hot! It **doesn't** hurt!"

But it **was** hot. And it **did** hurt. My skin turned lobster red, though it never actually blistered. Why was she requiring I lie to myself? In the innocence left of my childhood, I did not know, but in time I learned those lies of a manly facade well. And it breaks my heart to acknowledge that I passed them on to my own son.

* * *

I started kindergarten in Bingham midyear. As an outsider in this close-knit Mormon community, no one wanted to play with me. Nimble fingers molded every available piece of the clay—or slimed gaily away with all the obtainable finger paints—and all hands pushed me away whenever I came near the sandbox. There was nothing left with which I could play.

Finally, I spotted the teacher's pointer. When her hands then reached to take it away, I'd had enough. Scrambling onto her desk, I started swinging. She called in the principal. A fire raged in me, and though only five, I think it was that fire that kept them both from taking the pointer away. Discipline was the order for school in those days, and they could have taken it, maybe even used it. Perhaps they saw the fire was beyond the bounds of misbehavior. I don't know. The violence with which I flailed that pointer held them off until finally, Mom came to get me. I did not escape her fiery discipline.

* * *

Clearly, I could have turned out big-time bad. With my new mother's Jekyll and Hyde personality to teach me, it was a choice. For me, being a disturbed child was a sure thing. Yes, I learned anger. But meanness? It just wasn't in me. Unlike my brother, that was something I never developed. In the beginning, our experiences were much the same. In the end, we chose such different paths. Perhaps it was only because he did not have forty-five years to mature.

* * *

We moved to our own house in Sandy, Utah the following summer. It was to be our permanent home—well, on and off—throughout my youth. For a time, Dad stayed on working in the US Mine at Bingham. During the summer after my second grade, he quit and, with a few friends, went in on the lease of a uranium mine down south, in Utah's canyon country. The place was aptly named, Fry Canyon.

~ *In the Present with Big D* ~

I sit here before the glare of my computer awaiting Big D's inevitable comment. Yet, there seems nothing forthcoming; just a picture in my mind of an old locomotive, chugging away, and a figure stoking coal into the firebox of the boiler. Again I smell the acrid essence of Bingham Canyon. But wait—I know that grin!

"Yes. I was there with you then, too, Jeff, on those steps in Bingham Canyon. I held you close—you and your stuffed red horse—and loved you as no one living had the capacity to do. Though you did not know it, I stoked the fire of love in you, for with so many like you, it often burns out at such times. Besides, it is what was necessary for me to complete my end of our pre-existence deal." His laughter flows with the chugging of the engine. "Perhaps when next you feel the chill of another fear-filled heart, you will choose to remember your fire. Perhaps you will stoke that fire in them."

"Uh . . . thanks, Big D. I . . . I never knew."

"Just part of our bargain, remember?" He has materialized beside me and pauses to push his engineer's hat up at a rakish angle with one long, bony finger. "You chose to learn some great lessons—lessons love does not normally survive. So now tell them to me."

"Not sure what you're getting at here, Big D. Are you talking about that absolutely magnetic quality that all children possess simply by the wonder of things new, even to the wonder of someone of a different color? About how we learn the adult ways of prejudging everything and everyone by what we're told?"

"Sounds like you have learned something of the lies." His ruby gaze now seems very focused.

"Lies? Oh God, yes. Adults tell children so many lies!"

"Why would they do that?" His grin is harder to read now. Did I hear a chuckle?

"I don't think they do it . . . well . . . deliberately. Most are like old platitudes they just pass on without really knowing what they are saying."

"Like . . ." Now I'm sure I hear his amusement.

"Well, like: *'Don't you dare embarrass me; be on your best behavior. Stop being such a crybaby! Don't let them see your pain. Stop doing that. You want Mommy to love you, don't you? Only bad kids act like that.'*"

"Okay, so what is the truth here. What don't they know about what they're saying?"

Given that his naked skull is all I can see, why am I so sure his words are spoken tongue-in-cheek? "*Truth?* No, I'm uncomfortable with that word being spoken anywhere near this . . . this . . . *sick shit!* And why are you pulling my chain about it here, Big D?"

"Jeff, do you think it would ever be possible for me to pull your chain about it had you, too, not passed that same sick shit off onto your own son?"

"Uuuu-rrrghh . . . ," I groan. "Goddammit! You're right, I did. But that was before I knew about the truth."

"Yes, Jeff. You are no more—or less—at fault than they are." His grin is now sad. "So what is the truth? You've already laid out the lies. Keep it simple."

"The truth they are saying is this: 'I hold you responsible for my choice of feelings, and you get to hold others responsible for yours. Don't let anyone see your true self. Rather, put on a mask of pretense to the world. You won't be acceptable—being who you really are—allowing your true feelings, thoughts, fears, pain, sometimes even your love to show through. And above all, always remember: Our love is conditional upon you pretending to be who we want. And speaking of our love, it, too, is a pretense.'"

"I'll grant you that, Jeff, 'sick shit' it is. So what was the effect on your life?"

"I grew up building and learning to wear a facade. And as an adult, I seldom felt safe enough to show the truth of myself. How could I, not knowing who is behind the other person's facade? The sad part is that so few people ever truly get to love us because they, too, don't know who we are. Even Meg, my first wife—the love of my life—didn't know me. Shit, Big D, how can I fault her for not loving me back the same way as I loved her. Like nearly everyone else, I was fucked over and lied to in order to fit into this sick society. I couldn't show her who I was; besides, I'd long since forgotten. Was it the same with her?"

"Ah, Jeff, you know it was." Is that a tear I see coursing its way down the brittle bone of his cheek? "But with the writing of your story, you will discover exactly who you are. And by knowing the Spiritual Laws, you now know the truth of life."

"But why am I feeling more and more like a round peg trying to fit into society's square hole?"

"S'real simple: You just haven't finished drilling your own hole yet—and you've yet to help a whole lot of other folks do the same." His grin now seems to take on an aspect of seriousness, as does the tone of his next words. "Jeff, you do know that your acceptance by others doesn't depend on you fitting into anyone's fucking square hole, don't you? Your acceptance by them has nothing to do with you being unacceptable."

"Well, ye-yeaah. What are you getting at?"

"Jeff, your parents didn't adopt you because they wanted . . . *you*. No, they wanted the child they couldn't have. You were a surrogate, *and surrogates aren't the real thing*. Surrogates are *never* acceptable."

"But what about all those years growing up? They seemed to accept me. . . ." I shrug, confused. "They didn't disown me until I divorced Meg—'abandoned her,' as they put it."

"Did you, Jeff? Did you abandon her?"

"I suppose so, Big D." I sigh. "But I gave her all our assets and took all our bills—nearly $36,000 worth, almost a year's pay."

"You tell them that?" His gaze has now narrowed.

"No, they weren't interested in my excuses—didn't even give me the chance to discuss it." Again, I sigh. "Shit!"

"Truth? You want to know the truth, Jeff?" His gaze now cuts into me. "Truth is, you had the balls to do what they both wanted to do for all those years but didn't have the guts."

"What? But—"

"Yeah. You remember all the mean, nasty things she did to you and Mike?" He grins in amusement now. "You always thought that because she was careful not to let others, and especially not your father, see that she was hiding it behind her facade—and yes, she was. But he knew anyway because she was just as mean to him, only in much quieter ways."

"I never saw it."

"No, you wouldn't. She ruled you through her screaming fits and beatings, him through his guilt." He chuckles outright. "Your father was a man, a good man, but he was no angel. Like nearly everyone else in this world, they each married the other's facade—the one they showed each other to make themselves attractive. But with those we choose as our mates, facades don't last all that long, y'know?"

"Hhheee-yeah." I sigh, thinking of Meg and me and of our own sick, shit relationship, how it was after our own facades fell away. Me, the fear-filled husband so afraid of losing her that I let her carry my balls in her pocket for twenty-five years; her, so insecure that she required such control over me and, getting it, could neither respect nor certainly love me in that same manner. "Y'know, I didn't divorce Meg because I stopped loving her, Big D. It was because our relationship left no room for me to love her and still respect me."

"And your mother, Jeff? When was the last time you accepted her?"

The focusing of the twin lasers from beneath the bill of his engineer's cap seems to drill into me, and I take a long time answering. I sigh. "Truth is, Big D, probably not since those steps in Bingham."

"Are you willing to accept her now?"

"You mean deal with what has kept me from loving her?"

"Loving?" His eye sockets flash with humor. "No, you've loved her. It was trusting that you dared not do. You had good reason to protect yourself as a child, and you're an adult now. Can she now harm you?"

"No."

"Hmmm . . . what if you could know of the pain beneath **her** facade, Jeff?" He pauses, appraising me. "Think you'd feel empathy with her? Are you aware that her own mother thought the proper way to teach children was through those same lies and fear? She, too, didn't mean to be, but she was one mean bitch. Is it a wonder why your mother was mean, too? Didn't you just admit how you 'passed that manly facade' thing onto your own son?"

"Yeah, but I was never mean to him. And I've done my best to be honest and real and loving since—"

"Yeah, since when?" His tone presses me but does not mock.

"Well, since I met you there in that hospital and changed."

"Changed how?"

"I mean, the 'being real and honest with myself' part of our agreement, Big D."

"Yes, and . . ."

"And it has changed my whole life, as well as my relationship with my son."

"Your mother has never made that pact." The ruby glow in his eye sockets focuses laser sharp on me now. "Can you be okay that she may never be real and honest—or loving—with you?"

"Yeah," I whisper.

"Can you be okay that, like your ex-wife, Meg, the changes she sees in you now are so foreign to her that she can only label you as 'crazy'?"

"Ha-rrumph." I feel a need to clear my throat before replying—again, in a whisper. "Yeah."

"And face it, Jeff." The angular bones of Big D's own face are now only inches from mine. "You've only been whining about all the 'wicked witch' bad shit she did with you. Was she never nice?"

"Yes." I sigh. "When my father or other people were around, and yes, at other times as well, but that does not negate that her love was conditional—"

"True." Big D's breath now hisses in my face with the pungence of burning cinnamon. "Point is"—he pauses, holding me immobile with his burning gaze—"is your own love now conditional?"

"N-n-no!" I stutter, confused by his sudden anger. "I'm angry, but as you pointed out, she is my mother. How can I not love her?"

"Good, glad we got that cleared up. Perhaps now's the time to stoke up the fire of those embers. Might just melt the chill you still feel of Bingham Canyon—might even warm her some as well." The grin beneath his engineer's hat is the last thing to fade as he leaves me with that bottom-of-the-barrel tone of his final words reverberating in my ears. "Now that's the good shit."

Often others label us as cowards when they see our fear. The truth is, we are not until we, ourselves, label us so. Every human on the planet has fears. A fear is only an imaginary dragon in our mind. It generally starts as a little flying lizard sent by our higher self out of love to caution and warn us of perceived danger. Then it is blown up large by our conscious mind using the winds of possibility. We believe ourselves cowards, those of us who won't walk the dragon until it is, once again, a little lizard.

Redneck Spirituality—Book Two

Chapter Four

Fry Canyon

God, how I loved Fry Canyon, wild and remote beyond the imagination of my choicest dreams. Until Mom, Mike, and I arrived, there were no families there, just miners living in scattered trailer camps and shacks—damn primitive.

On the day we pulled in, a late afternoon monsoon shower brought respite from the heat of the summer. A hundred tiny waterfalls plunged over the sheer-red sandstone cliffs, stretching majestically high. The fragrance of sagebrush and cedar floated on the cool, humid, ozone-tainted air. Yes, the smell of the desert after a thundershower was to my young mind unforgettable.

The arrival of our family was like the bringing of civilization. Seeing us take to the primitive life so easily, the other miners' families soon began arriving, necessitating the building of a two-classroom school. Meanwhile, we kids had a nine-month reprieve, which we put to good use.

On long, dusty hikes, we explored the desert. Often braving the threat of flash floods from those late-summer monsoons, we seduced the shady sanctity of the canyons. Should our intrusion coincide with the sudden rage of waters between those smooth, sandstone walls sometimes a hundred feet or higher—though often only yards apart—we could not hope to survive.

In the wash bordering our campsite, we already were witness to those flash floods. They'd come rumbling with the churning of the boulders carried within their muddy froth. Coming, as they did, from miles up the dry washes, a clear sky was no guarantee of safety this time of year. It was with reverence we hiked there, almost as if we were invading the sanctity of Mother Nature's womb. Combined, it titillated a sense of naughtiness well beyond that of normal disobedience to our parents' strict rule of "no hiking in the washes."

I loved Fry Canyon, but of it all, perhaps most appreciated and prized was my growing collection of arrowheads and painted pottery shards. It stretched my young mind to think of how they were so beautifully crafted by ancient hands—hands long since turned to the very dust on which we trod. Fry Canyon was an ancient place. Yet, for an eight-year-old, it was full of fresh, undefiled excitement, danger, and discovery.

* * *

A few miles downstream in White Canyon, just to the north of Fry, we found a Moqui Indian ruin. Tucked in under an overhang on a canyon wall, the only way we could reach it was to walk out about thirty feet along a narrow ledge and then climb down another fifty, using some worn hollows in the cliff face cut there by ancient Indians as hand and foot holds. These ended beside a huge boulder sitting on a ledge. To get to the ruins below, one slid down, around, and under the rock like so many ants under a white sandstone brick. One slip, and it was a very long two hundred feet to the canyon floor. This was something Mike could really get into.

As for me, I sat on top and raged at the sudden, shaking stiffness in my arms and legs and the whirling in my head that threatened to send me skittering into the depths every time I attempted to descend. Below, I could hear the excitement in the voices of the older boys as they explored the mysteries of the ruins.

* * *

It was a wild and rugged place. Here, as in the cowboy movies, danger was a first cousin to death. Like the others, I ran over to witness the hubbub the day the *Happy Jack Mine* caved in. They brought the body down off the rim in the back of a dump truck, arriving just at lunch break, and laid it out on a table in the general store. The store served as a sort of community center and was just across the wash from our school at White Canyon. The body was covered, its outline showing plainly through the sheet, except where the head should be. There, the sheet was oddly flattened and painted in red. Then someone raised the corner for a look. For me then, the Wild West romance of Fry Canyon became sudden, deadly reality.

* * *

Fry Canyon was a huge box canyon about six miles long, varying from a half to two miles wide. All of the more prominent rock formations had names. One, shaped like a chair, could be seen way in the distance down White Canyon. That one was called *Jacob's Chair*. There was another up near the head of Fry Canyon, which was about three hundred feet tall. Its base was cone-shaped, but the top hundred feet or so was a twenty-foot-wide vertical sandstone cylinder. That one was named *Jacob's Peter*. Being completely flat on top, I shuddered, remembering my own experience. It appeared Jacob had been overly circumcised—must of been by one big-assed axe.

Lastly, about midway up the canyon, there was yet another. A free-standing mesa, it was about four hundred feet tall and shaped like a gargantuan pan mounded with food. That one, of course, was known as the *Frying Pan.*

One day, Mike, his thirteen-year-old friends, Willis and Billy, and I all hiked over to it. On the vertical south wall, we located a ledge that varied from a few inches to a foot wide. Angling up the face of the sheer cliff for about two hundred feet, it then entered a crevice, which rose the last fifty straight up.

Last in line, I made it only halfway along the ledge before my heels met only air. The wall was of smooth, orange sandstone with what looked like burnt oil trailers of black manganese stains, running down the sides. My rubbery limbs felt numb, and my head swam with dizziness as that rock face seemed to push the rest of me out into space. To the left and right, my grasping hands met only smooth rock. Glancing below, it looked to be a hundred feet to the boulder-strewn talus slope, though in reality, it was probably a mere sixty. Worse, there was a bend coming up where the rock face turned slightly inward and bowed out even more. Billy was just then humping his body around it.

Up ahead, Mike and Willis were climbing up the crack. Their backs wedged against one side, their feet against the other, they wormed their way up. Only nine years old, I knew I did not have their strength—my God, I had barely enough to remain upright. Backing inch by trembling inch, I made my way down.

Again, I'd stayed back, and I again felt very much a coward for not bringing myself to brave the heights all the way to the top. I would never see the names and dates written on a ledge up there. Some, Mike later said, went back so far as the 1860s. They were the unknown heroes of the Old West, scratched there by their own hands. My own name, borrowed though it was, would never be beside theirs like Mike's now was.

Then it came time for little brother Jeffrey to provide the amusement. It all began with Billy winging a flat chunk of red slate over the edge, arcing it toward me on the slope several hundred feet below. It splattered with a loud crack on a rock twenty feet above and to my right, showering me with painfully sharp shards.

"Oww! Hey! I'm down here, butthead!"

"Hey, look. It's the pus-pus-pussy!" Billy's remark floated down, accompanied by a bigger, more accurate chunk of slate. It narrowly missed as I dived to the side.

"Naw, looks more like a chicken," came Willis' faraway jeer. "Buk . . . buk . . . bu-kuck!"

"Yeah, a chicken," came a new, more hurtful voice. "Let's see if we can chop its head off!"

Then they all got into the act, winging plate-size flat pieces of slate, turning and twisting into weird, unexpected trajectories, bursting explosively all around. They laughed hilariously, prancing and chicken clucking, as I frantically dodged about, slipping and sliding on the sand and rocks of the steep slope.

Next, they began rolling big boulders over the edge. As my panic escalated, I called them every filthy name my fertilized little mind could conjure. That seemed to amuse them all the more, for still, the boulders continued thumping and skidding all around me, often just inches away.

Eventually, I tucked myself under a huge rock and waited for them to tire of their game.

The summer sun was hot, and sweat mingled with my tears of anger and humiliation—and something more. "Aw shit, Mike! How could you?" My lonesome moan brought no answer, save for the whump and rumble of yet another boulder careening past overhead, raining me with dust and pebbles.

* * *

The school our fathers built was done up first class. There were separate boys' and girls' outhouses in back, each with three holes. One day during recess, I was taking a leak when I noticed an eye peeping through the knothole in front of me. Shifting my aim, I drilled that hole with a stream of golden quicksilver, honed deadly with circumcised accuracy. An immediate screech erupted from the other side, and I emerged in time to see a girl named Judy stumbling away. Both hands frantically clawing at her face, she tripped and began rolling around, making all kinds of yipes and yowls, like a puppy that had just sniffed up an angry red ant pile.

The whole school gathered around her in amusement. That was the day I became known as **Dead Eye**, a nickname I always felt would have been better applied to her.

As for me, I never again saw Judy's, or any other eye, looking through that knothole. Guess they got my message: You just don't piss around with a straight shooter. Yes, perhaps there can even be a gift in having one's tallywhacker cropped.

* * *

Mike, Willis, Billy, and I liked to play poker in the bed of an old dump truck where we could be out of the wind. We were there one day when Pete—a boy my age whom we all disliked—began teasing Dead-Eye Judy, who's physique indeed resembled that of a very plump puppy.

"Fatty, fatty, two-by-four . . ." Beyond dislike, his voice grated against my concentration.

"Go away, lemme alone." Her whining was even worse. As usual, I was losing. Boosting myself up, I looked over the edge.

"Hey! You guys take it someplace else. We're tryin' to play cards here."

". . . Couldn't get through the bathroom door." He ignored me as he ran circles around her, poking her fat body with a stick. Her whining turned to shrieks as she squatted in the sand, her arms up, protecting her face from the stick.

"Hey! Cut it out, asshole."

Pete paused just long enough to stick out his tongue and wave a clenched fist, but for one insultingly stiff finger.

Reply enough. I jumped out of the truck and stalked over. Still grinning, he raised his fists, clearly expecting an easy victory. Everyone knew I avoided fights and never started them. He'd never seen me fight—but then, he'd never seen me angry.

Drawing near, I saw his mocking grin and didn't hesitate. Charging in, fists swinging, I managed to thump him several times before he broke loose. Raising a cloud of powdery dust, he stumbled to his trailer. Tears streaming and holding one eye, with his nose dripping blood across a split lip, he was no longer grinning. I let him go.

Climbing the steel rungs into that dump truck's bed, I heard Mike's chuckle and felt him slap my back. "Hey, nice goin', Jeff. You really kicked his butt good!" Standing on the clean metal of that bed, its surface scratched bare by a thousand tons of uranium ore, I saw something in his eyes that hadn't been there before.

"Yeah, ya better run home to mommy, ya chicken shit little fuck!" Willis jeered at Pete's retreating back. Almost fourteen, he was the oldest and sometimes used words even he wouldn't tolerate coming from us. "And next time ya bother us, we're gonna sic little Jeffrey on ya again!"

I hadn't realized how there was never really any code of honor that kept the three bigger kids from picking on us smaller ones. And why was it I was the one they would let go hiking with them? They simply were afraid we'd squeal on them to the adults—that is, all the others would but me.

Too, I suddenly understood the thing about the Frying Pan, and even the other time—the time they'd used me for target practice when shooting bird shot from a .22. It was Mike firing, puffing spurts of dust around my feet and off the rocks nearby. They laughed and jeered from the ledge above as, again, I frantically dodged around. I still carry a BB lodged in the rim of my left eye socket that I received as I peeked from around a boulder. *Yeah. They trusted me! They knew I'd never tell.* Suddenly, it didn't seem to matter how that trust might just get me killed.

"Jeff-rey!" It was Mom calling me to our trailer. I was in big trouble now. Pete's mom was constantly coming over, complaining about anything we did—real or imagined—to her "Precious." And here this time, I'd really made a mess of him. I shuffled over, hanging my head in my best "gee-I'm-so-ashamed-of-myself" rendition.

"Here, JW." Mother smiled—JW was what she called me when I'd done something right. She used the name sparingly. "I'm proud of you for sticking up for Judy. Here's a dollar. Just don't tell anyone about this."

I walked away, that big, silver coin riding solid in my pocket. But for its hard, heavy metallic reality as I fingered it, my experience of receiving it might well have been only a dream.

Of course I didn't tell anyone. The dollar remained our secret.

Nor did I tell her the real reason why I'd beaten up Pete. Hell, I didn't know the underlying true source of my anger—how his obvious disrespect was simply saying to me: "Coward! You are no one I need to fear." Does it ever matter what someone else says? The words in one's mind are always one's own.

What I saw in Pete was simply summed up in his grin. It was his red cape in the face of my bull. My bull didn't even think before trampling his ass. Yet, was I like Mike and his friends? In a way, I was accepted. But was I, too, a bully? Inside me, somewhere deep, something about it just didn't feel so good. Yet, for a part of me, there was no denying that kicking Pete's ass felt great! "Coward!" That silent word he screamed at me; was it somehow now negated? No, it still rang loud in my own mind.

Within my family circle, what I'd done was right and condoned, even rewarded. There was that secret dollar, there was that fraternal slap on the back from Mike, and there was that further acceptance from the older boys. I was someone they could bully without fear of being reported. And now, I was someone who would pass it on. *I was one of them now.* Accepted!

But the price? God! Was the price worth it? Mike certainly had a chunk of the bully within his character. I saw it, knew it, didn't like it—and now, it seemed, so did I.

But it was his bravado that scared me. It literally screamed to me of his agony and how he didn't much value life—not his, not even my own—while, too, it whispered, pleading for someone to just cherish him.

Did Mike ever see that there was someone who believed in him, uplifted him, loved him unconditionally—someone who, in the end, could not stop the inevitable. Ah, but back then, at the age of nine, of all this . . . what the fuck did I know?

* * *

Kicking Pete's ass was the easy way of dealing with those cliffs and with those outside myself who might call me a coward. Inside, it was a different story.

After having failed Mike on the cliff face of the Frying Pan, my nights became even more troubled. Waking with the banging of my head against the ceiling above my upper bunk in that dinky trailer, I'd listen sleeplessly to the silvery desert winds whispering lonesome through the cedars outside.

Except now, beside the gritty stink of sweat-laden socks smothering my sleep, the nightmares now carried a different theme. Helplessly, I would watch from someplace just out of reach, while Mike fell to his death. Or perhaps I would have a hold on him, on a sweaty hand or a ripping shirt. Always, I would be unable to keep the grip. Always, Mike died. Always, it was my fault. And always, sleep would then elude me. Although I knew it was only a dream, I could not rest again, but instead, lie searching mentally for a way I could have saved him.

Almost nightly, I thrashed it out with the walls, ceiling, and bedding. And often, when awakened by a few kicks from beneath—"Hey, dipshit! Knock it off!"—I would promise myself I would never let Mike climb another cliff without me.

* * *

Was Mike ever aware of my silent promise? I don't know. But, for the little time left us in Fry Canyon, Mike seemed to see my fears and looked out for me. Would he do so in Australia? We'd just learned we were moving there.

Kangaroos, wallabies, wombats . . . the outback of Australia would be the next place to where our father's work would take us. Out there in the "bush" were things other than cliffs with which to tempt fate—things just as deadly.

~ *In the Present with Big D* ~

"Well, Big D, am I missing anything?" It's been several days since I finished this chapter and he hasn't come, though now I feel him near. A vague sense of unease seems to surround me, like the darkness of the night—nothing but the embers of my campfire's coals and the desert all around me.

"Yes, it is well—that you feel this apprehension just now, Jeff. You certainly have missed something." Big D shows himself, the dim light off the coals reflecting off his bony skull. He still wears his engineer's cap and carries that same fun-poking grin.

"Okay, then give it up. I'm ready."

"Ha!" He chuckles. "That's what I like most about you. Whatever I request, you are game for it, though I know the sweat coats your palms." He holds his own bare-bones palms out as if they are a reflection of my own. "Still, you are not ready for all of it just yet."

"Is it so bad?" I swallow, trying to moisten my suddenly dry throat, and hear his kind chuckle again.

"Good? Bad? You know about good and bad." His bottomless gaze holds me; the coals in his empty sockets exactly mirror those of my campfire. "The KY jelly coated lies of judgmental minds—minds just spouting their slimy shit to fuck with your head. It could be a matter of the greatest upliftment . . ."—one lidless eye socket seems to wink—"should you choose it so."

God, but he loves the dramatics!

"Yes, I do know that one: **'Perception is a choice'** "—I quote from the laws—"but why won't you say?"

"Cowards? Bullies? Integrity? The truth about real men? Whoa! How about the truth about Mike's love? The truth about **your** love? Indeed, the truth about **you . . . about your whole world?** Yes, you have much to learn."

I can no longer see him and his laughter is fading, seemingly rushing away across the desert like some old western train. "Patience. You're right on track. Keep on a-chuggin, chuggin, chuggin. . . ."

"Wait, Big D! What do you mean '. . . much to learn?' Learn what? Goddammit—wait! Tell me."

His reply seems to mock. A repeat of his own words, it comes floating thinly as if on the wind, like the steam chug of an old locomotive. "Much to learn . . . much to learn . . . much to learn. . . ."

"Wait, come back!" There is now only a thin whistle of wind seemingly rushing through and around the yucca and greasewood of this Nevada desert, nothing more. "C'mon, Big D . . . shit!"

Any animal Man chooses to view as a threat, he will always attack, seeking to kill it first. The truth is, it is always in that endeavor wherein lies the greatest danger for Man. For this is his normal response to everything he perceives as a threat—including someone who thinks differently than he.

Redneck Spirituality—Book Four

Chapter Five

The Bush Down Under

My third grade was just finished when we left Fry Canyon. After a brief interlude with cousins in Orem, Utah, we joined Billy's family in Australia—this time in a construction camp amidst the grandeur of the high mountain ridges of New South Wales. Thick forests of stately eucalyptus stood close all around.

From those ridgetops began a wide plateau. The township of Cabramurra nestled there at the edge above us. In the near distance loomed large, the snowcapped peak of Mt. Kosciuszko. Hidden away in a hollow below it all, a solitary, stubby, bald hill topped our campsite and gave name to it—Kenney's Knob.

I never knew the source of that name. Kenny, whoever he was, had his "knob" also been cropped like poor Jacob's peter? The memory of my own circumcision at the age of three certainly made both names seem a little personal—at least personal enough to illicit a wince the first time I heard them. And why is it okay to name some landscapes after a man's personal anatomy, but not a woman's? You never hear names like Pussy Hollow, Vaginal Gap, or Big Nipple Mountain up by Forty-four Double-D Pass.

Dad was hired on by Billy's father as a tunnel foreman for the construction of an underground power station on the Tumut River. Billy's dad was the project manager for this part of the Snowy Mountain Scheme, which consisted of an intricate system of dams, water tunnels, and hydroelectric power-generating stations running throughout the Snowy Mountains of New South Wales and Victoria.

The place was beautiful, so rugged, mountainous, and all silvery green from the sun's reflection off the shiny leaves of the stately gum tree forests. And the air—so fragrant it was with the natural exotic essence of eucalyptus cough drops. Unforgettable, as it was also combined with the damp, earthy muskiness of the fallen leaves turning brown and moldering into the springy earth of the forest floor. Long streamers of bark swayed in the breeze, whispering against the smooth, towering tree trunks, like so many sunburns cooling in the forest shade.

Such was its presence that this was the area where, years later, the movie *Man from Snowy River* would be filmed. Dad, Mike, and I spent a lot of our spare time wading in the streams, spin fishing. It was great!

Fishing was something of a passion with my father. Except for a few "manly things," he was mostly absent from my life, never one to simply hold his sons close or to tell either of us he loved us. No such words ever crossed his lips; it would have been alien to his nature. True to his own upbringing, he thought that sort of thing would turn us into "tinker bells." A "real man" doesn't need any of that mushy shit at any age.

Back in Fry Canyon, Dad often took Mike and me poaching deer by spotlight. All the miners did it, that being the only way they had of putting meat on the table, as there was no continuous electricity for a freezer and the generator only ran intermittently. Compared to Fry Canyon, this construction camp was virtually a city. Power was abundant, though firearms were tightly controlled, so fishing it was.

I always loved my dad, yet the times I felt any close connection were sparse. These killing sports were the only "manly" things we did together. Around him, one could not show an unwillingness to kill an animal or squeamishness, no matter how beautiful the beast or how bad the stench and mess of a gut shot. The smell of it—and the feel of slime on our arms as we tugged away, ripping those guts from its dead carcass—that was Dad's way of teaching Mike and me to be men.

Everything my father considered as the mark of a man were things I abhorred, yet, he was my dad and I wanted him to feel proud. So I wrapped myself in that facade—even tried to enjoy the thrill of the kill and the time-honored pride of the hunter, providing sustenance by his skill and cunning. But sometimes, upon hearing the agony in the scream of a dying rabbit or watching the death throes of a buck, seeing the light of its life fade from those gentle eyes, my soul would grieve for what I'd done

And I'd put a few more bricks in the wall around my heart, the one which stood between me and the world, and even my father, this wall my father seemed to think represented the strength of a man. Sad the price fathers pay for making "men" out of their sons. And again, doubly sad: I paid the same price with my own son before I realized the truth.

How could I say I loved this man—my adoptive father—when the truth was I also feared him? As Spiritual Law states: *'There are only the two energies—love and all that is not love (fear).'* I know that those energies cannot mix. Perhaps the truth was it was me; I did not love.

To my eyes, my father was a strong-minded, physically tough, don't-take-no-shit-off-nobody type of man. He never whooped me. Mother did that.

Love—fear? It can be so confusing. Could it be only his anger, that while I loved him, it was only his anger I feared? Only occasionally displayed, it could almost be physically touched. The energy of it was damned real. But on that psychic energy level . . . hell, what did I know about "psychic?" When it came to "vapors of the mind" farts and the smell of wet dog or a gut-shot deer, those were the kinds of vapors about which I knew. Things so tangibly intangible, as the ability to feel the energy of others, are things I see in myself only now. No wonder I was confused.

My father's anger was like a time bomb with no hands on its clock face. Just a couple of times did I experience the explosions, and only once, personally. We were visiting cousins, sons of my father's brother. The three of them—younger, freckled, redheaded little shits—liked to tease me by throwing dirt clods. Knowing I was not allowed to hurt them, they had me outgunned.

Dad warned me in the car before we arrived, "If they throw clods at you again, don't you dare throw any back!" He paused to deliberately look over the seat at me in the back. "You hear?"

I sighed, knowing they would tease, given the chance. "Yes, Dad, I hear." I glanced over at Mike, wishing I was more like him. He was too much older to be a target. Besides, he would hurt them regardless of the consequences, and they knew it. At their house I stayed inside, that is, until Dad ordered me to go out and play. Sure enough, they were waiting with the clods. Dodging as best I could, I caught the biggest of the three. I held him with one hand wrapped around the back of his neck. He wasn't very big.

"Knock it off, ya little fucks!" I screamed. "Or I'll kick your sorry, little butts." Then, just to make the point, I jerked up until nothing but his toes touched the ground, then kicked him in the seat of the pants—hard. He winced and teared up, but as soon as I let him go, the response I got from him and the others was a virtual rain of clods. Some whizzed by, but others hit explosively against my arms, shoulders, chest, and even my head, bursting into clouds of eye-blinding, gritty dust. After running and dodging, rage building, I picked up a clod and let it fly hard at a leg.

The front door next to their big picture window burst open, and Dad came at me on the run. With his fist doubled up, he reared back and let loose a roundhouse that would have taken my head off had I not ducked. Maybe it scared him, too, for he didn't swing again, but his teeth were gritted as he said, "Go get in the car! We're going home now."

Gleaming alongside his anger, there was disappointment in his eyes. It seemed there was always disappointment whenever he regarded me. Why had he deliberately set me up to lose? And what would have made it a win in his eyes? Did he want me to be a take-no-shit-off-of-anyone kind of guy like him? Did he expect me to beat up on kids smaller and younger? No, I'd have to be mean like my brother.

That kick in the pants did no good. I'd have to hurt them. I would have to be an idiot not to see there was some kind of bet between my dad and Uncle Andy. Surely he didn't expect me to take the abuse in obedience to him? None of it made sense!

I never asked—just accepted that I was deserving of his disappointment—and he never mentioned it again. He gave me a direct order and I disobeyed, no ifs, ands, or buts. Asking for an explanation would have been a "but," the same as making an excuse. One did not make excuses to my father.

So it has always been between us, except for our time in Australia. In those mountain streams and lakes of New South Wales, we fished—Billy, Mike, our fathers, and me. We fished and did the male bonding thing, the only time in my life my father and I ever touched one another with something resembling love. It was the best we knew to do.

Perhaps that is why Australia is so sacred in my memory. Even the dying squirm and pungent slime of gutting fish was much more bearable, compared to the gutting of a deer or a gut-shot rabbit in Fry Canyon. Maybe my father saw that and was not disappointed.

Mom, who never liked being away from civilization, seemed to like the outback of Australia—most of the time. That is, until that morning when I went out to chop kindling. Both our cook stove and heater burned wood, and the kindling supply was one of my chores.

You'd think that living in the wilds of Fry Canyon would have instilled a better sense of awareness to my ten-year-old mind. But in stepping out the back door, we were both caught by surprise—that snake and I. It whipped its head back, poised to strike. There, only a foot between us, with one hand on the doorknob the other holding the axe, I froze. Nothing moved except for the flickering of a forked, purple tongue, flicking out twice, tasting my air. We both remained that way for what, maybe two or three seconds? With the pounding of my heart, it seemed an eternity. Then slowly, I backed the two steps into the house and gently closed the door.

As snakes go, it was weird looking: about four feet long, fat, and dark reddish brown. The last few inches of its tail sort of necked down real skinny, like someone had pinched it. Clearly, it was not to be messed with. From Fry Canyon, I knew the deadly possibilities of being nakebit so far from any real medical help. Back there, we only messed with baby rattlers—until we learned that the venom of baby snakes was the most poisonous of all. Even so, this snake, in any space, felt of real menace. Slipping out the front, I went to get help.

I ran next door to Billy's, looking to find Mike. Mom was there, chatting with Billy's mother. On that, I counted myself lucky. In a casual voice, I gave my ploy. "Mike, Billy, c'mon outside; let's walk on the stilts." Our stilts we made from two-by-fours, only instead of the foot chocks being set at a twelve- to eighteen-inch height like everyone else's, Mike insisted ours be set at forty.

Mike just rolled his eyes. "Don't bother us, Jeffy, we're busy." He only called me Jeffy to point out my 'little dipshit' status.

Ducking my head to his insult, and in a low whisper, I hissed, "There's a snake on our back porch. I think it's poisonous."

"Oh . . ." Mike perked up, then glanced over at the women who were still busy talking. "Okay. C'mon, Bill, let's go."

Mike knew exactly what a snake on our back porch would mean should Mom ever see it or just hear about it. Only two days before, she'd found a big, gnarly looking wolf spider on the kitchen counter. Arming herself with a can of bug spray and a frying pan, she'd wreaked havoc all over the kitchen, then collapsed at the table in tears.

It took Mike and me the best part of an hour to put all that busted crockery and the splintered, poison-soaked counter back into fair shape, all the while enduring her constant stream of anguish. Mom always blamed us for every misery in her life.

To hear her tell it, her life was dedicated to sacrifice for us. We knew the words well: "Ungrateful; lazy little shits; irresponsible; don't care about nobody but yourselves . . . You think it's funny, don'tcha?" We weren't smiling. But had it been anyone besides her, she would have been right.

*** * ***

When the three of us got there, the snake was long gone. Our curiosity, and mention of it to other adults, resulted in a secret that turned out impossible to keep and brought fear to all who heard. The snake was a death adder, one of the deadliest in the world. Yet, any danger it posed to us was worth it. Its venom or Mom's; we knew with which we preferred to deal. And the alternative—cleaning up mangled snake guts—was just not a chore either of us would have enjoyed, especially knowing the inevitable aftermath. We liked Australia, and didn't want to have to leave.

~ *In the Present with Big D* ~

I've been aware of Big D's presence while writing these last few paragraphs. Now, turning my head, I see him. "Well, Big D, it is the truth. Do you feel it too harsh?" I speak first to counter my unease. It is not like him to come so quickly, and the energy emanating from him now feels a lot like that of the death adder.

This time, he merely stands silent beside me; his gruesome grin is his only reply. Feeling somehow as if I've already hung myself, I try to lighten the mood. "I hope I'm not being too harsh in pointing out my mother's venom here."

"What is . . . just is. It is the venom of your judgments—and yes, blame—that makes something poisonous to your soul." I sense humor in his tone and also . . . what? Disappointment? No, sadness. Disappointment requires judgment, and Big D has never judged me. "Do you really want to turn those fangs upon yourself? You, of all people, Jeff, you don't see your own blame here?"

"Well, no. I don't see it that way."

"Again, Jeff, you break your promise. The fact you don't see it is why you are still among the living." He shakes his head and his next word sounds more like a sigh. "Look . . . we've already been over the issues—those you've been whining about concerning your mother. Now you're just blowing smoke up your own ass. Here, let me help."

The glow of his eyes now turns to twin lasers, and the shirt across my chest smokes and begins to burst into flames. "Aaaiiiii . . . shit! Stop, Big D—please!" I slap out the embers from the blackened holes in my best shirt and wince at the burning sting on the skin of my chest. "You don't have to be so damned dramatic, just tell me. I'm really not all that stupid."

"That's to be determined." The glow from his eye sockets now carries a deadly tinge, for I know that if I'm not honoring my promise, I'm putting my very life on the line. "Start by telling me what it is that has your hemorrhoids in such a pucker."

I glance down at the envelope, thrown carelessly into the corner of my computer hutch, remembering its sole contents: an article scissored from some religious magazine. It preached the thought that the only thing one's father bestows upon his son is his good name. It is her continued way of saying, "You besmirch ours with your very life."

"Hell, it's true. I am angry with her sick dramas. I do wish it were different between us."

"It?"

"Okay! I wish *she* were different."

His hollow chuckle surrounds me, chaffing me with the sandpaper of its mirth. "Is it any different with you, as with her?"

"Oh, hell no. She plays these goddamn silly fucking war games, trying to shame and control me."

"Same game, only you play it with remote silence." His stare now pins me, and I feel like a bug. "Yours is a cold war." The flaring coals of his stare burn now with the intensity of dry ice against wet skin. "War. You said it correctly. Now, what will it take for you to stop playing your own part in this silly, fucking hellish war—this *game* that you refuse to take responsibility for playing? Yes, just so, this *hell* you both are creating."

"What! What do you mean?" My words fairly hiss. "Shiiiit, Big D. You don't think I've a right to be angry?" I snatch up the envelope and fling it into the waste bin next to my desk.

"I'm going to give you a pass on that one—for now." He stands silent, soberly observing me for a moment. His chuckle then comes with that familiar back-of-the-throat tone, though more pronounced, accompanied as it is with his mocking grin. "Didn't you recently write something about Australia being 'sacred' in your mind? Why was that?"

"My father, that was about my father." I shrug. "So?"

"So are you aware that the article in your mother's envelope—now in that waste bin—was not *just about how she felt?* C'mon, Jeff . . ."

"Oh." I take a deep breath and let it out slowly in a sigh. "Uuhhhh . . . I see what you mean. My father also feels I'm not honoring his name."

"Ah, so now the smoke clears! Be honest. This chapter's about your father—and about *your* perception that you deserve to be a disappointment to him." His voice takes on a sharp edge, as if that bottom-of-the-barrel tone could ever be sharp. "Well, do you?"

"Oh Christ, Big D." I sigh. "Maybe I did back then, I dunno, but I damn sure don't now!"

"Well then, you're actually angry with them both but not willing to acknowledge it about your father, right?"

"Yeah." I sigh. "That's right."

"Then will you acknowledge that it is both of them whom you don't accept?"

"Yeah, Big D, you've made your point on that score. It's *both* of them. I understand."

"No, Jeff, you don't understand, and your 'pass' is now used up. It's time to prove you're 'not all that stupid.'" Despite his perpetual grin, I know he's not joking and requires an answer.

Lost in thought, my mouth hangs open. The moments pass, but nothing comes.

"Look, Jeff, remember the law: *'You are the creator of your life'*?"

"Yes, course I do. It's the number one law of all."

"I'm guessing that you don't remember the number two side of it—no pun intended."

"Guess, Big D. You never guess. And you're right, I don't know what you mean."

"That's because it is the side mankind sees as the ***shitty*** side—pun absolutely intended!" His grin now definitely mocks. "It goes like this: 'You are the creator of your life *... **but ONLY your own life.'** "

"What?"

"Yeah." The fires of his glee now fairly dance in those eye sockets. "You have to accept that others have the right to create themselves to be exactly who they want to be."

I stand silent, no reply possible to the simple, but unexpected, truth of it. He continues.

"It's okay for you to be angry—not okay to not be accepting." His grin widens. "The really smelly part here is: You can't possibly accept someone when you feel they are responsible for your pain?"

"Goddamn, Big D. Blame! You're right. I was blaming them for my anger."

"You got it. Blaming others is to not take responsibility. It is lying to yourself." His grin is now one of satisfaction. "To blame is something all humans have been taught. It's an unconscious habit—and one I expect you to break."

"Yes, Big D, I will." I know he hears the honest intention in my words. "And thank you."

"You do know that should it be a conscious thing, it will break our agreement about you being honest with yourself." He ducks his head to more directly focus the fires of his gaze, and oddly, I feel a chill. He continues.

"But right now, you need to address the question of honoring their name. What're you going to do? You do know that he does indeed see you as a disappointment, don't you?" He holds his hand out in a gesture toward me, and for a moment, he appears to be cradling a dog turd in his bony palm. "That's the real turd at the bottom of it all, isn't it?"

I almost chuckle at the crude analogy in his humor. So closely does it match my own that it seems to take the edge off the harsh meaning of his words and instantly dissolves my anger. "He's my father. Doesn't matter that we're not blood-related or that he doesn't accept me.

I love him and respect him. Sending him a dog turd would be like telling him to fuck off. That's just not something I'm ever going to do."

"Making people wrong doesn't work—never has. You know that. Still, the sentiment expressed in that article *is* how they both feel. In their minds, you don't honor their name. What options do you have?"

"I could do what my mother has always demanded, though my father never has—well, not verbally—until now." I grimace, recalling our recent phone conversation.

"So what's he demanding?"

"He wants me to go to my mother on my knees and beg forgiveness for being the cause of all the pain and embarrassment in their lives."

"That what you want to do?" With his grin now more pronounced than ever, he adds, "There's still the dog turd. . . ."

"No." I chuckle. "Pass on the dog turd. As for begging forgiveness, that would be a lie, and it would be to continue playing that stupid, fucking game."

"How so?"

"They are demanding control—demanding I take responsibility for how they're choosing to feel. If I do, then I'm, once again, playing my part in the game." I sigh. "No, I'm not going there with them, or anyone, ever again. Still, they are my parents and I do want to honor them." Again, I sigh. "Shit! Given what I've got to do now, it's not likely they'll ever see any honor in it."

"So what will you do?"

"There's only one thing I can do—give them back their name." I shrug. "And yeah, I know. It will only be seen as a big 'fuck you' every bit as bad as sending a dog turd." Picking the letter out of the trash, I stare at the blur of it. My voice now takes on a high, unnatural tone, coming as it does from a painfully tight throat. "Besides, I think it's time I had my own name, and not the one I had when my birth mother shoveled me off into that orphanage. It needs to be one I can honor as uniquely my own. It's the only loving thing I can think to do here. Is there a better alternative, Big D?" My shoulders sag. "I don't feel good about this being a win only for me."

"No. Unfortunately, there isn't. You need to *always* seek out win/win solutions, but **sometimes** there will be others who insist on being losers. *'Everyone is the creator of their own life—and only their own.'* Again, it is the law."

A tear rolls off the end of my nose and lands on the blackened ruins of my shirt as I sit slumped in my chair. "Just seems so sad that besides my son, no one in my family now sees any honor in me."

"There you are mistaken, Jeff. Though you were adopted, there are others in your extended family who aren't blind to the family dynamics. Some will understand and even admire you." He crouches down beside me, and I feel the steely bones of his arm cradling my back as his hand grips my upper arm in his bony embrace. "And I, too, see the honor in you. You can count me as family."

All children, given time, will grow. Some even six inches at a time, and sometimes, multiple times a day. Such fluctuation for a boy is usually called "puberty." Ah, it is a wondrous time in life to be a boy.

Redneck Spirituality—Book Four

Chapter Six

Tarzan's First Puberty

Every morning, the rickety bus hauled our motley group up those two and a half steeply twisted miles to the school at Cabramurra. "Motley" because mostly we were a rather ragtag bunch of "workers'" kids: immigrant workers enticed by the Australian government for this manpower-poor Snowy Mountain Scheme Project. Most of the parents were Italians, Greeks, and Romanians—just muscles to do the work. Their children? Well, the bus did carry with it a certain air of garlic and unwashed bodies.

The first one I approached was a boy about my own age. A little scruffy, his clothes were clean but worn, much more recently washed than himself. "Hello, my name's Jeff. What's yours?"

He cocked his eyes sideways at me, then leaned to the boy sitting on his other side. They had a whispered exchange in whatever foreign language they spoke, then he looked nervously at me and with his palms facing upward, he shrugged. I took it to mean he didn't understand and left it at that. Yet, later in school, the schoolmaster asked him a question and in broken, but understandable, English, he answered. The mystery was only solved later, when I realized he was afraid of me. We, the half dozen Americans, we were the bosses' kids—his father's bosses' kids. That position seemed to mean more to them than it did us. Then there was a language barrier. Whatever the issue, it quickly became apparent—we were all okay with keeping to our own groups.

School here was hard for me, and harder for the others. Being mostly of poor peasant stock, they were not very literate. In a way, perhaps they were the luckier ones. Wherever they were going in life, it had to be better than where they had been. So it was, I hung with my own group. Was I the snob for wanting to talk with someone who would answer me back, or were they? Sad, the extent of racial fear, but then we all participated.

I had my own problems to deal with. The mismatched school year set me back half a year to the beginning of the fourth grade. That was difficult enough on my ego, but then, the Australians had some weird ideas about education—ideas like school was a place to learn things and to hell with socializing. Testing meant I was given a question and was expected to write the answer, and to convey it understandably, correctly, and legibly. I could no longer rely on my short-term memory being jogged by multiple choice answers. Instead, I found myself working very hard for the first time. Using their old-fashioned nib pens, I hen scratched across the paper. Then, dipping again from the inkwell built into the desk, I hen scratched some more and later received only mediocre grades.

There was no excuse for me: I spoke English. Given the headmaster's aristocratic disdain for Americans, I validated the worst of it. While I certainly didn't want to be known as a "slacker" or "screw up"—they had a habit of "getting the cane"—still, that was who I became.

It usually began with the headmaster shuffling through papers at his throne of a desk, then barking, "Jeffrey Williams. This penmanship is atrocious!" With his finger flung out, pointing, he'd growl, "Go to my office." In the office, he'd take down the cane from its place of honor on the shiny gold of the brass hooks mounted to the wall.

"The Cane" was a bamboo stick about eighteen inches long and a half inch in diameter. This one was split several times down on the business end. We shared a very intimate love-hate relationship, that cane and I. It loved me and I hated it—that distinct, whooshing whistle it made just before the meaty slap as it laid a red-hot kiss across my open palm. On those chilly July days, midway through the Australian winter, mine was often one of the few warmed hands in that poorly heated schoolhouse. Toe curling, that burning sting was definitely an incentive to my learning. And the headmaster? Looking back, I seriously suspect that cane and I was what provided the only source of orgasm his shriveled-up, bony ass enjoyed.

* * *

Australian schoolmasters? They were mostly disciplinarians, their American counterparts, only caretakers. What both systems lacked, it seemed to me, were teachers— teachers whose joy and enthusiasm for our learning burned within their own hearts, teachers like Miss Amy from back in Fry Canyon. God, how I missed her, especially after the San Juan County School Board sent old lady Hatchet—the name actually was Hackett—to give her the axe.

Old lady Hatchet, with her long, skinny, wrinkled neck, beak of a nose, and the mean glint of her eyes through wire-rimmed glasses. She reminded me of a vulture. When it came time to read for her, I looked into those beady eyes and, remembering the sour disdain in her comments to the others, said, "No way! I ain't reading for *you*."

Turning to Miss Amy, she asked, "What kind of little cretins have you got here? Why, you haven't even been able to teach them manners. Then, shaking a bony, claw-tipped finger in Miss Amy's face, she fairly hissed, "The San Juan County School District has no place for an incompetent hussy like you. You're fired!"

There was a combined sharp intake of breath from the whole class, then a groan filled the room. Yet, no one braved to say anything— well, except me. I tried to go to Miss Amy's defense, but a high-powered official from the San Juan County School District just wasn't one to listen to an illiterate cretin like me. I have felt guilty all my life for getting Miss Amy fired. It is only recently that I realized that the word "hussy" spoke the bald-faced truth. To Miss Hatchet, the word meant, "I am jealous of a beauty like you!"

* * *

The misery I found there in the academic world was well balanced by the joy I took in Australia otherwise. So it was with the Tarzan swing. There was a tree that hung out over the garbage dump at Kenny's Knob. The bank below fell steeply for about thirty feet, steep enough so that trash and litter did not linger at all on the slope. Someone had tied a rope to the tree and we used it extensively.

Out we'd swing over the fast-sloping rift of that valley—out toward the gum trees, with their leaves and bark floating with the fragrant, earthy scent on the mountain breeze, a scent now slightly tainted by the garbage. Yes, we, too, floated on that breeze. For me, at that height, the heady adventure was mixed with a certain fear. It was something we'd been forbidden to do, and of course, we all did it anyway—until the day the rope broke.

Sure enough, Mike was on it at the time. I fully expected to see him die as I watched his flight, seemingly in slow motion for those thirty feet down. It ended in the trash against an old log at the bottom. His hand slapped the log with an audible crack. This time, it was only a broken left wrist—the arm bones bulging the skin inward made it look like his hand was put on crooked. In the years since Bingham, Mike had at least learned not to land on his head. However, it required a trip to Sydney to get his wrist set. Mike didn't enjoy the trip, but I did.

At Sydney, Dad left Mom and Mike at the hospital, then took Billy and me to get a room at a hotel. The next morning was spent by Billy and me at Bondi Beach. I did not know how to swim, so I waded in the shallows like a boob, while Billy swam out to the shark net. The swimming area bordered the open ocean, which was frequented by great white sharks.

In the afternoon, we wandered the narrow streets downtown with Mike now sporting his new, pure-white cast. Liberally interspersed among the small shops were English-style pubs. We peeked through the doorway of one and experienced the beer, piss, vomit, and sawdust essence of a truly adult place.

Before leaving our hotel room, Dad slipped us both a little money—me, enough to buy a throwing knife. Mike, now, I guess he rated something more, what with the misery of his injury and all. Entering the leather shop, he passed by the saddles and horse tack and went straight to the kangaroo hide stockwhips. One soon became his pride and joy, and my secret envy.

After almost two years, we left Australia. It was late 1958, and I was not yet twelve. This time there would be no straight through, thirty-six-hour flight only broken by the hour-and-a-half refuel in Hawaii.

I felt a pang of regret as I watched the Australian Coast slip into my past and into the mist out beyond the horizontal tail wing with its two upright side fins on that old Qantas turboprop. Along the way, we vacationed for several days in Fiji, staying at a resort away from the city. For our parents, it was the honeymoon they never had.

For me, it felt luxuriously exotic, like the sort of things rich folks would do. Those "rich folk places"—there would be more yet to experience. But it always felt odd, like we were just visitors to the experience. We were never rich folks.

But there in Fiji, Mike and I had our own bungalow, made mostly of log beams and braided grass panels. We slept in mosquito net-shrouded beds, and for the most part, our time was our own. Not knowing how to swim, I spent a lot of time with a swim mask, face down in the shallow lagoon, watching the fish. That night flight from there to Honolulu, on the Hawaiian island of Oahu, was misery. Even with all my days on the desert at Fry Canyon, I'd never been sunburned. Sitting in that darkened plane, everyone around me laid back snoring, drooling in their sleep, my back also drooled. As the blisters broke, the skin began to peel just like the dead bark swinging off the trunk of an Australian gum tree—yes, misery.

We stayed at the Reef Hotel on Waikiki Beach. Arriving at night, there wasn't much to see. But what I noticed about Oahu was the pervasive fragrance of flowers on the balmy, humid air. Everywhere we went was the sight and scent of flowers. While there, we took a tour of the island, ate pineapple fresh out of the fields, saw Pearl Harbor, and assorted other things tourists usually do. Of it all, the greatest thing I did was learn to swim.

Because of the sunburn, a lot of my time was spent in the cooling shade of the hotel's swimming pool. It was always deserted, as everyone else preferred the sun and the beach. I began by swimming across the corners of the deep end, and as my confidence grew, I started cutting the corners wider and wider until I could swim clear across. The pain of my sunburn lasted only days; its gift, for the rest of my life.

Arriving stateside, we stayed about a month with an uncle in Napa, California. While there, Dad bought a new '59 Ford Galaxy to drive back to Utah. The sleek, futuristic styling of a next-year model car was a big deal back then. Traveling back to Utah, people would point and stare. I wasn't sure I liked it. Drawing attention to myself at Sunny

Hills—now almost seven years in my past—always meant pain or misery to me in some way. My uneasy self-consciousness was not yet left behind. Hell, it still isn't. Yet, in a way, it was fun to find myself envied, even if that envy was only about the car.

Once back, our house in Sandy was still rented under a lease, so Dad, in turn, rented a house on 35th South in Granger. I was bumped up a half year in school, once again on track and in the sixth grade. Way ahead of the others, school suddenly became easy and stayed that way clear up through high school.

Dad leased a gas station in Granger and sold new and recapped tires. After school, Mike and I worked part-time at the station, pumping gas and mounting tires. There was never any pay—it was just expected in a Mormon family.

In our free time, we kids did a lot of bow fishing for carp and hunting rabbits in the marshes around Decker's Lake. I dearly loved my recurve hunting bow, so much so, that girls never seriously crossed my mind, except in the dark of night and the privacy of my hand and mind. But that was changing. Yes, I was beginning to grow, as the often embarrassing bulging of my pants would attest.

* * *

After moving back into our house in Sandy, and now in the seventh grade, there was a girl, Tina Richards. She was fairly tall, about five feet eight—important to me, as by then, I stood at six feet. Towering ungainly above the others, and skinny, I felt like a grasshopper at a cricket convention.

And Tina; there was much more to Tina. She was pretty—and built, from her billowy cleavage split by the straps connecting the cups of her bra, to the folded, denim stitching joining the shapely legs of her jeans. Yeah, Tina was built. Those jeans, stretched tight as they were, might well have been painted on. They seemed to cleave the space between her thighs in miniature redundance. Tina had great *camel toes*, as we guys called them. Yes, hers was the kind of body from which wet dreams are birthed.

Yet, the thing I liked most about her was how we could talk. We talked about almost everything, that is, everything except sex. Tina was a good Morman girl. And me? I was pretending to be a good Mormon boy, a requirement in a Mormon family. In-between sucking each other's lips until they were too numb to feel, I found her to be intelligent, sensitive, beautiful, and very sexy. God! She had everything.

* * *

We steadied for about a year and a half. Then gradually, however perfect, it began to feel a little like a rut. I had visions of growing up, marrying my childhood sweetheart, then always wondering if it could be any better with others. I wanted to know, to experience.

And perhaps, too, it might have been simply: I hadn't experienced Tina—not fully. There was always cloth between me and those breasts, and the 'Y' of her thighs was also never touchable.

Kissing her soft lips, holding her with my face buried in the sweet essence of her hair, I shared my feelings with her openly—as openly as was permissible for a good Mormon boy. I could not bury my face in her beard, smell her, touch her, kiss her lips there, or acknowledge those antsy feelings that were crawling up my legs.

We parted. Somehow I always thought we'd get back together sometime . . . well, later. But no, those kind of ants always have a habit of biting a fella on the butt, and sometimes, in later life, on the nuts, depending where he puts his dick.

I've often wondered what happened to Tina. Maybe that perfect rut would have been a great place for me to have stayed. Through it all, there is one thing I have come to know about her: For me then, Tina was perfect. It's been said that "a rut is just a grave with the ends kicked out." Truth is, life just carries us where we consciously or unconsciously want to be. And ruts? Ruts are dug by the heels of some knothead in resistance—like me.

* * *

As for the time when Mike broke his arm back there in Australia, his Tarzan-like life only served to reinforce my own sense of caution. Oh sure, I also swung freely from that Tarzan rope. I, too, felt the thrill.

But unlike Mike, it wasn't about cheating Death. Just to survive with a brother like Mike was thrill enough for me.

Okay, I'll admit it: maybe there was a little fear in the mix. Maybe having a little cautious fear is what kept me alive. Mike was devoid of it. It seemed he often created opportunities for himself to leave this world. Was leaving life in some courageously glorious way what he wanted, or did he just want his life to be fun?

Caution is a skill I learned because of Mike—a balancing act between possible joy and possible pain, life and death. And I love him for it. By watching his extreme example, I've learned to keep my finger off the scales. I think using caution in stepping through fear has little to do with cowardice. And fingers? Nothing to do with bravery.

And fuck! Maybe this is just me making cowardice okay in my own mind?

* * *

As for roaming the world and rubbing shoulders with the rich folks? We did that for a time. I never had much money, but remembering it now? Yeah! Just maybe we were rich. Maybe being rich has little to do with one's money and everything to do with one's thinking.

And me? Maybe my thinking needs to include a little more self-worth?

* * *

Puberty? For me, it was a time of heady excitement and ravenous hungers, most of which were lived only in one's imagination and satisfied in the palm of one's hand. It still was a time of great fun. Perhaps that is why I am enjoying my second puberty so much.

You know, the one most call post-divorce syndrome, middle-age blues, midlife crisis, manopause . . . only now it does not require the palm of one's hand. For it is the time in life when those matching hungers in a woman have finally been reached and made morally okay within her psyche. Or perhaps it is just how much time it takes for women before they are ready to unleash.

And me again? Sometimes it's hard for a guy to keep pace with a woman's sexual leash—sometimes not?

~ *In the Present with Big D* ~

"Well, Big D?" I feel his presence. "Aren't you going to interrupt this dissertation? Have you nothing to say?"

His laughter billows with that bottom-of-the-barrel familiarity. "Well, not about that last part, certainly." He materializes in the shadows of my den just beyond the bluish glow of my computer. "I wouldn't touch that with any bone. But the rest? That mushy crap about caution? Mike didn't teach you shit about it. True, he taught you about balance, but mostly he taught you to have fun." The ruby glow of his eyes flashes in merriment as he adds, "And by the way, where your motorcycle is concerned, your finger gets just a might sticky on those scales."

"What? I don't understand." *God! Why do I find myself saying that so much lately?*

"Perhaps you've got too much rattling around in your skull."

"Are you saying I think too much . . . or that I'm just rattle-brained?"

"Ha!" His empty eye socket seems somehow to wink. "Maybe neither, maybe both."

"Well, what then?"

"Simple honesty, remember?" He winks again. "What happened just yesterday?"

"Yesterday?" Instantly, my mind flies back to yesterday. Again, my ass is planted in the sand, arms hugging my knees tightly to my chest. My whole body is shaking with the draining of adrenalin as I sit in the shadow of a lone yucca—the only shade near this pull-off. I look across at my bike. Its sleek, powerful form, with its blazing chrome and eye-catching crimson-and- orange paint, leans casually against its stand. Like a drug to me, it sometimes deadens my senses to the realities of fragile flesh hurtling atop it down the roadway.

Bugs . . . and bug-smeared bumpers . . . God! I'd almost become a big one! It happened so suddenly. One moment I was winging by the line of semi-trucks, plodding their way like monster ants up the grade. The wind ripped around me at seventy-five, with an occasional unnerving side gust. Suddenly, I caught just such a gust—magnified off the flat front of a semi— and in the next moment was over the double line, trying to brake, but starting to go down into a side skid.

Then there was the Pontiac before me, its green paint and chromed grill and its driver's eyes. Even at a combined speed of well over a hundred miles per hour, I saw my death in those eyes. Releasing the brakes, I fishtailed past, yet it almost seemed. . . .

"You did hit . . . and you didn't." Big D grins, releasing me from the spider's web of my memory. "Don't you see?"

"See? See what?"

"It's all so simple." His voice has become loving, and I know he is again about to tell me something very profound. "Don't you know yet? Ultimately, your demise is up to me?"

"I thought it was about either quitting or completing my purpose in life."

"It is—then again, have you looked at who I am to you?" His eyes have begun a fiery glow. "You? Me? God? We are all one and the same!"

"The same?"

"God? The Creator? The Great, Omni-fucking everything? I know your personal belief is that God is literally made of all the energy of the universe. True?"

"Yes, true."

"And I know you believe that of it all, no matter the form of the energy, it is all of the essence of God?"

"Yes."

"That in that essence, you are all literally one and the same!"

"Yes, the higher part of us is, literally, God! This is my belief."

"What about me? Big D . . . Mr. Death, am I, too, God?"

"Yes."

"And one and the same with you? C'mon, Jeff, what do you think?"

"Well, sure . . . that's what I understand."

"No! You don't understand!" His gaze is now painfully bright. "You, like all mankind, prefer to see me as someone or something else! Some separate entity!" I feel mesmerized now in his gaze. "It's all so very simple. Do you really want to know?"

"Yes." Though I feel somewhat fearful, I open myself willingly and hear his snort of approval.

"God . . . you . . . me . . . this highest essence of your soul! This is who determines above all if you live or die. You live until the purpose of your life is completed." He pauses and time seems to hang. I can almost sense the eternal nature of it. Like a microbe under the microscope, I am the focus of his gaze. "Yes! You have a destiny. You will live until I, 'this highest essence of you,' see that you, 'your lowest conscious level,' have completed your destiny . . . or quit!"

Visions of a bed, a hospital room, and a talking monitor flash into my mind. I remember our bargain. . . .

"Yes, now you've got it: you made a choice—we made a bargain! I spared your scrawny ass then . . . ," he pauses to chuckle, "and again yesterday." I feel his ivory caress whisper across my cheek. "You reached out to me way back then in the pre-existence. Our agreement made back then has been binding."

"I don't—"

"Understand. I know you don't. For you, it did not go into conscious effect until after you quit on your destiny and found yourself in that hospital, facing me. You didn't make our bargain then." He pauses to chuckle. "You only reaffirmed it into consciousness. The life you now live is the one you had planned."

I can only gape as he continues.

"You, me, and that higher power most call God—on that level, we are one, remember? God knows everything, and on that higher level, so do we. On this conscious level, you think you are learning these things, and having learned, know. Thing is, you cannot truly *know* without experiencing. The plan here in life is to experience. ***This part of God's experience is called your destiny.***

"Big D, I . . . I don't. . . ."

"Let me make it real simple." The glow emanating from his eye sockets now flickers brightly, and there seems to be some special ecstasy now accompanying his words. "You, Jeff, along with all living beings, are ***the*** part of God that experiences and ***knows—life!***"

I blink and find my mouth is open and my jaw working, but no words are coming out. I feel his palm gently rubbing my back as he leans in to deliver his next words. Beginning in a whisper, they increase in volume as he speaks.

"You, Jeff, are special. You are ***sentient***—thinking, feeling, intelligent, self-aware—***life.*** And you personally have chosen to raise the bar on your own farther than most are willing. Hold true; there's nothing to fear. I am your most loving advocate. When your destiny is complete, we will go willingly!" His humor reverberates through my head with his parting words. Spoken loudly now, there does, indeed, seem to be a rattle to those reverberations. With them, he reveals something I must never forget. "Danger, caution, bravery, cowardice— none of that shit matters so much as how you feel about yourself. Again, hold true to the joys of your heart! ***Experience*** it all for yourself—for this little piece of God who now . . . ***knows***."

So often we, as men, equate sexual conquest with manliness. Why is this so? Isn't it true it is the women who let us? She doesn't really surrender—she accepts. Another equally macho fallacy, also requiring another to let us, is that if we can make another appear as "less than," then we appear as "more than." In both cases, we are only displaying the smallness of our mind—and sometimes, our member.

Redneck Spirituality—Book One

Chapter Seven

Hanging With Mike

On the summer following my ninth grade, Mike hanged himself. I never knew why.

The evening was uneventful there in our house in Sandy. I was in bed in my room upstairs, Mom in her bedroom next door, and Mike in his bedroom in the basement. Dad was in Greece.

Business was slow at the tire shop for Dad and his new partner, my uncle Andy. They needed extra money for expansion, and Dad figured another juicy overseas job would do it for them. The job was in the mountainous area of Northwestern Greece. Dad went ahead. We were to join him as soon as the campsite was ready for families.

I was nearly asleep when the noises began.

Wham! Wham! Wham!

Bolt upright in bed now, I wondered, *What the hell is Mike doing down there? Sounds like he's wailing on the gas pipes.* There was silence for a few seconds, and I began to relax back in my bed—

Wham! Wham!

"Goddammit!" I cursed softly under my breath. "Shit!" Ripping out of bed, I rushed to the stairwell leading to the basement. "Mike!" I hissed in a coarse whisper. "Stop it! You'll wake up Mom." We both knew how she was; nothing had changed there. Her angry tantrums only happened when Dad wasn't around, and of course, that was pretty much all the time just now. These days, Mom often harangued us for what seemed like hours at a time.

We knew the drill well. The key words hadn't changed: ". . . ungrateful, lazy, inconsiderate . . ." And we knew about all her aches and pains and how we ". . . just don't care." Perhaps we just didn't believe, for they would magically go away once we turned on the water works and shouldered the blame. Over the years, Mike and I got good at crying on cue. Oh, our tears were real, but only out of aggravation, not repentance. This night, I just wasn't in the mood.

No answer drifted back up, and after deliberating a moment, I turned to leave.

Wham!

Goddamn him! I stomped down the stairs. He was stronger, tougher, meaner, but God how I wanted to kick his ass! *If I'm going to pay the price with Mom, he's at least going to get a shitload of my mind.*

When my line of sight broke the level of the basement ceiling, I was looking straight into his room—and at his body hanging by the neck from a rope tied to the gas pipes. He was bare-butt naked, his face rapidly turning blue. Rushing over, I began a frantic search for something with which to cut him down. An eternity of ripping through his stuff produced a hunting knife. Supporting his limp body with a shoulder, I hacked at the rope above until, at last, it parted. Lowering his body to the floor, I noted he'd chosen to tie a hangman's knot.

Staying in character: the Wild West to the end . . . , I mused somewhere calmly in the back of my mind. Weird—the rest of my mind knew only panic as I began sawing at the rope along the spiral coils of the hangman's knot. So tight was it, and so far had it cut into the flesh of his neck, that I could not cut any closer without taking off an ear, or worse. When the rope finally sprang free, and with trembling fingers, I checked for a pulse. There was none! Nor was he breathing. He appeared dead.

Goddamn you, Mike! No . . . you . . . don't! My gut lurched as vivid scenes from my nightmares flashed across my mind. I gritted my teeth. *You won't slip through my fingers! You don't get to die—not this time.*

Mike's old British 303 rifle was leaning up against a support beam. Snatching it up, I frantically banged the butt against the rough-cut wood beam screaming, "Mom! Mom! Wake up! Get an ambulance.

Mike's hurt!" Then, jerking his chin up and back, I pinched off his nose and, with lips sealed over his mouth, blew into it. When after three or four breaths nothing happened, I rolled him over onto his front, quickly crossed his hands under his face, and began manual respiration, just as I'd learned it in the Scouts. Positioning myself at his head, knees up against his forearms, I rhythmically began pushing heavily down on his back, then rowing back upward with his elbows. Mouth-to-mouth was relatively new, something I didn't know well or feel comfortable with continuing—not with Mike's life depending on it. This I knew how to do.

It was probably the correct choice, as there was no heartbeat. Manually pushing on his back may have been a crude approximation to CPR, which was non-existent at the time. It worked. Mike coughed and began his first convulsing breaths just as Mom ducked her head down the stairwell.

"What is going on down there?"

Ignoring the tone of her voice, I ordered, "Don't come down. Just get an ambulance— NOW!"

Mike spent about a month down at "Happy Acres" while they checked him for loose screws. I don't know how many they found, but they let him out in time to go to Greece.

Why did he do it? It's possible it had something to do with a particularly sick book I knew he was reading. It told about how the Nazis were strangling people in the concentration camps. Mike was fascinated in that it described how the male victims would get erections as they died. Hell, I'd never known Mike to ever read a book, and why else would he hang himself totally nude?

Clearly, I'd saved his life, yet he never thanked me—or ever acknowledged it. No one did, nor did I want gratitude. But sometimes I wondered if, in reality, he was mad at me, so sullen he would become when I attempted to question him. Perhaps my suspicions about that book were true. Yet, concerning sex and hard-ons—that stuff we'd always freely discussed. And that book? He knew that I always kept his confidence. Why would he have a problem admitting that to me now?

So many questions still remain, even today. Why his surly silence? Did he feel I'd somehow made him look bad, proven myself the better son? Did he really die, and if so, what was his experience like? Whoa! If that were true, did he find the love and acceptance denied him in this life? Maybe I brought him back into this world against his will. Holy shit! Possibly it was some higher power that required him to return.

Did Mike have a purpose—a destiny I was forcing him to fulfill? Did it involve me?

Yes, the questions remain unanswered, all but that last one. Mike did, indeed, have a destiny to fulfill in my life. And who knows, perhaps also in the lives of others.

* * *

Dad's new job was as a shift boss for the diversion tunnel of a dam on the Acheloos River in the "Ozarks" of Greece. The site was some sixty-five kilometers north of Agrinion, the nearest town of any size. The people there were thought of as hillbillies by the sophisticates around the big cities like Athens. Mike and I later provided them a lot of entertainment—two Americans speaking in hillbilly Greek.

* * *

What an experience it was, our trip to Greece. The train rattled and clacked in tempo to the singing of the rails all the way from Ogden, Utah to Grand Central Station, New York. From there, we sailed on the Queen Elizabeth I, first class. It was her old maiden—her last—voyage. It ended at Cherbourg, France. From there, we boarded another train to Paris. And finally, early the next morning, we traveled Paris to Athens by plane.

* * *

Athens had an exotic air, so many people speaking a language unintelligible to us. It felt, well, foreign. Yet, we were the foreigners. They didn't seem all that much different. Their clothes were the usual: shirts, pants, shoes. Sure, no one wore tight blue jeans, wide belts with big, shiny buckles, or cowboy boots. The strangeness I noticed was in the smells of their cooking, and with it, their bodies. In Greece, it seemed all food was contaminated with garlic and swam in olive oil. The city itself was a strange mixture of ancient ruins and modern buildings, with sections of cramped, little shops and apartments poured in-between.

As the housing at the job wasn't yet completed, we rented an apartment in the same building as Billy's family. This job was another one that Billy's dad asked my father to come along on. Mike, Billy, and I soon found ourselves enrolled at the American Academy.

Most of the students were embassy officials' kids and Air Force brats. I'd never seen such an assortment of snobs. No stranger to rejection in my younger life, it was clear to me that these people had it down to perfection.

Mike, Billy, and I were just normal Americans. Our parents weren't high government officials or Air Force Brass. Hell, we weren't even rich. As we were nobody to suck up to, we were nobody to know. Needless to say, we didn't like it there. Our grades reflected it.

* * *

We often took the Athens subway out to the Atherton suburbs where the rich Americans lived. The kids our age met every Friday and Saturday night at a place they called the Teen Club. They played records and a few danced, but mostly everyone just sat around smoking and generally trying to out-cool everyone else.

Though we three had dicked around with cigarettes back in our Fry Canyon days, smoking now became a habit—one which I took pains to hide from our parents. Mike, it seemed, didn't need to. Some things not acceptable with me, with him, were expected. I was thirty when I finally kicked the habit. Mike never did. He didn't have my luxury of time.

* * *

There are two small mountains that mar the cityscape of Athens, or perhaps it is Athens that mars the landscape of the mountains. One is topped by the Acropolis, and the other, a few miles to the north, by a monastery. Our apartment house was just down the street from the latter. Around its base was a park with lovely footpaths, trees, and bushes—normal park stuff. It served as a place the unmarried lovers of Athens, and perhaps a few loosely married ones, used as their own personal motel. The ground beneath most of the bushes was paved with prophylactics.

The peak was crowned with a monastery, but below and behind it was a marble quarry. I was later told it was where the marble used to build the Acropolis was quarried. It was just Mike and I exploring on the day we found it.

Standing in the bottom of that quarry, its naked rock wall nearly vertical for maybe a hundred and fifty feet, Mike said, "Let's climb the wall. It'll be fun!"

I shuddered at the excitement glinting in his eyes. "C'mon, Mike, not another cliff; you know how I hate heights." Then, with futile hope, I laid on some guilty responsibility. "And if you do, you know I'm going to have to climb it with you."

He was already four feet above me when he gave his reply. "Okay then . . ."

It wasn't too bad a climb. The rock was rough with plenty of hand and footholds. When we reached the top, Mike looked at me, probably noticing the green tinge, and his next words had to have been said out of pure meanness because he grinned and chuckled before saying them. "That was fun. I'm going back down."

Like everything else in his life, I suppose Mike took my climbing with him that day as a challenge to his bravery, for once we reached the bottom, he hooked his arm with mine—did he see the trembling of my knees—and went in search of a better cliff. He found it on the back side of the monastery. About two hundred feet high, it had some really slick, mossy spots and a lot of fairly smooth, near vertical open rock. I hung right behind Mike until just before the top. Then came a place where I couldn't see the next hand or foothold and was too stretched out to move back. The paralysis of fear began to take hold, and I was sure my guts were about to be smeared all over this mountain.

God! How did I get myself into this mess? Is this it—the end?

Spread-eagled across this seemingly smooth rock face, I searched about with frantic eyes. My finger and toeholds were too precarious to move without a place to go. The cliff face was nearly vertical and I hugged it tightly, bleating out in a squeaky treble, "Mike . . . Mike! I can't move. I'm gonna fall!"

"Oh fuck, Jeff, just stretch out! There's a handhold to your right." There was a note of annoyance in his voice.

Body tensed and trembling, I cautiously leaned out, craning my neck. "Yes . . . I see it!" Hanging literally by a few fingers and toeholds, I fumbled out with my right hand and was still six inches short. "Uhhh . . . but I'm stretched as far as I can."

There was little strength left in my straining body, nor was my hold secure enough to make an all-or-nothing lunge. Hell, I'd just done that and knew with surety I couldn't go back. Instead, I hung there, feeling the moments of my life ebbing with my strength. Then, taking what I expected might be my last frantic look around, I saw only Mike's boots, six feet above, scuffle one more step away.

"Mike, I can't hold on much longer!"

"Aarrrghhh . . . shit! Just a minute!" Mike growled his disgust, then maneuvered down a few steps and extended his leg. "Here, dipshit, grab my foot."

Taking a hold with my left hand, I made the lunge. A few minutes later found us climbing over the low rock wall into the back courtyard of the monastery. We both sat down together on the flagstones, exhausted, our backs against the wall in the cooling shade. I looked over at Mike and saw the triumph in his eye and knew the adrenalin still rushed in his veins. It still rushed in my own, but unlike Mike's, it didn't rush in triumph. And in my mind was a silent prayer, *Please God! Don't let there be another cliff!*

We were still there, resting, when the heavy, wooden door from the monastery opened and out stepped a monk. Dressed in his black robes and tall, matching, upside-down stovepipe hat with its round, flat brim at the top, he seemed immersed in the world of his opened book. He did not appear to notice us right off as we rose and headed for the side gate. It must have been the clump of our cowboy boots, for his head jerked up. Eyes wide, his mouth fell open, aghast in silent surprise.

"Nice place you got here," Mike said in passing. Then chuckling, he slid back the locking bolt and unlatched the gate set in the high, rock, outside wall and stepped through. I followed, glancing back at the monk's still-opened-mouth astonishment as I closed the gate behind us. Walking along the path that led down and around the outside of that medieval monastery, I couldn't help but wonder if the sanctity of his courtyard would ever again hold the same meaning for him. How many centuries had it stood impenetrable to the likes of us?

* * *

Looking back, I realize that the one time I actually did save Mike's life, I got no appreciation. So why did I continue to appoint myself his guardian? That very act was just my mind's way of saying: *I don't hold you capable.* Is it any wonder Mike felt the need to demean me? But then, didn't I allow it? Didn't I enable him by buying into his act by looking at myself as weak and cowardly in comparison?

I believe this climb scared Mike as much as it did me. After all, what would he say if little brother, Jeffrey, ended up dead? My prayer was answered. He never again climbed another scary cliff when with me, and perhaps after that one, none of the others were frightening to me.

In trying to *save* Mike, maybe I cheated myself. Witnessing his demise, in whatever manner he chose, simply required more courage than I had. Witnessing his joy of climbing could have been exhilarating; he was damned good at it. Witnessing his inevitable death might have lent him more grace that way—for himself and for me—for it required a healthy acceptance of his choices in life. Was the fault mine that there was no such grace when Death did come to him?

Appointing myself Mike's guardian served no one. Again, there is that Spiritual Law: *'I am the sole creator of my life.'* But back then, I knew nothing about Spiritual Law. Besides, I could never accept that Mike was the sole creator of his own life. My God, that would require me to be willing to face my life without him, alone. He was my one remaining connection to who I was—to family.

Even so, nothing I ever did made him live his life differently. None of it served to keep him in my life any longer. No, Mike was Mike—someone who just naturally took every opportunity to piss into Death's face.

The question is, are we ever really any more than just witnesses in other people's lives? If they live any differently than they would want, because of us, isn't it just a pretense we witness. Between Mike and I, it was only his truth that I witnessed. I know this because every time I asked him not to piss into Death's face, he just pissed into mine—only at the time, I just didn't see it.

* * *

As for this time right now, I see clearly that I am beating the crap out of that word "witness." It is so hard to accept being just that, a witness, to the life of someone you love who is killing himself, and you can't stop it. Mike has been gone more than fifty years now, and I still miss him. Despite all who have come through my life since, I am again, alone.

I loved and admired Mike. Much of who I am now is because of what I saw in him. But I don't know if he ever lived his life any differently because of something he saw in me, something he wanted to change in himself.

~ *In the Present with Big D* ~

"Mike did . . . and often. It is to your credit that you don't know it."

"Big D, you're here a little early, aren't you?"

"Of course . . . I'm always here when you need me." His voice comes loudly, from behind my shoulder. I swivel my chair to address the misty shadow of him.

"Okay . . ." Not being sure why I need him just now, I decide to humor him. "Well, what do you think?"

"Hmmm . . ." I get the impression of him pursing invisible lips. "Looks like you nailed it. I'm impressed!" There comes a faint clacking as his shoulders shrug.

"What? You're not going to get mad at me, or tell me how little I understand about this chapter?"

"Are you living your dreams?"

"Yes."

"Following your joy?"

"Yes."

"Being exactly who you are?"

"Yes."

"Being honest with yourself—even right now?"

"Yes."

The rapid-fire question and answer session now suddenly stops, just as my Beretta 92 sometimes does when it stovepipes on a poorly reloaded bullet. Big D regards me silently for just a moment, and I get the feeling he has just jacked the slide and released that useless shell.

"Then why would I be angry?"

"I don't know, Big D." Somehow my question feels a little lame. "It seems like you always are."

"Always were, yes—before that hospital room. We are always angry whenever we're being unfaithful to ourselves, but then, everyone gets a little time before I step in." His soft chuckle resounds from that oh-so-familiar bottom of the barrel. "And you *do* know that you've used up yours"—he ducks his head meaningfully—"*don't you*?"

"Well yes, I t-t-think I do." Somewhat unnerved, my tongue seems to stumble over itself.

"Yes, I know you *think* you do, but you have only touched on it." His voice now holds amusement. "Now it's time to take it deeper."

"I don't understand . . ."

"Is it any wonder your soul would anger when you deny it its joys? Or when you don't follow the path of your life's purpose? Or especially when you lie to, and are traitorous to, yourself?"

"Oh, I see . . . Yes, I did all that." Relieved, my excitement quickens. "God, yes! And I understand about following my joy and being honest with myself, and why all that is part of our bargain. And yes, back then, I was very angry—"

"Everyone does this 'anger' game." He grins as he interrupts me. "And few are honest enough to know it. Like you then, they look for someone or something 'out there' upon which to unleash that anger. They carry it around like a loaded gun and use any little excuse to pull the trigger. Ha! Even you still carry a little anger about your brother's choices in life. And while it doesn't amount to more than a BB gun, even you still take an occasional potshot."

"Yes, I see that. And it's so dysfunctional—"

Again, he interrupts. "Blame in any form is . . ." His pause is pregnant, his gaze now intent. ***And no, you don't see.***

"See w-what?"

"How you came into this conversation pointing your BB gun at me."

"What? No, I didn't do—"

"Jeff, face it. You aren't as conscious as you *think* you are."

"What? How so?"

"Yeah, exactly. *'What'*—what does it mean to be *conscious*?"

"Uh . . ." I pause to collect the jangle of my thoughts. "It means to look within yourself and to know the truth consciously about yourself—and how you are living your life. It is about taking responsibility for all of it."

"Try this then. You came to me just now, expecting my anger at some illusionary failure about you, wanting to blame me ahead of time for it. You the victim: I the perpetrator." His laughter echoes and reechoes into silence. His next words ring sad, but clear. "Then you even tried to paint me as some dark, sickle-wielding savage—who killed your brother."

"No! Not me . . . ," I begin in quick protest.

I hear his answering sigh. "Ah, but it's true. I am that to you—the part that ultimately handles the darkest dishonesty of every person alive. In the end, when facing the sickle, no dishonesty will survive. But then, you know that very well. Yet, you prefer to blame me for your painful lie that I played an undue part in your brother's death." His words now change and lovingly caress me in a kind of melancholy. "Hell, some have called me 'The Grim Reaper.' But, given our last conversation, do you really think I deserve that kind of reputation, or to have it validated by you?"

"Oh shit, you're right. I was blaming you. But—"

"Don't sweat it, Jeff. I will not fault you, this time, for not being honest with yourself."

"But I am being honest—I really am! The price of breaking our agreement is much too high."

"Again, did you not just admit coming into this conversation trying to *blame* me for some silly shit? And then again *blaming* me for killing your brother? Don't you know the key word here is *blame*? And *blame* is simply another word for 'dishonest.' That's twice in this chapter you've been dishonest—three times were I to count your statement that you 'really am' being honest."

"But . . . but . . . ."

"Jeff, Jeff, let's not get pissy," he chides. "I said I wouldn't fault you. You *are* following your joy, and all the rest of our agreement, but for this. Besides, you're only human. Like all humans, you're not so consciously connected to your soul, especially when blinded by your pain." His bottom-of-the-barrel tone somehow seems to have a certain added huskiness. He sighs and, shaking his bowed head, continues in a heavyhearted, and somehow hardened, voice.

"There is something we need to get straight, right now." He looks up and pins me in the fiery, almost violet, flames of some deep emotion. ***"Blame is the insidious bitch of unconsciousness. She is a bitch you don't get to fuck with, ever again."*** To repeat: "I won't fault you this time for your unconscious, carnal indecency. Nor did I fault your brother for his meanness—or for all that pissing in my face. He, also, was blinded by his pain."

"But you are the same 'Death' who visits others. You did take my brother, didn't you?" Even as I say it, I can feel the ice crackling under my skates.

"C'mon, Jeff. Don't you start pissing in my face. We've been over this." He chuckles, this time without humor. "Remember? On this level, you, me, all of humanity are part of God. We are ultimately one and the same. We all play our part. Yours is to do the living. Mine is to run the shuttle bus—oh, and the sickle." His words end with another chuckle and a sizzling swish. His feigned practice swing almost sends me scrambling backward over my chair. "This sickle is more like a shepherd's crook. No. Like all the rest, he did his own dying. I merely gave Mike a ride home."

The ice breaks, plunging me into the icy realization of truth. I can only gape at him as he continues.

"Have you ever considered that maybe the pre-existence pact he made with you was simply completed?" He pauses to bend down, placing his grinning countenance only inches from my own. "You've already admitted that much of who you are is because of your brother's contributions—even his death. And you"—he pauses once more as if to emphasize a point— "don't you realize how much you taught your brother, simply with the courage by which you live your own life?"

"Courage, Big D? I don't consider myself courageous. You know that." His features now dissolve into a mist, leaving only his last words distinct, but mysterious.

"Yes, I do know. Keep on writing. . . ."

I shudder at all the fear-filled, chickenshit things I've admitted so far—and at all the rest yet to come.

What one person may feast on as a delicacy, another finds repugnant in the extreme, usually because someone once told him it is so. It is not about what tastes good, nurtures, or gives growth. It is only about prejudice. So it is when one does not think for oneself in life. Is it any wonder mankind is so slow to grow?

Redneck Spirituality Book Four

Chapter Eight

The Ozarks of Greece

The job's living accommodations was a newly minted little town at a place called Kremasta. Located on a mountain plateau above the dam site, there was a little meadow in the center, green with grass and dotted silver with the lighter, almost metallic, sheen of several olive trees. It separated the bosses' residences—our fancy white cottages—from the drab, gray workers' barracks. Behind it all to the east rose the granite peaks of a high mountain range.

The dam was to be built in the gorge downstream of the junctions of three rivers. The main one, the Acheloos, ran narrow, clear, and deep. It is said this was the river named after Achilles, the ancient Greek hero. Or perhaps Achilles was named after the Acheloos River. We didn't know, but then we really didn't care. We just loved that river. When not shoveling through the drudgery of our correspondence courses, we roamed the countryside—usually at the river, on the river, or in the river.

With Bill—Billy from Australia and Fry Canyon—there with us, we were again an inseparable threesome. One of our favorite activities was to float the Acheloos, wearing only cutoff jeans, tennis shoes, and scuba masks, just floating along, watching the fish. There were some as large as four feet long. In one spot, we could swim right through them. They'd move over gracefully, barely out of reach, and let us pass— probably thought they were being courteous to the disabled.

We usually took the rapids feet first, on our backs, and facing downstream. Of course, Mike did manage to find just one that looked outright suicidal, one I wouldn't do. It wasn't out of fear that I refused. Hell, I didn't fear the water, but here it posed an extreme danger. We used no floatation vests, and the boulders breaking through the turbulent surface were huge. If anyone was knocked unconscious, and no one saw and fished them out, I shuddered to think. Among us three, no one accepted that role of guardian, except me. Hell, no one even recognized the need, but me. Yes, me—again, Mike's self-appointed savior.

The foamy white of these rapids ended at the end of the ridge, where it turned and emptied into a gorge, abruptly transforming to blue-green sapphire with the deep, untroubled waters. The sheer walls rose forty to fifty feet high. I stationed myself on a slightly lower outcrop, jutting out over the water. Being both high enough to see the rapids and near the bend into the gorge, it was the only logical spot from which to stage a rescue. From there, I watched their progress as, whooping in glee, they bumped and dipped along in the churning foam. The rapids soon spit them, without serious injury, into the calm waters below me.

"Yeah! You really missed a great ride, little brother." Mike's voice barely carried over the crashing of the rapids. "C'mon in!" It was his challenge. He knew very well my fear of heights. Clearly, he didn't believe I'd overcome it. Was he wrong?

There was little danger; no stupid chances here in leaping from this perch, a mere forty feet up. But looking at them—so small down there—my breath seemed to catch in my throat, and my legs trembled. The very thought of jumping brought a creeping paralysis to my limbs. My hand on the boulder alongside, so steady just moments before, now wanted to cling, to let myself down onto trembling knees, and to crawl from the edge.

"Yeah? Well, you missed a great jump." Giving myself no more time to think, I leapt. For a long, whirling moment, I hung suspended.

Then my sneakers hit with a splat, and suddenly I was very deep in the chilly depths, stroking hard for the slow-moving surface. Reaching it, I coughed. Water gushed from my sinuses, draining out my nose.

"Woo-hoo!" screamed Bill. "Way to go, Jeff. That looked like fun."

Mike grinned in wicked glee. Me—I just gritted my teeth, knowing that, once again, he'd goaded my actions.

Bill's eager outburst struck me as odd. He'd always played a silent Tonto: first to Willis' Lone Ranger in Fry Canyon, and now to Mike's—dependable, supportive, but silent, except for unexpected glimpses, now and then, into the profound. I'd touched some unknown, silent something in him to bring about this noisy support of me. I did not know what.

And I'd set a precedent, one I soon came to regret. Diving from that cliff became one of their favorite things. Me? My mind could never get to the triumph or the ecstasy. Mine would catch somewhere just past fear at a place called "relief"—and then only after the climb up and the survival of each jump.

* * *

One day we found, and caught, a small snake in a shady pool alongside the river. About two feet long, it was a nondescript, grayish brown with darker blotches running down its back, much like any other water snake we'd ever seen. We were walking down the road, passing it back and forth, letting it slither about in our grasp, when we passed several Greeks dressed in grungy work clothes, obviously just getting off the afternoon shift. All shrank back except one. Stepping forward, he grabbed Mike's arm in a vice-like grip and gingerly plucked the snake from his grasp.

"Hey! What the fuck?" Mike's body language alone said we were headed for trouble.

Throwing it violently to the ground, the man snatched up his friend's shovel and flattened it quite thoroughly. We couldn't understand their excited gibbering, but one word kept coming through: "Vipeira, Vipeira."

Mike's onslaught was interrupted by my quick step into his path and hand on his arm.

"Mike, listen! I think they're saying 'Viper.'"

The Greeks merely shook their heads and rolled their eyes at one another. Their gibbering now took another tone as they turned to amble off. Other words now came through clearly: "Flacca" (stupid) "Americano."

"Hey, Asshole!" Mike wasn't through yet.

"Filli say tone calli mou," (kiss my ass) was one's parting comment. I didn't bother to translate.

Picking up the mangled carcass, Mike watched them leave through eyes seething with resentment. Then, with his pocketknife, he pried the mouth open. Sure enough, a quick twist of the blade revealed them: long, ivory needles hinged up against the gums—fangs. Again, another deadly snake had forgiven us our stupidity in favor of peace and, this time, paid with its life.

As for the workers, our relationships with them were not all so remote, or disrespectful. Other than this one time, I was never met with anything I did not feel was friendly. But then, I was always friendly; sometimes Mike was not. *"The energy out, does return in kind . . ."*

There was the language barrier, both for us kids and for our fathers. Running the work crews was exasperating for them. They depended heavily on interpreters. Dad's two interpreters? Well, they left something to be desired. With his urging, and to our delight, Dad found a solution that worked.

* * *

Stavros and Yorgos were their names. They needed a better understanding of English, and of Americans in general. We needed someone to show us around. We became their weekend tutors, and they, our weekend tickets out of town—or, perhaps more accurately, "to town." It worked very well.

Stavros became my favorite. An olive-skinned, average size man in his early twenties, we three towered over him. His dark-haired features and soft, brown eyes spoke of a gentle nature, belied by his perpetually grungy dark jowls. There was just something about Stavros, expressed in the depths of his eyes and in the kindness in his voice, which never left any doubt: he was a man to trust.

We spent Easter with him at his family home on the outskirts of Agrinion. It was a typical, though humble, marble block house with whitewashed trim and a gray, concrete tiled roof.

His mother was a little, old, gnome of a woman who dressed in perpetual black, complete with a black shawl, covering her thin, silver hair—widow's garb, as Stavros later explained.

There was an older sister, an attractive, smartly dressed woman with an aristocratic nose. The dowry for her marriage to a local banker was Stavros's proudest accomplishment. Now he worked for that of his younger sister, Christina, who was just fifteen—my own age. Without a dowry, she could never hope to be accepted for marriage into any respectable family.

Christina had her sister's good looks, minus any aristocracy. She also had her brother's soft eyes and gentle disposition. Out of respect for Stavros, and the family's hospitality, I put my hormones on lockdown and did my best to ignore her.

Between my hand being constantly crammed into a pocket of my tight blue jeans and my carefully styled and combed Elvis hair, Stavros confided that she thought I looked like "that Americano movie star, James Dean." My only concern was in hiding that sudden bulge in my front pocket every time she was around.

Then there were the two nieces: five- and six-year-old hellions, compliments of the banker. I found them delightful and played with them almost constantly. Besides, it allowed me the occasion to take my mind off of Christina—and my hand out of my pocket.

Easter in Greece is the big holiday of the year. Like every other Greek family, Stavros's roasted their Easter sheep in their front yard beneath the spreading arms of a shady fig tree—head, eyeballs, and all. On a separate spit alongside sizzled a shish kebab of chunks of meat and other unidentifiable things. Stavros called it Souvlaki.

Treating us like visiting dignitaries, he took us around to meet all his friends. As was the custom, we were served a chunk of Souvlaki everywhere we went. Along with it went retsina, a really distinct-tasting wine—a taste which I found needed some acquiring. While mutton, too, had never been a gold star item on my favorite foods menu, after the fifth family and the retsina acquired, I kind of relaxed into my new role and just enjoyed all the kind attention and notoriety.

That night, Stavros's mom served up a real delicacy. It was a watery soup, with little chunks of rubbery stuff bobbing about with something that looked much like macaroni. Leaning close, I asked, "Steve"—Stavros by now wanted to adopt the American version of his name—"is this macaroni?" I picked one up in my spoon.

"I don't know what is this 'macaroni' thing you speak. That is the insides thing where all the foods the sheep eat goes through."

"Oh . . . okay." Keeping my face as neutral as possible, I placed the spoon in my mouth and with only a few cursory chomps, swallowed the rubbery fare down quickly. I preferred not to ask about the other ingredients. Surprisingly, not knowing didn't bother me all that much, although I was rather relieved when they didn't honor me with one of the eyeballs. Mike and Billy were, after all, older, and age does have its advantages.

Afterward, there was a home-brewed liqueur called Ouzo. It tasted like licorice and burned like cayenne. With the fumes of that Ouzo tickling the back of my nose, my American prejudices just evaporated. Perhaps some foods are simply enjoyed best in the dark—without the light of prejudice.

* * *

Ah, yes: *"Perception is a choice,"* and like all choices, can be made with a simple conscious change of mind—or maybe a sip or two of Ouzo. Back then, those choice delicacies served in our meal were relished by Stavros. He sucked them down noisily without spoon or straw and from the edge of his bowl.

And then there were my choices in the perceptions I held about myself.

~ *In the Present with Big D* ~

"Yes . . ." Big D kicks in now, interrupting the flow of my writing. "Do you see the evolution concerning those views you then held about yourself?"

"Of course; it's clear I've changed." I wonder at his sudden intrusion, his need to interrupt.

"It is not my need." Big D cocks his head down and to the side. The glow from his empty eye sockets now looking at me from that angle carries the same hint of rebuke as does his voice. "Didn't you, yourself, interrupt your story? Didn't you bring it into the present? I said I would be here for you whenever you needed me."

"I don't know that I need you just now—and stop reading my mind!"

"That's not possible. Have you forgotten again just who I am?" His voice is like the clearing of mist, fading to clarity with every word. It is his form, standing beside me, that now begins to fade. "But it seems your choice, just now, is not to read mine. So sad; I was about to tell you another one of life's great secrets."

"Goddammit! Don't you dare go away after laying something like that on me." My anger is real, a choice I am making, though I know not why. "Stop playing fucking games with my head!"

"'Fucking games?'" His sockets suddenly flair hot, as if the door of a blast furnace has opened into my face.

"Yiiiiieee . . ." My scream is involuntary, as are my hands, now up, trying to shield my face.

"Again, you forget just who I am. If you wish to exist even one breath more, I require respect and esteem!"

The issue of his words, combined with that burning anger, provokes a far worse agony in me, almost as from a chain reaction within the nucleus of my existence: *shame!* It takes a moment to catch my breath. "You have it! I'm sorry! I don't know what—"

"But you do know. You have nothing if you don't have respect and esteem between your consciousness and your soul. To disrespect it consciously is to say you no longer want this life. By God, you may not exactly see me as your soul, but you better consider me as everything in-between! You've always had a problem with those in authority, but I am **not** your authority. ***We are you, and you will have self-respect!***"

"Yes . . . yes, I will. I . . . I do. And I do want to know about all of life's secrets." My ploy is at least as much a diversion as a genuine hunger to know. "Tell me, please!"

"And honesty . . ." Big D continues, ignoring my words of appeasement, though the agony has eased. "You have less than nothing if you don't have honesty." Like muddied water in a stream, his anger now seems to have run its course, to be replaced with something new, something that flows silent and sad. "You are up against the lies mankind has always told himself to avoid knowing, and owning, life's secrets—secrets illuminated by the laws, but which you keep in darkness from yourselves." I feel his sadness, know it as a timeless wilderness, filled with eons of bleakness and savagery. He continues.

"Do not ask of this secret to appease. Ask only if your consciousness is willing to accept true responsibility. Seeing this one secret will surely shine a light into the darkness behind which you hide. Are you ready for all it may reveal?"

I pause to gather my courage before answering. "Tell me."

Big D takes a long moment, arranging his butt bones comfortably across the mess of papers on the side of my desk, then fixes me in his gaze. "Okay then, here it is: *'**You always have exactly what you want in life, your wants are chosen by your every judgment, and your judgments, together, make up your point of view.**'* "

"What? What does all that mean?"

"Ha . . . you are so typical. Always making the simple things hard, and the profound things, you want to see as simple." He pauses, and I hear his rib cage rattle merrily. "It just means that if you want something better in life, simply make your judgments more lovingly. Living life or tasting food—if you want it to be good, don't first judge it bad."

"Well, how do I do that? Isn't it necessary to judge? Don't we keep ourselves safe by judging?"

"True—and you also keep yourselves limited by it."

"Well, don't we have to limit some things . . . I mean, c'mon, Big D, aren't some things, or some people, just plain evil?"

"No."

"Look, I'm missing something here."

"Yes, I know. Consider this: *'What is of true evil in this life is created in the process of determining what is good and what is bad.'*"

"What?"

"That's right! And speaking of 'right'—it is the same with 'right and wrong.'" My mouth now hangs slack as he continues. "Consider: If mankind knew nothing of the concepts of 'good and bad' or 'right and wrong,' could there ever be 'evil?'"

"Well . . . ahh . . . no, I suppose—not the concept of it anyway. But wouldn't man still sometimes do harm to his fellow man?"

"Probably so." He chuckles. "And in your effort to make something profound into something simple, you miss the point."

"Which is . . ."

"Consider: What if instead of 'right or wrong,' 'good or bad,' there were only 'loving or unloving,' 'safe or unsafe?'"

"Uh . . ."

"Then if someone were to deliberately hurt another, you might judge him as 'unloving' and 'unsafe' to be around, correct?"

"Yes?"

"Could any action you might then take ever be about revenge?"

"Wow! I'm beginning to see what you mean."

"If everyone just forgot their judgmental concepts used in determining evil, could evil even exist?" The cherry glow of Big D's gaze has taken on a hue of merriment.

"That's not likely to happen."

"True enough. You can only erase evil from your own life. 'Good and bad,' 'right and wrong'—it is these very concepts, these inane judgments, that give birth to the reality of evil in your world." His form now dissolves to a vapor, leaving behind his final cryptic words, clearly intended to haunt me. "Your religions teach it. And of those who have no religion, most believe it. But the fact remains: This is where evil is created. *'Each and every person now armed only with the judgmental concepts of 'good and bad,' 'right and wrong,' is a 'Typhoid Mary' of evil. Each must cure themselves.'*"

"Good, Big D—you're right."

"Good? Right? I'm . . . 'right'? SHIT!" He roars back into sudden clear view, shaking his sickle in aggravation. "I just repeated myself *four fucking times*, and even *you*. . . . Oh . . ."

He stops and stands silent for one long moment. "Good one, Jeff." Then, shaking his head as if in admonition, and with the sound of one long, disgusting fart, he fades, leaving behind. . . .

Whooo-eeee! Even as one hand whips back and forth, fanning my nose, the other self-consciously reaches back to assure myself that my shorts are empty.

Perception is a choice. Yet, how much of our personal worlds are governed by the choices made by generations past? We are born into a prison built brick on brick by each of our ancestors. A prison without doors, but which to sustain life, needs to have a few windows. Though perhaps heavily barred, and set up high, they at least let in necessities—food, water, air. . . . I think our Creator provided us each a spoon with which most simply eat their gruel. Yet, if we cherish it and polish it, we can hold it up and sometimes catch a reflection of the truth through those high bars, or perhaps even use it to dig our way free. That spoon is called honesty, self-honesty.

Redneck Spirituality—Condensed From Book One

Chapter Nine

Reaching Through the Bars

Why is it that Americans don't seem to want to admit we all defecate—we shit? Few want to call it such and find it vaporously embarrassing to discuss, especially around others of the opposite sex. Strange that for such a natural function of life, it is something we often ignore, pretend we don't do, and when nature demands, certainly avoid mentioning openly in mixed company—unless first we delicately paint it pink, as in "powdering one's nose" or "making a pit stop."

It was the same for me. From an early age, I had what amounted to a phobia on the subject. I found it was a damn embarrassing and unpleasant experience to use a public restroom where there was no assurance of privacy. In Greece, I discovered myself suddenly alone in my sentiments. The rules of Greek society were vastly different in the toilet, compared to those of any other shithouse in which I'd ever been.

But back in 1963, that clueless "me" was planning on spending another weekend as a guest of Stavros at his home in Agrinion. He knew nothing of those rules. That "me" was feeling slightly on edge, and although his stomach churned just a little sideways, he refused to let it stop him from having the weekend adventure he'd been looking forward to with Mike, Bill, and Stavros—and more importantly, someone very special.

Stavros left for town the previous evening. It was just Mike, Bill, and me boarding the beat-up little country bus that morning with its load of peasants, their children, a few chickens, and a goat. Feeling vaguely out of place, and very uncomfortable with the gastric possibilities, I gritted my teeth and ignored the signs of the disaster about to befall me.

It was a beautiful, clear, cool summer morning. The air was fresh and sweet with the scent of olive trees as we boarded the dilapidated country bus and left Kremasta, dragging behind our very own dust cloud. As we rattled and bounced along that dirt road, my stomach began to churn, almost as if in sympathy with that old bus and its goat droppings dancing up and down its dusty isle. Then, just before the little town of Acheloos Vlasios, the pressure began to build—fast—the kind of pressure which clearly says, "Don't you dare fart! If you do, it's damned sure to have a lump in the middle."

In less than five minutes, I was squirming in pain. There was an outcropping of rocks coming up on the downhill side of the road. Like some wounded crab, I scuttled up to the driver and told him, mostly in urgent motions, to let me off. He didn't understand the pretense of my pantomime until I stopped pretending and began clawing at the door. Then he stopped the bus and opened it.

Clear of the bus, I motioned vehemently for the driver to move on. For a second or three, he just sat there, staring, then the bus lurched forward. I surely didn't want anyone—concerned or not—following me, as clutching my stomach and stooping in pain, I scurried off behind the rocks. Once out of sight, I immediately dropped my drawers, squatted, and with a cry of relief, literally sprayed the rocks behind me. Alleviated of my burden, I began fumbling in the pockets of my pants, now in a heap around my ankles. We always carried toilet paper, as the local sources could not always be relied upon.

Perhaps it was the soft bleating of the sheep, or the tinkle of their bells, which drew my eyes upward. In a flash, I took in the small herd of about a dozen scattered before me, but what held my attention were the soft, brown eyes of a very pretty young shepherd girl sitting on a rock about twenty feet away. There was a definite twinkle there. Clearly, she was holding her amusement by a pretty fair choke hold, and in her struggle, it was winning.

Ears burning, I ducked my head and groaned. Then, with as much dignity as could be mustered, I wiped myself, pulled up my pants, and stalked off, hearing behind me the release of her strangled peal.

Back on the relative flat of the rutted dirt road, I looked right to where it disappeared through its narrow-cut bank on the ridge, and farther, to where it scribed the flank of the far mountainside, miles off in the distance. To the left, the road traversed into the loins of the mountain, then back out again onto the flank of the next ridge, a quarter mile over as the pigeon flies. To go that way, I'd have to take the turkey walk around. There were no vehicles in sight.

For a long moment, I turned and looked out off the mountain to where it briefly flattened into a rolling, green plateau. The white houses—homes of the bosses—and long, gray workers' barracks could be seen surrounding the base of the water tower of Kremasta. I thought of the times I'd climbed that tower with Mike. He liked the view from where it stood at the edge of the gorge of the Acheloos. Just now, I would have preferred that giddy view to the one I had here, some two miles straight across and up the mountain. By road, it would be at least ten. Still by road, I would not again pass by those sheep. With a sigh, I turned left and began walking home.

I'd not covered a quarter mile when a car pulled up behind, honking. It was Mike. He managed to get the bus driver to hold the bus at the village just around the bend, then hired a car and came back for me. Yes, getting back on that bus was embarrassing, though not nearly so much so as looking into the eyes of that shepherd girl who'd watched me texturize that rock.

In Agrinion, Stavros met our bus. When we explained my dilemma, he stopped at a Kios, a street vendor's shack, and bought some little black pills. They looked like nothing more than charcoal, but did the trick. I was so relieved, for I had a date with Maria. Stavros had arranged for us to meet at the movies that afternoon.

Maria was tall and slim, with a womanly promise in her ample, fifteen-year-old breasts. Her hazel eyes and delicate porcelain features were framed by midnight curls—moonlight on a marbled Greek goddess come to life. God, she was magnificent!

Maria's older sister and cousin flushed out our hand as dates for Bill and Mike. In the darkened theater, we took up half a row with Stavros, Maria, and then me on the aisle.

With the theater dark, and the movie flickering away through the tobacco smoke, I did what I'd always done and thought expected of me now. I tested the waters of Maria's feelings by slipping my arm across the back of her seat, then casually dropping it onto her shoulders. Maria squirmed quickly forward, out from beneath it. Confused, I rested it back on the seat. Stavros's shaking head caught my eye, and I raised my eyebrows in question. His hand lifted mine off the seat, and another shake convinced me to retrieve it.

For long moments, I sat in addled embarrassment, staring straight ahead at the screen while out of my side vision I observed Maria slowly settle back. I felt like some klutz who just bumped into the Venus de Milo. All eyes in the museum seemed on me. Could I glue the arms of her embarrassment back on? And why did they break off so damned easily anyway?

Stavros leaned across and whispered, "Jeff, I need to pee; maybe you come with me."

Out in the lobby, Stavros led me into the restroom. Lit by a single bulb, it seemed to possess all the carnal rankness of a swamp. An open-faced stall to the left of the entrance faced a long, metal, whiz-trough-from-hell, which appeared to be glued by its own scum to the length of one wall. The commode, I noted, was the usual single-molded concrete slab with a recessed six- inch hole between two flat foot pads set slightly higher. A bucket of water stood beside it—for those with bad aim—and there was even the luxury of a roll of toilet paper. I was about to ask about the missing hand sink when Stavros turned to me.

"Jeff, you can no touch Maria like that. Only bad girls do that in theater. People think her whore, you do that."

"My God! I didn't know. We do it all the time in America." I turned and slapped both hands up against the cleanest wall and leaned forward, hanging my head. "Jesus, she must think I'm an idiot."

"Is okay . . ." His hand patted my shoulder. "I think she still like you. Come on, I still have to pee."

I was standing at the trough, aiming my yellow stream next to his, when I caught a flicker of motion from the corner of my eye. Someone was using the shithole. Shaking the last drops, I casually turned my head. It was Maria! She squatted there, her panties around her ankles, and was looking me in the eye.

Confused, I jerked my eyes forward. Frantically, I stuffed myself away and zipped up. Then, with a pained hiss of breath through gritted teeth, I backed it down and more carefully rezipped. Stavros was already done and stepped past behind me, while I stood fumbling with my crotch. As he drew near Maria, she spoke a soft query and he stopped in front of her stall, the perfect picture of ease, as he answered.

Me? I kept my face respectfully averted and waited, my back carefully placed to the side wall of the stall. As they talked, her voice sounded of a soft, urgent concern, his of calming assurance. Very few words did I understand. Then Stavros slapped my shoulder, "Come, Jeff . . . is good—she still like you!"

In the lobby, I turned to him. "Steve, what the hell was that all about? Why did she come in there?"

"She come to pee." Eyebrows knitted, he cocked his head to look up at me. "You don't see that?"

"But . . . shit! Why didn't she use the ladies' restroom?"

"What is this you mean 'ladies' restroom?'" His hand held palm upward, he gestured in the direction of the doorway we'd just come through. "Is only one restroom."

Quickly, I glanced around. He was right! There was only one restroom. Just then, Maria joined us. I knew my face was flaming, but I forced myself to look at her and smile, as together, we turned to go in.

"Jeff, that is a very funny term." Stavros chuckled. "What does it mean, 'butt shit?' You say this a lot in America? It does not make sense."

"What? Oh." I snorted in self-realization. "That's something I guess I say a lot. It only means, 'I wish I had known.'"

"Oh, is interesting . . . 'Butt shit!' I think I like this term."

Back in our seats, Maria took my hand and held it low between us. We finished watching the movie in the Greek way.

* * *

Afterward, we all walked down the road leading south, out of town. It was the main highway and paved, although in this rural area, few people owned cars. Once outside of town, we again held sweaty hands under the afternoon sun. Maria walked between Stavros and I, well behind the others. We seldom had to surrender the blacktop to traffic.

Most of the Greek words I knew were of those crude "men" things—nothing I could say to Maria. So I communicated with her through the touch of my hand on hers and the lovesick mooning of my eyes. Yet, the incident still troubled my mind, and I wanted to better understand her culture and what was morally acceptable.

"Steve, why do you have prostitutes here if they are so unacceptable?"

"They are for the single mens—or just the poor mens." He seemed a little uncomfortable, and not because of Maria. She understood nothing of English.

"What's wrong . . . you don't want to talk about it?"

"Is okay. Is just something we not much speaking about." He smiled. "But everybody here know. You just don't know. So I tell you what you want know."

"Thanks." I reflected a moment. "What do you mean 'poor men?' Is that poor 'married' men, too—and what do rich men do?"

"Yes, all poor mens." He paused as if to collect his thoughts. "Rich mens don't go much to the prostitutes; rich mens have mistress. Every mens have needs. Just we don't speak about it, but these things everybody do."

"Yes, but wives? Can't they meet those needs?"

"Sometime, but many time marriage is arranged by family. That man, he may not want that womans."

"Oh . . ." I thought about it a moment, feeling discomfort with the sweaty clinging of my shirt—and of something else. "What about the married women? Don't they have the same needs?"

"That very bad." He shook his head, his face wrinkled. "Very much bad. Good womans never do!"

"What about single women, like Maria here?" Maria glanced at me, now aware we discussed her. I smiled. "Doesn't she, too, have needs."

"Oh, Maria very good womans." Stavros, too, smiled at her, and we all crowded to the side as a small truck clattered by. "She not married"—he shrugged—"so is okay. Unmarried womans often do. Just no one must know."

"But what if she gets pregnant?"

"Yes, that sometime very bad. If man's family don't like her, they no get married." Again he shrugged. "No mens then wants to marry with her."

"Well, then what would she do?"

"Oh, she become prostitute, but Maria very pretty, probably become some man's mistress."

Maria was looking back and forth between us, and I suddenly realized the conversation had turned grave. I smiled my reassurance, and her eyes dropped shyly from mine. Realizing how much reputation mattered to her, I determined I would not again bring stain on hers.

At the first thick orchard of olive trees, we turned off the roadway. I soon found myself alone under a tree with Maria and wishing I'd asked Stavros what was expected of me. He'd simply said, "Stay here. We will come back later."

We sat down together, still holding hands. I wondered if this was all they did. *What if I were to kiss her, hold her, touch her sweet body. . . . God! Is it possible we might even make love?* That last thought brought an embarrassing, large lump into my pocket. *But what if someone sees—her sister, cousin, Stavros, or maybe some olive farmer checking his orchard?* I sighed. *No, I must not.*

And so I talked to her, though she understood not a word. I told her how my heart yearned for her and how beautiful she was to me; how parts of me now ached to touch, to kiss, to know her. She sighed and seemed frustrated with my inability to communicate. So I told her about the hormones now raging, hopelessly wishing she could understand, that she would reach out and touch this aching need now bulging my tight blue jeans. Yet, from my experience in the theater, how could it be morally acceptable for us to actually touch one another? And so I held back my touch, even my kiss, unwilling to further embarrass her, hoping she would somehow guide me in knowing what I could acceptably do.. When Stavros finally came, her tone as they spoke sounded almost angry, and I knew that whatever was expected of me, it was something I had not done.

On the highway back to town, Maria now paced on the far side of Stavros. He nudged me.

"Why you don't make loving with Maria?" He nodded her way. "She want know."

"What? How could I? What about her reputation? What if someone had seen?"

"No one would have seen."

"But what if she got pregnant? I didn't want to ruin her whole life."

"You don't have the rubber?"

"No!"

"Doesn't matter. You father very nice man; Maria very nice girl." He shrugged. "They make marriage, she get pregnant."

"But Stavros . . . I'm only fifteen!"

"Doesn't matter. You father rich. You have no problem."

I thought about my parents and their Mormon sense of responsibility. Yes, they might take her in, but accept her? I turned it over more in my mind. It felt sticky. Yes, they might even have come to accept it of her, but never of me. I gazed over at Maria. Her eyes—now unreadable—wouldn't meet mine as she stared down at the roadway.

Stavros watched me, then spoke to my frustration. "I think Maria not want to see you again, Jeff. She say she think you afraid."

"But . . . shit!" I gritted my teeth in frustration.

"Yes . . . butt shit," Stavros agreed.

My eyes, too, now dropped to the pavement. The late afternoon sun teased a trickle of sweat from between my shoulder blades, and my balls still ached from the sustained strain of my hard-on, now soft. Ironically, I knew if I'd used it as my ruler, I might have measured up.

Stavros was right. I had affronted Maria for the last time.

~ *Looking Back* ~

In retrospect, was it possible Maria and I were soul mates? Had she, too, felt that inner quickening? I think not, for there was little strength in the bond between our hearts. Perhaps we were just two people caught between the moralities of one another's societies—clueless. That I could know her in her most intimate moments, see her pee or even defecate openly, but not share even the slightest hint of ourselves romantically, or especially sexually, with the same open honesty was incomprehensible to me. I think she was merely a stimulating teacher, someone to give me a lesson in my becoming someone else's soul mate.

My experience of her has taught me something about honesty, about stepping past the dishonesty of one's culture—a lesson that would soon serve me well elsewhere. Back then, neither of us had the maturity or courage. I wonder if she would now?

Our worlds are changing. Mine now has a hit TV show that flaunts the idea of unisex restrooms. I wonder what hers has?

~ *In the Present with Big D* ~

"Ha!" I jump as Big D's megaphone chuckle blasts into my left ear. "Is that all you got from this part of your story?" His grin seems mocking.

I shake my head and gingerly rub at my ear before answering. "Well, I thought it was kinda deep." *Why do I feel such a need to defend myself?*

"Yes, why do you?" He answers my unspoken thought. "I serve as your mirror, reflecting you as your soul knows you need to see. Uncomfortable sometimes . . ."

"Oh."

"'Oh'? Take—it—deeper." His voice drops an octave with each word.

"What do you mean? How much deeper can I go?"

"Perhaps, then, the word is 'where.'" Still low, his voice now becomes gentle. "Where are you at today? Maria didn't understand you, and in that, you chose pain. Where is there misunderstanding in your life today? Where is there, again, such pain?"

My mind seems to shift a gear. Ah, yes, my mother—and my trip just last week to work things out with her and my dad back in Utah. Suddenly, I find myself there, again facing her venom.

"How could you just abandon your wife?" Her face is screwed up into an ugly, red grimace.

"But I didn't just—"

"Shuuuttt-utt-ut! There's no excuse . . ." Her hand flies up, palm opened out before my face, then clenches dramatically into a fist. "I can't even face the family, knowing they know about this! And the church—I haven't gone in months. Oh, I'm just so ashamed of you—"

"Mom, where's Dad? How does he feel?"

"You leave him be. He's out back in the shop, working. He doesn't want to see you!"

"Does he know I'm—"

"Aaargghhhh! Her scream comes from deep down, as much a growl as a scream. It seems to carry a hint of hysterics. "I said, he doesn't want to see you." She speaks with her eyes bulging and jaw tightly clenched. I am very familiar with the signs. Her anger is now barely under control. "You . . ." She pauses and, like an actress in an old silent movie, clenches both hands into fists and shakes them in my face. "You who shit on his good name, then threw it back into his face—go . . . now! You are no longer welcome here."

"Yes . . . now you're there." Big D's words of encouragement seem to draw me back into this time and place.

"My mother won't even try to understand. . . ." There is no mystery why my letters remain unanswered. My pain is about the "where" she's gone with me.

"Ah, but perhaps she can't." Big D's robes swirl in sooty mist, as if sucking up the very light with his gesture. Somehow, it reminds me of how my mother is with love. "Maria, steeped in her own Greek traditions—did she understand?"

"But we all make the choice of our perceptions . . ." I quote the law. "My mother chooses not to understand. Well, doesn't she?"

His eyes glow in reproach, and he regards me silently for a long moment before answering. "Not all make those choices consciously. Some need to grow in wisdom a little, you know, before having even the ability to hear and understand." His shoulder blades clack as he shrugs.

Big D is always correct, but this time he has lost me. *Is there something here I don't have the ability to understand?* He reads my unspoken query and answers, "Oh, you have the ability! You have it because you know your life is all created by you! And, because sometimes . . ." His bony index finger taps me meaningfully on the chest before transferring back to his own with a soft clack. "Sometimes—just not this time—you choose to listen to me." His grin reminds me of Grandma's old double-decker organ. "Look, didn't you feel embarrassed when you texturized that rock in front of that shepherd girl?"

"Well, no shit!"

"No, it was a *lot* of shit!" He chuckles. "And what about when you saw Maria squatting over that shithole, taking a whiz? Did you then feel embarrassed?"

"Yes?"

"So? Did they appear embarrassed?"

"No. It was normal for them. Elimination is just something they know we all need to do. They don't have our hang-ups."

"Yes . . . exactly! But did you understand that?" His hand, now extended toward me, flips over. "And if you had, would you have been so embarrassed?"

"My God!"

"Yes, Jeff." Big D chuckles. "You can call me that, if you like. I complete that connection for you." I ignore his gentle jab.

"My mother hasn't the understanding to be other than ashamed of me right now!"

"Did she ever?"

"No."

"Did you do anything other than what you needed to do—than was necessary to continue to live your life?"

"No."

"For her, it's not even about you, is it?"

"No."

"Knowing this"—his voice now blurs with a brassy kindness as it rumbles up like soft-blown notes from a trombone, played from the bottom of that barrel—"does it need to hurt so deeply?"

Feeling good about sex requires an element of love. But let's face it—with many men, it is not their soul, not their heart, not even their dicks, but their ego that does their fucking. I believe it is always so, until we learn how to love and to make love. Until then, sex is just an orgasm of the ego—an e-gasm. Problem with e-gasms? We men are the ones who get slimed, and no quick swallow is going to clean up our mess.

Redneck Spirituality—Book Four

Chapter Ten

Virginity: The Other Side of the Tracks

The next day, Stavros took us to a seaport town farther to the south called Messolongi. It was supposed to be an outing to the beach and museum with the girls, but Christina was sick—and of course, her sisters wanted to stay and care for her. Hearing the news, Mike and Bill both snorted their disgust.

"Way to go, numbnuts!" Mike said, winging a cuff toward the side of my head, which I effectively managed to block. Bill just made evil eyes at me. Although they didn't have intercourse, they both communicated without reservations with their girls the previous day. And today, they both had rubbers.

Still, Stavros wanted to show us something of the culture. Messolongi was a town of which all Greeks were particularly proud. Way back in its history, it had once been laid siege by the Turks, but the courage of the Greeks had prevailed. None were taken alive. For me, it was a mystery why mass suicide would be something of which to take such pride. But then, I wouldn't know what life would be like for a survivor. Was it a brave or cowardly thing? Maybe the point was in the big "fuck you" it said to the Turks. So we made the bus ride and even trailed through the local museum. But the museum and the mostly empty beaches were of little interest to Bill and Mike. Later, in a poorer part of town, they discovered something that did titillate their interest.

"Hey, Steve, what's that over there?" Mike's look was one of eager intent. I think he already suspected.

"Oh that . . ." Stavros's nose screwed up. "That is the brothels where the soldiers go. This town have army base, many soldiers." He now looked like he smelled a stench worse than the septic service truck, which just then was passing along the road. "Is not very good place for you to go."

Mike gazed out across the level, salt-encrusted, bare flats, past the hump of the train tracks. There were three shacks there, widely separated, alone and shabby. He looked at Bill and me, his eyes shining.

"Let's go see."

Bill shrugged his nonchalant acceptance.

Me? My protest sounded lame, even to me. "Why? We're not going to do anything there, are we?"

"Shit, Jeff! They're not gonna bite you." Bill joined in the laugh as I stumbled against Mike's shove. "Well, probably not, anyway."

Stavros's eyebrows were knitted together as one. "I don't think you fathers like I take you there very much."

"Don't sweat it, Steve, we'll never tell."

Stavros looked closely at Mike, then to Bill and me. He shrugged and nodded.

Inside the first shack, the room was clean, but still sparse and dingy. The whitewashed wall held no pictures, only a small shelf holding a few bottles above a wooden table. On the table was a large washbasin, a few folded towels, and a pitcher of water. The only furnishings other than that were a few rickety chairs scattered around the walls.

Mike was still a virgin, a shameful status he desperately wanted to change. He entered the room eagerly and gazed about, almost with a sense of reverence. Bill was just game to do anything Mike did. Then the young prostitute emerged from her chambers. Pretty enough, she wore only a bathrobe, her ample wares showing clearly through its opened front. Me? I took one look into the empty depths of her eyes and felt nothing erotic toward her. This woman didn't want me. She seemed devoid of passion for anyone or anything—not even for the few drachma we would put in her hand. How could I feel passion for her? What I did feel was a pang of shameful disgust with Mike's next words.

"Hey, check out those tits!" The bulge in his pants spoke largely of his differing attitude. "This one's mine."

It took perhaps all of five minutes, during which time we waited in the outer room with the prostitute's maid. The maid's features and hers were much the same, except for maybe twenty years more actual age, then forty years of physical sag, and then a couple of hundred years more in her eyes. I wondered if she was the mother.

Watching her as she mixed a liquid into a large bowl of water, I asked Stavros, "What's she doing?"

With a look of mild contempt, he made several cupping motions to his crotch. "She is making the douche . . . for not to have the baby."

"It was great!" Mike fairly burst through the door sporting a huge grin. "You going next, Little Brother?"

"Naw . . . I'll pass."

"How about you, Bill?"

"Hell no! Not after you greased it all up." Bill's look was of mock disgust. "I want a fresh one."

The next was a little plain and a lot dumpy.

"What do you think, Little Brother?"

"Pass again."

"Bill?"

"Me, too."

The last was older, maybe in her mid-thirties. Like the others, her eyes spoke nothing sensual to me, despite her well-proportioned body. Bill spent a solid half hour in her private room. I thought his grin a little forced, when afterward, Mike slapped his back.

"How was it?"

"Great! Yeah, just great!" The tone of his voice now matched his grin—forced., But Mike didn't seem to notice.

"Little Brother?" The term was wearing. "You going next?"

"Pass."

"Well, how about the chubby one?"

"Maybe next time."

"Might be a while before you get another chance to break the pit outa your cherry, Little Brother." Mike thought he was being cute by then pointing at my crotch, the lump being conspicuously absent. "Or, maybe not . . ." he added.

"I'll wait . . . and knock it off with the stupid 'Little Brother' shit!"

"Aw-ooo." Mike mussed my hair, causing me to stumble against the doorframe on my way out. At least he didn't further embarrass me with another comment about my crotch.

Later, Bill confided in me of how he didn't enjoy it much—said all she did was lie there, farted once, and picked the pimples on his back. Sometimes Bill told me things he'd never tell Mike.

And Mike . . . maybe he just got one with a real itch to scratch. He really did seem to think it was great and razzed me about it for several days.

But Mike did not have the last laugh. About a week later, back home in Kremasta, I found him sitting cross-legged and naked on his bed, using a can of bug spray and a pair of tweezers.

"Wha-cha doin', Mike?" I said it as if I didn't know and did my best to repress a grin.

"What does it look like, smart-ass?"

"Looks like you're spraying gonads and picking crabs." I could no longer stop that grin or the chuckle that followed.

"You best just haul your ass out of here, 'fore I start kickin' it!"

Mike eventually "fessed up" to Mom and Dad about those "dirty toilet seats" and went to the company doctor for some DDT powder. I didn't point out to anyone about how, since we'd left Athens, the only toilets I'd seen with seats were inside of our homes. No, when it comes to using Greek toilets, crab lice can't jump that high. I'm sure Dad knew that, but he wasn't saying anything to Mother. With Mike, he was closing ranks. Shit like that was expected—of Mike.

For me, Mike's experience pretty well summed it up: There was sex, and then there were crabs. To me, the two just didn't mix well. Besides, I now knew why they called it "hand lotion"—and it wasn't for dry skin. Far better my hand lotion and dreams hearing the moans of well-satisfied women, if only in my mind. Yeah, far better those dreams than the reality of paying someone to pretend to enjoy me, or scratching my back while I scratched her crabs—a pretty sad form of jacking off.

* * *

Yet, jacking off? Sex? Loving? What it all meant to Mike and Bill, I never knew. Was it only about self-gratification? More important to me is what it all means to a woman. For them, is it only about his selfish gratification, or does she want it, too? That question is one that still rattles around in my skull, even today.

~ *In the Present with Big D* ~

"You hit it right on its little head there!" Big D's remark drops into my mind, a lighthearted snicker. "Sex happens either in love or fear, and in each is a different experience."

"I never know when to take you seriously."

"Okay then, let's get serious." Now standing solidly before me, he fixes me with a penetrating gaze such that I cannot look away. "You said you '. . . took one look into the empty depths of her eyes and felt nothing erotic toward her.'" He drops his head and shakes it back and forth, as if in disappointment. "C'mon, Jeff, 'empty depths?' No! You saw directly into her soul. Maybe back then you weren't conscious of your own psychic gift for feeling the energy of others, but you are now. Now tell me, what did you see? What did you feel?"

It takes me a moment—remembering her back then—then the answer comes pouring out. "I saw pain, I saw sorrow. Hell, I don't know if they were the same as she saw them, but I saw her unmet dreams and felt a sense of her love being rejected. And me? I didn't want to be just another prick, puncturing the sanctimony of those sacred dreams with my selfish greed." I take a deep breath and let it out in regretful disgust. "What I did not see back then was how the example of her life would soon challenge the truth about mine by pointing out that same cruel greed in me—but my soul saw it." And then, thinking of how it all would fit still later, I feel the tears begin to fall. My throat suddenly tight, I croak, "Meg . . . my Meg. I wasn't so much different with her, was I Big D?"

"Ah, Jeff, with Meg you were very different. With her, it was in the space of love, not greedy, selfish fear. Your soul offered hers something she had never known. And for a time, she accepted it and grew. More to the point, for a time, you gave to her and grew."

"Yes." My shoulders shrug, and both hands make a sweeping gesture outward from the wrist before I put it all into words. "But she, too, is in the past."

"Yes . . . and life only happens in the now. Let's talk about love and fear as it is right now, and about the laws."

"I'm not sure I follow you here, Big D, but I've studied the shit out of the laws, and I think I know a few things."

"You think so?" I smell the essence of scorched wood and know I am out of line. He continues. "There are things you know in your mind, and things you know in your heart. This thing I would tell you now, you don't know in either place. And slipping in a little attitude to confuse and avoid the issue doesn't get it with me." His eye sockets now glow intently. "Now! Do you want to hear?"

"Yes." There is truth in his words. I feel an unknown discomfort and sigh. "Tell me."

"All right. To recap the law: *'The energy out returns in kind,'* right?"

"Right."

"The next law is also about the energy. *'There are only two kinds of energy: the energy of love and the energy of all that is not love—fear.'*"

"Yes, I remember those laws; pretty simple, those two."

"You think so?" Big D's smile now seems to mock. "Then tell me—what is fear and what is love?"

"Fear is anything that doesn't feel good, is harmful or destructive, and causes one's soul to diminish."

"Wow!" Big D raises invisible eyebrows. "You see the negative shit very well, but what about love?"

"Well, love is what feels good."

"Some would say vengeance feels good."

"Yes, but love, in itself, is never actually harmful to anyone."

"'Actually?' Do you mean that some might perceive it so?"

"Geez Big D, I hate to be playing this same old tune, but . . . there is my mother. Apparently, she feels harmed by my honesty these days. And my letters—there have been no answers."

"So it is only the honesty of it that some might perceive harmful?"

"It seems so."

"'Seems so?' You don't know?" Big D's grin definitely now mocks me. "Would you have nurtured or ever given your mother the opportunity to grow in her own life—or just in her understanding and closeness to you—without the honesty?"

"No. Did all that dishonest pretense shit during those first forty-five years. Tried to be who she wanted. . . ." I grunt in disgust. "Didn't work!"

"So your letters were sent in love and honesty. Did they nurture you?"

"Yes."

"Okay, let's look at it." Big D's eye sockets now shoot sparks like two red Fourth of July sparklers. "Love feels good, is never given with intent to hurt, requires absolute honesty, and nurtures the giver, but not necessarily others."

"I think that is a fair assessment."

"Then could the first law also be said: *'The energy out is received—and perceived—back in kind?'* "

"So . . ." It feels as if the dark cloud overshadowing my mind has moved on, and the sunlight is streaming in. "You're saying my mother has never accepted me. Until she wants to love, she cannot see, much less accept, mine."

"Yes." The sparklers seem to focus into red pinpoints of intensity. "Do you see how it is for her—how it is really her own mother's fearful rejection that she sees love as being? Can you see that it is, at its least, her cry for love?"

My mind seems dumbstruck for a moment before I finally reply. "Yes . . . yes, I can."

"Can you love her anyway, knowing it is only in the space of yours, or someone else's, that she has the most opportunity to change this about herself?"

"What?" I bluster. "You doubt I love her?"

"Love her? Then what about expectations? Real love carries no expectations. Can the expectations of its being returned from the person to whom it is given ever be placed on real love?"

"Of course not!"

"Then why do you expect it of her?"

"She is my mother."

"Motherhood, too, happens either in love or fear, and in each is a different experience. Take away the connection of birth, and it becomes simply a choice. She has never been loving. She has merely— through you—had that opportunity. That is the promise you two made before you, either one, ever drew breath." The intensity of his gaze sharpens painfully hot. "Does she not keep her part of the bargain?"

"What do you mean?"

"Do you not also have the opportunity to learn *real* love?" He pauses one of those deliberate pauses before continuing. "You know . . . without expectations?"

"Oh. Yeah, I see what—"

"No, Jeff. You *don't* see. This is just another of a long string of opportunities wherein you've had this same lesson in your face."

"What? I don't see it—"

"C'mon . . . isn't that what I just said? Think, Jeff. Think about Meg. Is it possible you had this same pre-existence agreement with her? And with her, you learned it in your heart. But you seem to have gotten this lesson ass-backward. Don't you think it's time you acknowledge it in your head"—Big D reaches out and thunks one painfully hard finger against my forehead— "and let go of all this fucked-up pain?"

"Owww—shit!" I pause long enough to rub the sting of it and give myself time to think. "Yes . . . yes, I see it now."

"What, Jeff?" He ducks his head, the glow of his sight shifting upward, now coming from under the inquisition of invisibly raised eyebrows on his bony eye ridges. "What do you see?"

"With Meg, her 'love' was only a fear-filled need to feel secure, using me. Mom's was a fear-filled need to be a good Mormon momma—also using me, but never wanting me, the surrogate, for a child of her own. With Meg, I was the surrogate for the husband she couldn't have—for the guy she loved before me."

I bow my head in resignation, my throat aching. I croak. "Neither one has the capacity to actually return my love. I accepted it about Meg, without even thinking, and now need to accept it with my mother." I sigh. *Crap! I thought I had a handle on all this crazy 'mother shit' with that last chapter. Here I am again, still whining about it.*

I wipe a sleeve across my eyes to soak up the frustration. Then, with my vision cleared, I look up only to discover that Big D is nowhere in sight. Yet, I hear his reply clearly, as if spoken directly into my ears.

"Yes, exactly. It's all 'crap'—all shit—that has nourished you. Might help if you were to begin seeing how everyone who has ever played a part in your life has nourished you." There comes his amused chuckle. "Sometimes it stinks, and in handling, it feels slimy like shit. But in reality, it's so much more."

I know that law, too, and state it to myself, silently. ***"Everyone and everything in my life is there for my greatest good—a gift from my Creator."***

Just so, Jeff. His thought floats back in kind, silently, on the river of my mind. *Like I said, it is so much more. This lesson is not so much about love and not being loved back. To love is always the correct choice; it's a no-brainer.*

"What else could it be about then, Big D?" His answer does not come right away, and I am beginning to wonder if he heard me. *Big D?*

I call to him in silent thought. Then his answer does come in not-so-silent exasperation that nearly blows out the eardrums of my mind.

COURAGE, Jeff! It's about having the courage to love FIRST, even though you know what it is like when it's not returned. It's about having the courage to face your pain. You would not be human if you did not choose such pain.

He is gone now, leaving me feeling as if my mind is still inside some big-assed church bell, reverberating. And I am *done*—done whining about my mother and done mourning Meg.

Some choose to spend the rest of their lives mourning the loss of a loved one—and many view it as a loving thing. The truth is, mourning is not about love. And for most, it is a natural and healthy thing. It is about us dealing with, and moving past, our pain in the fact our life no longer includes them. Yet, for some, it becomes about us using that loved one as an inviolable reason for not having the courage to live life as it is now. How does one talk honestly about such an unflattering thing as cowardice in the face of one's pain? Is it so much different than cowardice in the face of one's fear? Or is it the same?

Redneck Spirituality—Book One

Chapter Eleven

A One-Fingered Wave—Mike's Goodbye

Just as they impacted the whole nation, the bullets that killed Kennedy also impacted me. In those latter days of '63, our whole nation was changed. Yet, unlike most, I did not cry. Nor did I cry for Mike. With the bullets that killed him, the change was also deep and personal, but it seemed only so to my life. But then, I'm getting a little ahead of myself.

Mike and I flew back from Greece early. Back in Utah, school was beginning and we didn't want to be late—or so we were told. I stayed behind with Cousin Red at Aunt Annie's in Draper. Mike went on to Cedar City to enroll at the junior college there.

Only a few months younger, but a grade behind me, Cousin Red was the closest I had to a best friend. We were together in Fry Canyon, although back then, he'd never been included in our circle: Mike, Billy, Willis, and me. As mentioned before, his father was my dad's partner in the tire shop. Red and I had connected in those, our indentured, years and now picked up what Greece interrupted, including our family servitude at the tire shop. But on my first day back, Red and I were free and wanted to go swimming at West Jordan, some twenty miles away. Aunt Annie didn't have the time to drive us.

"It's okay, Aunt Annie. I have my Greek driver's license." I smirked, pulling out my airline ticket.

"I don't know . . ." Her mouth screwed itself to the side, studying it. "It's all in Greek."

I smothered my mirth and continued the joke, surprised she'd not caught on. Why would she? I was of legal age. Besides, she knew me—knew I didn't lie. Joke? Yes. Instead of calling my joke, she called the Utah Highway Patrol. My "Greek driver's license" was good for thirty days.

Red and I piled into her old '52 Ford wagon. Now the joke was on me. I'd never driven a car, and the gear selector indicator for the automatic transmission in this one was broken off. There was no way of telling which gear was which. Red sat in the passenger seat, cradling his chin with his right hand, his arm propped across the open window frame—the picture of nonchalance. Out of the uncovered left side of his mouth, he prompted me.

"Punch the gas petal twice and release it."

I did as instructed.

"Now turn the key all the way."

Cough, roar, gri-i-i-i-nd . . .

"Let go! Let go of the key. Damn!" Aunt Annie's look now held some anxiety as she watched from twenty feet away. "Okay. Hold the brake and shift down one notch."

Click—click . . .

"No . . . back up one."

Click—clunk . . .

"Okay, look behind. Are we clear?"

"Uh-huh."

"Okay. Let off the brake and give it a little gas."

We lurched backward.

"Stop! Stop! Whew . . . damn, that was close!"

I glanced in the mirror and was surprised to see the hood of the neighbor's car looming so large in the back window of that old wagon.

"Okay. Shift two down." Click, click, clunk. "Give it a little gas."

We were off! As the familiar sights of the neighborhood parted to flow smoothly around an unfamiliar steering wheel, I could hardly believe it. I was tempted to call the joke, but damn—this was just too much fun!

We went swimming that day, and to many other places over the remaining weeks, until finally, Aunt Annie caught on. I was relieved to find her sense of humor still intact. She always was my favorite aunt.

Yet, discovery did not come before some small proficiency in my driving—or at least it seemed—as fewer and fewer people were honking and shaking fists. We'd just smile and wave, usually with one finger. Surviving one's youth for some can be quite a feat.

Two months into the school year, Mom and Dad arrived back from Greece. With Mike in junior college, it was us three moving back into our house in Sandy.

Now a junior at Jordan High, I worked nights and weekends with Red at the family's tire shop. The job required a car, and we found ourselves co-owners of an old '49 Chevy. God, it was an eyesore! I would've taken a stick in the eye rather than face the embarrassment of claiming ownership. Whenever people asked, I always said it was Red's car. It was only a half-lie—or half-truth. Besides, I think he did the same.

Spurred by visions of having a car we could actually drive out of the closet, we decided to fix it up. After stripping the bumpers and chrome off, we sanded it down. Short on money, we used what primer paint we could find lying about the shop. Gruesome! The base color, once fungus green, now was coupled with several different shades of red and gray primers. The car was old, beaten, tired, and discolored and was now stripped naked of any chromed decency. We took a dubious pride in purposefully having the ugliest car in school—kind of like mooning in the face of all the rich kids and their shiny, new birthday cars.

It never got painted, nor did Red or I ever have a date in high school. We might as well have stayed in the closet with our car, though that is NOT to say we were interested in each other. We weren't bad-looking guys, and the automotive grease ingrained indelibly in the cracks and crevasses of our hands and under our nails didn't cause us to stink—at least not that an armpit check could detect. Still, for some reason, the girls gave us a wide berth, as dating went. I was gun-shy from being shot down a few times in the past; Red was just shy. So it was, we blamed the car.

It is just as well that our free time was spent working. My job, coupled with a tall, naturally awkward frame, combined to limit my dates to zero and served well to keep me out of a sticky spot or two. For me, the merest wisp of fragrance from a woman's perfume, a fleeting glimpse of cleavage, or the suggestible, budding fold showing through the fabric of jeans stretched tightly between rounded feminine thighs— that was all it took to stiffen my attention and require that hasty fist once again jammed into the correct front pocket.

I didn't know then just what it was that kept me from pursuing my interest in the ladies. I thought it was expressed—coming through to them with the frequency of my glances, or the way I had of showing up in the vicinity of a selected few, slinking around like James Dean— cool and perhaps a little covertly mysterious. Somehow I believed they knew of my interest. And maybe they did and were creeped out. None ever made the first move. As a male, putting my feelings on the line was my job. But for me, I turned wrenches instead. Standing in the grease, beneath a couple of tons of car, seemed somehow safer.

I wonder if James Dean, too, had been lonely? Had he, too, faced his Marias? The Maria in Greece was the second to hold that name— and that disdain—for me. There was one earlier. She was my next love interest following Tina, way back in junior high. A very pretty young lady of Mexican descent, her full name was Maria Martinez. Some of the guys had shortened it to M and M—applicable, though for her, the shell only looked like candy. And inside, too, there was nothing sweet.

I was enthralled with her dark eyes, olive complexion, and the graceful sway of her body. After weeks of consideration, I implemented my approach. Slipping up alongside as she crossed the junior high PE field, we paced together in silence through grass still wet with early morning dew. Secretively, my hand sought hers and passed a love note. She'd taken the note just as secretively. Then, for the next few days, I waited and wondered what her answer would be and how it would come. Several days passed with no response. I did it again—and again, no response.

It's clear my infatuation played out rather romantically. No doubt Maria was flattered, but was she taken? On the third attempt, I made the mistake of dropping the secrecy. Two of her friends were with her.

Maria turned to me, her face wrapped in an ugly scowl. "Don chu effer bodder me akin weechor stupeed, fuckeen, eema-chur leedle nodes! Why wud I effer be een-tor-esteed een a beeg, skeenny, domsheet like chu, hannyway?" With that, they all three turned and flounced away, their every nuance mimicking outraged disdain.

I stood there with my mouth open, feeling, and perhaps looking, exactly like what she called me. Maybe for a time—a long time—I bought into her belief. I was, indeed, six feet two and a bit lanky back then. That part didn't hurt, but a "dumbshit"—too "stupid fucking immature" for the likes of her? Those words did. Were they the same ones as in Maria's mind in Greece as well? Ah, so much wasted concern to put on ourselves, worrying about what others think. Too much control to give to someone who doesn't even know of it—or care.

* * *

As I was finishing my high school days, Mike was not doing well in college. After falling in with a bad crowd and flunking out, he and his roommate came back to Salt Lake and got an apartment together. Mike went to work at a garage in the city. He'd changed. I didn't like the manners of his friends. Mike, too, now seemed to hold all others in a sort of crude contempt, including me. Just before Christmas, Mike got fired.

A month before, he'd given Mom a string of cultured pearls. I don't think even Dad had ever given her anything so impractically expensive. A day or so before Christmas, Mike visited home. When he left, they'd disappeared.

How often I've wished he had only stayed. Could I have helped him deal with his life? In the early morning hours of the twenty-ninth of December, I awoke to my worst nightmare.

"Jeff . . . Jeff . . . wake up!" A gentle shaking, "Wake up!"

"Ummm . . . wha . . . what is it?" I squinted in the light from the hallway. An icy chill touched my awareness and brought me instantly awake as I caught sight of my parents' faces. "What's wrong?"

Dad said, "Jeff, it's Mike. . . ."

"Oh, please don't blame us!" Mom broke in.

"Mike's dead," Dad continued. "The police were just here and told us."

That brought me bolt-upward in bed. "H-how. . . ."

"He's been shot—"

Again, Mom interrupted. "Oh, I hope you won't think it was because we were bad parents," her voice broke in a strangled sob, "that he's dead!"

Why would she think that? I wondered silently, then asked Dad, "What happened?"

My voice sounded like a badly connected telephone line. Did it carry the guilt I felt in my mind? Guilt, because with the news had come a strange relief. Could they see how I truly felt? Shock, yes. But sorrow? No . . . only relief—relief that I hadn't been there, and it wasn't my fault. I'd not failed him. *God! Am I some kind of unfeeling monster? Why just relief?*

Then, recalling Mom's words—had she, too, felt the same way about Mike? Had she taken it on her conscience that somehow she also was responsible to be his savior? Did she share this same guilty relief? No, her guilt was of something else.

For me, Mike's death hit like a blow too hard and fast to immediately feel anything except that stunning, guilty relief. It was no surprise as, like a smashing fist, it was always clenched and poised in anger, and always in plain view. I'd always known this blow would come—and violently.

It was much later when came the sorrow . . . and loneliness. I felt it keenly; like my soul was dry and shriveled, tough like the desert, desolate, without tears. Mike was my brother. We were connected in the heart and through the blood. No one else could share his place with me, and I loved him. Who we were was now extinct—except for me.

Eventually, I heard the story directly from the creep Mike roomed with—word for word in proud, intimate detail—and knowing Mike as I did, I could surmise the rest. They broke into a high school together; supposedly, there was some money kept in the office. They didn't know about the night watchman, who called the law.

Rounding a corner in the darkened hall, they came face-to-face with a cop. Mike carried a single-action Ruger .22 caliber pistol. There they were, only ten feet apart, both holding their arms out, both sighting down the quivering barrels of their guns.

The cop screamed, "Police . . . drop it!"

"N-n-no way! You drop yours!" came Mike's squeaky reply.

It wasn't clear who fired first, but suddenly, the hallway was filled with the muzzle flashes and thunder of two pistols spitting fire and death. Mike went down, his legs folding like brittle limbs on a dead tree, blasted by the .38 caliber tank round that shattered his spine. But he continued shooting. Frantically thumbing back the single-action hammer before firing each shot, he managed to put three slugs into the cop's stomach before his gun was empty. With the first hit, the cop staggered back against the wall and, using it for support, continued emptying his weapon. Then there was silence, broken only by the clicking of two revolver hammers falling on spent casings. In the end, the only sounds remaining were Mike's final, gurgling gasps, accompanied by the faint, scratching noises made by his fingernails against the cheap linoleum in that school hallway, as with his last involuntary spasms, he died.

Yes, the creep told it all to me in intimate detail, like it was some sort of gory adventure to him. He went on to explain in heroic delight how he then made his escape. The wounded cop was seated against the wall, his gun empty on the floor beside him, dumbly staring at his bleeding gut, brushing at the blood with nerveless hands. The creep told of how he slung his tire iron through a window and followed it, diving boldly out between the jagged remains. With police lights now flashing all around their car, he ran off into the night. They were waiting when he reached their apartment.

He whined about how they'd roughly tackled him to the ground, cuffed him brutally tight, and then held him for hours of interrogation. I felt no sympathy for the creepy cockroach and saw nothing heroic about his slimy, little ass.

* * *

It took several days for the coroner's autopsy and Mike's body to be released to the funeral home. At his viewing, Mike lie there looking somehow small and fragile in the copper-toned coffin. My parents asked me to choose between the two—one was cheap, the other, cheaper. I picked the more expensive one. Even though we were just back from a very well-paying overseas job, my parents—true to their good Mormon upbringing—were frugal.

It made me wonder if they also pinched a few pennies with their choice of morticians. The stitches showed clearly where Mike's lips were sewn shut, giving him a faintly fishy, almost gruesomely comic expression. True, his mouth had always fallen wide open naturally in his sleep. My own jaw muscles clenched with the grinding of my teeth as the people filing past made all the usual remarks and condolences, while their children spoke the truth.

"Oh, such a terrible thing to happen. So sorry for your loss." Then the inevitable, "If there's ever anything. . . ."

All while their little boy pawed curiously at Mike's nose, "Oh, Mommy, he feels just like wax!"

Then some of Mike's trashy friends showed up, dressed in Levis, giggling and joking. One—the girl he'd been boinking—remarked to her friend, "Oh, doesn't he look so natural? Just like he was sleeping.

Who'd know that just a few hours ago, they were sawing his . . . oops?" Then came a fluttering of insincere eyelashes in my direction.

It seemed they were having a great time, and I saw no respect for Mike in their demeanor. It took a real effort in self-control for me to keep from tearing the four of them up and stuffing their heads up their own assholes—fitting for them to see themselves the way I was seeing them.

* * *

The first days of the new year, 1964, were smudged lightly with falling snow and a gray, frigid haze. For me, the night of that viewing felt much the same. Inside, there raged a cold, deadly anger that threatened to spill into the frigid void of my tomorrow. Seriously wanting to lash out, I had to leave for a while—to just get away—before it would all explode.

I abhorred violence, but this night, I knew with a surety that such violent capability was definitely within me. I would gladly have filled in Mike's grave with the broken remains of his dysfunctional friends, then topped it off with a cop. That he was in a hospital fighting to survive meant nothing to me.

In a phone booth, I tried to call that cop, not even knowing what I wanted, only that I hurt and wanted to heap some of my pain off onto him. They say "Men don't cry; they get angry—and they get even." I shed no tears, and wasn't anger supposed to be hot, like flames? For me, it was something cold, like an icicle through my heart, somehow turning me frigidly mean. I wanted to strike out, and he clearly seemed the appropriate target.

We never spoke; the hospital wouldn't let me through. Just as well. I'm sure I would've regretted what I'd have said, and, depending on his reply—and my need to be right—perhaps even the things I might have done. Taking my private war to him would have cost me my soul, along with my freedom in life. Even if I did manage to avoid incarceration, somehow I knew that holding on to that kind of energy would consume my life—and didn't.

~ *In the Present with Big D* ~

"Wow! Until now, I didn't realize I had so much going on, with Mike's death and funerals and such." I sit back from my computer. "Big D? I can feel you near. . . ."

Now it comes to me, a certain whiff of burning cedar. Somehow it seems to be Big D's signature greeting whenever I am overstepping. "Quite an ordeal you made of Mike's funeral, don't y'think?"

"Yes, I suppose it was."

"Do you know that some thought it was the most beautiful funeral they'd ever been to?" Twin glows and a toothy smile appear now and are slowly filled in as Big D's features take shape in the chair next to my hutch.

"What? Who?"

"The girl Mike was 'boinking,' for one." Big D's grin gapes. "She saw the love in you for Mike and wished someone felt that way about her. Her sick humor was only a cover for her pain."

"Oh."

Yes, 'oh.' Kinda puts a different light on it, doesn't it?"

"Yes." I sigh. "It does."

"You know, Jeff, someday your own final breath will caress the heels of your soul. It's been a while now since that hospital room. Have you given further thought to your own funeral?"

"Well, I don't want any gruesome viewing, or grave, or spectacles of wailing grief. . . ."

"Jeff! Hold on. Like most, you're real clear about what you don't want. My question was about what you do want."

"Oh . . . yeah." I stop and just sit for a long moment, putting it all together in my mind. "Well, after they take the parts they can use, I want my remains cremated. I want my funeral to be a celebration of who I was. I'd like it held somewhere in the canyon lands of Utah, or perhaps on Lake Powell. Later, maybe after people have dealt with any pain, or messy feelings, they could just play a few meaningful songs, say a few honest words, and dump the ashes. Then I'd like it if everyone would party: hot dogs roasted on sticks, campfire burgers, dancing, and the sound of laughter." I pause a moment, picturing it. "Perhaps I'll be there in spirit and take part. They'll hear me in the songs—songs perhaps accompanied by a whisper on the wind. They'll see me in the wild, stark majesty of the canyons and mesas; breathe me in with the scents of pine, sage, and cedar mingled on the desert air. Perhaps they'll even witness my passion in the summer thundershowers and know true nurturing, as once did I, with the passing of the rains." I stop. "God, Big D! I seem to be waxing rather poetic here."

"As you said, you have a lot of feeling riding on this. Are you ready to take it on home?"

"You mean that even after all that ooey-gooey, I'm still not going deep enough?"

"Wide and slow does not always mean deep." Big D's grin widens. "Narrow it down some; like that gorge of the Acheloos, keep it slow and deep. And remember, we miss too much when life rushes fast. The rapids can be risky and fun, but there is never any depth to them. Go deeper, Jeff. You know how it's done."

"Okay . . . well . . ." Fingers touching thumb, and slowly releasing a deep breath, I center myself, counting down and relaxing into my old, familiar, alpha meditative state, using the three- second Silva method. "I know that funerals are really for the living; the dramatic, often hypocritical, shows of sorrow and caring, or spectacles of personal flagellation and blame. . . ." I pause to take another deep breath, then letting it out, I shrug a kink out of my neck before continuing. "I just want mine to be something different, Big D. Something in honor of me; something fun. And joyful, you know?"

"Yes, I do know." His laugh is low and somehow wistful. "And you've already said as much. Why do you repeat it?"

"Shit . . . you're right." I sigh. "I did already stress this point. Does seem pretty silly to keep on repeating it. I don't know why I'm so attached to others not mourning my passing."

"Ha! Inside, you do. It is just not the way of man to make funerals anything other than an opportunity to express their pain. Funny thing—it's not only about their pain about someone being gone from their life. More to the point, it's simply that they, too, will die. To choose joy at your funeral would require that they see the meaning—the contribution their own life has made—and to be okay with their own death. Ah, but this you know, from personal experience, maybe?"

"Yeah, you're right again. But do you have to rub it in my face?"

"Yeah, Jeff, think I do. You have gained a little knowledge prompted by personal experience. "But you don't yet **know** what it is I just told you. And speaking of which. . . ." His gaze seems to pin me down. "You do know how life turns to shit whenever you break the Spiritual Laws, right?"

"What? Which one? I don't see it."

"Have you forgotten the *Law of Control? 'Nothing, nor no one, can make another feel anything they don't choose to feel.' "*

"Yes, okay . . . hmmm . . . you got me." Smiling at my own insecure need to control, I continue. "The ceremony will be set up my way, but where others may take it in their own minds and feelings— you're right, that's not my concern."

"As for that cryptic '. . . don't *know* what you know' thing I mentioned? Here's another of those laws you've been ignoring." The coals of his gaze have softened suddenly. *"Emotions are the words of the soul and are fueled by its unmet needs."*

"Uhh . . ." My grunt is an involuntary thing, as this law hits almost physically. It leaves an aftertaste of something bittersweet in my mind—a mind now opened.

"Yes . . . exactly, Jeff! You still have a need to know your life has mattered." His laugh is joyous.

"Yes, it's true." I sigh. "God! Will I ever get this need of mine met? It feels as if I've wasted so much of my life."

"Not wasted, exactly. Life is always perfect—always giving you the perfect opportunities to grow. It's only your reaction to life that sometimes is not so perfect. Your need will be fully met. Once you learn your lessons, you will have paid for the limo ride. Your funeral will simply be an opportunity for others to get their own needs met, and for some, maybe even a lesson or two. Whether tears of joy and celebration, or of sorrow, guilt, and fear, your funeral just gives them an opportunity to feel their emotions. It will have little to do with you. Some may only show up to flirt with the chicks at the party."

"Yes." I chuckle. "No doubt."

"Funerals don't mean shit! It is not what comes after your death, but only where your life has reached into theirs that you really touch others. For you? You have and will yet touch many. And because of what they see in you, some will change their lives. Later, in the lives of everyone they, too, will eventually impact, that touch will then carry an element of who they have become—and with it, a small essence of you, forever."

"My God, Big D! That's kind of scary."

"Ha! Doesn't have to be. If you want to feel good about it, all you need do is stay honest with who you are and live in the energy of love. This is the simple secret of all greatness."

"Oh, in these last few years, maybe my life has mattered—some. But greatness? I don't see greatness in me."

"One's greatness is something one never sees outside of the ego." He shrugs. "It is well you don't see it. As for your funeral? Whether one or a thousand show up, you have touched many more than that. They just won't all know it." His toothy smile now seems to hold great passion. "Besides . . . I'll be there to celebrate it with you, as will Mike and others. Afterward, we'll ride those fragrant breezes, even play amidst the lightning bolts, and laugh with the thunder of the desert monsoons. It will be our tears of joy nourishing the desert that day. For you, your funeral will be exactly as you visualize it—as poetic as you want it to be."

Everyone lives in their own reality, and no one's looks the same. I must be willing to open my mind to yours if I want to know you. Otherwise, I'll just see someone who looks like me. The funny thing is: I won't recognize me.

Redneck Spirituality—Book One

Chapter Twelve

Grantsville's Finest

Mike's death was not even a hiccup in the world around me. But for me in my world, there was a sudden, silent loneliness that defied all explanation—a loneliness no one seemed to feel but me. Even though Mike had been off in school and I'd not seen much of him for almost a year, that was inconsequential to the fact, I would now never see him again—ever.

Still, there was Red and me. Red and me at school, Red and me at work, and through it all, there was still the '49 Chevy. It, above all, seemed to bind us together. We called it "The Scumbucket." Just seemed like the fitting name.

There was a grease pit across from Jordan High called "Burger Time." My smoking habit required I hang out behind it with the garbage during lunch. It was a habit I kept well hidden against my parents' Mormon ideals, but mainly, it was also against school rules. This hideout was where all the *bad asses* hung out.

Yet, I didn't fit in. I had not the meanness associated with their characters. They kept to their own group and, except for the company of smoke-free Red, I smoked alone. They respected our size enough to leave us alone. I was now six feet four and weighed a work-hardened two twenty. Red was not much smaller.

Soon we found ourselves with a comb-wielding shadow named Dick Newman. A wannabe badass, Dick was always ready with some heroic story from his past. We found him entertaining and took him in with a wink—except for the time we were out drinking and caught him pretending to drink while pouring our precious booze out one of the holes in the Swiss- cheese floorboards of the Scumbucket.

Weekends, when not working, we often went rabbit hunting. One day, we were coming back from a hunt in Skull Valley. Following a Cadillac at eighty-five, we were approaching Grantsville when a white car whizzed by from the other direction. There was a flash of yellow, and I recognized the beehive emblem of the Utah Highway Patrol. Silently I groaned, as in the rearview mirror, I watched him brake and swerve around into a U-turn, his red spotlight on.

"Damn!"

"You're not gonna run, are ya?" Red's voice held the beginning of panic as I pulled out to pass the Cadi.

"Naw, but the Cadi's speedin', too. Maybe he'll get the ticket and not us."

The best I could push out of that old, straight six was ninety-three. The driver of the Cadi refused to slow. By the time I got around, we were just blasting by the 35 mph sign on the west end of Grantsville. Hitting the curve at sixty and slowing, I felt my heart come to rest somewhere around my left testicle. Sitting at the side was the town sheriff. I hauled it on down to thirty-five.

"He's coming," said Dick from the back seat, confirming what I already knew from my mirror, "but he hasn't turned on his reds!" I could feel his fear—knew it was about the price he'd pay with his dad back home. It was something not even his bravado could hide. I felt it, too.

"I know . . . I know . . . just keep your damned nose out of the back window and your eyes open for a garage or something we can pull into and shut the door. Something—anything!" If I could just get out of the sheriff's sight. . . .

I made a quick right; well, kind of. My brakes were well roasted and went spongy. I did manage the corner, only a little to the left— actually, between the stop sign and the ditch.

Getting out of the sheriff's sight soon proved an obvious impossibility. And outrunning him? The Scumbucket hadn't the power. We'd once managed to evade the game warden when chased for spotlighting rabbits one night. That was only because after cresting a hill and out of sight, we dodged down a handy side road. Shielded by a few cedar trees and with our lights out, it made a good rabbit hole to hide in as the warden went roaring past. But that was not an option here. We threaded our way around the residential section at the required twenty-five, with him right behind. There were only a few blocks in any direction before the town started to peter off into the desert. Finally, he flipped on his reds.

The constable, I'll call him Officer Fife, reminded me of old, stringy rawhide. From the gleam in his eye, I knew he meant to nail our own hides to the door of the Grantsville Courthouse. As a sign of good faith, I got out and stood by the car, waiting as he hobbled up, doing his best police officer swagger. I still don't know how he managed that. He glanced through our back window and saw the guns on the seat. Now his eyes were really gleaming. With his hand on his revolver, he drawled.

"Wha'chu boys been up ta?"

"Uh . . . just been out to Skull Valley, rabbit hunting." I knew my grin was a little sheepish.

"Ain't no rabbits here 'bouts."

His accent didn't peg him as a native of this one-bishop Mormon town. Still, something told me he knew the truth, so I didn't bother mentioning the twenty or so Jacks we'd shot. Somehow, I just didn't think he'd be receptive. Besides, I figured he was planning on using big enough nails on that courthouse door. I wasn't asking for a crucifixion.

He thumbed open the trigger strap on his holster and squared his stance. Without taking his hand off his gun, he said to Dick and Red, "You two . . . git out t'car . . . come out dis side, an' keep them hands in plain sight." Once they both obeyed, he continued. "Now put yer hands on t'hood—feet back—n' spread 'em."

Then he turned his attention back to me. "You, Boy . . . bring out them there guns," adding, "re-ull slow now . . . one ut a time . . . re-ull keerful now." Each phrase was spaced ominously, as with each gun I complied, laying them across the roof of the car.

"Now open t'ak-shins . . . les have a look-see at them breeches," he drawled. "Wanna make sure t'ain't gonna go off, don't cha'know?"

To me, it sounded like what he was really saying was, "Go ahead, sucker, draw!" I was careful opening each firing chamber—very careful—especially so, since while it was happening, there was a call coming over his radio. It was a highway patrol request to stop a '52 green-and-brown Chevy. They were off a few years, but without its chrome, the Scumbucket could well have been a '52. Luckily, Officer Fife was either hard of hearing or too absorbed in his rendition of Marshall Dillon to notice.

"Okay, now Boy . . . lemmy see yer lie-sins n' regis-tra-shun."
He took one look at the faded registration and said, "Thars sumpm'
phoney 'bout tis. They jus' don't give 'em out blank lak' kis."

Badly sun bleached from its perch on the visor, the writing was
unclear, but the number printed on the corner was okay. Red started to
point this out, only to get a finger pointed in his face. "Shu-t-t-t . . . shut
y'r mouth, Boy! Wusn' talkin' to ya."

Then to me, "Spread 'em, cross t'hood!" he ordered coldly, then
patted all three of us down. Finding nothing, he moved his search to the
car. In the trunk, he found a spare generator core and some tools. Now
his eyes were not only gleaming, but he was starting to lick his lips.
Perhaps it was to keep from drooling.

I could almost hear him thinking: "Oh boy! Stol'n car . . . stol'n
tools . . . stol'n auto parts . . . guns. . . . Oh boy, I'm a hero. Thank'ya,
God. I've done caught me some re-ull desperados!"

"Why fer ya drivin' 'round my town? Ya lookin' ta steal
somethin'?" This was Dick's forte. He piped in before we could answer.

"Oh . . . uh . . . we were just looking for a friend who lives here."

"Wut-sees name?"

"Uhh . . . er . . . ah, John."

"Sheet, Boy! Tha' don' tell me nuthin' . . . wut-sees las' name?"

"John, uh . . . Smith . . . uh, John Smith."

I ducked my head and winced as Red looked over, silently
rolling his eyes.

"Ain't no John Smith lives here 'bouts. I knows ev-body in this
here town." And likely he did, despite his accent.

"Well, yeah, but . . . ah . . . he just moved here."

"You boys is lyin' ta me here! We jis call tis here regis-tra-shun
in, n' then we'll find out." He paused to give us each a meaningful eye
where we leaned spread-eagled against the car. "Don-chu boys move
now, hear?"

By then, I knew we'd really made Officer Fife's day. He looked
thirty years younger, as he fairly danced back to his car to call in a
license plate check to Salt Lake City. He just stood there, grinning
happily and chuckling to himself as he waited for his answer.

When it came, I watched his face fall. He walked slowly back to us, his head down, looking at the ground. Without looking up, he handed me my papers and growled, "Git outa here!" We wasted no more of his time.

Loading our guns back up, we piled in and moved off. Red, sitting next to me, turned to see if the officer would follow. He didn't. Before Red swiveled back around, he reached out and thumped Dick on the side of his head.

"What? What? What was that for?"

"Jesus Christ!" Red growled. "Why didn't you just say 'Joseph Smith'? Dumbshit!"

"What? What d'ya mean?"

Red wiped his hand on his pant leg and exchanged glances with me. I shrugged, then glanced in the mirror at Dick, now busy restoring his wayward strands of greased hair. I replied. "Dick, sometimes it's just better to tell the truth—and we pretty much were until you dropped that load of shit."

"What d'ya mean?"

"What do you think if I'd just told him, 'We weren't sure if we were slowed down enough when we hit the speed zone. We thought if you figured we were locals, you wouldn't give us a ticket.'"

"I think he'd have given us a ticket."

"Yeah . . . well . . . we're lucky you didn't get our asses thrown in jail. Don'tcha know it's a felony to lie to a cop?" As long as we knew him, Dick never did get it.

Working and rabbit hunting were not the only things Red and I did with our time together. It was during these high school years when my love for rocks and gems really began to blossom. Red always loved them, too—at least the collecting part. We spent a couple of weeks every summer camping out on the western desert of Utah, mostly around Topaz Mountain in the Thomas Mountain Range or at the Dugway Pass geode beds. Dick's mother wouldn't let him go. He said it was because she didn't trust Red and me. I believed him, at least the part about trust. The little shit lied so much, who knows how much of his shit he'd blamed on us.

For us, the desert was like a restroom sign to a man with diarrhea. There was never anything we were happier to see, and we were always in a rush to be there. The smell of sage and cedar, the thrill of finding gemstones, crystals, and arrowheads, their weighty feel and natural beauty resting in our hands. These were the gifts of the wastelands.

Headed out across the wide desert stretches, just Red and me; dirt roads cutting vast panoramas between the towering naked peaks and ranges; open vistas, hung with early morning haze, all promising a hot day—and freedom.

And of course, there were the nights. Sitting around a cedar fire, the taste of roasted rabbit, illicit beer, and smokes, all embellished beneath a carpet of stars with the telling of our life's special stories. Such were the very best of times for me.

At Topaz Mountain, the ground literally sparkled with small, clear, sun-bleached topaz crystals. For the delicately colored pinkish-yellow ones, it was necessary to climb the craggy peaks and break up the tough, gray rhyolite rock with crack hammers and chisels. Though grueling, hot work, we loved every minute. We always went home all grimy, sweaty, and deliciously, odorously grubby.

~ *Looking Back* ~

There is something about the desert which always brings peace to my soul. I think it has to do with man and his judgments. There seems to be a duality about man. It lies in the boundaries of his thoughts, in the way he limits himself. He sees life as if it were a single piece of string with something always at each end: right and wrong, good and bad, righteous and evil. Why couldn't the cord just as well be endless, like nature? Nature just is, and in "being" with nature, I find peace. What would the world be like were mankind to let go of judgment and just "be?" For me, that is the world of the desert. In that world—in that space of natural completeness—I feel so insignificantly a part of it all. Then is when the overwhelming problems of my life also become insignificant, and easily seen.

I have often sat on a precipice overlooking the confluence of two deep canyons and listened to the messages of the wilderness. Like the ancients who left the flint chips littering this spot, I like to think I, too, have seen the natural wisdom of the earth as written in the manganese stain on the cliff face across the way:

Peace is the natural way of being.

Other times, it floats as a spiritual vision on heat waves against the effortless horizon:

Condemnation in our judgment is not natural
Prejudice is a disease most often taught in our youth,
an infection only cured for the few who learn to think for
themselves.

Although judgments obviously are necessary to my personal reality, and in keeping myself safe in the world, still, there are limits those same judgments always put upon my thinking and, therefore, create my misconceptions. And maybe—bottom line—they simply just flavor my thinking. Is it positive or negative, uplifting or condemning? How does it all serve me in life?

As to other people? When I don't listen to the things they tell me—their beliefs and opinions, their personal truths—I am blinding myself. I'm cutting myself off to things I can't see about me, to a learning I could have, and won't. I believe that old axiom: Change is the only constant in the universe; if I'm not growing, I'm dying. Can my mind grow without looking at what I don't want to see? Perhaps it is about listening to the beliefs of others, then doing my own thinking.

Officer Fife, Sr. had a special part in teaching it all to me. The thieving scum he perceived us to be were not who we were—not that we were any angels. I'd look him up and thank him for making me aware of my own life's misconceptions. But he must be gone from this world by now and probably can hear me just fine.

* * *

When last I saw Dick, we all three were in the army and on leave. Red and I were both draftees, and Dick, of course, had joined. Red was in a signal outfit headed for Vietnam. Dick was fresh out of basic training and sporting his uniform, complete with wishful decorations: a couple of service ribbons and even a unit commendation. In addition, there were two expert weapons medallions, a truck driver's medallion, and an infantry braid, all but two of which—fresh out of basic—were impossibilities. Did he think we wouldn't know? No, Dick hadn't yet got it, and maybe in the end he did. Maybe he found a place where he fit in, and maybe he became the hero he always wanted to be. The last I heard of him, he'd made sergeant; the last I saw was his name on the wall.

Red, I saw again two years later. He'd finally taken up the smoking habit—just not of tobacco. The man he'd become was moody. We didn't seem to have much left in common, and we never again connected.

~ *In the Present with Big D* ~

Again, the essence of sage and cedar comes now to my mind, so strong that it overpowers my lighted incense burner. There is a stirring that seems to be happening just outside edge of my vision.

"Yes, it is me."

"Big D! I wondered if you would come this time."

"It is good to see you thinking for yourself. You are right on track." Amidst the darkened swirl of him, I get the impressions of his grin and his engineer's hat. "Just one question, though."

"What?"

"When are you going to pull the plug outa your butt and relax a little?"

"What!"

"It's not that it ain't true, Jeff, but maybe you need to read over the last few pages of this chapter—all that stuff about the duality of man, judgments, growing or dying. . . ."

Picking up the manuscript, I do as he bids. "Yeah, I see it. Sounds constipated . . . preachy, even."

"You could become a preacher. Church would be a great place to dump a load of shit, and a lot of people would probably come to wallow in it. You do know that preachers are paid to tell folks how to live their lives—folks who don't want to think for themselves."

"Okay, Big D, I hear you. I'll rewrite it."

"Naw, just leave it. Y'know there are some folks who will skip all this discussion between you and me. They just want an interesting story—maybe because it helps to make their own life more interesting."

"But we discuss some deep shit."

"True, and they aren't ready to hear about the meaning of life— not yet. If they ever get ready, maybe then they'll get out this book and read the parts they skipped."

"I suppose."

"Y'know, Jeff, not everybody who reaches that place in life where they meet me find, as you did, that they aren't ready to give up. Most don't realize that they've already given up, and so dying's all that's left." The darkened misting of him swirls as if to leave, then pauses and firms up solid to my view. "Besides, I will not fault you your need to purge just now. Between the motorcycle and your meditations, you've spent a considerable time on the desert of late."

"Oh God, Big D! My Meg . . . my parents . . . my old friends . . . everyone from my past life is now gone. Well, except for my son, and he lives 3000 miles away. I didn't expect the price to be so high!"

"Is the joy you find in living the freedom of your soul worth it?"

"Yes."

"Through it all, have you not offered them an alternative to the control they seek?"

"You mean . . . ?"

"Yes, exactly." He places his bony right hand almost reverently across his rib cage where his non-existent heart would be, and adds softly, ". . . your love."

"Yes. Not once have my dealings with them come from any space that was not love."

"And . . ."

"And I don't know if they simply can't see it—or don't want it."

"Yes. For something to be given, it also requires an acceptance." The heartbreak in his voice matches my own. Then, as if to illustrate his final words, he fades from sight. "In a society so steeped in the control of others, even when present, love is a precious, but often invisible, commodity." The last I see of him is the glow of his right eye socket as it winks prior to his final words. "Some folks will never see the love you offer them with these, our intimate discussions."

There are no secrets, just things we refuse to see consciously. In my higher mind, I know everything about you—and you, me. On that level, there are no secrets. And on that level, we are so much more than we can ever consciously conceive.

Redneck Spirituality—Book Two

Chapter Thirteen

Graduation Night

For me, graduation from Jordan High School went off like someone else's silent fart—one for which it seemed I had been assigned blame. Yet, in my feeble attempts at denial, I, too, began to smell something about me and the fact that I had no female relationships, nor many close friends. I could not deny my social life did indeed stink.

At school that last day, the buzz in the halls was boisterous with who was going to what party after the ceremony, who else would be there, and of course, how much and what kind of booze would be brought. My only close friends consisted of Cousin Red and Dick Newman, and they were still juniors. I walked those halls, and though I knew those around me, somehow, I walked among them as a stranger. Was this last day of high school the way it would always be for me? *Will I always be a stranger to everyone I think I know? God, how can I make this be different?*

"Hey, Jeff, I'll be over at Rick's tonight. He's gonna have a keg party. See ya there later."

"Yeah . . . great, Marty!" *How do I tell him I'm not invited?*

"Jeff! Yo Jeff. I got it. I scored a quart of vodka."

"Great, Kev! Whatcha doing with it?"

"Whatcha think . . . taking Paula and some orange juice and going to Memory Grove."

"Sweet! Enjoy 'em both." *Certainly can't ask to come along on his party.*

"Hey, where you going tonight, Jeff?"

"Ain't decided." *Surely someone will invite me somewhere?*

No one did. That evening found me sitting alone in my half-owned '49 Chevy. Its colors shone dully, but bravely: light green spotted with primer, gray and brown, under the neon lights of the Murray Frostop. I had, through no minor effort, finagled some beer. There I sat in all the glory of my newly won freedom and adulthood, eating ripple-cut French fries with special Frostop sauce and drinking beer through a straw. Someone once told me you could get more effect that way. I was just beginning to wonder what my party-of-one would do to top off the night when Lisa Bender and Lois Wayne pulled up alongside. They were in Lisa's mother's station wagon.

I'd known both since the sixth grade. Lois and I had endured the weekly school dance lessons together. She'd always fought with the other tall girls for the rights to dance with me. Back then, I was the only boy who was tall enough to suit them. At the time, it was somehow imperative to her. It never concerned me as to exactly why. Now, in high school, Lois was no longer considered tall. Though not unattractive, she was just a little light of lung. And certainly, she would have been better looking without the horn-rimmed glasses. She did, however, have a great personality, and I liked being around her. Besides, it was closing time, and the beer was beginning to take effect. So I was glad when Lois struck up a conversation.

"Hey, Jeff." She smiled. "What are you doing here?" Her eyes were sparkling, Lisa's, avoiding.

"Hi, Lois. Hi, Lisa." Lisa was the prettier of the two and I always felt attracted. Her response toward me was no different than usual for girls of her ilk: a quick nod, a distasteful flash of eye, quickly covered by a mascara-coated slip to the side.

"I would have thought you'd be at some party, whooping it up and breaking hearts." Lois's eyes told me she believed it.

"Yeah, right! You have to be invited first."

"Well, I expected you'd have started your own."

"Thought about that . . ."

"Yeah . . . well?"

"Nobody accepted, so I got a few beers and I'm celebrating alone."

"Well, you never asked me. I would have come."

"Too late now." I grinned. "I'm about out of beer."

"Doesn't matter; I don't drink beer anyway?" It was not a statement, but a questioning proposition.

"Does that mean you want your heart broken?"

"Might want to check out that possibility."

Damn! The girl has spirit. She was beginning to look better and better to me. Still, Lisa was the prettier. . . .

"Lisa, would you want to join the party?"

"Not for me." Her shake of head looked more like a shudder. "But Lois is a big girl now." Lisa was looking much less attractive.

"Say, Jeff, why don't you take me home? We could check out my dad's rock fireplace in the basement. Those rocks come from all over. . . ." Lois paused. Her implication seemed clear when she added, "You know?" Did she know geology would be my major at the University of Utah? I didn't recall ever having told her. No, it had to be more. Tonight there would be heavy breathing between the two of us, alone in front of that fireplace. Hot damn! To graduate my status as a virgin—hers, too, if I knew Lois. What a great ending for graduation night.

A short time later found us there, in front of that very fireplace, only I wasn't breathing heavily. In fact, I was doing my best not to breathe at all. Lois's father was standing next to me, explaining from where this and that rock had come. And Lois's father was a bishop in the Mormon Church—the same church to which I belonged and in which it was a sin to imbibe alcohol. I didn't want to breathe any beer fumes on him. Worse! I didn't want him knowing the reason both my fists were stuffed into my front jeans pockets.

Looking back, I wonder: What if he and I were having our conversation consciously, in real honesty—soul to soul? On that level, our conversation was much different: *Hello, Mr. Dad. Yes, I'm young. . . my hormones moan and groan, even howl, a serenade to your daughter. Her small, firm breasts, pert nipples, lithe body, raise the want, the expectation of my loins, a desire for a meeting within—within her by me. I know you, Mr. Dad . . . 'cause you remember me. I am your worst nightmare and your fondest dream. I am your most memorable memory. So you take up my time, keeping me in this space, discussing your stupid . . . fucking . . . fireplace!*

* * *

The summer after graduation was spent working at the tire shop, fulfilling the family's expectations. Our pay, mine and Red's, was still a dollar-fifty a day—"for lunch." Pocket money was dependent on need. Except for our occasional weekends on the desert, we had few acceptable needs. The next fall, I attended the U of U. As with high school before, the working only moved to the nights. Dad took another overseas job that year, this time on a dam in Victoria, Australia—a place called Khancoban. Did he really feel my education was that much a drain on the family resources?

My college days were short-lived. The first term I loaded myself up with some of the most difficult subjects possible. Then I spent all of my spare time at the campus coffee shop, affectionately known as "The Huddle," occupying my time with blackjack and bullshit. The next two terms were spent in striving and study. My tour boat was no longer set on "cruise," and while it was in full reverse, it continued straight ahead with its rudder still locked on Vietnam. The war had suddenly developed an insatiable appetite, and it took a 2.5 grade point average to stay off the USDA's—United States Department of the Army—prime beef list.

It was during this time that I and a young lady named Gail lost our virginity together one night. Blindingly fast, it happened in an awkward jumble of elbows, knees, and passion. I found myself staring at a surreal slick spot, with a dot of crimson, on the cold, hard basement floor, while my ears heard the rush of water down the sewer pipe from the upstairs bathroom. Like some sudden, mutual, spasmodic fit, it left one of us bleeding and the other in sexual withdrawal. *Was this it? My God . . . was this the big deal to which I worked so hard—now in the past, so quick and meaningless? I could have had more fun jacking off with a chunk of liver, and I wouldn't have felt bad for the liver. It wouldn't have been screaming, "Owww, ahhhh! It hurts! It hu-r-r-r-r-r-r ts . . ."*

* * *

I was under eighteen and considered a minor when Dad took the job in Australia. This made me eligible for a free trip. Because my grades were not high enough, I was required by the draft board to get a special dispensation to travel outside the country—or so they seemed to think. I gave them several months' notice and called often to inquire, but when the time came to leave, I still had no authorization. I called from the airport in San Francisco:

"Selective Service . . . Murray Office."

"Hello, may I speak to Mr. Kleules?"

"Yes, this is Mr. Klueles."

"Hi, this is Jeffrey Williams. Has the board given their permission for me to go to Australia yet?"

"Look, Mr. Williams, you're going to have to have more patience. We on the board don't meet again for another two weeks. We'll try to consider it then."

"It's been three months and I'm out of time."

"Mr. Williams . . ." He sniffed audibly, as if his nose had just discovered something brown stuck to the sole of his shoe. "Yours is not the only case we have to consider."

Just then, there came an announcement over the terminal speakers: "TWA Flight 767 . . ."

"Okay, fine. Look . . . they're calling my flight. Just send your answer to me in Australia. You have my father's address."

~ *Looking Back* ~

Yes, I got some sense of satisfaction with the way in which I handled the situation. Yet, I'd clearly set myself up to lose. Unlike many of my classmates, I was lucky in that I didn't lose my life, my body parts, or my peace of mind somewhere out there on the blood and mud of a Vietnamese rice paddy.

That draft board was typical. Utah was never a hotbed of dissension during the Vietnam War. I think it was from the way we were raised. In general, we Mormons turned over our minds to what the church said was right—our lives, too. We paid our tithe to the church, and then we paid in service, some to the point where it took up their lives. For the church would require it, in God's name, until we had nothing left for ourselves.

And of course, it was the law that we paid a tithe to the government, too, wasn't it? Like our church, we also believed that going to this war was the *right* thing to do. When asked to give of our service, we young men considered it our *duty*, few realizing that our *duty* and the *right thing* are merely figments from someone else's imagination. Few truly understood what was purchased with our lives. Few parents knew who it was that benefitted from the blood of their sons. It is what always happens when people won't think for themselves.

The government said it was *right*, so we gave . . . , and they accepted our lives to use as they pleased. We never asked the questions: Did any of them give, or lose, their lives? Was there any threat to God or country? Or was it just someone's thirst for money and power?

~ *In the Present with Big D* ~

"Horseshit!"

"What?"

"Yes . . . 'horseshit!'" Big D reiterates. "True as it may be, this has to do with what's already nourished that horse *out there*. What about you, *in here*? All I hear is blame and victim; I hear nothing about how this understanding nourishes you now! So, yes! Horseshit!"

"'Nourishes me now?' What does that mean?" My eyes probe the darkened room for him. "And I don't fucking appreciate your . . . 'horseshit!'"

"Whoa!" The word comes like the striking of a match, and the air around my desk seems to suddenly smell of sulphur. "You best turn around, Son, you're speaking out the wrong end." As if by the flaring of a match, he is now illuminated at my side. "You are the part of me that's clueless. I'm the part of you that knows everything!"

"Of course—you're right! Forgive me. Don't know what got into me."

"Look . . . swear all you want, just lose the attitude. There is no *right* or *wrong*, except what rattles around inside your skull." Again, his familiar grin. "And *forgiveness*? It's just a personal need of judgmental people. I need not ever forgive you; I never judged you *wrong*. But disrespecting me? Now, that is something that simply doesn't work."

"Yeah . . . okay. Look, I'm sorry, Big D. The 'horseshit' stuff kinda set me off."

"Yes, I know. It was your mother's favorite expression. Your father preferred 'bullshit.' They said them often to keep from getting real with you, especially when they didn't want to look at what you were really about for them. Kind of like now."

"In what little they've spoken to me in recent years, I've heard those words often. But I thought the points I was just making were important and valid."

"Let's just shovel this barn out, one turd at a time." The humor in his tone feels reassuring. "It never works when you look at your problems as being formed by anyone but you. What is, just is. The problem part is entirely of your creation. Ha! Truth is"—he cocks his head and seems to wink sagely—"governments rarely serve man, and churches rarely serve God."

"Y'know, you've just said my whole speech there in one sentence." It almost seems to lighten my mind to think of it in such simple terms.

"When I came for you in that hospital, did you look to your church or government to help you?"

"No."

"Perhaps sometime the rest of mankind will see how very insignificant churches and governments are in the grand scheme of things and quit assigning so much deadly power to them, like you then did."

"I see it; won't even try to deny it. It was me who played their stupid game—played it without thinking and without consulting that part of me inside that didn't feel so good about it." My mind feels as if it has just emerged from the shadow of another one of those pesky clouds. "Shit! I played my own mindless part in the death of every soldier who died in Vietnam. Like them, I gained a lot of self-respect for being willing to put my life on the line for what I thought was right— never mind that my thinking was nothing short of 'fucked up.'"

"Doesn't it feel good to say it again, but without the blame? And by the way, the ending of this chapter is similar to the last. Reads like a fart in the elevator. Now . . . what is that saying about you?"

"Well, for one, it is only other people who think I stink. I no longer do."

"Yeah, Jeff, it is good that you don't care what others think." I get the impression that his permanent skeletal grin has suddenly widened. "Besides being none of your business, it is an impossibility to care and still be your authentic self. But you know it says a lot more than that."

"Sure. I think it says I'm growing. It's got to stink to others when they realize I don't just accept their personal beliefs but, instead, think for myself. Right and wrong are just words of judgment that often don't even come close to meaning the same thing to everyone. No matter from which end it is spoken, it's going to stink. Why do people have such difficulty in seeing things as simply 'loving' or 'not loving'? Sure, I'm seeing how my church and government had me believing their lies, and I'm taking responsibility in knowing the truth of it now. I'm learning to just live by my heart and not play my part in other people's silly, destructive games."

"Ah, 'loving and not loving'. . . ." Looking at his frozen, ivory countenance, I can almost see the arching of invisible eyebrows. "You have many whom you love wanting to play those destructive games with you of late. They are not so happy that you no longer play your part."

"Like, who in particular? That covers pretty much everyone I know from my past."

"Your parents. They've both taken on a great deal of pain, so much so that it might kill them in their old age. Such drama! And all because of how you choose to live your life."

"Will it, Big D?" I can't help but swallow hard. "Will it kill them?"

"Ha! 'It' won't do shit! You know that." He leans forward, his posture intent, yet his voice for all its passion is as a soft caress. "I mention it only because you've sworn off whining about them and would never bring the subject up. It's just not what you want to do. Nevertheless, yes . . . they likely will die, their lives a twisted mass of ineffectual control and pain. And in their minds, you are to blame. They choose this rather than to love and accept you and your right to be you. I can't stop your pain, and I can tell you clearly: Don't buy into their bullshit—or horseshit."

"Is there anything I can do besides live those lies they expect of me?"

"Love them . . . hold them capable. . . . They might surprise me— might even decide to accept responsibility and call for the limo ride for later. You did, you know?" Big D's fleshless hand brushes the moisture gently from my cheek. "Hell, besides me, pain is man—and womankind's—greatest motivator, self-inflicted though it may be. That they still live says they have not yet made their choice. They will either learn the life lessons you have provided by example or give up in blame and take the shuttle bus." He cups my chin, holding my gaze locked to his for one long moment before adding, "You've discharged your prior-to-life agreement with them; be okay with their decision."

I nod my head, unable to trust my voice just now.

"And you did it with courage and love." With a wink from the blazing coal in one eye socket, he is gone.

Integrity is a gift given to me that only I can give. When I am in integrity, I honor me. There is a certain integral strength in me, such that I need have no heroes *out there*, for I am a hero *in here*. This is what I know. This is what others see, and it matters not if they honor it—at least not to me. And yet honor me they will, both in respect and trust.

Redneck Spirituality—Condensed from Book One

Chapter Fourteen

Make Me a Man—A Stout-Rodded Man

The letter said, "*Greetings,* from the President of the United States—"

I said, "Oh, shit!"

After vacationing most of the Australian winter at my parents' place on the Murray River in Khancoban, I'd gone down to Ballarat, Victoria and arranged to attend the Ballarat School of Mines. It was a very prestigious, world-famous college, somewhat comparable to our Colorado School of Mines. The letter awaited my return. My mother's face was grim as she handed it to me.

This was one of those more obvious forks in my road of life. I had a choice. Would I tell the draft board where to stick it, along with my citizenship, or would I go back and enter the army? In the grand scheme of things, I, too, was wondering if my country's honor was dying. Would I become just another chunk of gristle for the meat grinder called Vietnam? Much as I resented the draft board's heavy hand in my life, and the obvious lack of integrity amongst its leaders, there was no contest.

My induction into the army took place at Fort Douglas, Utah. The sergeant reminded me of a bulldog: short, squat, made from chiseled bone and muscle. Pacing restlessly back and forth before us, stomach in, back straight, he moved like someone with a stick up his butt. His disposition certainly seemed to confirm it.

"Single line! Right here! Now! Move! Move!" We jumped to his bidding and soon had a line of sorts formed. Slapping his pants leg periodically with his clipboard, he passed down the line, pausing momentarily to transfer that slapping motion to the crotch of one man standing too far forward. "I said . . . line up!" The man's ass shot backward with a cough, followed hurriedly by the rest of his body.

"Now place your belongings on the floor in front of you and strip to your shorts! Now! Move! Move!" Naturally, some of us were reluctant. "Get used to it, Girls! Move! Move!"

"Now, from your left, count off in twos!" We began our count. "One, two, one, two, one. . . ." Someone wasn't paying attention; his conversation with the man beside him was interrupted by the sergeant's clipboard.

Whomp!

"Wassamatter, Boy? Didn't your momma teach you what comes after one? Two! Say it!" The man rubbed the side of his head and repeated a sulky two. As the count continued, the sergeant stepped in close, so they were almost nose-to-nose. "Better you straighten up and fly right, Boy! You don't want to tangle assholes with me . . . do you?" The clipboard's flick was accompanied by another ass flinching backward, then a sick shake of the man's head.

"N-no."

"That's 'No, Sergeant' to you, Maggot!"

"No, Sergeant!"

"Good!" The sergeant stepped back away. "Now, again: from your left, count off in twos!" This time, the count went without any problems.

"Now! Ones . . . line up here! Twos . . . here, facing each other! Leave your belongings where they are! Quickly, now! Move! Move!"

Our two lines were about eight feet apart. We stood there in our skivvies looking at each other—a comical assortment—one muscle-bound bod of steel, but most, soft and pudgy. No one was laughing. He continued, "Now, peel 'em, bend over at the waist, and spread your cheeks!"

There we were, like two opposing lines of brown-eyed Cyclopes. Accompanied by the sergeant, a doctor with captain's bars on his white lab coat ambled along behind us, tapping each on the butt with his pencil to indicate when we could straighten up. His tap on the man next to me was answered.

"Pfffutttt . . ."

In a blur, the sergeant jerked the man backward, out of line by his hair. "Stand at attention, Boy!"

The man straightened, but there was a smile on his face.

"You think it's funny to fart in the Captn's face, Boy?"

"Ooh, Tharge, you're thuch a ba-rute!"

The sergeant's fist was interrupted on the back swing by a quick move from the captain.

"Sergeant! A word in private, please."

Together they stepped to the far end of the room, where the doctor clearly told him something he didn't want to hear. The sergeant's jaw muscles were clenched when they returned.

"You think you're clever, Boy, but it ain't gonna work here. Whachur name?"

"Kevin."

The sergeant moved in close. I was one of the few who heard him whisper softly, "Kevin, this 'fag act' ain't gonna keep your sorry ass out of 'Nam. You're in for a world of hurt, Boy!"

Next, we were told to stand with our feet shoulder-width apart, our heads turned to the side, and to cough as the doctor stuck his finger up one nut and then the other. The thing I found most irritating was the pleased look on his face. Did I hear a chuckle at Kevin's cough, which sounded more like a seductive moan?

Afterward, we were allowed to dress. Then, as a group, we took the Oath of Allegiance. It was a relief when they didn't make us do this, too, with our skivvies at half-mast. I guess they thought it deserved a little dignity. Nevertheless, it felt to me a little like thanking the rapist.

* * *

We arrived in El Paso, Texas by a military-chartered commercial airline and were immediately bussed off to Fort Bliss. I could feel a sense of something huge impending in the predawn blackness of the night as we glided by the long, twinkling lines of perimeter fence lights. Looking at them from within the green confines of our lighted military bus, I wondered how long it would be before I again felt free. Through the opened crack of my window, the cool desert air smelled of wild freedom. Then, after being ordered to close it, I wondered how long it would be before I again felt free. Aside from the route to and from the base, I still, to this day, have never seen El Paso. While there, El Paso never felt of any kind of freedom.

Whoever named Fort Bliss had a truly sick sense of humor. The normal ten weeks of misery and dehumanization for us was crammed into eight. The lords of the base wanted us enumerated, inoculated, indoctrinated, immoralized, demoralized, mechanized, circumcised, and whatever else it took to make us soldiers—by Christmas. And they were determined we would not miss one ounce of the misery.

Those eight weeks seemed like eight months. Every second of our lives was rigidly controlled. The least infraction, real or manufactured, committed by me or just one of the group, brought immediate pain and strain, usually in the form of push-ups. In the first week, screwups called for ten to fifteen four-count push-ups; by the sixth, it was sometimes fifty. We called cadence to our suffering: "One . . . two . . . three. ONE!" *Down . . . up . . . down.* "TWO!"

Sometimes, as individual punishment, the push-ups were done on the blocks: two concrete pads, the one for the feet being about twelve inches higher than for the hands. An alternate torture was the front-leaning rest, or the up position of push-ups held without movement. This was usually an individual punishment, as it took time. The unlucky shit would be ignored so long as he remained rigidly in position, while the rest of us went on about whatever misery we were doing at the time.

Several times, I saw Kevin and other guys give up in tears. While some looked at them in disgust or ridicule, I knew their suffering intimately and worried if I would be next to succumb.

In the four times it happened to me, I felt lucky, in that I did not voluntarily break. There was one time when I blacked out on the parade ground during PT—physical training. We were all in the front-leaning rest position, compliments of another of Kevin's fuck-ups. I was only out for a few seconds before I awoke with blood gushing from my nose and Drill Sergeant Wheatzel climbing my butt.

"Get your sorry ass back in position. Wassamatter, Pussy, you need your mommy to wipe your nose for you?" The sergeant loved his work. "Well, she ain't here, and you best stop bleedin' on my parade ground!"

I stayed there—my elbows locked, shoulders locked, knees locked—and with a thousand pounds of meanness sagging my butt, watched my boyhood drip away in steady, crimson drops. My body was strung like a power line with one downed pole. It trembled and jerked spasmodically, a hundred thousand volts of grounded agony there for perhaps a thousand moments more. Finally, the general order was given: "Form up! You, too, Pussy."

Kevin was the albatross of our platoon, so many infractions did they hang on him, and through him, we, too, often suffered the penalties. Eventually, he was put in the hospital with a chipped cheekbone—compliments of someone's entrenching tool. The owner of the tool went to the stockade, and while no one spoke of it, in our hearts, we all thanked him. We never heard from either again.

For me, my positive experience of basic training boiled down to one incident. It all started during morning chow right after the PT incident. That day found me in the very back of the chow line. By the time I processed through getting my tray filled, all the acceptable seats were filled, leaving only the empty table next to the one where the drill sergeants all ate.

No one ever wanted to sit in close proximity to them, especially to Sergeant Wheatzel. Part of his introductory speech went, ". . . It's been said that were the weasel but made as big as man, there wouldn't be a single, goddamned human left on the planet. Now, I may be a lean, mean, green, fighting machine, but don't you dare let me hear you calling me a weasel!" His fellow drill sergeants all did anyway. I sighed and sat down across from my platoon's drill instructor, Sergeant Peterson. I was, therefore, unavoidably close enough to hear the conversation he was having with Sergeant Wheatzel—and yes, the men in his platoon called him Weasel, of course behind his back. He was small and lean, had rat-like facial features, and a downright mean disposition.

"Peterson . . ." His chest was puffed out, and he was not given the normal respect afforded another of equal rank by placing "sergeant" as part of the salutation. "You gotta stop coddling these jelly donuts you call a platoon."

"They're all good men, Weasel."

Sergeant Wheatzel's face darkened. "They're pussies, and you're gonna get 'em all killed! Not one of them will be hardened enough to handle the shit they're gonna face in 'Nam."

"They'll handle it—"

"You mean like this long, skinny cockroach behind me here?" His thumb jerked over his shoulder toward me. "Passed out on the parade ground all limp and drippy like a used-up cunt. Why, give me a day with him, and I'd have him crying for his mommy."

Sergeant Peterson stood abruptly and, picking up his tray, turned to leave. Then, glancing over at me, he stopped and turned back. Setting his tray back down, and with his knuckled fists holding his body steady, he leaned forward, right into Sergeant Wheatzel's face. His voice was so deadly quiet that I barely caught his words. "He didn't quit, did he?" His last word was as a soft breath, and I wasn't sure I heard. Did he say *". . . Asshole?"*

If anything, the training became harder, but it helped to know the sergeant had our backs. While I became toughened physically, I was also developing a very unhealthy resentment and fear of those in authority over me—well, except for Sergeant Peterson. This was the choice I made as a result of my experiences and, I don't know, perhaps it was the choice the army intended for me to make. I just know it wasn't a good attitude to carry on into my later civilian life, as I was still unwilling to fully accept that authority.

On my last day at Fort Bliss, when I opened my footlocker to start packing my duffel, there, in the top tray, was a jelly donut wrapped in cellophane, sitting on a paper plate. Looking around me, I noted Sergeant Peterson about to go out the doorway. He flipped me a "see ya" kinda salute and I responded. Mine had the perfection of the full military version. I've always remembered that moment with fondness, as I never saw him again. A salute is a sign of respect between those in the military, and I was no longer a trainee.

I've often heard it said about the army that, ". . . it will make a man out of you." For me, I became a man despite the army. And the jelly in my donut? It was no longer soft enough to come squirting out my ass like diarrhea under pressure. It would never again embarrass me.

* * *

After basic, there was a short leave for Christmas. I spent it with Cousin Red's family, just bumming around and occasionally helping out at the tire shop. Although Dad was in Australia, it was still a partnership between our families. Then I was off to Advanced Individual Training—AIT—at Fort Huachuca, Arizona, there to be trained as a light truck driver. After basic, Fort Huachuca was easy. Our days were spent learning to drive the two-and-a-half-ton, canvas-topped 'duce and a halves.' Our nights were usually spent drinking low-octane, three-two beer at the Post Exchange—PX.

One evening, I found my name again on the duty roster—kitchen police for the third time in a week! I'd learned early in the army not to complain when things were not fair, but it never stopped me from feeling picked on and angry. That evening, cross-eyed drunk, I managed my way back to the barracks and passed out cold on my bunk. Roused out at 0400 hours for KP, it seemed a toss-up between my headache and thirst as being my most miserable misery. We always kept our canteens slung over the ends of our bunks, and grabbing mine, I guzzled most of the contents. It did wash away the taste of the Mongolian horde, which seemed to have trooped through my mouth the evening before; washed it away but left a bad taste all of its own. As I screwed the lid back on, I shuddered. *Ugh! My God—tastes like piss!*

Later, while slinging biscuits and gravy on the serving line, there was snickering going on, pointing in my direction. Some passing me seemed to be chuckling. I hurt too much to pay much attention, but then came the remarks.

"Nothing like a good-night whiz, eh, Jeff?"

And, "Sure is nice to have those bunk bars over the urinals . . . something to hang on to when you're plastered," wink, wink.

I didn't understand what the hell the joke was all about. Then Dan, the Texan who bunked below me, came by.

"Dan, what the hell is everyone snickering about?"

"Ya'll don't remember?"

"No!"

"Well, ya got up jus afore lights out n' somehow mistook Jerry's footlocker fer the urinal. Ya plumb soaked the poor dude's duds."

I was still mentally debating the possibility they were all *putting me on when Jerry came by.*

"Drinkin's mighty thirsty work, hey, Jeff?"

It was with great effort that I stayed on my side of the counter, but by the end of the day, I'd dropped all thoughts of revenge—fair's fair. To this day, I still don't remember doing the deed.

* * *

On our fourth weekend, we were allowed passes. Mostly everyone, myself included, took off for Nogales, Mexico. In those days, I did a lot of my thinking from an alternate ego. Like the rest, I was determined to find the finest-looking babe in town and make her howl louder than my hormones. There was only one problem: there weren't any fine-looking babes in Nogales, at least nowhere that I could see. I spent the evening going from bar to bar, drinking whiskey with the guys. One of them, in fume-laden terms, summed up the babes of Nogales: ". . . butt-ugly whores!"

Eventually, I was ready to lower my standards. I'd never bought a whore before and now wanted the experience—or thought I did.

Perhaps the alcohol, mixed with the hormones and the army, had somehow changed things for me since that day in Messolongi. Or perhaps, I just wanted to be a hard-drinkin', hard-sluggin', hard-dickin' macho soldier like the rest of my buddies.

Midnight would not wait. Soon, it was nearly time to start back. Dan, in his characteristic drawl said, "Whatcha doin', Son, savin' y'r self fer marriage?"

"No, I guess not. I think I'll just take the next one who sits on my lap and asks for a whiskey and a fuck. That seems to be the program."

Almost instantly, I regretted my words. No sooner were they out than there was a woman on my lap. And she was fat and she was ugly, and she said, "Buy me whiskey, let's fuckee!" all in the same breath.

Oh, did I mention breath? It wasn't real attractive, either. After I'd paid the bartender for the drinks and room—and the girl for services to be rendered—we went out back to her little cubicle. She slid out of her dress.

Oh, did I say 'slid'? I meant 'popped.' She unzipped the single zipper down the front, and with a grunt of satisfaction, kind of popped out of it. She looked to be about seven months pregnant and a hundred seventy pounds ugly. We got in the bed.

I don't know—it might have been all the whiskey. It might have been that I just wasn't particularly attracted to pregnant, ugly whores with bad breath. But clearly, it was apparent my hormones weren't howling. They weren't moaning. Hell, they weren't even squeaking.

We tried everything. She played with it. I tried fantasizing about other women—even about jacking off. Nothing worked. I left, too embarrassed to even argue for my money back.

I suppose that when whiskey talks, men often make promises they cannot, in good conscience, break. And as for women? Ladies of the evening often become scags in the morning's light.

~ *In the Present with Big D* ~

I sit here, thinking back over this chapter, and I just don't know what to say. "Big D, show yourself; help me out here. I know you are with me. I feel your mirth mocking me."

"No . . . not mocking." I feel a light touch of ivory upon my shoulder. "It is just the enigma of your words."

"Enigma? I don't understand."

"'Ladies of the evening often become scags in the morning's light'?" He pauses for effect before hitting me with it: "Anyone in particular come to mind?"

"No . . . no." As I say it, in my mind there forms a picture of Meg. I shudder at the implications. *But she was different! And we haven't come to her in this story yet.*

"Ah! My point exactly!" His laughter comes with such passion that it rattles my own bones. "It is the grand enigma of them all." He has moved around to stare with an insistent glow into my eyes. His ivory digits still grip my left shoulder, almost as if he knows I need supporting in what he will say next. I feel a great, nameless foreboding. "In your mind, you have already given a name to your foreboding," he continues. "Meg."

"Meg?"

"Yes, Meg. You don't even want to look at that one"—his chuckle is soft and somehow loving—"do you? Even now, and it's been four years that she's been gone. And remember, you've sworn off mourning her."

"But not Meg!" I feel my eyes involuntarily misting. "She was not the same."

"Ah, but she was! She is! Ha!" Big D laughs. "Meg is every woman! That whore in Nogales was every woman! And even every man! You know this in your head, just not in your heart. You . . . are . . . all . . . the . . . same!"

"'The same?' Yes, but . . . oh shit! It's all so confusing!"

"Yes! The same . . . equal! It is an enigma how you can all be beings of such absolute magnificence that your conscious minds have not the ability to even conceive, and how your 'consciousness' has such little courage as to allow so little of it to come through into your daily lives. The only difference between that whore and you is that consciously, you have a little more belief in yourself." Big D smiles his mocking grin and adds, ". . . but not much."

"Yes," I duck my head and groan. "No wonder this chapter feels kind of . . . off."

"Oh, but there is still more to see here."

My head jerks up as if by its own accord. "Like what?"

"Well, take the training received in the army. Were they really training you to be a man? Does a real man ignore all pain and pretend it doesn't exist?"

"No."

"Then are you saying he has the courage to acknowledge it, walk through it, change his mind about the mental stuff, and accept and deal with the physical?"

"Yes, I'll agree with that."

"Would you say that a real man obediently and blindly accepts the orders of his superiors?" Big D's gaping grin now carries a tinge of satire. "Indeed, does he have superiors?"

"Hell, no!" I feel anger at the obvious abuse my country made of its soldiers. "No wonder there is such atrocity associated with war. I was being trained to see ugliness in others, to hate them, to be desensitized to their pain, and to subjugate myself to my 'superiors' mindlessly!"

"Yes, you were training to be a killer." He pauses to let it sink in. "To you, then, and to the army, that woman in Nogales was just a fat, ugly, pregnant whore to be used by you." His eyes flare brightly a moment, then he adds, "Just as your country would use you."

"Yes . . . so it seems."

"Perhaps it was not for the alcohol or any lack of courage that you couldn't get it up." The light in Big D's eye sockets again reminds me of sparklers and my childhood joy on the Fourth of July—only with a reddish hue. He continues. "Incidentally, you honor yourself because you have never accepted the blind obedience required of a soldier to be a killer. Your hesitance would have gotten you killed had you gone to 'Nam."

"What!"

"Yeah, you never knew it, but I saved your scrawny ass then as well."

"But . . . but—"

"Surely you don't think the military handed out 'sole survivor status' to everybody whose brother got killed outside of the military and in the commission of a crime—well, do you?"

"But my parents applied. They told me so years later."

"They were denied—until I put the fix into a certain captain's ear."

"Look, Jeff." He pats me on the shoulder. "Just know that you honored yourself when you came back from Australia in answer to your country's call. Just as the founding fathers, you, too, risked no less than your all. I wonder, though . . . if they again asked you to fight in someone else's war, in someone else's land, where there is no threat to your own, would you step forth now?"

"Big D, I've grown. Honoring myself now would look very different from then."

When your hormones groan and you're thinking with your little head, remember: It has no compassion. It will always want to move in the direction it's pointed—sometimes forward, sometimes back.
Redneck Spirituality—Book Four

Chapter Fifteen

I, Predator

It felt pretty good to wear a bright-red, diamond-shaped unit patch on my left shoulder. After Fort Huachuca, my first real post was to the 5th Supply and Transport Battalion at Fort Carson, Colorado. Ah, a regular outfit . . . and a patch that said I finally belonged. Soon, there were yellow, private-first-class stripes also.

Alongside the towering eastern scarp of the Rocky Mountains, Fort Carson stretched forth between the portals of NORAD—the North American Air Defense Command facility inside Cheyenne Mountain on the west—and Peterson Air Base to the east. In the event of a nuclear war, it was a comfort to know our toast would be first to be burnt.

Although, as a truck driver, my job was to haul equipment, most of my time was spent between pulling maintenance on the trucks, KP, and guard duty. About every other weekend, we marched in parade. I often wondered at the true purpose for those parades. Maybe the general's wife had a new hat to show off, or perhaps there was a visiting "dicknatary." I only knew that for us, they were a general bummer.

After six months, I put in for duty in Korea. I'd heard about how good it was there. Fort Carson was simply no great adventure. It would have been easy to put in for Vietnam; those who did could be gone nearly overnight. But somehow the thought of blood, guts, gore, and death just did not seem very romantic or in any way beneficial—especially if they were my own. By then, I'd rubbed shoulders with enough "genuine war heroes" to know the truth about the glory and romance of war.

We could always tell those who had served in 'Nam: there was some solitary *somethingness* which set them apart, or perhaps it was more of a *missingness*. It almost seemed as if the essence of their very soul had somehow been violated and was now withdrawn. During the Saturday morning formations, often they were presented with some medal or other: a Bronze Star for bravery under fire or a Purple Heart for combat wounds received. The commanding officer would read the glorious descriptions of their brave acts, hand over the medals, handshakes, salutes—a regular ceremony.

I didn't understand at first just why it was treated so soberly and then unacknowledged afterward, why no one said much about it. Then one day it was Spec-Five Jennings from my own platoon who received a Bronze Star. His bunk was next to mine. I saw him sitting there on his footlocker after Saturday morning inspection, just staring at his medal. Most had skipped lunch and were already headed for the bars of Colorado Springs. We were alone.

"Jeez, Jennings,"—unless we were the best of buds, we always used last names, and 'Nam vets rarely wanted to be buds—"I didn't know you were a genuine war hero!"

His head jerked up, features tight with anger, then they seemed to loosen a touch. "Williams, you just don't know . . . 'less you been there, you can't fucking know!"

I sat on my own locker across from his and studied him a moment. I saw his tears of frustration and didn't know how to respond. "Tell me, Jennings, I really want to know."

"Can't be explained . . . shit! . . . fuck! I feel like Judas," he said, looking down at his Bronze Star. "Judas was used . . . but fuck! Even Judas was paid off in silver!"

"You betrayed someone?"

"Jesus, Williams, you just don't get it! I . . ." He rolled his eyes as if at a loss. "Look, we . . . ." His fists are clenched and slowly raised, somehow ineffectually, only to drop limply with his next words. "We betrayed the whole fucking world!" With that, he rose and stomped off into the latrine, winging his medal into the trash can in passing.

No, for me Vietnam was not somewhere I wanted to be. It wouldn't have mattered anyway. Unbeknownst to me, there was that "sole survivor status" granted to my parents. I was not going to 'Nam.

The wheels of government turned slowly in the army—when not turning around Vietnam. Eventually, they turned out my orders for Korea. I had two weeks' leave coming, and again, spent it at Cousin Red's. There was a girl staying there, a friend of my cousin Judy. Her name was Janet.

One evening found Janet and me down in the basement, alone. It all began as a game of "I'll take this off you, and you take something off me, and we'll see who chickens out first." Soon it all swung free, and still, the game continued. Under my fingers, her nipples stiffened. Likewise, she found a handle of her own. I nibbled on her neck. She blew in my ear. I put a hand between her thighs and tickled her, on the inside. We moaned, we grunted, we squirmed. We ended up bathed in each other's sweat—and a rather large puddle of something even more slippery. I told her withdrawal was neither the most satisfying form of birth control, nor the safest.

The next day found us at a drug store. Condoms, then, were not out on open display. They had to be asked for from the druggist. I'd heard horror stories from friends about holier-than-thou druggists refusing to sell to young people. Salt Lake City is the kind of place that lends itself to preaching. For the price of membership, anyone who wants to can preach in a Mormon Church. Some druggists were even known to preach right there in the store—in front of God, you, and all the other customers.

Thoughts like these were running through my mind as I parked in front. I looked through the window. *Oh God! There was a lady behind the drug counter. Geez, what do I do now?* Then, looking over at my companion, I very coolly announced, "I'm buying!"

I smiled, Janet smiled, and I handed her the money. Her smile faded. Eyes bugging, she shrieked, "B-b-b-but, you don't think I'm going to. . . ."

"You want it? Go get 'em." I stated it in studied nonchalance, then watched as she ripped out of the car and slammed the door. *Oh well . . . I* sighed. *It was fun while it lasted.* But to my amazement, Janet had a set of balls and went in and made the purchase. Looking back now, I have to admit how sometimes, I was a real prick—which brings me back to Lois.

While I and the lady with the balls were working our way through that package of condoms, I was also dating Lois—from my high school graduation night. She hadn't forgotten me. As usual, I paid my keep at Aunt Annie's by helping out down at the tire shop. Lois often dropped by to ply me with cakes and cookies. The next I knew, I was dating her; funny how such things work. Clearly, Lois had a weakness for me. I pressed it for all it was worth.

Whatever the fantasies going through her mind may have been about me, she had always acted as a nice Mormon girl. Me? I just wanted to nail her—bad!

Our dates involved some pretty heavy petting—hell, more like stroking. Lois, being small breasted, was extremely sensitive, so touching her in that area was strictly out. I guess she felt that somehow meant she had to grant me other liberties, which was just fine with me. I massaged and tickled, caressed and stroked, and by the second date had managed to snake my hand past the elastic wall. The guys called it "stinky finger," but the aroma that wafted to my nostrils seemed only to speak of the finest essence of womanhood. Soon my fly was open, and Lois, her eyes wide, was taking un-Mormon-like liberties of her own. Had she never seen one before?

I think in the end, it was when I told her about how I was aching for her that finally swayed her. I don't know what women have that would correspond, but she seemed to understand how "blue balls" was more than a concept.

My flight to Korea awaited me the next afternoon, and this was our last opportunity together. The drive-in movie now over, we stopped randomly on a darkened neighborhood street to neck. It was about two a.m. Would all my hard work culminate in the ultimate experience, hopefully for us both? My member was sheathed with the last remaining rubber as we jockeyed for position on the front seat of Aunt Annie's old ford wagon. It strained at rigid attention awaiting Lois, who crouched poised, her virgin gash gleaming in the moonlight just inches above. Slowly, she lowered herself, and as her warm wetness softly touched my manhood where it stood in the arctic chill of the winter's night like a missile on the launch pad, I exploded. Grunting with embarrassed disgust, I ripped off the rubber, rolled down the window, and threw it out—all the while hoping Lois hadn't seen and wouldn't know how little control I had over myself.

"Just forget it . . . we're not going there tonight," was all I said before driving her home in frosty silence.

Standing on her porch in parting, Lois broke the silence. "I'm glad we decided to wait." I quieted her with a kiss and left her then to think what she wanted.

The next day, I found out that Janet—the lady with the balls—could count and had been anticipating our last rubber. I've never seen a woman any angrier than she when I told her I couldn't remember where I last put it.

Later in Korea, I received Lois's first letter. It gushed with her love. She told of how she would wait for me, and too, of how she respected me for waiting for our marriage before having sex. Reading it, seeing myself through her eyes, I felt a rawness in the pit of my stomach, as if I'd been kicked. I had not said I loved her, nor certainly had I asked her to marry me. But I knew that in her eyes, my actions did not require the verbiage.

Still! Stringing her along in hopes of making my dick feel good? God! Was this what it felt like to be the lowest worm in the outhouse? How had I become so cruel? Worse, how now to break it off without her hurting more?

And now there was a Korean woman, one who, in the mahogany reflection of her exotically slanted eyes, had hypnotized my heart. This woman I wanted as I'd wanted no woman before. Wishing it did not have to be, I knew my "Dear Joan" letter would be painful for Lois. This time, there was just no other way than honesty. I simply stated, as gently as possible, how I'd met someone else and now our relationship was over. She wrote back one brief letter, pretending indifference, and telling me it was okay, saying how she'd also met someone new. Like a police spotlight through a Venetian blind, her pain showed clearly between the lines of her words. I, being the culprit, never answered.

~ *Looking Back* ~

Many times I've wondered what became of Lois, of how much pain she might still carry in her heart because of me. Understandably, pain was the choice she made back then. I just hope that, like me, Lois has learned not to carry it inside and has released it. When I knew her, there was something bright and shining—totally delightful—about her spirit. I hope she has not allowed her experience with me to dull or tarnish that in any permanent way.

And Janet . . . did Janet need to do the same, or was her revenge enough? Through my cousin Judy, she'd extract it soon enough. Still, how many men in her life since have paid the price of my insensibility? How much anger does she carry toward men from her experience with me?

Of Lois and Janet? I've thought of both often over the years. Even still, I would have trouble facing either in honesty. How does one live with the despicable actions of one's life. The completion may be only mine. I cannot make it so for them. For me to bring my relationship with them full circle to forgiveness, love, and completion, what is required is for me to acknowledge the truth and then forgive myself.

So, Lois . . . Janet . . . I was an asshole in my treatment of you both.

~ *In the Present with Big D* ~

"Jesus Christ, son!" Big D's voice startles me. My fingers jump from the keyboard as if flamed. "Get down off the cross and take a fucking break!"

"Big D! What do you mean? Are you saying that I'm trying to be their savior?"

"Yeah, that, too." His bony butt rattles as he takes a seat on the edge of my desk. "Trying to crucify one's own self just doesn't work. Hell, what do you do when it comes to driving that last nail?"

"Are you serious, or are you just cracking jokes?"

"Would you like to be the first in history ever to see me hurl?" He catches my quick glance toward his sickle, where it leans against the wall. "No, Jeff, not that. I refer to my lunch, of course. I find it downright nauseating when someone who knows better tries to accept responsibility for other people's experience."

"Yeah, but the way I treated those girls. . . ."

"Wasn't very loving, I agree!" He grins. "And yes, you were acting like a prick!" A soft clatter like ivory wind chimes accompanies his shrug. "Fucking is just one of the three things pricks were made to do directly; making babies is an indirect thing. Now, have you forgotten the law?"

"Which one?"

"Well . . ." Big D drops his head, and his hand clatters in mock resignation against the bare bone of his brow. "You know you weren't in their lives to cause pain? Everyone does that to themselves."

"Ah, yes! I know that law: *'All emotional pain is self-created, and all physical pain carries a necessary ingredient of self-creation.'* "

"Just so . . . and what is the law concerning why you shared some time together?"

"Ah-ha! Know that one, too. It goes: *'Everyone in our lives is there for our learning.'* "

"And what did you learn from these ladies?"

"All this concerning them has never felt good to me." I pause a long, thoughtful moment before continuing with my answer. "From them, I learned that I want love from me to feel good—not just physically, but to be loving."

"Has it?"

"Yes! I have to say it has. Since then, it has never been a dishonest taking." There is a certain joy in just saying it. "And yes, I've done a little mutually enjoyable fucking, but mostly, my lovemaking has been loving."

"Ah, so you prefer to use that thing for *loving*?"

"Well, yeah . . ."

"Perhaps, then, it is about knowing the difference. Could it be, *that* was the true gift of these two women? Many men live their entire lives just *pissing* and *fucking*." Big D's neck bones creak slightly as he nods, and the glow winks briefly in just one eye socket. "Can you accept that your gift to them, received or not, was of equally great potential— no apology needed?"

Our higher self—that part of all humanity which is of God—knows: The experiences in life we need for our growth will always be presented to us for our learning until we open ourselves to the lessons. Those reoccurring happenings in our lives, we need to be especially aware of and to look at. If we don't accept the lesson, it will only show up again more forcefully—more painfully—the next time.

Redneck Spirituality—Condensed From Book One

Chapter Sixteen

The Land of Curly Nose Hairs

Our arrival at Kimpo Air Base was nothing like I'd pictured. A sooty haze hung heavy in the biting December air, masking the sun with the essence of coal, a smell that was instantly noticeable with every breath. Simultaneously, the moisture in that breath froze the hairs in my nose.

Shuffling in line with the others, I stepped from the plane and started down the tall, steel-grated steps of the boarding stairs. For a moment, my mind drifted back to my childhood—to the chilly, smoke-filled air of Bingham Canyon and to those front porch steps of so long ago. For all its distance in both time and space, I felt as if I was back there in Bingham, and it did not matter that nothing else looked the same. A brief, involuntary shiver passed through my body, and somehow, though surrounded by so many other strong, virile men all clad in the same dark-green, Class A uniform as mine, I did not feel a part of something large and strong. I just felt small and weak, and alone.

Herded into a hangar, we found our duffel bags were stacked unceremoniously in one huge pile. After pawing through and locating my own, I joined the long line snaking about the inside walls. It ended near the door, where a portable cloth screen was set up. Here we were required to receive a gamma globulin shot, supposedly to ward off a disease caused by mites in the local grass.

I don't know why they bothered with the screen, or the shot. The screen provided almost no privacy, cutting the view from only one direction as it did, and the grass was buried under snow and ice—but then, that's the army.

One by one we filed up to the screen with our duffel bags in tow and dropped our drawers to receive the shot. The hypo and needle were huge, like something one would expect to see being used in a horse barn. With every dozen or so men injected, someone would be sure to pass out cold.

It was a strange feeling to see a large, muscular, macho military man drop in his tracks like a steer on the kill floor. I think it had a lot to do with the fact that as we approached the curtain, our eyes were naturally drawn to the needle. Almost hypnotizing was it to watch as it sank into the fleshy buttocks of those ahead. Then, as the plunger was crammed down, the milky fluid within swiftly disappeared into a newly formed knot on that poor bastard's bare butt.

Those who fainted usually came to right away and were led stumbling off to sit in a chair. The medics seemed to take it all in stride, only showing annoyance once when the needle was broken off in some sergeant's ass as it went crashing earthward. Of course, this meant they'd have to dig it back out, hopefully before he regained consciousness. They weren't pleased.

"Shit! Gaw-dam things are supposed to bend, not break! Shit! Mother . . . fuck!" I heard the medic's disgusted curse as he worked his pliers on the bare butt of that sergeant out cold on the floor, only two places ahead of where I stood. Holding up my loosened Class A pants in one hand, my duffel in tow with the other, I could only grit my teeth and await my turn, hoping it would not be me next on the floor.

There followed a rather painful bus ride, a few klicks—kilometers—to a compound where the "in transit" barracks were located. Once settled in, I had just enough time to make chow call at the holding company's mess, an army term which, in this case, was an apt description. Then, after grabbing a shower, I wandered down to the local Enlisted Men's—EM—Club with a few of the guys.

The place had a rather exotic air: booze flowed freely, shots clinked gaily, and there were women. Most were with dates, but there were half a dozen business girls who'd somehow gotten signed in at the gate—undoubtedly for a price other than money. Circulating freely among the unattached men, they drank a lot, laughed a lot, and disappeared a lot for fifteen or twenty minutes at a time, and with different GIs. I soon learned the boiler room was quite a busy place.

Eventually, one sat down next to me and struck up a conversation in halting English. She was quite pretty and would have been attractive, except for her heavy makeup. It gave her a rather garish look, kind of like an oriental Tammy Faye Baker. Also, her breath was heavy with an unfamiliar spiciness that was somewhat unpleasant—hell, unpleasant doesn't describe it. It curled the newly thawed hairs in my nose. I later came to know it well as the smell of kimchi, the Korean national dish.

Kimchi is made from varying degrees of fermented Chinese cabbage laced with garlic, hot pepper powder, and sometimes dried minnows and other assorted treats. Most of the classier girls had learned to tone down their breath to a mere eye-watering level by brushing their teeth and tongue right after eating. This one hadn't.

"Hi GI! You belly handsome, strong man." She placed one hand on my thigh as the other groped at my biceps. "You maybe looking for pretty gorl?"

"Yes, you are a pretty girl," I acknowledged, "but I'm not looking tonight." No need to say I was not attracted.

She seemed pleased with my compliment, so much so that her hand on my leg now began to creep crotchward while the other slid innocently down my arm.

"Can makie you feel belly good—"

"No you don't!" I grabbed her wrist just in time to extricate my gold ID bracelet from her grasp before she turned and fled. Watching her go, I shook my head.

"Not much class in that sperm bank," remarked the Spec Four beside me. I looked him over, noting the round, red-and-black hourglass patch on his shoulder, his Nordic blond features, effervescent eyes, and open grin. I liked him. "You new in-country?"

"Yeah, just got here, and you? What about you?"

"Short timer. Been here about eleven months. I drive the cattle wagon for the Seventh Admin." His humor was infectious. "I'm just here to pick up a load of fresh meat for Camp Casey in the morning."

"I'll be seeing you then. I'm headed for the Seventh S and T."—Supply and Transport Batattalion. I stuck out my hand. "Name's Jeff Williams!" I noted his name stenciled in black above the shirt pocket of his fatigues—Fletcher.

"You can call me 'Fletch.'" He shook my hand as he rose to leave. "Be seeing you; gotta turn in. Oh! . . . and Williams . . ." He paused, a look of distaste on his face. "These are street girls. They don't even let them work the clubs in the ville. Slip your penny in their slot, and it'll be dripping with interest before the week is out."

I sat there a while longer, just soaking in the ambiance. *Colorful place . . . interesting people*, I thought, then finished my beer and called it a night.

* * *

The next morning found me on Fletcher's bus headed north toward Camp Casey. Located about twenty-five klicks south of the Demilitarized Zone—DMZ—it was at the railhead supplying the area.

The terrain we passed through near Kimpo Air Base was mostly snow and ice-covered rice paddies, with a network of raised pathways lacing everywhere. There were occasional rounded hills, most maybe five hundred feet high. As we proceeded northward toward Seoul, the terrain became more and more hilly.

We crossed over the Han River on the outskirts of Seoul. Being iced over, it provided a major recreational attraction. Hundreds of people were whizzing around on the ice. A good many of them were wearing what looked like white surgical masks over their mouths and noses. I wondered if they were afraid of catching a disease. Later, someone told me TB was a concern, but mostly they were protecting themselves from the bitter cold.

All along the Seoul side of the riverbank was a shanty town where thousands of people lived in shacks made from whatever pieces of trash they had been able to procure and hang together. Seoul obviously had more people than could be comfortably handled.

The streets of Seoul were a trucker's nightmare. I gained a healthy respect for Fletch. People, cars, bicycles, three-wheel motorcycle trucks, and van-size kimchi busses all swirled around together, vying for the same space, every one of them pretending not to see the other—especially us in the GI bus.

Yet, when crowded, they always seemed to give way just enough to keep from being run over. Fletch crowded often. It almost seemed as if the whole city was in the streets, playing "chicken."

We had only one incident; I won't call it an accident. A man was tooling along on a bicycle loaded with crates of chickens. They were stacked about eight feet high and four feet wide. It was an amazing trick to see. The man dogged along directly in front of us, purposefully refusing to give way. I thought it an interesting way to play chicken, what with using the real thing. Eventually, Fletch got his break, and as we roared by, he clipped the crates. The man on the bicycle went down. He was immediately back on his feet, dancing a jig of fury, all from within a cloud of squawking chickens, broken crates, and feathers. Fletch just grinned and chuckled to himself repeatedly. In fact, it seemed to make his whole day.

Past Seoul, the terrain became somewhat mountainous. "Somewhat," in that the mountains weren't the lofty, majestic mountains of my native Utah. But nonetheless, they had a grandeur of their own—just on a much smaller scale. We traveled through numerous small villages, then through a larger town called Uijongbu, pronounced we-jong-boo, where there was a crossroads of two well-traveled highways. Continuing on north, we passed through several more small villages until coming to the next large town, Tongduchon. It was situated alongside the Seventh Division's Camp Casey, our final destination.

Along the way, I was struck by the extreme nudity of the mountains. It was easy to see how the war, fifteen years earlier, had pretty well devastated Korea. The torrential downpours during the monsoon seasons hadn't helped matters by washing away most of the topsoil. There were very few trees and not much brush.

I'd already noticed the occasional sight of peasants walking alongside the highway, harnessed under wooden pack frames neatly piled high with huge bundles of dead twigs. Sometimes they walked in twos and threes, but usually alone. It was mind-boggling for me to imagine just how far they must have trekked, and the difficulty of collecting so many twigs in the scarcity of these mountains. What a meager living to be surviving on. Fletch seemed to take a special interest in my education. I sat on the aisle in the first seat behind him and often leaned forward against the short, separating partition, placing myself almost alongside to ask him my questions.

"What's with all the branches?"

"Kindling," Fletch answered. "They need it to get their charcoal bricks lit."

"What do you mean, 'charcoal bricks'?"

"Standard heating and cooking here is all done with round, charcoal bricks about eight inches in diameter and maybe another eight in height." He pointed at the smoke drifting from the chimneys of some homes in passing. "Smoke circulates under the floors for heating," he explained. "Works pretty good, except. . . ." He paused a long moment as if lost in thought. His eyes seemed suddenly to have moistened.

"Except what?" I finally prompted.

"Except it kills them off like fleas . . . whole families at a time." His jaw was clenched, and I now noted a definite tear in his eye. "Lost my Yobo that way."

He didn't seem inclined to continue, yet something told me he needed to. "Yobo? What's that? Tell me about it." I spoke softly, and when he remained silent a moment more, I added, "I'd really like to know."

"'Yobo' in Korean is sort of like saying 'wife.' We were going to get married. She was pregnant with my child." The tear slid seemingly unnoticed down his cheek.

"How'd it happen?"

"Gassed . . . carbon monoxide! Happens all the time." He ground the words through clenched teeth. "The floors often leak. Kills hundreds, maybe even thousands, every winter. You'd think the stupid fucks would have learned!" He smiled bitterly and wiped an angry hand across his eyes to clear his sight. "Koreans are a hardheaded lot. They don't like to admit when they're fucked up. They can't take being wrong about anything!"

"Your Yobo, too?"

"Yeah . . ." He hacked as if to clear a tightness from his throat, and his next words ran non-stop, almost as if he wasn't sure he could get them all said. "Bought her an electric heater. She said it cost too much. Wouldn't use it—even when I gave her extra money to pay for electricity. Money was pretty important to her. She wanted a big, fancy wedding, and she was always taking her family expensive presents every time she went home." He shook his head, and I noticed his knuckles had turned white where he gripped the steering wheel. "Stupid, fucking, foolish pride! They all have that 'saving face' shit going; remember that."

"When did it happen?"

"Last month . . . was gonna re-up and stay for the paperwork. Now?" He shook his head. "Now I just want to get the fuck out!"

"I'm sorry, Fletch," I said softly. "I'm sorry this happened to you." We both stopped talking then and were silent the rest of the way.

When we finally arrived, Tongduchon proved quite a large town. A jumble of gray, cement-tiled roofs and drab, wooden-framed shops and houses, it was, nevertheless, clean and orderly. My eyes probed its streets and alleyways. All except for this blacktopped main highway, all the streets were paved with frozen mud.

The overwhelming number of businesses seemed to consist of bars and brothels. Among them were scattered a few souvenir, jewelry, and tailor shops. It appeared the whole town was set up to cater to such as me. Still, I wondered at my feelings. I was excited to explore it all, yet there was something that did not feel so good. Was it that it had a certain transient air, as if no one really expected to actually live there very long? I'd seen that same shabby air about every GI town in the states. This one was, at least, neat, clean, and orderly. Looking back, I'd have to say it was simply that Tongduchon was the face of greed. Perhaps it did not cater so much to us GIs; rather, we were, in reality, the banquet.

In town, the prostitutes were thick on the streets, and Fletch seemed disposed to repeat his warning of the night before.

"Watch out for these street girls. They're the lowest rank echelon of whores. If they don't pick your pockets, they'll get your throat slit, or at least give you a case of crabs or dick-drip— or worse."

"You seem to be talking from experience."

"Yeah, I've ripped my share of pipes off the shithouse walls, but that was all before I met my Kim." His teeth gritted momentarily white, and I saw him consciously let go with a slight shake of his head. "Anyway, don't be thinking the bar girls are that much better. You don't have to worry about the slicky boys slitting your throat, but the rest still goes."

"Slicky boys?"

"Yeah . . . gangsters, hoods, thugs, pimps. Don't look like much, but most know Moo Duk Kwan or Tae Kwon Do, and they're mean. See that bridge?"

"Yeah?"

"Been a lot of GIs cut up and thrown offa it." Watching me, he chuckled. "My advice is get a steady—a Yobo. It's the only way you stand much of a chance with the women round here."

As our bus slowed down to make the turn through the main gate of Camp Casey, six or eight girls began running alongside, smiling, waving, and making offers through the windows. By now, most of the windows were down, and GIs were hanging out, jeering, and drooling.

The jeering was good-natured and seemed to follow one of two veins: Either the GI was telling the girl he was too big for her to handle, or he was hollering for his buddies to strap a board across his ass 'cause he was going to jump this one or that.

The girls, for their part, were making equally obscene references to the GIs in their pidgin English. It was a little difficult to understand what they were saying, but the meaning usually came through clearly by the way they were waving and flaunting their wares, by rubbing their tits and crotches, or, as in one case, bent over with her dress flipped up to show off the charms of her bare tush.

"Hey, GI." She pointed over her shoulder. "You don need whorry fall een dis poossy! You onny need whorry you don fall off! Ha-ha. I tink you too o-gul-ly for otter side eh-nee-whay."

* * *

Camp Casey took up most of the east side of the valley. To the west of town, between the tracks and the river, was A Company, the organizational part of the7th Engineers Battalion. B Company—my assignment, where most of the actual trucks and equipment were kept—was located on the road to Munsan-ni, about a half klick away across the river to the southwest. Our compound marked the end of town.

The working end took up the north two-thirds of the compound. The orderly room/commander's office, arms building, commissioned assholes' quarters, mess hall, PX, and EM Club were all arranged in the center near the main entrance. Our troop quarters on the south end consisted of fifteen-foot-tall and forty-foot-long Quonset huts. Like galvanized road culvert pipes cut in half, they were set in three lines. Squatting in the middle was one of the few buildings not made of tin: the latrine/shower house. A square thing of cinder blocks, it sported a conventionally peaked roof of green tar paper shingles. A tall, chain-link fence, topped with concertina wire and marked every hundred yards with guard towers, surrounded the whole galvanized, tinfoil collection.

My duties consisted mostly of driving the five-ton tractor trailer tankers that delivered fuel to several smaller fueling and lubrication rigs. Sometimes I'd service the temporary fuel storage bladders set up at our construction sites in the area to the north along the DMZ. Other times, I pulled the low-boy flat trailers, carrying assorted pieces of heavy equipment between our compound and the sites.

The duty in Korea was everything I'd been told. We had ROK—Republic of Korea—troops assigned to the American army. They bunked alongside the rest of us. Their duties consisted mostly of guarding the compound. They were called Katusas, and I never met one

I didn't like. They were generally pretty upper-class people, as they had to have some kind of connection to get assigned such soft duty. We had no worries about the local thieves getting inside our compounds. They were well aware the guards would shoot if given any excuse.

We had houseboys who would make our bunks, do our laundry, and shine our boots—all for the modest sum of about seven dollars a month, including tip. Even sweeter, there were Korean locals who did the KP duty as well.

As for parades, there were none. We had real jobs to do. And besides, there was no one around to impress. This pretty well took care of all the pet peeves we all had about stateside duty, but the real clincher for most was that there was more pussy around than they could shake their dicks at.

For me, though, I wasn't doing any shaking. The memory of Nogales and the high incidence of dick drip here was enough to keep me out of the brothels. Fletch had only confirmed my own views. I didn't even like to go out to the bars to drink. Like Nogales, there was always some woman wanting to squirm her ass into my crotch every time I sat down for an OB—Oriental Breweries beer. The tagline hadn't changed much, but the accent had. "Buy me whees-kee. You mebbe wan go boom-boom?"

* * *

Instead, I took up karate, Moo Duk Kwan style. My instructor was just starting out and didn't speak any English. I was his first and, for a long time, only student. It made for a strange teaching style. Everything was shown to me, and I seldom knew the name of any of the moves or sometimes even their purpose. If I was learning one of the blocking techniques and didn't understand it, or just did it wrong, I was likely to learn the lesson by painful demonstration. The next time was generally a lot better.

I also learned to be accurate. When sparring, if I accidentally nailed the instructor or didn't sufficiently pull my punch, I would usually find myself blowing a little unexpected wind out of one end or the other.

For amusement in my off time, sometimes I'd buy a bag of candies at the PX, then standing at the perimeter fence, lob them over, a few at a time. Little kids would magically appear out of nowhere. I got to be pretty popular with them.

Other times, some of us would hang out at the river side of the compound. If the weather was good, there would be some 'business girls' washing clothes in the river.

It was an interesting process. First, they'd soak the garment in the water, then rub it down with bar soap. Next, they slapped it down on a rock and whacked the hell out of it with a stick. Then, back in the water it went to rinse and wring, then on to the next item.

Sound boring? Not really. You see, they were well aware we were watching and would put on quite a peep show. After all, they were in the business. We could sometimes get some very entertaining, but good-natured, bantering going on with them, mostly through gestures and pidgin English. It would go something like this:

GI: "Hey, Baby-san . . . *Kundingi lockie lockie joh-ta.*" (You've got a very nice ass).

Girl: "No *can channa* (can do), GI. No fuckie . . . dat end. You mebee need boy, yes?"

GI: "Oh no, Baby-san, you just fine."

Girl: "You not so fine, GI. You havva beeg o-gul-ly Amereecan nose!"

GI: "Yeah, Baby-san. You know what they say? Big nose . . . big feet . . . big *chaggie* (penis). . . ."

Girl: "You no havva big *chaggie*, GI, you havva littul bebby *chaggie!*"

GI: "Oh yesss, Baby-san . . . have big *chaggie* . . . give you nine inches . . . make you hurt ree-al good!"

Girl: "Nine eenchees? Hah! Mebee you have put een tree time . . . geeve nine eenchees. Hort? Heh . . . you mebee have heet een head witt wock . . . mebee den hort!"

And so it would go, sometimes for hours. The insults would fly, as would the hand and body language. Very seldom would anyone take offense. It was simply entertainment, and occasionally, some connections would be made—for later.

* * *

I'd been barely a month in-country when Jerry, a short, skinny, old Spec Five veteran seemed to take a liking to me. We found ourselves in the EM Club one Saturday afternoon, guzzling beer together. Jerry's Yobo, Soon Yi, one of the more mature business girls, was with us. While Jerry was off in the can, she asked if I'd be interested in steadying her friend, Miss Pak. I declined, but she was pretty insistent—said her friend really needed a steady and that ". . . I teenky you likee hor. She belly pwitty likee you, you know?"

"N-no . . . oh, no!" Looking down from her pretty brown eyes with their fine, crow's feet lines, down to the even finer spider web of wrinkles above her pendulous breasts, where they somehow had come to rest over my arm, my mind went blank. I could only stutter out that if I wanted a girl, I'd just go to the ville.

"But you nebber go ville, Cheff. Mebbe you just no likee gorl?"

With her breasts now fairly undulating across my arm, I knew my eyes were bugging. All I could do was stutter a denial. Then, hoping to distract her from my other parts, now uncontrollably disloyal to Jerry, I muttered, "I just don't like VD."

"Oh no, Cheff! Dis gorl . . . she belly kind . . . wor-yal . . . no butterfry (cheat). You steady, Mees Pak, neffer have whorry—VD!"

"I'll think about it."

"You better no tinkee too rong!"

Over the next two weeks, three more of the "attached" guys recommended this same girl to me—unasked. And, too, I kept overhearing her name mentioned in passing conversations. In fact, two other Spec Four drivers seemed to be having a running dissertation about who would steady her. Specialist Butz, who bunked next to me, had recently given up on his plan to re-up and stay in-country to marry her. I hadn't paid it much attention, other than to note how his buddy, Flannigan, was pestering him about taking her over as his Yobo. It seemed the lady wanted nothing to do with either.

On the night before he was to rotate out, Butz broached the subject to me as I sat cross-legged on my bunk, nursing a cigarette and reading a novel. Clad only in a bathrobe and wearing a pair of thongs, he paused to sit across from me on his bunk before heading for the showers—two huts down the board walkway.

"Williams . . . I hear you might be thinking of steadying Miss Pak?"

"It's just a rumor, Butz, why do you care?" Obviously he did from the way he was worrying his towel. Sitting on the edge of his bunk, he twisted, pulled, and plucked his eyes on it, rather than on me.

"Well, look . . . she won't have anything to do with me or Flannigan. I just want you to know that you can't do any better than her." He stopped twisting to look earnestly up at me. "Look, I care about her. I'd just hate to see her get hooked up with some of these assholes around here, you know?" He got up and, clutching his robe, braced himself for the frigid dash to the showers. "Think about it, will you?"

"I will . . . sure."

Saturday night found me in the EM Club, again drinking beer with Jerry and Soon Yi. This time, when Soon Yi brought up the subject of her friend, I was more open to the idea.

"Okay, Soon Yi! You and every Yobo in town seem to want me to meet Miss Pak. So, I'll meet her."

"Good!" Soon Yi grinned, fairly wiggling with anticipation. I could tell she really liked this Miss Pak. "You come compound fenz . . . outside you hootche . . . ten o'crock tomorrow. You see I no *kugi-mar* (liar)."

~ *In the Present with Big D* ~

I sit here watching the curser blink, thinking about that first meeting with Miss Pak, or Meg, as she came to be known. Then my mind falls strangely back to Fletch, and I wonder how he has coped.

"When you knew him," Big D answers my thoughts, his voice loud in my ear, "he was a man in great pain, was he not?"

"Shit! Will you stop sneaking up on me like that? Nearly jumped out of my skin."

"In time, Son . . . in time you will." I hear his soft chuckle and feel his piano-key grip on my shoulder, yet turning my head, I see nothing but the books on my study wall.

"Where are you?"

"Here, Son, I'm always here . . . you don't need to see." There comes a slight squeeze. "But what is it about Fletch that you wish to know?"

"I wish I could have helped him, and I'd like to think he is now all right."

"Oh, you did—in just being there to listen, you helped in his healing."

"I suppose so, but I wish I could have done more."

"If you could go back to that moment now, what would you do? What would you say?"

"I think I would hug him and tell him of how I share his sorrow, having now known Meg in my own life. I'd say to him: 'What you found with your Yobo was beautiful. Take the essence of that into your life with your next woman and cherish it. When you think of your Miss Kim, thank her for her gift of it . . . to you.'"

"So you see similarities of his Miss Kim to your Miss Pak—your Meg?"

"Oh yes. He, too, asked his woman to change. And she, too, was unwilling. Both had that stubborn Korean streak!"

"Ah, but there is a great difference in what he asked of his woman: He asked her only in his concern for her life to change something about what she did in hers."

"How is that different?"

"You, Jeff . . . you asked Meg to change something in her mind, and you asked it to suit you in your life."

"What?"

"Yeah, you asked Meg to understand you and to be of support in your life."

"Yes, I guess I did. But what's the big deal with that?"

"To understand you, she would need to see you differently. She would need to change the way she thought about you, and that, Jeff, would have changed her whole life. You asked Meg to have the courage of a butterfly!"

"I don't see it."

"Jeff, let's be honest about the way she regarded you, particularly those last years. The unmistakable message you heard clearly, but tried so hard to ignore, was simple: 'I'm okay—but you're all fucked up!'" His unseen fist firmly shakes my shoulder, as if to awaken me. "To get honest with herself enough to even see that one would require that she own her half of the relationship—how she, too, was 'fucked up'—and that would have changed her whole life."

"I don't see that it would have been so difficult. . . ."

"Jeff! Listen to me!" His grip has tightened. "The honesty about your own life that you could no longer ignore in that hospital was simple: Your life wasn't truthfully serving you; in essence, it was indeed 'all fucked up!'"

"Yeah, I see your point. I was living a lie."

"Your impetus to change was your very life—your need to continue living it. Hers? Hers was only her relationship with you, and that, she thought, was just fine. It was your relationship with her she thought was fucked up. Yet, the change to her world would have been just as great for her as yours was for you. Now do you see the true scope of what you asked of Meg?"

"Yes. Shit . . . and I see that I had no right to ask it of her."

"Oh, but it was your right. A person must understand their mate and must be the biggest part of their support system." His grip now seems to caress. "Don't blame yourself that Meg was unwilling. You did what you needed to do."

"Oh God, yes! I see it now, and I'm done mourning her loss. But it still hurts that she had such a poor opinion of me."

"Ah, Jeff . . . the security she found in you. She told you about it—every day for some twenty-five years. You just wanted it to be more." I feel his arm slide around to cradle my shoulder in a loving embrace. "Just remember, what *you* found with your Yobo was beautiful! Take the essence of *that* into your life with your next woman and cherish it. When you think of your Meg, thank her for her gift of it . . . to you."

Our strength in standing by our beliefs must always be tempered by a willingness to look at what it is we believe—to recognize just what is it about us is served by that belief. While our belief systems guide us in life, they also limit. Growth is about releasing those that don't serve us well and adopting those which do. Sometimes our "strength" in holding to our belief can cause us to lose that which is most precious to us. This process is called "foolish pride."

Redneck Spirituality—Book Four

Chapter Seventeen

Meg's Story

The heat of the summer had not yet broken. The morning's cool respite was interrupted by the cries of a newly arrived baby beneath the thick, straw thatch of the last hootch on the rutted mud road leading out of Wansankun in North Korea. It was the first week of August, 1950, and the war was barely five weeks old. The communist leaders all sang praises of the troops, saying victory against the American oppressors of the South was imminent. Yet, the baby's parents felt only a foreboding of disaster. Such was the world into which they brought this child.

Indeed, the world changed over the next few years of war. Many men died—white, yellow, even brown and black—and women and children, too. Their blood all ran the same color, enough to fill a great scarlet river. Then there were tears—tears enough to drown the oceans. Times were not easy for the survivors, either. This child was a survivor.

Her given name was Pak, Me Gong. In Korea, surnames are always spoken first. When I first met her, she was introduced as "Miss Pak." Yet, "Miss" anything was not a name one calls someone intimately, nor was "Me Gong" something palatable to the American ear. I knew her as Meg. I'll call her Meg from here.

Back then, a babe in arms, Meg spent her first three years in caves and bombed-out houses while the shells whined shrilly overhead.

In those years, it seemed as if the ground always shuddered and the air growled of constant thunder. Sometimes it was not always as of a distant, ominous danger. Sometimes the blasts were deafening, the dust leaping up to blind and choke while the air rained dirt all around. The first half of her seven formative years was filled with fear and hunger—and the stench of dead bodies. She was among those miserable hordes eventually fleeing south, away from the communists and the death they brought.

She was still too young to remember it well when the fighting stopped. Nor was she aware how, as a refugee searching for scraps to eat, she'd gained her freedom in the South, only to lose it again at the age of fifteen—both terrifying events in her life.

Her family settled in Pusan, a city on the Southeastern Coast. Her father earned their living selling confections and renting umbrellas and tubes at the beach. And life returned to normal.

Meg's mother was a very beautiful and genteel lady, the kind most spoke to using the formal language of respect, even though such was usually only reserved for one's elders. It was, understandably, her early influence that molded Meg into a like manner. Never coarse or vulgar, Meg always acted very ladylike. Among Korean children, it was an acceptable practice when one needed to whiz along the road to school, or anywhere, they simply dropped their drawers and went for it—not so, Meg. During meals, when most people's chopsticks poked freely in the same bowl—not so, Meg's. Meg had a natural aversion for filth of any kind. She particularly disliked the boogers on the upper lips of some of the other children.

At the age of five, her mother became sick. Eventually she died, agonizingly, her stomach distended with a tumor, as if pregnant. Yet, between them there remained a special bond. Even past death, Meg's mother watched over her. On occasion, she was the dim figure who waited in the twilight between the outhouse and the front gate on Meg's arrival home, floating there, her feet never quite touching the ground. Sometimes she came in the night as a loving face, hovering near as Meg lie wrapped in her quilt on the heated floor of their one-room hootch. Meg and her father moved often, and her mother's ghost always followed, comforting Meg and haunting her father, though Meg was the only one who saw.

Wishing to be alone in his travels and his pain, her father, Chae Dong, took to drink. He arranged for Meg to be taken into his brother's family. Meg was old enough and would not be a burden; her baby sister was not. The baby was left on the steps of a Pusan orphanage. Then, as he was leaving, Meg put up such a heart-wrenching fuss that Chae Dong was unable to go without her. For a time, they traveled together: just Meg and Chae Dong—and the ghost.

* * *

In the years following, Chae Dong did his best to find a new wife and mother, but no one could quite compete with his memory of that ghost, nor stay long near its protective spell. Most who served as Meg's mother were shallow, mean-spirited souls who only wanted money and a good time. They had no room in their hearts for another woman's child. Finally, a widow from the mountains of the North, one whose greatest beauty was not of intelligence or anything outwardly showing, came along. This woman did have a loving heart. Her name was Chong Nan. She knew what it was like to have unacceptable blood. This kind soul was acceptable to the ghost.

Years earlier, Chong Nan's first husband was taken from their farm by the Japanese to be used as a slave laborer. He never returned. Times were tough then for Chong Nan and their child. Her husband's family would accept the child, it being a blood relative, but not Chong Nan. Chong Nan had nothing, was nothing—just another widow woman in a country full of them. Her husband's family owned the farm. With no farm, no rights, and no food, she was forced, of necessity, to give her daughter over.

Not long after Chae Dong and Chong Nan were married, he left to find work. He was to be gone for only a little while. The little while turned into many months.

In the town, there lived a rich, childless couple who were quite taken with Meg. They knew of Chong Nan's plight and approached her with the proposition of raising Meg as their own daughter. To Chong Nan, it was very obvious they were able and certainly appeared willing. With them, little seven-year-old Meg could have a much better life. Finally, with no word from Chae Dong, no food, and no prospects, Chong Nan agreed. It would be so, but only until Chae Dong returned. Chong Nan could not find work, except as a live-in maid. For such a job, having children was not acceptable.

Although she was given everything a child could want, and endlessly pampered, Meg was not happy. Nor would she bond with her new parents but waited for her father. One day, while squatted over the hole in the outhouse, from out in the courtyard, she heard her father's booming voice. Without pausing so much as to wipe, she went running to his arms, screaming, *"Apogee! Apogee!"* (Father! Father!).

* * *

Life was good for the next few years. With the money he'd made, Chae Dong bought a small neighborhood grocery store. After two years of prosperity, again, the money went into something bigger—a partnership in a rock masonry company. As a contractor for the government, they built retaining walls on road cuts and building sites. Chae Dong was well on his way to wealth when his partner embezzled it all and disappeared.

Embittered, Chae Dong, still a drinking man, became worse. In his obsession for revenge, he spent the next several years, and all their money, trying to track down his old partner.

There were some bad times. Meg, at the age of thirteen, had to quit school and get a job to help support the family—now including two younger half sisters and a half brother. Meg loved school and was avid in her learning, but in Korea, school cost money and there was not enough. Korean parents put all their future hopes in their sons. Ok Buk, Meg's younger half brother, would be the one going to school—the one who would be expected to provide for the family's future. This was very hard for Meg to accept. How could her father not see her worth?

Meg found work in a light bulb factory. Fitting, for though being a natural beauty, it was from the inside out that her light really shined. Men were like moths to it. As a schoolgirl, she'd always been very shy with the boys. And, too, back then, those who hung around had always been sent packing—usually with her father's boot prints showing in embarrassing places.

Now, suddenly a woman in an adult world, Meg had no idea how to react toward men. For nearly two years, she lived a recluse, except for the company of a few girlfriends. There was one fellow, though, who seemed to be very gentle and understanding—not at all like the macho acts put on by all the others. Meg finally relented and accepted a date to an amusement park.

Their date started out very well. They had a great time together, playing all the games and eating all the goodies. Then, on the Ferris wheel—disaster. All her thoroughly enjoyed goodies ended up not so enjoyably in his lap. It was Meg's first and last innocent date.

By this time, Meg was approaching sixteen. Her body was nearing that of a woman—a very attractive woman. She answered an ad for a job as a hostess in a coffee shop for Americans, who, as everyone knew, were very good tippers. It would mean money enough to help her family in style. Now that would really put a crack in her father's stone-headed opinions. Living with him was becoming increasingly difficultAs for the job, there was a catch. Meg did not have the money required for the transportation, room rental, presentable working clothes, and food. Ah, but not to worry; that could be advanced against her earnings.

Meg soon found herself on a bus with several other pretty, and also very naive, young women. They laughed and joked about all the wonderful things they would do with their lives now that they all had such great jobs. The awakening came with their arrival at Tokoree.

There were only two roads into Tokoree. The one for general use was a narrow-rutted dirt track leading over the mountain and connecting to the main highway between the larger towns of Uijongbu and Tongduchon. The other was the paved main road leading through the American Army's Seventh Division, Camp Casey. Available only to Americans, it began at the main gate in Tongduchon and ended at the back gate in Tokoree. Down this road every evening came swarms of GIs, each with only two things on their mind: drinking and fucking—these being the sole purpose and reasons for Tokoree.

* * *

If ever a place could truly be called the asshole of the world, it would be named Tokoree. Situated in a desolate, treeless crack in the mountains, Tokoree was a grimy little town whose center of commerce was composed of one grungy whorehouse bar after another. In both the atmosphere of its spirit and its actual air, there was a definite septic odor.

The people inhabiting it were, in short, the feces of humanity. The leaders of the town—its most outstanding citizens—could be viewed as no better than vultures, preying on the rest. Or perhaps more simply, they were the parasites in the feces.

It was into this cesspool Meg stepped when leaving the bus that warm, summer midafternoon. She was met by a middle-aged *Mamasan* in a beautiful, green silk dress. It wasn't the woman or her dress that impressed Meg, rather her eyes. They were the color of rusted steel. And her gaze, when it touched, felt like a breath of winter. With growing apprehension, Meg followed this woman into one of the local establishments. She did not yet know that the term "Mamasan" here was not an old Japanese term of respect, but rather one of fear for young girls such as her.

Meg had never seen a place like it and didn't fully fathom its function. She knew only that she didn't like it, its dark dankness, or the smells of vomit, urine, and spilt booze. She especially didn't like the looks she was receiving from all she passed. She felt like a piece of meat in a butcher shop window.

That day, as Meg stood in the bar of that foul-smelling brothel, learning of her place in the scheme of things, her knees felt weak and her stomach—like her spirit—was rebellious.

All the fear and horror of her infancy again threatened to overwhelm her life. *"Chungmar hagee shidoyo!"* (I won't do it!)

With surprising strength, Mamasan grabbed Meg and slapped her into tearful silence.

"You owe me money!" she hissed, her little pig eyes gleaming just inches from Meg's own. "If you don't pay, I'll have you thrown in jail and the police will have their way with you anyway." Then, yanking on Meg's hair, she dragged her out back and locked her into one of the eight-by-ten-foot cubicles off the back courtyard. It was to be her home and workplace for a time.

* * *

That night, a Sergeant Conan from the Seventh Infantry came to town, got boozed up, and bought himself a night with a virgin. He didn't seem to mind when she didn't understand what was required of her and ignored her screams and pleas when eventually she did. After he was done, Meg lay sobbing weakly, bleeding from wounds that were more than physical.

In fact, he liked the feeling of power it had afforded him as he'd quenched his dark hungers. She'd been painfully tight against his penis, not like that slut, his ex-wife. He still held her parting image in his mind, mocking him from the bed—his bed—where she'd lain with those three grunts, their bodies a jumble of sweaty flesh. She'd laughed as he slammed the door and ran into the dark of a Fort Bliss night.

But this one . . . this one had not mocked him. His every thrust had been echoed in unison by a squeal of anguish. Her body had, all the while, thrashed ineffectually—like a child's beneath his far greater weight, striving only to get away, to escape the horror. No, this one certainly had not jeered about the size of it.

He marveled at the freedom! No one could touch him—no one! He'd paid for it. It was legal. Ah, you couldn't get this kind of freedom back home.

Now, anger spent, he saw her fear and loathing as she cowered in the far corner away from him. Hugging her knees, she shielded her tattered childhood with her legs. With opened palms, she hid the shame on her face, covering all but her eyes. They blazed with a fear-filled rage, and something more—something behind it—a look of childlike reproach? Vulnerable, yet it carried an oath of invulnerability. Like a sword of infinite sharpness held before her, it seemed to say, "You'll never hurt me like this again!"

Looking into the eyes of her wounded, defiant soul, he felt a sudden pang of remorse. A thought filtered down through the boozy fumes of his mind, and he felt a sudden need for her to see him differently. No, he really wasn't such a bad guy.

Pawing through the heap of clothing on the floor, his fumbling hands found the pockets of his khaki pants. From his billfold, he extracted a bill and held it out. Her only response was to shrink tighter into herself.

"Harumph!" he grunted, swaying dangerously forward. "Not good enough for ya, eh?" Then reaching back in, he ripped forth two more. Then again, when she wouldn't respond, he stuffed them with clumsy fingers into the crook of her arm.

"I'm really a pretty nice guy; everyone says so. You'll see." He paused to swig from his bottle. "Generous n' good lookin, n' all the ladies like me. You'll see. N' the guys . . . all the guys respect me, Sergeant Conan. Yeah! Gonna take care of you. You'll see."

Meg understood none of his mumbles, and when he passed out across the bed, she stayed in her corner. She looked at the money he'd given her. The weird-looking Military Payment Coupons—MPCs—would they be enough for a bus ticket somewhere? She knew better than to try it tonight. Mamasan's slicky boys were watching her closely, and besides, they had her clothes.

After that first night, Meg watched and waited for her chance. She'd managed to exchange those fifteen MPCs, then hide it away—about 4,000 Won. It would have to be enough. Three weeks passed, and she now wore clothes and worked in the bar with the other girls. Finally alone and unwatched, she sprinted for the bus stop. It may be she couldn't go home, but anywhere would hold more dignity for her than this. She'd find a place where no one would ever know.

Waiting her turn in the small crowd loading the bus, Meg felt an arm encircle her waist. Her quick intake of breath was halted by a sharp prick of pain against her stomach, just under the ribs. A voice hissed into her ear, "It would be very easy to put this knife through your heart." Meg looked down at the arm and saw a gleam of steel beneath the wrist. "Come quietly, or it will be so." Looking much like two lovers, they stepped from the crowd.

* * *

In the back room at Mamasan's, just fifteen minutes later, they began Meg's torture. Yet, Mamasan was no fool. She would never damage her merchandise, at least not its appearance. Meg's head was forced into a tub of water and held there until she felt her lungs would explode. When she was finally let up, the air fairly shrieked back into her lungs. Her hands tied behind her, she was at the mercy of Mamasan's three slicky boys. Bent over the tub as she was, coughing, choking in great gasps of air to ease her burning lungs, she hardly noticed her clothes being cut and ripped from her body. To her it seemed the worst was over, but then there came a slickness probing the privacy of her behind and the smell of cooking grease.

"She-pally-marl, ke-sickia . . ." She cursed them for the mongrel curs they were and struggled with renewed strength.

The one holding her head down only grunted, then sneered into her ear, "Stupid Americans! They may like your pink little cherry, but it's not near so much fun as a nice, tight purple prune. . . ."

Then, as the first penis pierced her sphincter, the screams rose involuntarily, only to be cut off each time by the water, repeatedly, until finally, half alive, she was again locked away in her hootch.

* * *

There is nothing like brutality to firm one's resolve. Meg bided her time. Since that first night, Sergeant Conan had returned often. Once he could see through the fumes, he'd found her to be modest, well mannered, and beautiful enough to take away any man's breath. Sergeant Conan promptly fell in love.

For one hundred seventy MPCs, and a little extra for food and room rental, he bought sole rights to Meg. This was no greedy little slut just out to make a few easy Won. This was definitely someone of class. Mistaking Meg's submission as meaning she felt likewise, he started through the jungle of red tape involved with a GI/Indigenous marriage.

That Meg would never want him after what he'd done never crossed his mind. How could she ever bring this brute home to meet her father? Meg knew her father—knew that in his typically traditional Korean viewpoint, it would be better she die an anonymous, lonely suicide, unknown, unnoticed, unexplained. Far better that than the whore bride of some GI.

But Meg was a survivor and was making friends with some of the others. She didn't like this "catching GIs" but did what she was told. Mamasan often wanted her to do it with GIs from other units and sometimes certain Korean officials. Of course, it was all behind the sergeant's back, but it paid her 500 Won—about $1.87—every time. Money was the only light showing Meg her way to freedom. It was good that Mamasan saw it only as greed.

Then came a stroke of luck! One of her new friends was steadying a GI who was being transferred to another unit of the Seventh Battalion. She would be moving over the mountain to Tongduchon. They struck a bargain: Meg would be this older woman's maid in exchange for smuggling her out of Tokoree and giving her room and board until she could find something.

It wasn't very long until Meg again learned another valuable lesson in life. This woman, who seemed so kindhearted and charitable, didn't believe in waiting to receive her rewards in heaven. One day, Meg made an innocent remark, which carried a hint of suggestion that perhaps this woman wasn't being completely fair toward another friend, and learned one didn't cross so charitable a kind heart. Meg found herself on the street, possessing only the clothes on her back.

* * *

No food, no money, no bed, Meg looked at the street girls infesting every corner and shuddered. Was she now one of them? There was a place she knew of, the Miss Kim Club. It was clean. The Mamasan didn't import her wares, took an honest cut, and dealt fairly with people.

Almost immediately, Meg met a GI from the Seventh S&T, a Spec Four named Butz, who wanted to steady. Meg agreed to become his Yobo. He'd only been in-country a short while, and being lonely was looking mostly for companionship.

Butz wasn't a lot to look at. Of average height and build, his face still retained the ravages of puberty. That's not to say he was ugly. Certainly, his was not a face that would scare the flies from the outhouse. But Butz was fun to be with. Meg found herself learning enough English to be understood. They went to movies, on hikes, on bus trips, and often just wandered around the Ville together. They talked a lot, and homely as he was, in her enjoyment of their relationship, Meg fell in love.

Being a "steady girl" or "Yobo," Meg was paid forty MPCs every month. One day, mid-month, after they'd been together nearly a year, Butz brought his friend, Flannigan, to their hootch.

"Meg, I'll be leaving in six weeks, and Flannigan here," Butz jerked a thumb toward his friend, "is going to steady you from now on."

In the light of the single electric bulb, Meg looked from Butz's pimply face to the smooth, dark, handsome one of his friend, and the questions buzzed silently through her mind. *How he can just leave—no tell me first? Flannigan—why he think I want steady Flannigan? I nebber like him anyhow. Who make this plan? And when?*

"Look, Meg." Butz continued when Meg didn't respond. "I just want to make sure you'll be okay. Flannigan's going to pay me the twenty MPCs and take over for the rest of this month. I'm going to need the money for when I get home to my fiancée."

"Phree-on-say?"

"Yes . . . you know, my girlfriend back home. We're going to be married soon as I get back."

Butz—married? How could he no tell me? True, we nebber talk about marry, but still— Again the thoughts buzzed like bees, only the last one stung with white-hot pain. *What do he mean, Flannigan pay him to take over?*

"What! You think me ke-gogie—some dog meat down in butcher shop? You think you sell me?" Snatching up her biggest pot, Meg advanced. "Get out . . . boths of you . . . get out!" After they left, Meg latched the door and spent the rest of the night sobbing uncontrollably.

Butz must've realized what he was giving up, and how in both fact and appearance, he lived up to his name. Too, maybe he just stopped and looked at the picture of his girl from back home. Over the remaining six weeks, he came to Meg's door many times, crying, pleading for her forgiveness. He even offered to re-up for another tour, if only she would marry him. Strange how such a short time before, this would have meant everything to her. Now Meg swore vehemently to herself: she would never allow herself to be vulnerable to any man—not ever again!

For those six weeks, and more, Meg stayed mostly drunk, drinking portaju and playing cards every night with her friends. The rest of the time she slept—and cried. The money was running out and reality settling in. She knew she'd have to do something soon. She knew it, and her friends knew it also.

One of them, Soon Yi, had already done something. She'd noticed a new guy at the B Company Engineers, watching him throwing candy over the compound fence to the children. Such a man could not be a bad person. That evening, she urged her boyfriend to invite him over to their table at the EM Club. During the conversation, Soon Yi asked him a few questions about his love life. She'd found out: "yes," he was lonely; "no," there was no one waiting back home stateside; and "no thank you," he didn't want a Yobo. Then when her steady, Jerry, was off unloading his beer, she leaned over close and asked, "Cheff, you say you want boom-boom you go ville—but you neffer go ville. Maybe you just no likee gorl?"

"Look . . ." His face was now scarlet; he seemed at a loss for words. "I like girls just fine. I . . . well . . . I just don't like VD." From her vantage, she glanced down past her ample breasts draped so casually over his arm. Looking into his lap, she knew he spoke the truth.

* * *

Soon Yi began a campaign involving all of Meg's friends. They had their steadies approaching this GI, telling him about Meg's beauty, her good nature, what a great friend she was, and about how she needed a steady. After only a few weeks, her plan came to fruition. On a Saturday evening, his curiosity apparently prevailed. He agreed to a meeting.

That Sunday, about midmorning, Soon Yi came pounding on Meg's wooden-framed paper door. Meg answered, sliding the door aside and squinting into the sudden brightness. The evening before had turned into another all-nighter of drinking and playing cards. When Soon Yi stopped in to ask if she wanted to meet a man, it seemed like a good idea—then. Now was different. Just now, Meg's head ached. She didn't want to meet anyone and certainly didn't want to think about steadying.

But Soon Yi persisted; hadn't she promised, given her word? Finally, Meg gave in. Throwing on an old, baggy, black sweater, she ran a comb through her hair and with dragging steps followed her friend down the hill to the compound fence.

As they approached the wire, Meg could see a man there, waiting. He was very tall and a little thin, and he wore the usual army fatigues with the eagle patches of a Specialist Fourth Class. Meg saw how his face was gentle looking and handsome—almost to the point of being pretty.

She did not like the "pretty boys," feeling them to be sissies. And most of the other GIs she believed only looked tough, while inside they were just foolish children. Americans, she'd discovered, were not so strong inside. Somehow, with this man, something felt different. Meg's appraisal was taken in quick glances as she came down the pathway. For the most part, she kept her eyes averted. The aching head, the taste of dirty feet, all blended into this bloated, puffy day. Certainly, it did not seem a good day for meeting a GI. Yet, seeing this one, Meg suddenly found herself wishing she had taken the time to fix her face or at least brush her teeth.

Now at the fence, Meg heard her friend make the introduction and knew she had to look up. When she did, it was directly into his eyes. Their color was of the deepest blue, a shock since she had expected them to be like the washed-out blue of most blue-eyed Americans. That kind always reminded her of the round, staring, dead fish eyes in the market.

Though she understood very little as he spoke, she felt a longing for some nameless something she had never known. She learned his name was Jeff, and though she could easily see his shyness, it did not feel of weakness. Instead, there was a strength that seemed to uplift her somehow. Life no longer seemed so hopeless, nor did she feel so tired and used up. And as they conversed through the chain link, Meg came to realize this man she wanted to know better—much better.

~ *In the Present with Big D* ~

There is little to be said for this chapter. It is about Meg and necessary to the story only. Without knowing these things, one would likely never know who Meg truly was. Yet, reading over it, I am reminded of some cheap romance novel. This chapter doesn't seem to fit with the rest of this story. Perhaps it's because it is divergent from my own. Something about it just doesn't feel—right.

Big D did not come to me with the ending of this chapter, and strangely, I didn't want him to. Still, I cannot help but wonder, does he ignore me? Is it because this chapter is not really my own story? Do I overstep myself somehow in telling it?

Mulling it over, I turn my head sharply, looking to the bed stand, toward the only light in the blackness of this long, sleepless night. It glows there, a cold-blue light—2:30 a.m. Then suddenly, I am aware of red tinging the edge of my sight. Turning back, I see something there at the foot of my bed, two consuming, red glows amidst a swirling, deeper darkness and an occasional gleam of ivory.

"Big D! Is that you?" He gives no immediate answer but leaves me to soak in ominous silence. "Look . . . my writing is not done, my purpose in life is not yet fulfilled, and I am still following my joy—well, aren't I?" My words seem to stumble over themselves.

His voice comes to me now as a deep resonance almost beneath the threshold of my hearing and speaks to me through my bones. "Yes, I'll agree. You need not fear my sickle, though it is not entirely true of late—that part about the 'joy,' anyway." His voice with each word seems to focus somehow until it is sounding almost normal. Could normal ever describe his voice? "I come only because you need me. With your restlessness now, you ask for me, though before, at the ending of this chapter, you denied me. Why?"

His last word is a demand, and I know I must give him truth, so it is with deep reflection that I answer. "It's about Meg. She's been gone for some time now, and I know I still love her. I swore I was done mourning, yet it has been painful to write about her. I denied you because I didn't want to face your truth."

"My truth is your truth, and this chapter is not all about Meg. Nor is it all about the truth." The glow from his eye sockets seems to bore right through me. "What is it truly about?"

"Well, it is the story gleaned over many years with Meg. I believe it is the truth."

"Then it is what Meg said was the truth—and colored by the way you wanted it to be."

"No! It is the truth!"

"Every word? Even the conversations?"

"Well, of course I did need to fill in some of the cracks."

"Ha!" Big D guffaws. "I like your choice of words!"

"Yes . . . well, okay." I shrug. "I told the truth the best I know it."

"Hold it right there!" It feels as if a switch is thrown, and I now face two glowing, red heat lamps. "When you're *filling in the cracks* with me, what I hear is *fuck the truth!*—and incidentally, *fuck me!*"

Stunned, I have no reply. He continues. "I am as your soul! Nothing but absolute truth works for me." The intensity lessens slightly. "The story you just told is partly who Meg wants to be, partly who you want to see her as being. You nailed it earlier—a la-la-land dime romance. You see Meg through the sunglasses of a blind man." His voice softens. "It is always so with those we love."

"Ah, shit . . . you're right, Big D. Though I don't want to admit it, it's true. I know I am biased." The glow, too, has now softened. "Look, I'll just leave it out. This whole thing seems kind of corny anyway."

"Let it be."

"Then I'll write it again in honesty. Just help me to see. . . ."

"No. Leave it in la-la-land. The romantic essence for some—the very charm of love—is found in its wondrous blindness. Now, are you sure you want to see it in honesty?"

I don't know why he gives me this chance to avoid the truth. It seems so unlike him. I give a hesitant "Yes," and of course with Big D, there is no thought he does not hear. He addresses my unspoken question.

"In coaching another, you are only an unwanted intrusion, unless you have a clear contract. They must acknowledge that they want to hear. Otherwise, you are only trying to save them from the life they want to live. People resist that." His eyes seem to flash with humor as he continues. "With you and me, it is different. We have a clear contract— and you know it. Still, you have avoided this part of yourself for a very long time. It requires your compliance, clearly and willingly. Now, are you ready to hear it?"

"Yes!"

"Good! Now . . . was the woman you met at that fence chained down in slavery?" His humor remains, but his gaze has intensified.

"N-no, but—"

"As an adult, was she the creator of her life?" I see a glint of grinning ivory. "Remember, it is the law."

"She was a child when it all began. . . ."

"True! Harsh lessons. And children are the closest thing to true victims in the creation of their lives." There is a tenderness now in his tone. "But even then, was her soul not really giving her the lessons she needed in this life? Did those lessons make her less or more?"

"I think more, but did they need to be so horrible?"

"That is between her and her soul. 'Horrible' for her is not for you to determine." Again, a flash of ivory. *"Life is always perfect, just as it is,"* he quotes. Then he adds, "Mankind has such blind judgment about this law."

There is now a vagueness to his glow and I feel him leaving. "Why are you going? Aren't you going to help me with this?"

"You ask, but when I propose the truth, you respond with excuses. I will ask it one last time: Was the woman you met an adult, and was she the creator of her life?"

"Yes! Yes, we all are."

"Was she not creating a life of prostitution,"—the glow from his eye sockets is intense— "even with you?"

"Yes," I answer softly. "And I like to think it was different with me."

"It was. And though it has been so long ago, in her mind she does not see herself as anything more than a rented cunt—even to this day. And as you well know, how you see yourself is your truth. That she could never see how you always held her in your highest esteem was on her, not you."

"Then how was it different with me? I don't understand."

"Reread the last couple pages of her story. Can you see the white horse? And the sun shining off polished armor? The sword and shield?"

Switching on the nightlight, I grab the manuscript and do his bidding. "Yes, I see it now!"

"Just so . . ." Now with the light, his gaping grin and glowing eyes have faded almost from sight. "Again, as you know, no one can save another from their life. It is always created according to their own views. You know this, yet with Meg, you still try to save her, to slay the dragons of her mind." His chuckle carries a note of jeer. "What happened back then is *what was*, and what was *just is* and will never change. You both have such resistance to the unchangeable. For her, the past gives birth to her dragons—dragons you can't save her from creating. And, too, you know that saving is never appreciated.

"Yeah, Big D." I sigh. "I know that."

"And you know that Meg saw you as her knight in shining armor, riding to her rescue. Even so, you know she will never appreciate you. Hell, what was it she told you there at the end when you were fighting so desperately to save your marriage?"

"Yeah, I remember. She said, '*You*—not me—need to go to marriage counseling. You're all fucked up. . . .'"

"*But* . . ." His grin now mocks me.

"Yeah, she always ended that one with, '*but I'm okay.*'"

"Yes, rather than face her truth, that lie became her mantra." I see him no more, but his words continue, resonating clearly in that familiar bottom-of-the-barrel tone of his. Yet, with them comes a tenderness quietly mixed in with the hard truth. ***"Life is always perfect."*** He repeats the law. "In searching for the perfection, there is always healing along with the hurt. But after thirty years, aren't you starting to get a little bow legged from riding that white stallion? And under the scorching light of truth, isn't that polished armor beginning to get just a little hot? Where Meg is concerned, haven't you already fallen on your sword enough times? Have you not screamed out in agony with it and washed your conscience clean with your tears?" He pauses to chuckle before laying on the harshest of his truth. "You are done with all the moaning and mourning. Isn't that what you said?"

"Yes, Big D, I did say that. And I feel I've—"

"Then in the perfection of this time, right now, don't you think you ought to get down off that fucking horse?" My mouth now hangs open at the steel in his words. I feel a soft caress of ivory digits across my cheek as he delivers his last words, softly now—earnestly. "You loved her with a passion few are ever privileged to know. In that . . . you were *never* fucked up. And that love you gave to her—it deserves *no* regrets."

When the flashbulb of fresh love goes off in your face, sometimes you trip over things in your way—things you don't see. Sometimes they are things you put there, then don't look at. Always there is a dazzling haze left in the backlash of that flash that hides the picture. You determine how long that haze will last. Some couples stumble through life together, forever. Others learn from the pain of their falls, look at their self-imposed obstacles, and gain the true gift of insight. With insight comes the ability to run, to move faster and farther in one's life. Sometimes the gift is accepted by only one, whose heart, for a time, cries as it is carried away by life.

Redneck Spirituality—Book Two

Chapter Eighteen

The Flashbulb of Fresh Love

There I was, Sunday morning, waiting at the perimeter fence as Jerry's Yobo, Soon Yi, came bubbling down the footpath. Her charge in tow was wearing a baggy, black sweater and appeared somewhat sleepy and disheveled. Hanging her head, she partially walked, partially was dragged down the hill. Clearly, she would have preferred to be elsewhere, as did I.

As they approached the fence, Soon Yi said, "Cheff, dis Miss Pak. Evvy one calla hor Meg."

Those words were all I remember of Soon Yi, or even of her presence after that, though eventually, I realized she'd gone. For in the next instant, I found myself looking into two of the most beautiful eyes I'd ever seen, mahogany pools of wonder with a reddish tint where the sunlight penetrated their depths. They blinked once and seemed to widen slightly. For a long moment, they held me speechless, unaware of all else—the rest of the world just didn't matter. If the eyes were the window to her soul, hers was perfection. I just didn't know at the time that there could ever be something like wounded perfection.

Then I became aware of her face: equally beautiful, framed as it was by bangs and a shoulder-length flow of black hair. It, too, glinted deep red where the morning sun shone through. Her body was one of slender, willowy grace.

My memory has always been in a haze as to just what I said when I was again able to untangle my tongue. Mostly, it seemed I asked her questions about herself and kept asking, for though her answers revealed little, the very interchange kept her there before me. She seemed to understand little of what I said, her answers coming in oddly strung words, or more often, just shy monosyllables that sounded like "uhhmmm." It was okay that she did not understand me. It was just that in that moment, she was there in my life—a pleasure to look at—and her voice was sweet to my ears. Finally, with a sense of barely restrained excitement, I extracted a definite "yes." She would sign in with me that afternoon at the front gate and accompany me to the EM Club.

There was nothing else but her on my mind as the next three hours dragged by. I asked myself all of the questions: Did I really want to take on a woman for money, and one I didn't even know? Was I man enough for a beauty such as her? God! What if she rejected me? Or worse, gave me some horrible, cock-rotting form of VD? And money? It would take a large chunk of my meager count of MPCs.

Yes, the questions swam like piranhas through my mind. My ego was not immune to their bite, but those mahogany eyes were. They still held me steady in their gaze, and something in them seemed to caress my very soul. At lunch in the Mess, I spotted two guys, who I knew had Yobos, and made it a point to sit at their table and pump them for information.

"Johnson . . . Miller, what's up? Thought you'd both be in the Ville with your Yobos!"

"Yeah . . . well, night duty . . . you know?" Johnson grunted, shoving his half-eaten tray aside in disgust. "I'll just be glad when they pull this wild hair outta their ass about rushing us to haul equipment to finish these bunkers on line Papa"

"Yeah!" piped in Miller. "What the fuck do they think we need a second line of defense for anyway? If the North jumps us now, we'd just wind up nuking the bastards; only thing that would stop 'em anyhow."

"Hey, guys!" I grinned. "I don't want to dampen your moods here, but you remember that Miss Pak you told me about?"

"Yeah?"

"Uh-huh?"

"Well, I'm seeing her this afternoon." Now was their turn to grin. "I'm thinking of steadying. Just thought you'd give me some pointers on how much to offer."

They both glanced at one another, and for a moment, neither seemed willing to answer. Then Johnson said, "Well . . . thirty MPCs is the going rate. . . ." Miller nodded his assent.

I looked from one to the other, aware that there was something missing. "Is that what you guys pay?"

Again, the look, then Miller answered. "Well, I'm marrying mine, so for me, it's different."

I looked to his friend. "What about you, Johnson?"

"Well, yeah. Mine gets a little more 'n that, but we've been together a while. Point is, if you offer more 'n thirty, she'll think you're a doofus and take advantage."

"Yeah," agreed Miller. "You don't want to start out at more than thirty."

"Thanks, guys," I said, then fell silent, watching from one to the other as they went on about their griping. Their words flew past my ears, as sipping at my coffee and chewing my cardboard sandwich, I thought about Miss Pak.

Their reactions to my question were curious. Did they think they were doofuses because they obviously paid more? Still, they both agreed; thirty was the going rate. That being so, well certainly, I didn't want to be thought a fool. Yet, there were ways to slip Miss Pak more. The money didn't matter to me. Just spending time with this beauty was my only intent—hell, a little extra money or gifts just to show her how much she meant to me. Truth was, I wanted her to love me. Our relationship, however it went, had to be about more than the pay.

That afternoon, I watched Miss Pak approach the gate. Her red silk dress shone in the sun, accentuating the grace of her movements. Yet, there was uncertainty there, too, like a doe testing the wind for predators.

She had applied her makeup very lightly—not at all garish like Miss Tammy Faye Kim down at Kimpo. Somehow it was no surprise. Miss Pak was something beyond all the women in my meager experience. Her appearance, the grace in her movements, and the way she spoke in her beautiful, soft voice all shouted out, *class*! She was like a diamond amongst the rhinestones—maybe not flashy, and maybe not quite polished—but the real thing.

I escorted her to the EM Club where we joined Jerry and Soon Yi. We ordered. Jerry and I had burgers; the girls, chicken. Then we made small talk over beers and sloe gin fizzes until our food came.

Like our orders, I gravitated toward Jerry with my conversation; Miss Pak, toward Soon Yi. Too shy to talk directly, our eyes did a little dance of stolen glances. Our dance lasted all the while, before and during our meal.

I was fascinated by her every movement, her every nuance— even the slim grace in her fingers as she picked the meat from her chicken. It was a distinct difference from the way Jerry's girl, sitting to her left, was wolfing hers: gnawing and slurping at the bare bones, then with stubby fingers, breaking them to suck the marrow.

Finally, Jerry and Soon Yi went off to play the slots. At last we were alone. My intention was to play it cool, yet instead, my eagerness stomped clumsily all over my tongue.

"Miss Pak . . . uh . . . well . . . look, Soon Yi said you wanted a steady." It tumbled out, sounding like a question.

She smiled shyly and nodded. "I . . . Meg. They calla me Meg."

I asked bluntly, in a rush, "Meg . . . uhh . . . would thirty MPCs be enough?"

She ducked her head and looked away over toward Soon Yi for a moment. Was that moisture on her beautiful eyelashes? I was about to reformulate my question—maybe offer more—but again she nodded. I saw, but in my excitement, didn't question or further take note of her unhappiness. Mistake? Perhaps. But for that moment, I had what I wanted.

Jerking the bills from my pocket, I pressed them into her hand. She drew back, embarrassed by the exchange of money. It was something I quickly realized should have been done in private. Again, I was struck by how different she was from the other girls. They would simply have sucked the money up and thought no more of it. Yet, from her expression, it was no secret she hoped for more. It was almost one of dismay. But it wasn't a concern. Hell, it just gave me more room to show my generosity. For me, this was a great adventure—for her, survival.

Day passes were never a problem. Depending on the schedule, we could get them almost any day and, in fact, nearly every evening.

Kind of like Cinderella, we just had to be back to the compound by midnight. As life in the army would have it, the roster came out with me on the night duty, hauling equipment to Camp Hovey on the DMZ. It would be three days before I would manage to see Meg—long days and nights filled with anticipation. Visions of her wafted constantly in and out of my consciousness.

On the fourth evening, Meg met me at the gate. She smiled, took my hand in her small, delicate one, and led me quietly down the road about one hundred yards. Oblivious to the milling of people on the roadway and the busy shops across from the compound—amidst the confusion of their unintelligible gibber—I saw only Meg. There was a narrow path to the right. We turned and followed it up through the jumble of hootches built along the hillside.

Before going through the gate at her own apartment, Meg pointed out the *pionso*, or outhouse. We were to share it together with several of the neighbors. It was situated across the alley and consisted of a little, tin-roofed shack with a 55-gallon drum cut in half and buried in the ground. There were two boards laid in parallel over the top to squat on, with a six-inch gap between them. I took one look and decided I'd use it in an emergency only—and certainly never when drunk. That thought opened possibilities at which I found myself shuddering.

I knew from experience of how the waste was disposed. They would dip it out, two "honey buckets" at a time, hang the buckets on a shoulder yoke, and trot them down the narrow alleys to a "honey cart" left on the roadway. The cart, when full, would be taken out to a rice paddy somewhere and the contents spread as fertilizer. I'd met people carrying honey buckets in alleyways before and knew it was always wise to give them the right-of-way. They were going to take it anyway.

Our hootch was built together with one other—kind of like a duplex of two single rooms. The roof was of the typical gray cement tile, and a low, four-foot-wide veranda, or porch, ran the length of the building. It stood at door level, about two feet off the neatly swept and packed earth of the courtyard. Meg motioned me to sit on the porch, and in her soft, broken English said, "Please to remove shoes, please." She said it surprisingly well, and I knew she'd been practicing.

While unlacing and removing my combat boots, I watched her graceful movements as she slid off her own shoes. Then, squatting in front of the little, wood-framed paper door, she slid it slightly open, reached in, and withdrew a pair of rubber slippers. "These, edywa shoes," she explained. "Fo you, Cheff . . . my Yobo." She finished softly, hesitantly, as if offering me an honor she wasn't sure would be accepted.

I felt a warmness touch my heart as I took them from her and tried them on. They were not large enough—not even close. Meg took them from me and attempted the feat herself. Worrying at them, she tugged and pushed, her face set in determined concentration. Although my size-eleven feet are fairly small for a six-foot-four frame, they were considered gigantic there in Korea. These were the largest size available.

Watching her, squatted there in front of me, I was touched by her disappointment. Clearly, she'd been anticipating my delight at the thoughtful care she took of her new "Yobo." I reached out and gently squeezed her shoulder.

"It's okay," I said as our eyes met.

She understood "okay," followed as it was by a shrug with raised eyebrows—the universal language for, "Oh, well . . . shit happens." Brightening a little, she ushered me through the door.

The room was not large, about the size of my own bedroom back home. There was a small, double-bed mattress made up against the left wall. In the far right corner sat a wooden chest for clothing storage. The floor was of yellow linoleum and felt quite warm to my stocking feet. At the center of the room, surrounded by a little, low-wire fence, stood a real luxury—a two-and-a-half-foot tall, cast iron, potbelly stove. Meg reached up and pulled the string on the single electric bulb hanging from the ceiling, glanced around with obvious pride, and smiled at me. I nodded my approval.

She handed me a pair of pajamas and gestured for me to put them on. I removed my fatigues, handing them to her, one at a time. She, in turn, almost like an assembly line, neatly folded and stacked them in a pile by the bed. As I unclothed myself down to the skivvies, I was aware of her stealing quick little glances, although for the most part, she kept her eyes demurely averted.

The pajamas fit, after a fashion. They were the large/fat size. Though the sleeves didn't reach much past my elbows, nor the legs much past my knees, they were comfortable enough. I sat on the bed in my new pajamas and watched in appreciation as Meg produced a hot plate and began cooking Korean noodles. She moved with a sort of liquid grace, her hands deft and sure as she went about her chore. In comparison, American women suddenly seemed bulky and ungainly to me.

We ate in shy silence, Meg with her graceful, little chopsticks and I with my spoon. The noodles were delicious, although watching her over the rim of my bowl, I could have probably eaten worms and not have noticed. Worms were supposedly a delicacy in Korea, and while I didn't believe it, that was the rumor.

After we'd eaten, she washed the utensils in a big bowl of soapy water she'd left heating on the hot plate, then carried them out into the frigid twilight to rinse at the well pump in the courtyard. I squatted at the door and slid its light, wooden frame open, just enough to see. Touching its delicate paper covering, I wondered briefly at its ability to keep out the cold. Then, seeing her there at the pump, I felt a warmth as she glanced up, her eyes meeting mine, and I knew it didn't matter. With her, this frigid winter would not touch me. Back inside, she dried and stacked everything in the corner.

Next, Meg put her nightgown on over the top of her clothes. Then somehow, she managed to remove her clothes from within it. Though not my preferred way of watching her disrobe, still, I found myself impressed by her modesty. It did not dampen my desire as, when sliding between the covers, she crept into my arms. Her body trembled against mine, and clearly, it was not from the cold of the Korean night. It took no fool to see that she was as nervous and shy as I. Realizing I knew next to nothing about her, suddenly I had an unquenchable thirst to know everything about this magnificently exotic woman, for I did feel I knew something of her heart.

Awkwardly at first, we began to converse. Her English left a lot to be desired, but as we talked, I found myself becoming very comfortable with her. Her full name was Pak, Me Gong, and she was from Tongbu, a town near Seoul. It had only been a little over a year since she'd left home; I'd suspected as much from her poor English and heavy accent. When asked her age, she didn't answer right away. Instead, she questioned, "How ole . . . you . . . Cheff?" I told her twenty and Meg replied, "I ole-so twen-tee . . . Cheff." She obviously wasn't being truthful, and I suspected she just didn't want to appear young and naive. Somehow, this meant a lot to her, so I didn't press it. Truth was, she'd just turned seventeen.

Meg didn't like "catching GIs" but admitted being a steady wasn't bad. She'd been tricked into coming to a nearby town by the promise of a good job in a coffee shop. Once there, however, she'd been forced into prostitution. I asked her, "Why don't you just go home now?

I'll help if you need me to." Somehow, I was naive enough not to realize she would then not want to see me.

She turned her head away for a long moment, and I saw a glimmer of tears. Her answer was choked, "No . . . now dur-tee: no *can channa.* Fat-ter no wan now! I . . . shame heem! No more can lib fat-ter hootchee . . . neb-ber!"

Holding her, stroking her thick, black hair, I told her through the blur of my own tears, "I don't think you're dirty. You only did what you had to. If you were my daughter, I would want you back—no matter what!"

She turned and looked at me, tears streaming from bottomless eyes, and simply replied, "Diffnt, Korea."

We lie there, just holding one another for a long while. She was not wearing any perfume, yet the clean, natural fragrance from her body, her beauty, and the nearness of her was having its effect. We kissed, and my hand sought her breast as if on its own accord. She flinched away. We both knew what was to happen, and I could see how Meg, for her own part, was not as eager as I. This was not the way I wanted it to be, so I contented myself with stroking her thigh and waist while we kissed some more.

Her body was perfect: breasts not large and pendulous, but rather smaller, more pert and firm, with nipples that jutted slightly upward and to the outsides. A perfect hourglass figure, her waist was small enough that I could spread my hands around her and touch my thumbs and middle fingers together. Her hips swelled out full, her buttocks, round and firm. Overall, I could not detect an ounce of fat or flab anywhere on her body. She was utter sensuous perfection.

In time, her body lost its tension and slowly began to respond to mine. She still stiffened whenever my caress came too close to her most private parts. I was determined Meg's experience would be as enjoyable as my own. I wanted it to be right.

Eventually, she indicated her readiness by the hitching of her nightgown and opening of her legs. There followed a moment of awkward fumbling, due partly from my own inexperience and nervousness, and partly from her being a little dry—her natural state.

But with a blush, a giggle or two, and a dab of moisture from her tongue, I soon found myself enfolded by Meg's warmth.

For a long moment, we lie there not moving—I, just soaking up the sensations fully. Then I began a slow, rhythmic stroking of her body, inside and out. My weight was supported by my elbows, my body gently touching hers, caressing her full length as we moved. My face was in her hair, and I breathed in the clean, sweet aroma of it.

Our passion grew with the pace. Every thrust of mine was met with an equal thrust from her. Eventually, her heels were doing a little tattoo on the backs of my thighs, almost as if she could pound me in deeper. I felt my orgasm rising from way down inside and knew in my heart that Meg was ready to receive. Raising up, stiff armed, my body arched tautly above hers as spurt after spurt transferred between us. A low groan escaped my lips, and I looked down to see that her eyes were shut in tight concentration. When they opened, they were clouded, unseeing, and I wondered what it was she saw. Certainly, it was not me. Then suddenly, they cleared and came to rest on me, and I saw something there—a surprised gratefulness and a healing of some sort.

Had she climaxed? No man always knows. Often, in the back of his mind, will be the question, a slight doubt: "Did I really satisfy her?" Yet, looking into her eyes as we lie spent in one another's arms, I knew, without a doubt, for her, too, there was something special about it. And I suspected—no, I knew—that whatever in her I'd touched as such, I was her first. My heart sang with the joy of it.

Sometime later, Meg roused and stepped out of bed. As I languished in a haze of relaxed contentment, I heard her pouring water and knew she was cleaning herself. Then suddenly, she was there beside me, urging me to sit up and scoot to the edge of the bed. Kneeling before me, she wedged a bowl of warm, strong-smelling blue water between my legs.

"Muss creen now," she explained. Then, with a clean rag, she slowly, almost tenderly, began washing me. In no time she had my attention, or rather, *at attention*. I took the towel from her hands and held out my arms to her. She came to me with a willing smile, and we again slid between the sheets and into one another's arms.

This time, our lovemaking held no urgency. It was now in tenderness that I advanced and retreated—tenderness and a certain silken, lingering luxury, all reflected in my gaze, now, too, locked in the depths of hers. Meg met each thrust with a throaty whimper of pleasure. My orgasm, when it came, was every bit as intense for me as the first, yet somehow it felt more of love than lust. Again, our eyes locked together, shining, and there was no cloudiness now in hers.

~ *In the Present with Big D* ~

I sit here before my computer, going over these words and phrases, wondering if I have put forth the essence of how it all began with Meg, if I have given how it was between her and me an honest shake. It is always hard to see reality when one's emotions stand in the way. My gaze lingers on the brilliance of the screen so intently that I am not aware of how the dimness of this predawn hour has become even more so. I first notice the black swirl of Big D's familiar presence only with his soft words.

"You loved her to the core of your being, didn't you?"

My body gives a slight start, but I have become familiar and knowledgeable enough with the bald truth of him and am no longer uneasy in his presence. With him, the lies I tell myself are all I need fear—or rather, my unwillingness to see them.

"Yes, you are seeking the truth here," he continues, having read my mind. "Do you still feel cheated sexually by Meg?"

I glance quickly up over my shoulder at the twin glows there, which now light my night with ruby fire. "No, hell no!" I protest. "Those are the feelings of a victim and I am no victim—not anymore."

"Then why is it you protest?" He chuckles softly, and I feel his bony knuckles nudge my shoulder. "Just what is the truth here? Of what do you still feel cheated, if not of sexual fulfillment?"

"Well, I guess it was that *she* was not sexually fulfilled by *me*."

"Guess? There you go 'guessing' again!"

"Yes, you are correct!" My words now come with conviction. "There is no guessing there. The fact that she did not take her pleasure says it clearly; she was not sexually fulfilled by me!"

"This was never about her, you know? And concerning her fulfillment? For you, that definitely is a guess." The softness in Big D's voice now grows firm. "Of what do YOU feel cheated?"

It takes me a moment before the answer coagulates with any firmness in my mind. "Emotion . . . my emotional needs were never met."

"Name them! What are these needs you had unmet."

"God! I loved her so much! I needed to feel needed." A tear falls unheeded. "Cherished,"—another lands in my lap—"even lusted after!"

I take in a deep breath and drop my head as it whooshes out. "Hell, I guess what I most needed was to believe she felt the same for me. But. . . . she didn't."

"You were all that with her."

"But I didn't feel it! She never told me . . . showed me." My voice hangs-up on the hurtful lump in my throat. "Goddammit! Why wouldn't she orgasm with me? Was that first time just a fake show?"

"No . . . you touched something special in her." The glow of Big D's gaze has softened through the blur of my tears. "But she has her own painful needs. She, too, wouldn't step past them, and you did all you could to nurture her."

"What? What do you mean?"

"She'd been hurt." The twin glows of his eyes tip to the side, and my mind is aware of unseen raised eyebrows. "Her need was to feel invulnerable to men; you know that. How could she turn emotional control of her body over to you?"

"Y-yes . . . shit! I just never saw her pain—something else she never let me see."

"So who cheated who here?" The glow flickers with a certain merriment.

"We cheated ourselves."

"Yes . . . if you choose to see it that way." The flickering of his humor has increased, and I know there is much more to understand. "What if she gave you a great gift here, in your sexuality? What would it be?"

I think aloud. "Well, it's true. In all those years, I had to seduce her every time, and I had to last longer and be more artful, creative, and spontaneous. . . ." I smile in fond memory. "I also became very familiar with the ways she liked to be touched and the things I could say and do beforehand to prepare her mood." I pause, feeling the stirring once again down low. "Yes, I'd say that I always managed to get a response, her body to mine. With or without her orgasm, I could raise her passions.

"Say it!" Big D whispers. "Say it with true appreciation!"

"Yes!" I feel it and know what he means. "Meg taught me to be a damned good lover!"

"Haven't you been told that often enough"—he chuckles softly before ending—"lately?"

If it is in my life, it is my creation. All emotional pain is created in my own mind, and always when it is dwelling in my past. Whether five seconds or five years, the event has already happened. How can it be my own creation, you ask? Why would I create such pain? The gift of our pain is in the lesson, the miss-take. It enables us to remember not to create the same mistake again. We are simply built to succeed. We cannot succeed when we are unwilling to own our pain.

Redneck Spirituality—Book One

Chapter Nineteen

Of Drippy Noses

The next two months ripped by in a frenzy of happiness. Being in fresh love is often like that for a man. My days were spent driving the countryside, seeing and experiencing many sights foreign to me—sights now colored with the essence of Meg. The land now held her beauty in its own stark, frozen way. I saw those peasants anew as they trudged from the hills, yoked with their wooden backpacks, carrying those huge bundles of sticks. Those burdens now became those of Meg's ancestors. Even the honey carts, distributing their bounty to the rice paddies, now seemed to nurture my own soul. As my truck swept past the little children on their way to school, Meg was among them. Occasionally, when one would be squatting beside the roadway relieving herself, I would briefly wonder why I could not visualize her as ever being that one. Yet, Meg was there. She was always there.

Yes, I took it all in, the bustle of the towns and cities, people hurrying about their lives. They might be on foot, or bicycle, or crammed solidly in the little kimchi busses. Everywhere there was the honking of horns—and always, I thought about Meg.

Even the smells seemed new and exciting, though not always pleasant, especially the spiciness of kimchi, so pervasive on everyone's breath. I had not acquired an immunity, but an acceptance that was no longer hard for me to do now that it was connected with Meg.

Outside, hanging forever in the icy-sharp air, was the scent of the burning charcoal, so similar to that coal smoke of Bingham Canyon. Where once that scent was associated with frozen steps and the fears of an unacceptable child, Bingham Canyon now was only a remote memory. Rather, now that smell was of Meg and of our frosty nights together, wrapped in the warmth of our love.

Often, Meg and I would stroll the village market, past the pungent, sweat-decay essence of dried fish and squids, hanging row upon row to either side. Past the meat shops, whose skinned-naked product hung grisly in the windows, always before they incited a quick tug of resentment and memories of pets from long ago. Yet with her, even gaegogi—dog meat—was somehow acceptable. Yes, I took it all in and loved it, just as I loved her.

Then there were the nights. Some were still spent in the earnest endeavor to learn karate from my silent, mutant-ninja, Korean instructor. Perhaps I learned better, given his mute, though often painful, ways.

But the other nights were spent with Meg, eating the little delicacies she cooked: batter-fried potatoes, yams, and squid; rice and thin-roasted *bulgogi* meat; deep-fried *yaki mandu* dough envelopes, holding cabbage, meat, and noodles; potato and pinched-noodle *tsujabbi* soup; thick delicious vegetable chowders spiced with curry—all of it washed down with *makkoli* or *portaju*, the wines of rice or grape. And later, there would be Meg's arms and Meg's bed. Yes, I loved it all. Army life was suddenly enjoyable.

On our weekend romps through the ville, hand in hand together, sometimes we'd take in a movie. Although I couldn't understand much of anything said, I enjoyed the movies with Meg. Koreans, as a people, seemed steeped in those dramas of past tragedies, especially those of lost love. Perhaps deprivation has been a part of their culture for too long. Did Koreans always have to suffer, even for love? It seemed so, for nearly always in their romantic movies, the hero died and the heroine lived on to a long and lonely life. Those movies seemed only to elicit tears, and always did so from Meg—and even sometimes me.

Was it an omen of our relationship to come? If so, I didn't see it. My mind had not yet fixed on the obvious, nor recognized the depth of my growing love. In the intermissions between the emotional slam-bam of reels, little kids lugged boxes of ice cream up and down the aisles, shouting "Ice kikki! Ice kikki!" I laughed as Meg haggled with them over the price, unwilling to let them cheat the GI. I did not yet understand how an "ice kikki" intermission for some provided such pitiful detachment from their lives. For them, the breaks were pleasant, unreal interludes—ice cream and candy—and then the pain of lost love must again flicker across the screen. And their lives . . . were those movies like pleasant, unreal interludes, or did they represent the pain of their real lives?

Oftentimes, we would climb the hills or visit the numerous Buddhist shrines and temples. Whenever I would pull out my camera, the little kids would gather, as if by magic, to get their picture taken. They were occasionally a nuisance to the solitude of our love, but seldom for long, for there was always such joy in their clowning and posing.

On a soul level, I knew it almost from the start. This beautiful woman, this kind, magnificent soul in whore's clothing, was the woman with whom I wanted to spend my life. Clearly, she'd only done what she had to do. It was not who she was; it was just something that happened to her. I thanked God that it did. Yet, as for our love? It would take a traditional Korean tragedy to bring out my full intention. Yes, I, too, would come to know well the deprivations of my soul. Perhaps it was necessary before I would love her in my personal space of glory. Isn't "glory" always about overcoming?

* * *

We'd been together less than three months when I first proposed to Meg. It wasn't that I hadn't thought about it, but to consider actually doing it? At the time, the thought system in place in my mind went something like this: "Yeah! Here I am, a rich American—well, American anyway. Good looking . . . lots of prospects in life . . . what young woman living in a backward country like Korea wouldn't jump at the chance to marry me? Besides, she loves me!" No, inconceivable that, should I ever actually ask her, her answer would not be a given.

Just the evening before, my CO, the company commander, gave his required monthly lecture aimed at discouraging such GI/indigenous marriages. He'd rambled on about how even the steady girls were still whores, that these marriages very seldom lasted, and that these girls were just out to use us poor GIs.

His rambles, at that point, took on an edge of raving. I could see he was certainly putting some personal energy into it. Perhaps it had more to do with his mail from home than with the welfare of us poor GIs. After all, when someone gives you five cents worth of aggravation, and you give back ten bucks in change, then you're never mad at what you think you are.

Still, I'd watched the other girls and had to admit how possibly—for some—he might have a point. I didn't see it, however, in Meg. In her, I saw a beautiful, caring woman, doing her best to survive and helping her family whenever possible.

That night, lying beside Meg, propped on one elbow, I marveled at her beauty. Thick ribbons of shining midnight framed the oval crescent of her face. The deep, red brown of her eyes was veiled by dark fans, exquisitely slanted above broad cheekbones. I could not resist the pull of her full, ripe lips and leaned forward to nuzzle them with my own.

"Meg, you are so different from any other girl I have ever known."

"Oh? How is dis so?" Meg's voice carried a note of curiosity, and something more— something hesitant, something insecure.

"Well, it's like sex!" The word drew a blank look; I continued. "You know, making love?" Still blank. "Boom-boom?"

"Ah, yes . . . I unner-stand 'boom-boom.' Yes, go on. How is like this sex?"

"Yes, well . . . back home, sex is like some kind of game. You have to say the right things, go to the right places, own the right car." Meg's look was again confused. "You know . . . a car they are proud to be seen in. And you have to spend a lot of money showing them a good time."

"You own car, Cheff?" Meg seemed overwhelmed with all I had said.

"Yeah, sure, everyone does back home." She seemed dazed by the thought. "The point is, you have to pay the price . . . you have to make girls proud to be seen with you before they will make love."

"Oh, I ol-ways proud be seen wit chu, Cheff. You belly pretty mans!"

Her quick hug brought a warmth to my heart. I knew her words were sincere and kissed her long and hard in response. Yet afterwards, there stood a pensive silence between us, and I could tell she was chewing inwardly on something. Finally, it bubbled forth. "Cheff, is it not the same here . . . wit me?"

"What! What do you mean?"

"Well, don't you ol-ways spend moneys . . . show me good time?"

"Yes, but it's no big deal. . . ."

"Well, don't you ol-ways pays the price?" I had no idea what she meant, and my confusion left me without words. "Don't you ol-ways pays me every months?" Meg finished, a look of shame twisting her pretty features.

"No! Meg, it's not the same." I looked into her eyes and saw she wanted to believe me, but didn't. "What I have with you feels so good . . . I . . . well, I don't ever want it to end."

Still, her look said she didn't believe me, but something in me suddenly snapped. My God! *I believed it—every word.* Turning to her in earnest determination, I said something totally unexpected by either of us.

"Meg, will you marry me?"

She didn't answer right away. Whatever reactions I might have expected didn't happen. Instead, she looked down for a moment and seemed, if anything, even more confused and unhappy. I could see there was a battle raging inside her pretty head. Then she simply said, "No."

"N-n-no?" I stared at her, my mouth hanging open. My pride, my vanity, my deepest feelings, all now flattened out—smashed like a big-assed June bug across a windshield. How could she refuse so simply and flatly as that?

"W-w-why?"

Meg didn't answer, and after a long moment of silence, I laid back, suddenly alone and confused, on my side of the bed. It seemed inconceivable she would not want me. Did she, too, not feel this sense of absolute joy in just being with me? Apparently not! My God! How was it possible I had read her so wrong? Finally, she rolled over close, and I could hear the tears in her voice as she touched my cheek with real regret.

"I no wanna leef Korea . . . habba famaree here . . . send famaree money . . . I help."

"I can help them . . . just as soon as I get out of the army and have a good job. Why, we can help them together. We—"

"Famaree need me now," interrupted her simple reply.

I held my own reply. The thought that I could support her—nothing this side of hell would stop me—but her whole family? That was not something I could shift into. That reality wasn't within my realm of conception. Wrapping my head around taking on a wife was never conceivable before Meg. Still, a part of me was glad for her rejection, and another part of me now knew a sorrow it had never known. Such is the difference between the heart and the ego: one's love and one's fear. My heart knew no such fear, but my ego. . . .

I tried. Over the next few weeks, I tried to change her mind, but no amount of logic would dissuade her. Why did she have to help her family? She had so little now, and besides, wasn't she the child? And her family—the family who did not even acknowledge her, this "dirty GI whore?"

And me? In my mind, they were not my responsibility. Yet, perhaps they had to be, for Meg saw them as hers. It took that next month for the lesson to come home in full maturity.

* * *

It was cold that morning. The fuel oil can for the stove in our Quonset hut once again had run dry. I threw back the OD green army blanket and sat for a brief moment, shivering on the side of my bunk. Then, as I reached for my fatigues, there came a sudden realization that the end of my pecker was much colder than the rest of me. Looking down at my shorts, my jaw dropped with the discovery of some ugly, yellow stains.

Later that morning, I was processed through with the rest of the drippy dicks, also reporting to the Med for sick call. Eventually handed a little plastic cup and a glass slide, I was told to wipe the ooze off on the slide and then to take a leak, saving the first spurt in the cup. While turning to leave, I noticed that the slide was crusted with stains already. I turned back to the sergeant, interrupting his instructions to the next in line. "Hey Sarge, this slide's got crud on it! Can I have another one?"

Now, though army latrines generally don't have stalls, the army does have ranks. There are some people who, if their rank is higher, you just don't shit with—not in any manner. This was one. Clenched knuckles propped his upper body as he leaned across the table and told me in more understandable terms.

"Get your sorry ass, and your leaky dick, into the latrine." He paused, leaning farther until his nose almost touched mine. His next words were machine-gunned loudly, "And—do—as—ordered, soldier!"

I did as ordered. Fifteen minutes later, the sergeant read from a list and issued further orders. "The following men form a line before that door! You will be issued your first of three VD shots." As he read down his list, I noticed a funny thing: No one, it seemed, had lucked out.

I knew that every GI has the right to see a doctor, and though knowing it wasn't wise, I requested one anyway. The doctor didn't seem to have a much better disposition than had the sergeant. He sat there at his desk, polishing his captain's bars, and managed to look up at me, down his nose. After listening to my explanation about the dirty slide, he sneered, "So what makes you think you don't have gonorrhea?"

Keeping a straight face, I lied through my teeth. "Sir, I haven't had a woman in over two weeks."

I should have known better. He handed me a petri dish and said, "Okay, put some discharge in this."

Now, there hadn't been all that much discharge, and besides, I'd just taken a leak. No matter how much yanking and milking I did, standing there in front of his desk, I couldn't produce. This seemed to please him immensely. He stood up and shrugged into a white lab coat complete with captain's bars. Picking up a rubber glove, he said with a grin, "Okay, drop 'em and bend over."

I didn't feel good about the grin, nor the gleam in his eye, as he watched his hand slide into that glove. When he crooked his index finger and the grin widened, I knew I was in trouble. Reluctantly, I did as told while he opened a jar of Vaseline and took a generous gob. Without adieu, his finger stabbed, then latched on to my prostate as if it were a bow string. TWANG! With a hoarse yelp, I headed for the ceiling. I produced. I really produced!

As he snapped the lid over the petri, his eyes reflected the ice of his tone. "This culture will be ready in three days, and it better be negative. Now get your slimy ass out of my office and take your shot!"

A little shaken at the implications of my lie, there was again a vague sense of dread in me as I took my place at the end of the shot line. Remembering Kimpo, this one, indeed, felt like some weird deja vu treadmill as the guy in front of me, now finally taking the needle, fainted out, dead cold. Thrashing over the screen, he headed toward the floor. The obviously inexperienced Korean Katusa medic, still holding the syringe, went with him. With a yelp from the Katusa, all ended in a clattering heap. If they were generous with the gamma globulin at the airport, they were no less so with the penicillin.

* * *

The next two weeks, I was restricted to the compound and had to take that horse shot every day for three days. They gave me some red pills that set me to pissing in psychedelic orange. If, indeed, it was the clap, it must have been a very light case. I wasn't ripping the pipes off the latrine walls every time I took a leak—not like some of the other guys.

Later that first day, I arranged to see Meg at the fence. Looking at her through the chain link was one of the saddest, hardest things I've ever faced. She was unable to look me in the eye. I could not keep the quiver out of my voice as I passed her one final gift. "Here, take this money. You need to get yourself checked out for VD."

"I did . . . I hord . . . I go doctor . . . check out. I no habba BD!" Her tone sounded truthful, though guilty.

I insisted. "I do. Take the shots anyway." Then I added sadly, "You know"—I paused to swallow the hurtful lump before continuing—"I didn't butterfly on you. There's only been you." It was true, and I knew she knew it. Then I asked, my voice cracking, "Why, Meg?"

For a long time, she wouldn't look at me. Finally, her eyes rose, deep wells of agony, "It oly wonz . . . oly wonz rieutenant."

My eyes did not waver from her face. I could see the tears on her beautiful eyelashes as hers again studied an unseen ground. I sighed, then again choked back that persistent knot in my throat. "You know I won't see you anymore." There didn't seem to be anything more to say except "goodbye."

I turned, and as I walked away, there were tears in my own eyes.

* * *

The third day, when I reported for my final penicillin shot, I again requested the doctor. After waiting for about an hour in the regulation army waiting line, the medic ushered me into his office. I came to attention in front of his desk and saluting, said, "Sir, Specialist Williams; I'm here requesting the results of my culture test." Casually, he waved me back a salute. Then, looking at me distastefully over his steepled fingers, he smirked. "Ya can't have it. The incubator overheated and burned it up." He grinned briefly at my look, then waved his hand as if dismissing me.

I ignored the wave. Although I had no desire to sharpen his archery skills, I persisted. "Sir, I'd just like to know the truth. Can I take another culture test?"

One side of his mouth lifted in a grimace, and his tone as he replied was aimed a non-com moron. "Look, you've just taken several million units of penicillin over the past three days. Whatever was there is gone now. I won't waste my time making another culture." He was right. Leaving his office, I realized I'd never know.

~ *Looking Back* ~

I had my suspicions about that culture and since have learned to live with them. Still, in reality, those suspicions were just an excuse—a cover—something to focus my mind on so that I wouldn't have to look at the real issue: I'd contracted some form of venereal disease from Meg. It didn't matter if it was a NSB (non-specific bacteria), a simple urinary infection, or if it was the clap (gonorrhea). It was still a VD, and it was in my life. Yes, Meg had cheated—so easy to blame her for it all, weep in my beer, and just move on. But the real issue, the one I was avoiding—couldn't even see—was pretty simple: How did I create venereal disease in my life? Of course back then, I wasn't big on accepting responsibility for my life. The words in my mind went more like, "Why me? Why me and my Meg?"

Yes, now I can see. Like some typical Korean romance movie, Meg had set herself, and our love, up for martyrdom. And I'd played my part oh so well. But exactly what were the parts? I didn't then see them, but I was about to.

Yes, my creation here in the landscape of my life was about to be drilled home. In it, I would learn something about forgiveness; and in it, too, I would accept the lesson—and gift—of this experience.

Ah, shit! Even still, over thirty years later, I resist why it had to be so—the typical Korean tragedy. Yet, I know it was all perfect. I am who I am because of it all. Still, sometimes in my memory, while dwelling on the death of a place called yesterday, I just want to hold her and thank her for her gifts, just once more—again.

~ *In the Present with Big D* ~

Another chapter is over, and I sit here before this glowing screen. Again, it is in the dark of the early morning. Knowing that in five short hours I will leave for another day of turning wrenches, I feel a growing tension in the back of my neck. It seems to match the lump again in my throat. Yes, again—and after so many years.

Sitting back into my chair, I take a deep, cleansing breath and drop naturally into my meditative state. The lump dissolves, yet the tension has increased. Now it turns to a bony massaging—hard, yet gentle.

"Big D! I did not know if you would come."

"Yes, I'm here."

"What have you to say? What have I missed?" My eyes flutter open.

"Shush now." My eyelids suddenly feel so heavy, too heavy to remain open. "It is well you are beginning more and more to mentor yourself. Not many men would be willing to look at their own responsibility in what happened. You're getting the gifts of Meg's lessons here in spades. But what you no longer have and need now"— he pauses as his bony digits pinch out the tension from a particularly tight muscle—"is love."

I can barely hear his words now, yet it doesn't seem to matter. A warmth is spreading outward from the steady kneading of his hands upon my shoulders—so steady, for a time it seems to encompass me within a cocoon of contentment until, eventually, it merges with an insistent buzzing from somewhere off in the distance. As my eyes open to the light of day, my body is feeling surprisingly refreshed. From the bedroom in the back of the house, the clock alarm still sounds its message, heralding another day of repairing cars. And in the back of my mind, I question how much longer I will heed it.

The greatest gifts life teaches us are nearly always the most painful. When you are finished with choosing the pain, then look for the joy in the lesson. It is there in balance.
Redneck Spirituality—Book One

Chapter Twenty

"I Boom-Boom Oly You"

My mood was no better than the gray overcast that day as I slouched, bar to bar, through the Ville with my buddies, Les and Crip. Those two weeks on restriction were long and miserable, and though now past, I found I was not much happier. My sullen hands were crammed into the warmth of my pockets, only escaping this day for an occasional beer. Now, trudging through the muddy grit between establishments, the misting rain threatened to seep through the ever-darkening green of my Class A uniform, and I was sorry I'd not worn my overcoat. The nerves of my anger abruptly tightened a notch with the intrusion of a rasping hiss from near my elbow.

"Hey, GI, you wan see live sex show?" The man was in his mid-twenties, scruffy, with a porcupine-looking haircut.

Caught off guard, I flinched slightly and resisted my impulse to roundhouse kick his pimply Korean butt into next year. Instead, I casually brushed my hip pocket, checking for the presence of my wallet. It was still there. Glancing down, I noticed the unmistakable, lumpy, first two knuckles of a karate expert and knew his teacher hadn't been blowing smoke and selling belts. The way my life was going, had I given in to the darkness of my mood, he'd likely have wiped this alley with my sorry butt. "Oh, Christ," I growled. "Get lost!"

"No get lost," he continued, unruffled. "Belly good show. Oly two hunna Won (about seventy-four cents) . . . two gorl . . . maybe you wan gorl after . . . *can channa*!"

Knuckles or not, the temptation was back. If I hit him fast and hard . . . well, I was bigger and stronger. Les broke in, "Hey! Why not?"

Crip followed with, "Shit, let's check 'em out."

Urgh! I groaned inwardly, but outvoted, deferred. "Oh hell, why not?" I shook my head, wondering why I felt so uncharacteristically aggressive. With my attitude, I knew I'd be lucky to get back to the compound without first getting stuck with someone's knife. Funny thing—for the first time in my life, I didn't really give a shit!

The show was worse than expected. All four of us sat crowded on rickety, beat up, old chairs around a bed, which took up most of the space in the back-alley hootch. Two rather unimpressive women had been sitting on the bed, talking, as we'd entered. Cutting their conversation almost mid-sentence, they stood and with silent, practiced efficiency, shucked their bras and panties. Climbing onto the bed, they immediately launched into a mechanical pantomime of oral sex—something most Koreans considered as being totally filthy and depraved. In the close confines of the room, it was obvious they were not making contact—just getting close and making lots of noises while hiding behind shoulders, hair, and thighs. The pimp fairly squirmed in his chair with nervous excitement. The satisfied grin on his face almost seemed to say, "There, I created this. It's right on the leading edge of moral depravity. Man, we're really giving these GIs what they want to see!"

Me? I just sat there, my chin in hand, and heaved a sigh, idly wondering if my day would feel any better if I switched to drinking Korean Gin—or weed. Now that would be a first for me.

"Shit! I want to see the real thing." Crip said, and suddenly lunged forward. Grabbing the one on top by the back of her head, he fairly buried it between the other's legs. She came up hacking, spitting, and screeching in rage. We all three began laughing so hard that tears ran down our faces. Slapping him on the back in hilarious appreciation, we left amidst a hail of objects being thrown by the two raging women. The pimp was already gone. He, too, had known when to leave.

We didn't go far—less than a block—before choosing a bar at random and going in. As usual, our butts were barely on the chairs when there were three bar girls at our elbows, batting phony eyelashes and demanding drinks. We ordered up three OBs (Oriental Brewery beers) and whatever whiskey (tea) the girls were drinking. They waited only long enough for the drinks to come before making the usual "You wan go boom-boom?" pitch. Les, whose hands had been busy, stood up, revealing a crotch that appeared suddenly to contain something resembling an Idaho spud. He and his girl quickly disappeared together into the back, both groping their obvious connection.

Crip just said, "No, Baby-san . . . not interested." His girl quickly left and was replaced by another. I merely shrugged and shook my head, yet mine stayed, sitting next to me, quietly sipping her tea and watching me. I ignored her.

Crip seemed to find the new girl more to his liking. They sucked one another's lips only a few minutes before leaving. I remained sitting there in silence, drinking my beer. The girl finished her "whiskey" and asked for more. I would have refused, but I knew she'd just be replaced by someone else until they'd all had a whack at me. A few beers to fill the emptiness was all I wanted, and having them peacefully was preferable to making an ass out of myself. Anyway, the company was quite attractive, and I felt comfortable enough just sitting there with her. It was during the middle of the day and the place was slow. Even the jukebox in the corner was turned down low. Quietly, the girl began to talk.

"You no likee me?"

"Yes, you're very pretty."

That brought a smile, but she cocked her head, a look of speculation on her face. "Maybe you likee boy instead? Is okay . . . can channa."

"No, I likee you just fine," I assured her, perhaps too quickly, for her grin widened, and I knew she'd been toying with me. "Look . . . I just no want boom-boom right now."

"How you likee steady me?" she asked, moving in closer. "I likee you. You belly pwitty."

I was about to blow her off, but something in the intensity of her eyes stopped me. Out of curiosity, I asked, "How much?"

"Seek-sty MPC," she replied quickly, a hopeful smile brightening and erasing some of the harsh experience from her pretty face. Her eyebrows were raised with unexpected expectancy.

I chuckled, not really interested. In the pay line each month, when those cheap-looking substitute dollars were finally counted into my hand, they amounted to only eighty-nine Military Payment Coupons. Still charmed by the vulnerability beneath her brazen words, and at the same time touched by the sadness of her life, I continued the charade. "Hah . . . no way! Thirty is the going rate."

"Tirty! No can leef tirty MPC!" Her studied indignance dropped then, and in a nonchalant voice, she continued. "But is okay, I steady you tirty—oly boom-boom on side." She paused a moment for effect as her hands stroked the muscles of my arm. "For forty-fibe MPC, I boom-boom oly you."

My head snapped up, and the beer slipped unnoticed from a nerveless hand. My chair, which had been unconsciously tipped back against the wall, thumped solidly back onto all four legs. My mind screamed out in silent, frustrated accusation. *You dumb shit! What did you expect? You cheap-ass-dumb-fucking . . . shit!*

Hoisting my sagging jaw, I lunged to my feet. The girl was wiping at the beer stains on her dress and cursing under her breath. Only murder now showed in her eyes. I fumbled a bill out of my wallet—a ten—and pressed it into her hand, feeling a small satisfaction in knowing it was her cut of several days fucking that she wouldn't have to share with the establishment. Then, grabbing both sides of her face, I slapped a wet one on her forehead. She stood, gaping, as I ran out the door.

Although it was about a mile and a half, I didn't stop until I reached Meg's hootch. She was there and, to my immense relief, was alone. I must have looked insane—a man possessed—all sweaty and disheveled, pounding on her little, wooden-framed paper door, panting and wheezing out her name.

Upon opening it, Meg stared, speechless, her forehead wrinkled with concern. Eventually, I caught my breath enough to manage the question that burned within, "Do you still"—gasp, choke, cough—"want to steady me?" Her face lit and with a squeal, she threw her arms around my neck in answer. I collapsed back onto the porch, Meg in my arms, and me, just loving her.

When my heartbeat finally steadied, I laid it all out: How I would start giving her at least forty-five MPCs a month, and sometimes more, whenever I could. Then, losing myself in the richness of her eyes, I told her what my heart had ached these past weeks to say.

"Meg, I still want to marry you . . . if you want me."

Her eager arms flew around my neck. "Yes, I wan marry witt chu, too!"

* * *

No matter my joy, no matter how suddenly *right* my world was around me, there was still the army. The next day, I made an appointment with the chaplain. It was the first of a long line of requirements to marry a Korean National. The chaplain gave me an appointment. Then, upon learning my reason behind it, he changed it for one several days later. When it eventually happened, for him it meant only giving me a lecture.

Sitting there in a too-small, straight-backed chair, fatigue hat in hands, I listened until finally he finished with, "C'mon, Son, you know that what these girls here do is unclean in God's eyes. They're just whores, every one. You don't want to take someone like that home to meet your momma and daddy, now do you, Son?"

I stared at the disdainful curl of his lips and concentrated on keeping the fists, now twisting my hat beneath the cover of his desk, from flying the distance between. He was a "man of God" and an army officer, so I gave him my required respect in silence—a silence that now stretched a longer moment than it seemed he was comfortable with. He added, "Well? What do you say, Son?"

Against all I knew of the army, I replied, "Sir, do you want my honest opinion, man-to-man . . . you know, 'off the record?'"

"You can always speak honestly with me, Son."

"Sir, I don't believe your God is the same one I believe in."

"There is only one God, Son." He said it with all the assurance of a department store Santa defending Christmas.

"No sir!" I was finished playing his game. "My God sees the love Meg and I hold for one another and blesses us for it—even glories in it! Whatever she's had to do, it's no worse than I would have done. My parents will accept her if they will accept me."

"Well, that may be so"—his tone now held a brittle quality, like icicles poised to drop—"but you're going to find that the army takes a dim view of its soldiers marrying foreign prostitutes. This will ruin your career!"

For a long, surreal moment, our eyes remained locked. I resisted the impulse to laugh, then broke the silence. "Sir, are we really off the record here?"

"I said it, didn't I?" His eyes bulged slightly and a jaw muscle clenched as he thrust his face expectantly toward mine.

"Sir, I don't intend to re-up. I was drafted into this shithole, and I think the army sucks just as badly as does your God."

There was dead silence, except for a slight grinding of teeth and the sound of a knuckle popping from where whitened hands gripped his desk. Again, we stared in silent inflexibility over his ornate, black-enameled, personalized desk plate. Carved and inlayed in Korean mother-of-pearl, it read: Cpt. Don Kharibet, Chaplain - 7th Inf. Battalion, Camp Casey, Korea. Somehow it seemed way out of place, what with the spartan military furnishings—the simple, useful desks, chairs, and filing cabinets of this office building.

Yet, it was no more so than the look on his face just now, compared to the title "Chaplain" behind his name, carved out in mother-of-pearl splendor across its face. Finally, he ended the interview, his words hissing through clenched teeth. "Well, it doesn't matter. It will take at least ten to twelve months for the paperwork, and you don't have that long!" There were only seven and a half months left in my tour.

* * *

I left his office, shaken. This was not my view of life, liberty, and the pursuit of happiness—God and country and all that shit. Where were the freedoms I'd always believed were mine? It was then I began to question it all, to feel personally, the truth of it all. The war was in full rage in Vietnam, and so many of its veterans—people I rubbed shoulders with daily—seemed so bitter. It was then that I began to understand why some heroes' medals ended up in trash cans. This was what it felt like to watch one's country shit on all it said it held sacred.

True, I had fought in no battles and had been given no heroes' medals. But in just answering my country's call, I, too, had offered up my very life. Still, bad as his might smell, nothing justified my leaving my stench in that chaplain's office. Yet, my stink with him carried no substance; mine held no power over his life.

Nor had I then understood anything about Spiritual Law— especially this particular one, which I was breaking: ***"The energy out returns in kind."*** I would yet smell the return of the essence of my shit, just as, eventually, my country would hers.

That day I thought a lot about Spec Five Jennings back at Fort Carson, about the army's glorious description of his heroic action that had earned him his Bronze Star—the same one I watched him fling into the trash. I'd retrieved it, thinking he'd want it back sometime. I had kept it for him, even after he'd tried later to explain it all to me.

"Jesus, Jennings!" I'd said. "I get it that the army sucks, but don't you feel you've earned that medal?"

"Son," he'd replied. He was only about ten months, plus a century or so older. "You just wouldn't, no, you *can't*, fucking understand. I've seen men with their bodies blown to shit; seen 'em dragging their intestines through the mud; seen 'em tryin' to stuff 'em back into their bodies with hands that ain't much there anymore. I've smelled the stench of guts and gun smoke, heard them screamin'—screamin' such that just hung in your ear and couldn't never be drowned out by exploding mortars or the gunfire.

"No . . ." He paused to take in a deep, shuddering breath, his eyes clouded by some inner terror. "It ain't me that don't deserve. Shit! You just can't understand! You never been there."   He was right. Back then, I couldn't understand his words, nor the hurricane I saw in his eyes as his voice broke just before he stalked off. It wasn't anything I hadn't heard in nearly every B-grade war movie I'd ever seen. Except this was real—right here in my life! Hopefully, I'll never know the full truth of it—not as he did.

But now I was beginning to get an inkling. I understood how it was never about his deserving, or even the deserving of those now dead. I now saw, and agreed, my country didn't deserve them wearing those medals and glorifying this fucking war.

What I did not yet see was on an even deeper level—the survivor level. This deserving man's refusal to wear his medals was much more personal. Indeed, it was more than just deserving; it was about believing he deserved to be alive while his fellow comrades were dead.

And now, there was I, no longer believing in this man's army for the reasons I'd thought. It was *not* about me "fighting for freedom." Rather, it was simply about my country's control over another that I questioned, as did I question my own place in it all. If North Korea jumped the line, we had the nukes to handle it—and we'd surely use them. We'd have to, or they would get them.

So why was I here if not as a hostage? Battle fodder, just one of the thousands of American soldiers whose blood and guts and unlived dreams were the price someone "in power" was willing to pay to be right when they used those nukes. Oh, they'd be used, all right—in the name of protecting me. But likely, I'd be dead by that time.

Vietnam? That was different. Vietnam crept up behind the bastions of our country's ego. We died over there for the same stupid reasons—just that the body count had risen slowly and was at an acceptable hundred or so a week. Would it ever reach that critically unacceptable point? Likely not. There was just too much money to be made by all those corporate bastards selling munitions and such to the government—the same one whose officials they owned.

Control! Money! Certainly not freedom: That's what my country was all about. And control is just someone asserting their need to be right. Hell! Now I had this chaplain, and my CO, both telling me they were right—and that they knew what was right for me also. They didn't even want to extend me the freedom of choosing the woman I would marry. The constitution required it, but the army had its ways. Still, beneath all my self-righteous anger, I had no real reason to whine. The army did not have my squirrelly ass in Vietnam—dying. And me? I didn't even pause to wonder why.

* * *

That evening, back at the Quonset hut, I took Jennings' Bronze Star out of my footlocker. I understood now why he'd never want it back. In solemn respect for him, I placed it again into the trash.

As for the chaplain—he would not be the first "man of God" to tell lies for the sake of what he thought was right. So I checked with a couple of guys who were already married to Korean Nationals. They told me that ". . . No, you can cut the time to less than seven months if you have the money to grease a few palms—and if you can get your CO and the chaplain to back you."

Time, money, the CO, the chaplain . . . clearly, I would be starting with four strikes against me. Still, I did not stop checking until I'd found a viable way. Then I went to tell Meg the good and bad news.

* * *

She met me at the courtyard gate, the champagne essence of joy. Saying she had something to show me, she took my hand and, on dancing feet, urged me across the courtyard. As usual, we shucked our shoes on the porch. Then she slid back the door, and with a grand flourish of an arm, indicated for me to enter.

There, against the far wall, sat a shiny, black-enameled stereo cabinet. Like the chaplain's plaque, it was adorned with those typically Korean mother-of-pearl inlaid carvings. Beautiful!—though it was not the most ornate one I'd ever seen. Actually, it was a little on the plain side as such things went. But Meg was so proud as she lifted the lid and started Jim Reeves singing, "Please Release Me."

"Oh God . . ." I knew how much she loved music. "We can't afford this, honey."

Non-perturbed, she answered, "Oh, yes, is only ninety MPCs—feefteen now, ten one mos."

Sitting on the floor, I told her about the chaplain and what I'd found out that day—how I'd still marry her, only we'd have to wait until after I got out of the army. Then it would be just a matter of a background check made by the US Embassy and signing some papers. I explained that I'd come back after the check was done, marry her, and then she would only have to wait for her visa.

But it would all take time. She'd need money to live on from the time I left Korea until I could get a job and send more. She'd be staying with her parents, who now believed she worked for the Americans at the PX. And of course, I promised her that when we were settled back home, we'd help them, too.

"Honey, I know how you love this stereo, and you can have it if you want. I just don't know how we can do both. You need to decide."

Her eyelashes glistened as she gazed at its mother-of-pearl wonder. As she played her single record over and over that night, her hands lingered lovingly on its shiny surface. She wanted that stereo badly. And she wanted me. Soon the stereo was gone.

~ In the Present with Big D ~

A soft chuckle interrupts my reverie as I consider why the ending of this chapter doesn't feel right. Am I leaving out something important—something of which I don't want to look? Big D answers for me, speaking my thoughts aloud. "Yes, you certainly had a hard-on toward authority. You never liked others trying to control your life, did you? Has that changed much?"

"Yes and no," I answer. "Everyone has a natural resentment to those who believe they know more about how to run our lives than we do."

"Ah, then how is it you are different now?" There comes a momentary flash of iridescent colors as he dips his head into my monitor's screen. "I don't see it anywhere in here."

"Well, I am different!"

"How? Tell me exactly how."

Looking at him now, in the light of this day, he appears as an indistinct, sooty fog. Amidst a glimmering skull of bone, his dark eye sockets host two dim red glows. Confusion reigns, and in that dumb silence, there erupts a burst of scarlet laser, nearly blinding me.

"Focus up!" Though I can no longer see him, Big D's voice is anything but indistinct. "Much depends on what you say. And yes! I am the only ultimate authority over you. Just remember, I am a part of you; and like you, I am God—only consciously closer. Don't minimize or resent me."

"Yes, yes! N-no! . . . I mean, I will focus . . . a-and I won't resent you!" My mind is working frantically. I know that whatever I say, it must be the truth. "I . . . uh . . . I seldom now resist the judgments of others when they make themselves superior and me wrong in their minds."

"Yes, that's true," he answers. "You respect that it is their right to be 'right' in their own minds. What else?"

"I've learned to respond to those in authority in ways that serve me best."

"Wise move. Anger seldom serves there," Big D acknowledges. "What else?"

"Well, I've stopped trying to be accepted by every control freak in my life. I now see the resentment it once incited in me."

"Ah, yes! That's about not playing your part in their game." Big D's laugh sounds a little hollow. "Very liberating, isn't it?"

"Yes."

"You don't sound so liberated," he prompts.

"Well, the price has been costly."

"Yes? Tell me . . ."

"Some of those control freaks were those I loved the most in life." My answer now sounds hollow, even to my own ears. "They have all gone from me now."

"Yes, I know you loved them." My eyesight is beginning to come back, though with a heavy glistening. "Do you think they loved you?"

"Yes. They loved me the best they knew, but—"

"'But?'" comes Big D's perplexed reply. "You know how 'but' always negates everything said before it. What is the truth?"

"It doesn't look like love so much to me. It looks like control."

"What did it look like back then?" he continues.

I know he is going somewhere with this. "Well, I thought it was love back then."

"Then you've changed there, too? Does this mean they taught you how to love?"

"Why, yes! You could say that." I remember my mother and answer with some understanding, though cautiously, knowing he has not yet made his point. "It has helped in just knowing what love isn't."

"Then why all the pain? Why won't you just let them go with love and appreciation?" Big D's eyes drill me anew with ruby brilliance. "Don't you know that you always loved them far better than they loved you? And still, it was they who taught you about love."

"I don't understand . . ."

"You still don't get it?" He sighs before going on. "The only requirement of love is that it be given: Love never requires a return."

"What?"

"Look!" Big D shouts his impatience, and I am immediately aware that his anger can only be about some dishonesty or avoidance in me. "Love's true gift is always given to the giver and always by the giver. You give to yourself the feelings you want to feel about them. Love's about you; it ain't about them!" His words pierce me, and though I am not completely clear of their meaning, I know I soon will be. "Think of it this way." He throws a hand up, as if to shift to a new track. "How do you feel about spending all those years with Meg?"

"I loved it! I would not trade my having loved her for anything."

"Now, read back the last line of this chapter."

"'Soon the stereo was gone.'" My quote is answered only by silence. "So?"

"So how did it read the first time you wrote it?"

"It said, 'The next day, the stereo was gone.'"

"Wasn't true, was it?" There is a certain mockery in Big D's voice.

"Well, no . . . that's why I changed it." Somehow I feel defensive.

"Is it true now?"

"Well, yeah . . ."

"Really?" The very force of this single word nearly bowls me over. "How long was it . . . really?"

"T-two weeks."

"Well, now"—Big D shows his piano-key smile—"that sort of places you a distant second to Meg's need to please her parents, and just a slight scrape before her need to own that stereo, doesn't it?"

"Yeah, you could say that." I want with all my heart to deny it.

He continues. "Did this position change that much during your marriage?"

I consider his question a long time before answering, "No. I don't think so."

"Now, I ask you again: How do you feel about spending all those years with Meg?"

My words ring clear, and honest. "I still would not trade my having loved her for anything!"

"Woo-hoo . . . exactly so!" He bats my shoulder with a xylophone fist. "Now that . . . is the true essence of love!"

I can only grin, not clear where this is all going.

"And what of the woman you are with this day?" His gaze narrows in speculation, and I hear humor in his next words. "How do you stand with her?"

My mind comes back to the present—to her aqua eyes and the way I feel when I hold her in my arms—and then the scent. . . . It lingers pervasively on her breath. My answer cuts to the heart in honesty. "I run a distant second to her addiction: She is an alcoholic."

"Do you love her?"

"Yes."

"Enough so that you have addressed it honestly with her?"

"Yes."

"And . . ."

"And she hides it from me." I say it without any special energy. "Her drinking is a fact—one I have accepted she will not change."

"Would you spend the next twenty-five years with her?"

"No."

"Why not?"

I pause a moment, gathering my thoughts. "I want a woman who will love me as I love her—and love herself as I love me." I search for the words to clarify. "I deserve it! You know . . . equal love and equal honesty. . ."

"Ah!" Big D flings out one bony hand in mock surprise. "Then this, too, has changed. Is it possible that this is the underlying truth about love—the real truth that Meg has taught you?"

"Whadda-ya mean?"

Big D discerns my confusion. Though invisible, my mind's eye sees his lips draw back into a grim smile, fully knowing how confusion is the manner in which I often keep myself from seeing the truth. Strangely, he is not angry. His next words resonate in gentle empathy. "Loving and being loved has always been a hard one for you. You've never known another human being who was capable of teaching it to you in an open, honest, and giving way. It is for this reason that I will tell you this one, straight out."

Like Moses just descended from the mountain, he draws himself up before me. Cradled now, in the crook of one robed arm, is a stone tablet. The tip of his sickle arcs electric blue amidst a shower of sparks. These words it leaves in blood-red, molten slag:

Before one can love another, one must
first love one's self above all.

He looks up from his dramatic handiwork, and before continuing, asserts, "This you already know well, but there is more."

Before then, love is only need.

He pauses a long moment, as the words solidify indelibly upon the slab of my consciousness. Then, with a grin, he adds another postscript:

And like truth, love cannot exist
alongside dishonesty.

I look on in speechless appreciation. The truth in his words is matched only with his dramatic flair in their delivery. He chuckles once and squats down, the tablet has disappeared, and both hands now clasp the handle of his sickle as he leans forward comfortably upon it. His voice now is one of casual conversation.

"There is nothing I tell you here that you have not already learned. It took you those many years of loving Meg, and also these present short months of loving this new woman, to teach you all this. I have done nothing but cut through the confusion and clarify it in your consciousness."

"Yes."

"So, Jeff, you love yourself now. And you know what the truth is here concerning this new woman. . . ."

"Yes, Big D."

"Love her well this night, and tell her what she has done for you. Cherish her for it, before you go."

"She may not understand—"

"Doesn't matter; her soul will know. Love is not a conscious thing. And you, by your example, are exactly what she needs should she ever want to change her great neediness for something more."

When you want to hurt someone—when you want revenge—ask yourself: Is this what I would want to do if he were me? What if I were really doing this to me? For he is you, you know? And I am, too. You're hurting all of us. Like love, hurt is a feeling we give to ourselves. It, too, has nothing to do with others. And it, too, is felt by all. On that level beyond consciousness, we are all one and the same.

Redneck Spirituality—Book Two

Chapter Twenty-One

Hi-Ho, Fuck the Army

Perhaps the hardest lesson in the making of a man is that of forgiving his loved ones for being human. Is there anything that can make such learning any easier? For me, the answer was yes. I had already come to understand that my life, and the lives of those I loved, were all held in the hands of madmen. In the seeming helplessness of that, forgiving Meg was something I could do. It was my decision in taking back control of my life, to live my way—at least in the time I had while those madmen were deciding if my life would end in the name of freedom.

A step backward in time might be in order here. There were three events that happened in Korea shortly after I arrived and before I met Meg. They shook my world—in fact, they shook the whole world.

The North Koreans were in the habit of sending agents south to do dirty tricks. However, the South Korean people had their number. They were wise to the ways of the North and were not sympathetic. Even in a country of so many people, the agents of the North stuck out like bulls in rut. The two Koreas had been segregated so long that the idioms of speech had changed—something the communists didn't seem to know. They were easily spotted because they "talked funny." They'd been taught to expect their ". . . poor, oppressed comrades to the South" would welcome them, that they would believe them to be heroes in the fight against the ". . . oppressive capitalist Americans" and their "corrupt lackeys" in the South Korean government.

Though extreme, it was not out of character when on January 21, 1968, thirty-one North Korean commandos made an attempt to assassinate South Korea's President, Pak Chung Hee, at his residence in the Blue House at Seoul. Tongduchon was in direct line with the route between Seoul and the DMZ. So of course, when the incident happened, we were put on yellow alert. Most of the North Korean agents involved were gathered up within the first few days following the attempt. The South Korean interrogation techniques soon revealed the full details. Of course, once it all became known, the remaining few unsecured agents were of no further use, and upon capture were, in effect, dealt with on the spot. Just two days after that failed attempt, "Glorious Father" Kim Il-sung of North Korea had another orgasm of insanity.

It was late afternoon when our CO called a company formation—very unusual. I stood in line with the others as he explained the dilemma. He began in his most officious voice, though it seemed to quaver at times.

"Men, we are now on red alert. The North Koreans have just taken one of our intelligence-gathering ships in international waters off the coast. Given their attempt to assassinate South Korea's President two days ago, and the fact that intelligence shows their troops are massing at the DMZ, it appears we are all in for a shitstorm." He stopped to take a shaky breath, then continued. "Platoon sergeants will instruct you on preparations to bug out. Small arms will be dispensed according to platoon, beginning with 1st Platoon." Again, he paused and cleared his throat. "Men, sometime during the next day, you may want to pray. Platoon sergeants . . . huh-uhhh . . . take over!" After the clearing of his throat, that last word was more of a croak. Then, with a salute and an about-face, he strode off.

"First Platoon . . . fall out to the arms room!" Sergeant Slocum, my platoon sergeant, ordered.

"Second Platoon . . ." Sergeant Jennings began his own orders as we in 1st Platoon headed out. At the arms room, Sergeant Slocum issued further orders before we processed in line. "Once you draw weapons, report to me at the motor pool." Then, stopping next to me near the end of the line, he issued me my orders. "Williams, once you have your weapon, locate Sergeant Jennings and tell him it's 2nd Platoon's turn."

Supply and Transport battalions normally worked from a rear echelon base. However, also being only 25 klicks—less than 16 miles—from the DMZ, we didn't know how long we could remain in the rear echelon. That distance was about a minute and a half by jet, and in an all-out attack, we expected to be overrun by land forces within the first few hours. Would we be cannon fodder? Or, would we have time to bug out?

I did not feel the chilling threat of this reality until after I located Sergeant Jennings. I called out to him as he was entering the sergeants' quarters. He didn't seem to have heard me, so I followed him in. Reaching to knock, my knuckles connected with his door and it swung readily open. I was unprepared to see him, an old-time lifer, on his knees in prayer. He was someone I knew had served two tours in 'Nam, and I respected him for his good sense and courage. Now, seeing him there, kneeling before his footlocker, unseeing eyes cast upward while fear gushed down his face, I, too, was afraid. Numbly I stood there, my own eyes locked on him, and for a time, it seemed we two were the only true reality, as around us the world was filled with madness and the sounds of scurrying feet. From outside came the lieutenant's voice, now devoid of its Officer's Candidate School sneer. I did not know what he shouted; I heard only his fear. In my right hand, I clutched my weapon—an old, obsolete M-14. It was the first time I'd seen it since arriving. In my left was the one lone clip of ammo I'd just been issued. In my mind was one incomprehensible question: *How the fuck was I expected to fight with only one clip?*

I didn't know if the sergeant heard me knock. After that first long moment, I cleared my throat, embarrassed for my intrusion. "Huh-uh . . . uh . . . sergeant, they're ready for you at the arms room." Facing mostly away from me, he raised one hand, palm out, to indicate he heard. I left in haste.

I've no doubt, had the insanity escalated, our side would have eventually prevailed. Would we have used our tactical nukes? Yeah, for sure. Me? I could read the personal ramifications of it all in the fear of our officers and NCOs: They knew! Winning was something none of us here was expected to see.

Eventually, though, when the communists kept to their side of the fence, things again quieted. For several weeks, we trucked around those M-14s and our one clip of ammo. The order was: Don't chamber a round and don't squeeze one off, unless taking fire. To do so would result in an automatic court-martial.

Never were we issued anything more. There were no ammo boxes in our trucks, no heavy belts around our waists, no flack jackets, no grenades—not even machine guns protected our convoys. For that matter, we did not generally even travel in convoys. Nothing protected our asses but that one rifle and its single clip. After those two weeks, I never saw my weapon again.

About a week after the commotion quieted, I was on a supply trip for B Company. The village seemed unusually quiet. Except for a group of ROK (Republic of Korea) rangers standing at the side, the roadway was empty as I approached the bridge leading to Tongduchon. Before them, on the ground, knelt a Korean in civilian clothes, his hands tied behind his back. As I approached, a lieutenant stepped forward, leveled his .45, and pulled the trigger. His arm jerked with the recoil of the heavy automatic, and I flinched at the report of the muzzle blast. Simultaneously, the man's head exploded, and his body slumped to the right. Only small puffs of dust then rose in the early morning light to mar the sudden stillness of the scene, as one leg kicked spasmodically a few times, clenched once as if in agony, then relaxed into eternal stillness.

It happened so quickly, so unexpectedly, that all I did was goggle, mouth agape as my truck approached. The ROK lieutenant stared, without expression, at the body of that last-to-be-rounded-up North Korean assassin. He holstered his weapon as I came abreast, then his eyes rose and met mine. They were the eyes of a snake—cold and deadly. I felt an arctic chill blow from the nape of my neck down my back, much colder than the crisp air of that January day. The look on my face must have amused him, for his lips drew back in tight satisfaction. That smile and those eyes were imprinted indelibly on my memory during those few seconds. Many years have gone by since that day. I no longer recall his face; yet, that smile and the malice in those slanted, black eyes, are not misted by time. They remain with me in startling clarity—and I still feel the chill.

* * *

Shortly after that was when I met Meg, and my life in Korea lost all concern over such things—just unimportant shit. The freezing grip of winter began to thaw into spring, and with it then came my own private war under another kind of fire. It was an inner war to learn the lessons about forgiveness, acceptance, and love and how it pertained to Meg and me, and finally, about marriage and the army. Then came the morning I was singled out during morning formation and told to report to the CO after chow. That stink I left in the chaplain's office the day before . . . had it returned?

I did the official army routine. Upon entering the CO's office, I came to attention and saluted, "Sir, Specialist Fourth Class Williams, reporting as ordered, sir."

When he didn't return the salute, as he rarely did with the enlisted men, I dropped mine and remained at attention. Exchanging salutes was a form of acknowledgment and respect. As per regulations, it was required of us both. I did not take it as personal that the captain didn't respect me, or even look at me, as, with a grimace, he gave me a pained "At ease."

I'd learned to fear and distrust those in direct authority over me. Those who gave me respect, I liked. This was one I didn't—and he knew it. Giving him a reason to climb all over my ass was not the thing to do.

Without bothering to look up, he began. "There is going to be a four-week NCO course, and each company has to send a volunteer." He picked up his pen and seemed to be intently studying it, as he casually explained, "It's something like basic training, only for sergeants. I've decided to send you."

I'd heard about it already and knew exactly what was being left out. NCO Academy would be misery heaped upon more misery—enough to make basic training look like playtime in the sandbox. Moreover, it would take me away from Meg.

"Sir, I really don't want to volunteer," I replied. "I've only got about six months left, and I just want to do my time and get out."

His lips tightened and a jaw muscle popped. He ducked his head briefly, then raised it to glare, finally looking me in the eye. In his best "don't-fuck-with-me-boy" tone, he repeated, "This Company needs one volunteer—you're it. Dismissed!"

There was nothing more to say. With anger burning my gut and a matching glare, I abruptly clicked my heels forcefully together at attention and saluted. He'd again dropped his eyes to his desk, ignoring me as he pretended to absentmindedly thumb his papers while waiting for me to leave.

I wanted—no, I demanded—some form of acknowledgment and respect. It wasn't much, but it was something I could make him do. I remained there, solidly at salute, while about thirty slow seconds ticked by. He finally looked up with a grunt of irritation and gave me one of his "I'm-really-only-waving-at-a-fly-on-my-forehead" sort of salutes. Dropping mine with a flourish, and with parade-ground precision, I about-faced and stomped from his office.

All day I fumed, my guts churning with constant agitation. At lunch, the half cockroach discovered in my sandwich didn't add more than a gram of protein to my day. I would have been much happier had there been a whole cockroach I did—or didn't—find. My lunch stayed, but my guts churned on. Briefly, I wondered why this was all happening to me this day. Usually, the chow was excellent. The officers? Hell, I expected them to be assholes.

Most of the day was spent on detail, cleaning and inventorying the warehouse. With it finally over, I showered and, skipping chow, headed directly to the EM Club for an evening of serious drinking.

My fifth beer was just going down and my mind beginning to mellow when my platoon sergeant walked in. Spotting me in the crowd, he headed in my direction. I didn't like the look in his eye. It was the kind one gets for farting in the tent.

"Bad move, Slick; you've got night duty."

"Naw . . . c'mon, Sarge. You've got the wrong guy. I've been on duty all day." Sergeant Slocum was usually pretty cool. I thought he even liked me.

"Yeah, you, Slick . . . compliments of the CO." Sarge's face was grim. "You're delivering fuel to the bladder up north. Now . . ." He jerked his thumb over his shoulder. "Mount up!" He meant the temporary storage bladder at a new project near Camp Hovey on the DMZ.

"C'mon, Sarge. I've already pulled a full shift. I'm off duty— besides, I've been drinking. Surely the CO won't want to send me out now?"

"You're always on duty in this man's army, Son," he growled. "Now get your sorry ass in your truck. You've got three trips to make before you can hit the sack."

Is the whole damned world out to get me, or just that prick-of-a-CO? "Sorry-assed way to get revenge just for forcing a salute," I muttered.

"I said, move it, soldier!" Sarge meant business.

* * *

I still wanted to get drunk, and since Sarge didn't seem to care, I stopped at the PX and got a couple of six-packs on my way out of the compound. The loading dock of the railhead was at the north end of Tongduchon. By the time my tank was full, my truck was running about an hour behind the other three on duty that night. Each trip would take about two hours, up and back. We had orders to go south through Uijongbu, then turn north again to Chorwon where Camp Hovey was located.

There was a shorter route going straight north through "Chinese Tunnel" that would cut the time by about half. The problem was, it ran within a couple of hundred yards of the DMZ. Our CO had forbidden us the nighttime use of this route. He didn't like his trucks or equipment coming back with bullet holes in them.

All this weighed heavy on my mind as I pulled up to the gate exiting the depot. Obviously, I wouldn't be hitting the sack before 0400 hours this night, nor would I remain there past wake-up at 0600. Knowing the asshole my CO was, I expected it would be so for many nights to come. One usually learned early in the army not to piss off the wrong man. That man could usually be recognized by the polish on his insignia. With such a man, it is the only thing he can hold to that says he is better than you. My CO had very shiny brass. It shined with the same magnitude as the chaplain's gold cross. Briefly, I wondered how well the two of them knew one another.

At the gate, I stopped. I looked north, then south, and with a hearty "Hi-ho, Fuck the Army," I swung out and headed north.

~ *In the Present with Big D* ~

Looking back over this chapter, there seems so little upon which I need comment. It is mostly facts and events that fill in or are needed to set the stage to better understand the chapters to follow. Though resentments, as just described, no longer boil in my life—certainly not like then—it's late, and I'm tired. So with a hearty "Hi-ho, fuck it all," I'm off to bed.

"Au contraire, Son! This is not at all the place to say 'fuck it.'"

The words reverberate in deep base off the walls of my den, seeming to come from every direction at once. Big D's entrance then follows with more drama than usual, arriving with a howling, as if in a wind from the mouths of many tortured souls. Condensing before me into his familiar, tall, black-robed form, he is plainly visible while sharing that same space with my computer hutch. Yet, Big D's presence seems just as tangible—or more so. And strangely, too, he hovers above a vast ocean of silent liquid upon which barely a ripple disturbs its quicksilver surface. Strangest of all, neither reality seems to negate the other, but rather exist together perfectly.

"Whoa! Okay, I'm not so tired after all." It's true, for despite Big D's ominous entrance, I am immersed in an energy that feels of infinite warmth and love. "Is there something more here that needs to be discussed?"

"What about man's cruelty to man?" Big D now begins to glow faintly with a strange radiance not reflected but rather absorbed and re-emanated from the liquid all around us. "Isn't there something you now know—something you wish that ROK lieutenant had only known?"

"Ah, yes, of course." How could I step past this one with just a crude "fuck it?" Looking at him then, I formulate my answer with deliberate respect and honesty. "I wish that lieutenant had only known that on a higher, unconscious level, we are all literally connected—that what we do to one another, we also do to ourselves."

"Exactly so." The glow has increased. "We are, on that level, as a drop in the cup of humanity."

My eyes are drawn to his sickle. There, along its edge, is a dark, oily sludge, creeping down and congealing into a sickly brown drop upon its tip. I watch, fascinated, as it suddenly drips onto the liquid surface below. It hits with an explosive hiss, releasing a stench that assaults my senses, exactly like the bloated carcass of a dead cow I once chanced upon in Fry Canyon. I was naive enough to stab it with my trusty hunting knife. Once again, I feel the explosion of slime and crawling of maggots upon my skin—only with a thousand times the intensity.

The touch of that drop exploding on that quicksilver surface releases a roiling, brown-tinged wave, which immediately expands outward with a glow of sickly yellow light, seemingly to infinity. Then it is gone, leaving only a noxious smell that feels of shame and lingers only for a moment. My eyes raise questioningly to the impassioned glow of Big D's.

"Yes. That ROK lieutenant died today." The hood of his robe nods in solemn acknowledgment. "His was a long and painful death of cancer. What that man did was akin to defecating in the cup. Further, the Cup of Humanity is that from which God drinks. Humanity is as the experiential essence of His tea."

I am aware of the loving warmth surrounding me. It seems again unchanged. "But where did it go? I no longer feel the energy or smell the stink of that man's life."

"This love is the only thing that can erase such stench," Big D answers. "Just see that your passing does not leave such a memory, for the mind remains"—he gestures about—"God is forever."

"I won't."

"You won't?" His question mocks me. "You just did! Never again say 'fuck it' in indifference to cruelty." His laugh rings of irony. "That ROK lieutenant knew cruelty well. He experienced it as a young boy during the war. His whole life was bent on revenge. Treasure his poor example when next you're tempted to revenge . . . or to ignore another's cruelty."

"I will, Big D."

"Then treasure, too, the lesson he teaches you."

"Lesson?"

"Yes . . . you remember the *Law of Thought Energy?*"

"Thoughts are energy. They exist, and create, in one of two forms: the energy of love or the energy of that which is not love— fear." I snap the quote off with ego-studied panache. Then, in hopes of diverting the energy in Big D's stare, I add, "Uh . . . I guess that lieutenant thought mostly in fear."

"General . . . he died a general." Big D regards me silently a moment longer before continuing. "Fear is as creative an energy as love. And true—this is the law that applies to him. But the other law he illuminates here applies to you."

"What law?"

"This law you have never heard of, until now. Love or fear? Yes, there are only these two energies. And then there is something else. I call it the *Law of Abdication*. It states: *'A third state exists in the space of no energy. Called 'indifference,' it is the opposite of both love and fear.'*

"For in that space, one is not performing the basic agreement one has with the Creator: to live and to feel, in love or in fear. In that space, one makes no difference in the world—except for the loss of that which they could have contributed, had they cared.

"Like blame is the abdication of responsibility, indifference is the abdication of choice. These are the people waiting in line at Death's shuttle bus stop. Like you were in that hospital, they are just waiting to die. The only difference between you and them was that, at that time, you weren't saying 'fuck it.'"

"Ah, I see . . ."

"No—you don't *see*!" Big D's words seem to shout in my head. With them, once again I smell the stench. "You just now said 'fuck it' to this man's cruelty, just as you said it back there in Korea."

"What? What do you mean?"

"Did you say or do anything about it back then?"

"Well, no. What could I do? The man was dead." I shrug. "It was their country . . . their affair."

"It was you who died there, too!"

"I don't see . . ."

"What was it you just now said you wished that ROK lieutenant had only known?" His eyes burn as if into my very soul.

"Uhhh . . ." Confusion reigns in my mind.

Big D does not wait for me to get past it. "'. . . What we do to one another we also do to ourselves,' remember?"

"But . . . the man was dead . . . their country . . . their affair—"

"You could have reported it to your superiors; you could have told the whole world. You could have stopped the deaths of 3,682 more victims. You knew of his cruelty . . . and did nothing!"

"What 3,682 victims? How?"

"How do you think that ROK lieutenant rose so quickly through the ranks? He served three tours in Vietnam. The Republic of Korea also had troops there, y'know. Yes, he liked Vietnam. There he held many lives in his hands: friend, foe, and innocent. It took the deaths of that many people to make this 'hero' a general." Big D's words burn with caustic truth. "Many were innocent mothers and babies." He pauses to regard me in grim silence. "And that count does not include water buffalo. He loved killing them also. They were the assets the villagers depended upon to work the paddies. Some of that count he killed by starvation."

I have no retort but remain silent, slumped under the weight of his glare. He continues. "That ROK lieutenant fucked up—he let you see. Had you raised a stink, his country would have lost face, and he would have lost his rank." Big D's voice turns soft and loving, something his next words seem to negate. "Had I taken you that night in the hospital, do you think your essence would have tasted all that much better in the cup than his?"

I feel as though all my own ability to hold myself up is gone, that all that keeps me erect is the energy I feel from the pool surrounding us. "Oh God, Big D! Is there anything I can do to change this?"

"Just feel the love here around you and realize that your thinking just now has changed—*you* have changed. In acknowledging your part in this, you have just taken your stand. This is all you must do when you find yourself out of integrity: Place the change in who you are and acknowledge it to those involved. This is the true essence of the Creator's forgiveness. The energy will uphold you regardless."

If you are still alive, you have a destiny. You haven't yet finished what you are here to do—and learned what you are here to learn. And *you* haven't yet given up on *you*.

Redneck Spirituality—book Four

Chapter Twenty-Two

Nah... Nah... Na Nah... Nah

There was very little traffic. For the most part, the road was mine and I made good time. It was a straight shot north, and in what seemed only moments, I was nearing the DMZ. Now there was no traffic at all. Shutting off the headlights, I turned on the combat running lamps. They shed only a dim illumination directly in front, but the moon was nearly full and I had plenty of light. I began randomly speeding and slowing.

Was my CO using good judgment in forbidding us to use this particular road at night? No, that judgment came down from above. The Communist North Koreans did occasionally fire at us from across the DMZ. Sniper fire or mortars were not unknown to our troops there—only to people back home. Back home, such *incidences* would demand more of a response than the gods in our upper echelon were prepared to make.

Alone on that road, I was the only one in the world that night who didn't respect the abilities of the North Korean snipers. Or perhaps it was really respect for my own life. Certainly, it was not respect for those gods running our military. A few beers could have that effect on me.

Looking down that dimly lit ribbon of road, the hair stood up on my neck. Would my precautions protect me personally? Not likely. But then, I knew sniper fire would not be effective against a tanker full of diesel. Snipers were generally smart enough not to use tracers, and diesel fuel is not that flammable. Mortars were a different story. I had no wish to be flame grilled over a diesel barbecue.

My breath gusted in relief as I rounded the last turn into Chinese Tunnel. The ridge it center punched would from here on provide a screen between me and any fire from across the DMZ. I hadn't realized how shallow I'd been breathing, almost holding it, until I saw the dark maw of the tunnel and knew I'd soon be safe inside. Then, as its remote blackness swallowed over my truck, I realized suddenly: *My God! If they're sneaking about tonight, what better place for an ambush!* Switching my headlamps on full, my dread dissolved in the flare illuminating the empty tunnel ahead.

Tempting as I might have been as an entree, my arrival at Camp Hovey was without incident, occurring just as the third truck finished unloading. My own tank soon unloaded. The return trip was a backward retake, only at higher speed—all downhill, running unloaded. I was just pulling away from the dock at Tongduchon, reloaded, when the first of my cohorts turned through the gates into the fuel depot. This time, not pressing my luck, having twice pissed in the wind and, so far, still feeling dry, I swung south at the gate.

The trip through Uijongbu was uneventful. At the crossroads in the center of town, I swung my rig left and headed east, knowing the road would soon turn back north to Chorwon and Camp Hovey. The land was mostly flatland rice paddies. It, too, eventually turned, becoming terraced rice paddies as I climbed up and crested a ridge between valleys. From here on, the terrain would become more and more rugged and mountainous.

Coming down off the ridge, the road cut to the left. I downshifted, and my hands swung easily upon the wheel with each turn as it meandered along the hillside. Then, rounding a curve, I came upon one of our trucks, broken down alongside the inner cutbank. Braking and down shifting, I pulled to the right, intending to stop. With my attention diverted—and perhaps numbed a little by the beer—I didn't see the washed-out spot at the edge of the embankment until too late. Suddenly, my right front tire dropped sharply, and the steering wheel jerked in my hand with unexpected violence. It all happened so fast, I had no time to think. My reactions were purely automatic, totally without conscious thought.

As the cab tilted, the weight of 25,000 gallons of diesel fuel shifted in the tank behind. It was going over the side. There was no getting it back onto the road. To have even tried would have meant a rolling crash, my cab flailing about before being crushed under the tons of bursting, possibly burning diesel. Somehow, from a basic level of consciousness, I knew this. In that instant, I did the only thing I could have, and stayed alive—and I did it without hesitation. Yes, clearly, some power greater than myself has plans for me that have not yet been realized, for what I did in that instant was purely contrary to natural reactions.

In the back of my mind, I was aware of what lay to my right— that being approximately two hundred feet of forty-five degree embankment spaced with good-size trees and power poles and ending in a ditch before a half-frozen rice paddy. In that instant, I surrendered completely to what was happening. Not only did I surrender, but I also steered sharply right . . . and accelerated.

Many thoughts flashed through my mind on the trip down that embankment, so many, in fact, it almost seemed as if time slowed. I was aware of the poles and trees flashing by and of the ditch looming ever larger and deeper in my headlights. I didn't know if my trailer and truck would be aligned straight with one another when I hit the ditch. If it wasn't, I would instantly be jackknifed under the load.

And even were it aligned perfectly, was it even possible that the single, fragile-seeming, steel swivel pin on the tank trailer could hold? That pin was all that latched the fifth wheel, that big, greasy flat disc connecting my tractor to the trailer. It seemed impossible that it would not shear under the impacting weight of the massive, steel trailer plus sixty some odd tons of fuel.

At one point during that long trip, I looked up across the dim expanse of rice paddy at the hills on the other side—just dark shadows outlined against a star-filled sky. *Isn't my life supposed to flash before my eyes? Is this the last I will see in this world?*

Then, tractor and trailer in line, I hit the ditch. I was not traveling at quite a 90 degree angle to it, so my body was thrown violently right then left. My head struck the side window, spidering the glass and adding more stars to those in the night sky.

Then I found myself bouncing across the rice paddy. The engine was wanting to die, and I automatically began slipping the clutch, keeping it revved. Looking toward the far end of the paddy, I could see how the road sloped down to meet it and so swung left in that direction.

I did not want to be stuck like some beached buffoon of a whale. It would probably take several tanks to drag my truck from the soft ground of this half-frozen rice paddy. My hopes died with the engine when it eventually stalled, the batteries having been ejected by the same jolt that nearly ejected my head through that side window.

Still seeing unfamiliar stars and feeling weak and dizzy, I sat there, stunned and shaken, with the ebbing of adrenalin, one regret on my mind. *God, if I had just kept moving, maybe I could have made it back onto the highway.* Funny how such mundane issues can seem so important.

The other driver rushed over in a panic, scrambling up onto the running boards to peer in. "Are you okay? Are you okay?"

Gazing at him through the bloody spider web of shattered safety glass, I rolled down the window as far as its outward bulge would allow. "Yeah . . . I'm fine," I replied with an amused grin.

Calming, he wrinkled his nose at the beer fumes, then spoke curtly, "There's already a tow truck coming, so just hang loose." Then he stomped back to his truck to wait. I used the opportunity to gather up what beer was left and to stash it in some bushes on the far side of the paddy.

When the MPs arrived, one approached my truck and ordered me out. My feet had no sooner touched dirt than I found myself being flung up against the truck and roughly frisked. Glaring over my shoulder, I asked, "Is this the way you always treat accident victims?" In answer, he grabbed the back of my fatigue jacket and threw me backward to the ground.

"Don't you fuckin' move."

Disobeying, I sat up and, feeling vaguely surrealistic, watched him search my truck. I knew I was in trouble when he came out with a 'gotcha now' grin across his face—and an unopened can of beer in his hand.

"This your beer, Boy?" His superior smirk carried a Southern drawl.

"Not mine." I smiled back. "Never seen that before in my life. Oh, but you can drink it, if'n ya want," I finished, imitating his drawl.

"Git movin'!" Shoving me roughly, he forced me to climb the hill to his jeep. "Git in!"

"Whoa . . . wait a minute. I need to go get my logbook. It's a court-martial offense to be without it."

"Fergit yer fuckin' book! Git in!" The look in his eye told me he clearly wanted to use the baton now in his hand. I complied.

We were both silent until reaching the outskirts of Uijongbu, where he asked, "Ya wanna see a doctor 'fore I book y'r dumb ass?"

Obviously, the question was prompted by regulations, not concern for me—or for the large egg and the blood running down the side of my head. Definitely, he more than did not like me. The feeling was mutual.

"Yeah." My decision was made more because I knew it would put him out, rather than any personal concern.

We arrived at the I Corps Med at about one in the morning. Looking around, I was struck by a curious sight. Most of his buddies from the I Corps MPs were there, waiting in line to be processed. It appeared that there had been some sort of a problem with the chow in their mess hall. Now no one wanted to be more than a few seconds from a latrine.

Power tripping bullies . . . "What a poetic thing to happen to such a swell bunch of assholes." Whoops! Somehow that last thought had been spoken aloud. While inside, I knew there were some who deserved special respect, especially seeing now how difficult it must be rubbing shoulders with the others. Just what the mix was that night, I never knew. It's sure, there was at least one there looking out for the fool with a big mouth.

My general obnoxiousness was by no means endearing. In fact, it earned me a place at the end of the line. Accident victim—blood, bumps, bruises, head trauma, and all—I was the last to see the doctor. Too, it also insured I received no cooperation when I asked to notify my unit or for my logbook to be returned. Who knew where that went? And I hadn't yet filled in the crucial bullshit entries for the night yet. For all they'd know, I was on my first trip. It was nearly daylight when my turn came to be examined.

The doctor, a captain, seemed pretty concerned with the egg above my left temple and kept shining his light into my eyes, like he couldn't make up his mind. "How did this happen?"

"Well, my head kinda smashed the side window when my truck hit the ditch at the bottom of the hill."

"Ah, so you were in a wreck. Stand up."

I did.

"Now tilt your head back, extend both arms out, and touch the tip of your nose with your index fingers, one at a time."

Again, I did—no problem.

"Okay. See that line painted on the floor? Stepping heel to toe, I want you to walk that line."

Piece of cake. I was standing close enough to read as he wrote the report. After describing the head injury, he noted "possible slight concussion" and "fairly stable."

Unlike the MPs, the doctor struck me as a pretty decent sort. "Look, sir . . . I need to use your phone. It's been five hours, and even though I asked several times, the MP wouldn't let me make a call to my unit." I then added, in my most innocent demeanor, "I just don't understand what I did to make him so angry with me."

"Five hours! You've been here five hours? Let me talk to that MP."

Minutes later, while on the phone, I could hear the MP in the next room, getting his hemorrhoids trimmed by the captain. What with the diarrhea, I guessed he had a right to be sore. Finally getting through to my unit, my CO came on the line.

"Where the hell are you, Williams?"

"Uh . . . well, sir, I've been here at the I Corps Med all night."

"At the Med!" His voice blasted in my ear. "Do you realize we've had the whole area on alert—didn't know if infiltrators got you or what?"

"Sorry, sir. The MP who brought me here wouldn't let me use the phone. And he wouldn't let me have my logbook—"

"He what?" His words came with a sizzle. Maybe I imagined it, but the receiver actually felt a few degrees warmer as he continued. "You put that man on the phone . . . right now!"

Now it was my turn to grin as my CO finished the job on those hemorrhoids.

The sun was just breaking as we stepped out of the Med and climbed into the jeep. He hadn't spoken a word since he'd hung up the phone. But he was saying a lot by the way his breath hissed through clenched teeth; and too, his face was so red his ears fairly glowed. For some reason, he kept fingering the butt of his .45. Involuntary chuckles aside, I, too, said nothing.

At the MP station, I was read my rights and locked into a closet with a metal grill for bars until my sergeant showed up to collect me. This was the first, and only, time I was ever arrested. As I sat there watching what went on, I became aware of one odd-colored, oversize thread that wove throughout the fabric of these people's reality—that thread being how every single MP in the place honestly seemed to think *he* was better than every single one of *us* out there in the world. More than a feeling, it exuded from them to me like a foul odor.

I'd never felt I harbored hard feelings for the police, except maybe what was natural for the one who'd killed my brother. Yes, for a time, I truly hated that one, even though I realized how my brother left him no choice. That cop did what he had to do. My brother created his own life—and death. I knew even then, at some basic, though unconscious, level how holding on to my hatred could only harm me. The sharp edge of it had not been allowed to hack long at my soul.

Yet, sitting there in that cop shop in Uijongbu, looking out through the metal grating of the door, the memories flooded back. Again, I chose to hate. Perhaps it was triggered by the pervasive self-superiority of my captors. It was there eating at my gut when Sergeant Slocum arrived.

"Collect your scum and get the hell out of here," was the desk sergeant's remark as he released me to his charge.

With more bravado than sense, I retorted, "I'll just be glad to be breathing air that doesn't stink of MP—or was that diarrhea? Hell, same thing!"

Sarge clamped his hand over my mouth. "Shut up!" he hissed in my ear as he physically hustled me out of there. At the door, I looked back over my shoulder at four batons, now wrapped in four hands—hands obviously itching to tap dance those batons across my skull.

* * *

Why was it I always felt compelled to get in that last dig with every self-appointed tin god I came across? Why did I always take every opportunity to stick it to them? "I'm right; you're all fucked up! Nah . . . Nah . . . Na Nah . . . Nah."

~ *In the Present with Big D* ~

"Hello . . . Big D? Why don't you answer? I can feel your presence. It's been three weeks since I finished this chapter. Nothing more comes. Yet, somehow I feel you want more. Why do you leave me here to babble?"

His arrival begins as a gentle stirring on the outskirts of my thoughts that glides in on Teflon feet to stand audibly, but invisibly, before me.

"Ah, Jeff . . . what do you think this chapter is all about?"

"Well, I had thought it was a sort of reaffirmation that I have a destiny."

"Shit, Jeff! Anyone with a hunk of gristle between their ears has to know that. Anyone, that is, who has ever posed the question: *What's it all about?* You are not so different from others. I give a lot of reminders."

"Yes, I know, Big D. Time after time, I've felt your presence—understood it in the odds and in the tingling tightness of adrenalin following your passage. It was almost as if you walked around me, going out of your way to leave me here. But this time. . . ."

"Jeff, you don't know shit! Of course I steered your hands that night. But that is not what this chapter is about. Don't try to cloud the issue. Try understanding what you meant by '. . . that last dig.'"

"Anger; you mean my anger?"

"Sure, and yours often has a button marked 'Tin God.'" He pauses to softly chuckle. "You know, Jeff, anger is an emotion. As such, it is simply a message from your soul—the *Law of Emotion*, remember?"

"Yes, I remember: **'Emotions are the words of the soul.'**"

"And you know, Jeff, that anger simply says that you are being disloyal to yourself—to your soul. But some hold on to it and use it to hide that true responsibility from themselves. Much easier to blame someone or something outside themselves—to be a victim. Being a *victim* is not about the things that happen or what others do. It is always a state of mind."

"So?"

"So, Jeff, do you see anger as something of a weakness to be eradicated from your life?"

"Well, yeah . . . sure. Look, I know you're getting at something here. I just don't have a clue what."

"Ah, the folly of the *enlightened*. Most are just eggheads who know this shit in their heads. I expect more of you than mental diarrhea. I expected that by now, you'd know it in your *heart*."

"Uhhh . . . not sure what you mean." With his next words I see him, but only the bony plates of his face, the grinning ivory teeth and deep sockets each holding a fiery glow.

"What is, just is!" He quotes the law now in a voice that would have dwarfed Gabriel's horn. Simultaneously, his form bursts forth before me like the diesel exhaust of an old Kenworth engine pulling under a heavy load. His gaze now burns fiercely.

"Ow! Damn, take it easy on the ears! Yes, I know that law, Big D, but I don't see it has anything to do with anger."

"Could this not also be stated: **'There is no 'right' or 'wrong' outside one's own mind? And inside, it is only a lie.'**" His grin now feels somehow—grim.

"Well, yes . . . but again, what has that to do with anger?"

"And what if I were to add that it is the same with ***good or bad***?"
His white, calcified, finger bones tighten a bit where they grasp his
fearsome sickle.

"Well, again yes . . . but c'mon! We've gone over all this shit.
What could this possibly have to do—"

Swoosh!

His sickle sings through the air, cleaving several hairs to tickle
their way down across my frozen face, with not a breath from me to stir
their passage.

"I can teach like your *Mute Ninja Karate Instructor*, too, you
know?" He snorts, his gaze now flaming even brighter. "Is that what it
takes for you to learn? Fear? Pain?"

My mind springs into panicked action. There is no right or
wrong, good or bad? What is, just is? It all swirls around inside my head.
After several minutes of slack-jawed silence, suddenly, I just know. The
answer bursts forth:

"Everything has its place . . . its part . . . its useful function."

"Exactly!" His eyes now glow with unexpected warmth. "Your
anger is not something to deny, to rid yourself of shamefully, as quickly
as possible. It is to be felt!" The glow of one socket winks briefly. "As
you stated: It is your soul's message to you that you are being unfaithful.
Feel it, then lovingly—with no malice—do what you need to do to be
faithful. And lastly, let it go."

"Yes, I see. I get it."

"Oh, do you?" Big D's tone, coupled with his next words, again
sets my head awhirl. "Where in your life these days have you tasted
anger?"

"Well, yes . . . the bank. They've screwed up my account again.
Five times in as many months, I've had to go down and straighten out
their mess. I do everything they say, get it paid on time, but something
always happens—and again, they try to charge me a late fee! I've spent
hours on the phone, been passed from one person to another, then still
had to go down and spend more time in line waiting—"

"Whoa . . . ho! Hold on." Big D interrupts me with a chuckle. "Just let go of all the victim shit about them and ask yourself what the message is here—the one from your soul."

I stop for a moment, thinking. It doesn't take long. "I am helpless, stifled with this debt. It sucks up all my available cash and strangles my enjoyment of life."

"Hmmm . . ." Big D's red stare seems to sharpen. "I feel your hopelessness. You are indeed powerless here." The glow intensifies. "Why?"

It takes barely a moment for me to see it. "Because I just said it, even believed it. . . . There is that *Law of Spirit: 'Every word is an order to my soul.'* " I shake my head in mild self-reproach. "Our minds are built to make ourselves right. In saying it, I gave away my power, and worse, made myself a victim."

"Exactly . . . now why did you say it?"

"What? Well, I suppose because I was angry."

"No, the anger only serves to cover your pain. Your pain is that of an honest victim. You see, while everyone does set it up before coming into life, only children can be honest victims—and only when that is the experience needed for their soul's growth." His voice suddenly softens, and I barely hear his next words. "When was the first time you felt such helplessness, such a sensation of being smothered, as if your very life were being taken?"

"Ah, yes," I begin, just as softly. "Those stinking socks—and the despicable bastards who gagged me with them back in the Sunny Hills Orphanage!" My voice is now propelled by anger.

"Yes . . . back then, you were a child, helpless—a true victim." His words are still calm and nurturing, but now change to cut with the precise edge of a razor. "You are no longer a child. As an adult, you now know why—*you cannot grow past being a victim without actually becoming one.* When will you stop being a victim?"

"Right now!"

"Oh? How? What are your options?"

I almost feel surprised at the ease with which I list them. "I could make paying off this loan my most urgent concern in life. I could refinance, consolidate, and arrange to be paying someone who will treat me with the respect I deserve. I could find ways to increase my income, and maybe there is something I could sell that I no longer need. Hell, for that matter, I don't have much. I could go bankrupt and stick them with it all."

"Yesss!" Big D hisses, grinning, then seems to sober. "You could do all that, but there is one thing there that would not be loving."

"Yeah . . . I know that, but still. . . ."

"Uh-huh . . . now you're getting it. Anger is the fire that tempers resolve. Feel it, hear what it says, then decide your *faithful* course of action. Only then do you let it go, as it no longer serves." His grin widens. "If you want to eradicate something, try malice, as in that last option. Malice is the feces that lends stink to anger. It is a conscious choice—one that requires the misuse of anger." Big D now fades until all that is left of him are twin red glows. One winks out abruptly, then the other, leaving his last words to hang alone in the air. "Listen to your soul," his words now whisper, ". . . and choose to love."

When you can accept every man—weaknesses and all—only then can you truly appreciate the man that you are. Those "weaknesses" are merely the dysfunctions conjured by our souls to create the pain for change. Evolution? Change? Is it not the same? Another man's weaknesses, viewed in love, can only point to the magnificence of who we've become. But viewed in ridicule, we are blinded to who we've been—and more importantly, to the pain of who we are. It's about that *Law of Spirit: "Our choice of energies is only love or fear."* Ridicule is but a weapon of fear wielded by those without the courage to look at who they are.

Redneck Spirituality—Book One

Chapter Twenty-Three

"F" Troop

My little misadventure soon blew over. To my immense relief, the NCO School was out of the question. Instead, I was assigned to duty in the compound, running the steam cleaner for washing the trucks and equipment—simple, easy duty, especially since most of the drivers preferred to wash their own.

I missed driving around the countryside. The exotically strange, ancient newness of it all was something I'd cherished. But I didn't miss it too much; there was still Meg. I loved her. In fact, almost every night now, I loved her—multiple times.

I stopped taking Tae Kwan Do. My instructor was getting an extra ten-dollar fee every time I stepped up a belt and was stuffing them down my throat. Upon receiving a 3rd degree red belt—even though I purposefully arranged to be on duty and missed the test—I was done. Clearly, I wasn't ready for red, and I especially didn't want to advance to the next—the black belt—without earning it. I loved karate and could see that my instructor had it backward. He was supposed to be the milk sow and I the piglet receiving nourishment.

It was not such a disappointment. Although I enjoyed the swift, hard dexterity karate lent my body, and the sure confidence it lent my mind, those feelings paled compared to how I felt when with Meg. Whether we were enjoying the view, picnicking on the top of a mountain, or in bed wrapped in the throes of passion, there was a similar, heady feeling—just of different heads. Yet, in both my heads and my heart, I knew only joy when with Meg. I didn't want to ever be without her.

The spring greenery thickened and warmed into summer. Soon, the army transferred me to A Company, Seventh Engineers. I was assigned duty as an NCOIC—non-commissioned officer in charge—of the field shower section. I became what was known as the "acting jack," the temporary buck sergeant in charge of the shower-in-a-tent platoon. This simply meant wearing the stripes and having the responsibility, just not really having the authority—or the pay.

In the army's own form of corporate consciousness, they, too, kicked people upstairs for fucking up. I was responsible for all the equipment necessary for four field shower units, including tents, generators, boilers, six trucks, and five men. My job would have involved the decontamination of our troops in the event of nuclear warfare. As it was, though, the showers were only used on a couple of locations to service our troops at construction sites in the field.

My platoon consisted of the company fuck-ups. Unofficially, they called us "F Troop." All—myself included—had our orders "red flagged." If we screwed up again, we would not be allowed to leave the country, or the army, and that would be the best-case scenario.

My new CO said it clearly on the day I reported. "You better put a hard rein on it, Boy, or your next stop from here's gonna be the federal pen at Leavenworth, Kansas."

Yes, we were all fuck-ups. For one of my guys, PFC Kerney, a tall, lanky country boy, it was that he couldn't keep his pecker in his pants. Every time he passed a hole, he had to get it out and test the depth. Most of his time in the army was spent on restriction, suffering from a "runny nose."

Once, while on maneuvers, we were bivouacked about ten klicks south of Tongduchon in a little meadow surrounded on three sides by hills. The CO ordered my platoon to recon the hill to the north and to set up machine gun placements with overlapping fields of fire. I took

Kerney and another man and used the opportunity to take a short hike along the creek on the far side of the hill.

We hadn't gone far when we heard voices above the murmur of the stream. Rounding a bend, the lush underbrush opened into a clearing. There, squatted in the flow of the shallow stream, we encountered two young ladies, their backs to us, bathing. They turned, profiling brown, nubbed nipples on pert young breasts, their bare skin running in tightly tanned goose bumps across the bare expanses of their backs. That, and the charm of their butt cheeks spread wide just above the water, all seemed to attest to the chill of the early morning creek— and to a distinct impression, as if they were somehow feeling vulnerable to our bad-mannered intrusion. One's hair was frothed high in soapy bubbles as she worked it. The other held an old tin pan, ready to rinse. Both froze posed when they saw us. As they wore no makeup or clothes, I took them to be local farm girls.

"*Mian hapnida*" (excuse me), I said, feeling the heat from my crimson face, and continued on—but only for a few steps, for I found myself suddenly alone.

"Kerney . . . Donner, move out!" They didn't move, just stood there, both eyes and mouths wide. "Now!"

"But Sarge . . ." came their chorus.

"Now! You won't like it if I have to repeat myself." I seldom made my orders this forceful and they obeyed, stumbling backward along behind. Glancing at them, I somehow felt embarrassed for my country. "And goddammit! Give those girls the courtesy of some privacy."

Arriving later at the west emplacement, Kerney pointed toward the latrine. "Sarge, I got the trots . . . can I go?"

"Sure. Report to Canton and Green at the east emplacement when you're done. Donner, you're on this one with Critch." I turned as Kerney hurried off. "I've got a briefing. I'll check on you later."

I'd barely stepped from the first sergeant's briefing when the CO called me over to the machine gun emplacements on the hill. As I walked up, he pointed down the other side, his face an unreadable mask.

"Is that one of your men down there, Sergeant Williams?" My eyes followed his point, and sure enough, there was Kerney coming up the path.

"Yes sir, it is."

"Well, the colonel and I just watched him trade two blankets for some ass from those two business girls down there."

Oh, shit! I closed my eyes, shuddered, but said nothing.

"From both of them, that is!" The mask broke into a chuckle. "You're lucky the colonel also got a laugh out of it. So I'm not going to make *him* the issue—but those blankets *are* GI issue." His eyes narrowed. "Get them back!"

I stalked down the hill to where Kerney was trudging his way up.

"Been soaking your dick again?"

Sheepishly, he nodded.

"Great! The colonel was watching. Now go get those fucking blankets back, dumb-ass!"

"But Sarge"—there was a panicky whine in his voice—"I can't do that."

"The colonel says you can," I replied, hitching a thumb over my shoulder and showing no sympathy. "Now do it!"

Glancing uphill over my thumb, I saw the colonel and the CO watching from the top, twin gods, their hands on their hips. Like a trapped animal, Kerney's eyes swung from them, to me, then back down the hill. Slowly, his Adam's apple bobbed, then head hanging, he turned around.

Watching as he wrestled those blankets from the wildcat fury of the two screeching girls, I was tempted to lend Kerney some money. *Fucking officers are sure getting off on this*, I thought. Even at this distance, I could hear their superior snickers. My own sense of fair play said to make it right with the girls, but I resisted the impulse. This wasn't my affair, my responsibility, or my lesson. This was Kerney's problem, and he needed to learn to deal with it.

* * *

Another one of my little F Troop crew, PFC Green, didn't believe in showers. A towheaded boy from Arkansas, the prominence of his nose and bucked teeth was only outdone by the pimples surrounding them. For him, soap was like garlic to a vampire, though for him, garlic would only have improved his smell. He would—and did—wear his shorts until they rotted off. Several times we gave him GI showers, where we would drag him, kicking and screaming, and wash him down with brillo pads and scrub brushes.

Except for the first week or so afterward, it did no good. Eventually, I found a better solution in permanent duty at the only field shower we then had in use. It was set up near Munsan-ni, where Line

Papa was under construction. Line Papa was a system of bunkers and artillery emplacements located about five klicks south of the DMZ. It was to be our second line of defense against an invasion by the North.

This arrangement with PFC Green seemed to work to everyone's advantage. He didn't have to take any more GI showers, and we didn't have to smell him; and those who did wouldn't hang around using too much hot water. At least it worked for several months—until he came down with some weird disease. His nuts swelled up about the size of grapefruits. They shipped him home to a stateside hospital.

* * *

A third F Trooper, PFC Donner, liked to fight. He wasn't very good at it, but he never let a small thing like that stop him from trying to intimidate anyone he thought he could. He'd even tried it once on me.

We'd been working on equipment all that morning, when about 1100 hours, I realized Donner was missing. In fact, he'd been gone some time. Earlier, he'd said he needed to use the latrine and hadn't returned. I eventually located him asleep on his bunk in the Quonset hut. Regarding his fucking off as direct disrespect of me—as indeed it probably was—I was pissed. PFC Donner didn't seem to respect anyone, nor, in that moment, had I much for him.

"Donner, get your lazy ass off that bunk!"

He jumped, his eyes jerking open, visibly startled. He looked a little sheepish for a second, but then sneered, "You think you can make me . . . Sarge?"

Now I knew it was disrespect. "Donner, I don't need to make you. All I need to do is make you sorry you didn't."

He came off the bunk in a rush, but stopped short. It was only a feint to see what I'd do. I had taken one automatic step back to set myself in a "ready" stance. His next step would have brought a roundhouse kick that would have put him back down—hard. Instead of continuing the attack, he said insolently, "I'm goin', Sarge, I'm goin'."

"Damned straight you're goin'. You're goin' to be filling a whole lot of sandbags this weekend."

"Don't fuck with my weekends, Sarge." His eyes had turned mean. "I'll catch you down in the Ville . . . ."

"Yeah," I agreed, my eyes locked with his. "You can do that—if you want the pain. Or you can pull your weight around here—if you want respect."

"Work's that way," I added, pointing. He waited another defiant moment before breaking eye contact and moving off.

* * *

Vietnam had a way of changing people. Somehow, I doubted it was basically so with Private Critch, the fourth guy. He was a doper. Vietnam was his excuse for the addiction—and for an attitude. An extreme irritant to me, constantly stinking of pot and never quite sober, there was always a sulkiness on his face and in his voice.

I didn't like him and made no effort to hide it. He took it to be because he was black. In reality, it was because of his attitude. He always found someone or something else to blame for his every problem or failure in life. "Black" was his excuse of choice. I've often wondered if he showed as much cowardice fighting the war in 'Nam as he did fighting the one in his personal life. But then, who am I to call the courage of another into question.

Yes, I put my life on the line—faced down the bullet with the USS Pueblo—but that bullet did not penetrate my body. In its passing, that bullet was not even wind in my face. Never having been in Vietnam, I respected the courage of all who had—all except maybe Private Critch.

* * *

The last F Trooper's name was PFC Canton. Also black, he was a man of exceptional maturity. Although quiet and not easy to know, he was the one man in the outfit for whom I had the most respect and liking. In all the months I knew him, I could never figure out why Canton was put in F Troop. Perhaps there was some truth in the rumors about him and the black market.

We had big problems with the slicky boys stealing things from our field shower unit up at Line Papa. There was no perimeter fence or Katusa guards, so that made us easy pickings. One night, they stole an axle shaft out of our deuce-and-a-half truck while it was parked next to the sleeping tent. Funny thing—Canton was the only one in the tent that night. The thought did briefly cross my mind: Had he run out of money for his new Yobo's dresses? There was no proof, and where Canton was concerned, I didn't care. The next day, I took up a new shaft along with the mail.

It was a pristine, summer day. I'd left battalion late and was really enjoying the drive. At lunchtime, I stopped in at the nearest mess tent, which happened to be at the supply compound for the artillery.

Lunch was the usual fare: strong coffee, boiled potatoes, peas and carrots, meatloaf, and apple cobbler.

I'd never had any problem with army fare and was eating with gusto when three very scrawny-looking Korean Nationals came into the mess tent. The compound was only guarded by Katusas at night, and with our own security being lax as it was, they had simply walked in and were begging for food. It did seem odd. Starving Koreans? Here? It might be something seen in the shanty towns around Seoul, but here in the country? Here they had a way of looking after their own.

An E6 sergeant at the first table stood up. "Hey! You guys, get the fuck outa here! Go on . . . *Cutta chogi!*" (go there). He gestured toward the gate. They just stood in dumb, desperate resentment, their eyes skulking between his fat belly and his tray piled high on the table.

"Hey . . . whoa there, Sarge, at ease!" The mess sergeant—an E6 also—interrupted quickly. "This is *my* mess . . . *I'll* handle it." Over his shoulder, he spoke to a PFC on the serving line. "Hogard, give them a bag of grub and point 'em out the gate."

* * *

Possibly, I owed that sergeant big time. From the way it all shook out, I'm sure his act of kindness saved lives. On my return trip, a couple of hours later, I saw those same three scruffy Koreans handcuffed together with a fourth. They were being driven off in the back of a Jeep by the Korean security forces. Curious, I stopped in at the mess tent.

"Yo! Sergeant Curtis." I knew him, as I ate there fairly regularly. "What happened? You didn't have those poor bastards arrested, did you?"

Curtis just looked at me soberly and shook his head. "Never been to 'Nam, have you, Sergeant Williams?"

"What do you mean?"

"Did you see the way those guys looked at that dumb fuck, Bradley, when he tried to kick 'em outta here?"

"Yeah?"

"That's what it looks like when a man means to kill you."

"My God! Are you serious?" I searched his face, but it remained sober. "You really think they meant to kill us?"

"Bout as dead as roaches in the stew!" There was a crinkle just beginning at the corner of his eye.

"Naw! You're pulling my leg."

"No . . . truth!" The crinkle was now part of a grin. "I reported it to Ops. ROK Rangers caught them up there." He gestured to the hill behind the compound. "North Korean agents armed to the shorts—mortars, grenades, automatic weapons. More firepower than you can shake your dick at. And as you know, your dick is the extent of our own firepower right now."

"Did you know?"

"No."

"Well, those three who came down here weren't armed, were they? Why'd you feed them if you thought they wanted to kill us?"

"Sarge, I wouldn't refuse food to anyone who needed it bad as they did. Besides," his grin widened, "kinda hard for a starving man to hate someone who just fed 'em, now, ain't it?"

I learned later from Sergeant Curtis that those four were the remnants of a team of twenty-five agents sent down from the North. Their purpose was to set up guerrilla bands in the South. Believing they would find great support with the populace, they'd been badly misled. Whenever they'd contacted the South Korean civilians, they were turned in.

These four were the last remaining. Starving, they'd been on that hill for several days, arguing over whether or not to attack us and take the food. Instead, they trusted in our natural stupidity and lax security and just came down and asked. After all, what threat were we to them? Except when on red alert and expecting to die, we weren't even armed. It had been hard for those infiltrators to conceive that we Americans weren't protecting the South Korean forces from them. Hell, the South Koreans protected us.

~ *In the Present with Big D* ~

I've been looking back over this chapter, wondering where it has much meaning in my life. It's mostly about other people. What has it to do with my story? Does it fit in this book, assuming it is ever published? One of the things I've learned about writing is that if it doesn't move the story forward or perform some definite, useful intent, then leave it out.

Perhaps it doesn't matter, given the possibility this writing is only for me. Still, for me, the army was only a few short years of my life, yet it takes up a lot of ink here—maybe too much. Big D said I should just write what comes. But this? This chapter I'm thinking might be better left out—my finger hovers over the "delete" key. Again, it has been some days, and Big D has not seen fit to come to. Perhaps that is my clue.

"Don't you dare!" Big D's voice hisses directly into my ear, and I feel a vice-like grip on my shoulder. "This chapter illustrates perfectly the living of several of the best of the Laws of Spirit."

"Ow! Okay! It stays!" My hand goes instinctively to the pain, but meets only the knotted muscles of my neck and shoulder. They feel hard, like bone. "Please, let go!" I swivel in my chair out from under his grasp, and now, facing him, my eyes see nothing other than my den with its book-lined far wall. Rubbing and stretching at my sorely cramped flesh, I tentatively ask, "What do you mean? And please, stop teaching me so painfully."

"You said it before—your karate teacher's hands-on style offered you your best training."

"Shit, he was just selling me belts."

"No, Jeff. He taught you better than you know." Though I still can't see him, my brows knot in an unspoken question, which he nevertheless answers. "Doesn't matter. So far in your life, you have always learned best through your pain. Men are most often that way. It is one of those laws, you know."

"No, I don't remember that one. As I remember it, the *Law of Pain* states: *'All emotional pain is self-inflicted, and all physical pain requires an element of self-creation.'*"

DO—INNG!

"Owww, shit!" With a flip of his invisible finger, my head reverberates like a one-key marimba, almost as if Big D is sounding the tone for his reply. "That is correct—*that,* is what I am talking about: *'All emotional pain is self-inflicted, and all physical pain requires an element of self-creation.'*"

"But . . . shit!"

"'Butt shit?' How apt! Look, don't negate what I tell you with your 'buts.' You don't want to be saying later, 'But, if I'd only known—'"

I see him now. His arms are out, hands upturned in supplication, his shoulders raised in dramatic ignorance. My mind flashes back to a sweltering day in an olive orchard and the Greek goddess I once tried to touch, and wanted to love, but found my hairy, fear-filled balls were in the way.

"Must it always be painful or fearful?" I shake my head. "That seems like such a negative thing."

"It need not be." His laughter now echoes throughout the room. "Learning is the bottom line of it all. You will know you have taken a great leap in your evolution when your learning no longer needs to come painfully or fearfully."

"I fail to see how the *Law of Learning* applies all that much to this chapter, except maybe to my karate or to a few wildcat scratches inflicted on Kerney."

"Doesn't." Big D's grin flashes ivory beneath red, diode eyes. "And where it concerns you, what law does most apply in that incident between Kerney and the business girls?"

"Ah, yes! For me, that would be the *Law of the Savior: 'I cannot save another from, nor is it my birthright to interrupt, the process of another's learning.'* "

"Yes, and what did that mean in this case?" Big D's eyes are just a little brighter now.

"Hell." I chortle, still flexing my sore shoulder, and remember, "If I'd given Kerney the money to pay those prostitutes, no secret, I'd have never been paid back."

"Yes, just so! Saviors usually do get crucified for their efforts." The glowing diodes of his eyes have begun a familiar flickering, and I know I am being baited. "And Kerney didn't ask, but what if he had asked for some money?"

"Ha! I'd have refused. It would still have been about saving." I shook my head. "Kerney and I would have both known he had no intention of repaying."

"Would you have done it for Canton?"

"Yes, I would. Canton was a man of his word. I'd never have refused help to Canton."

"What!" The flicker of Big D's eyes has increased in tempo to a steady warmth, reminding me of a charged power cell about to be expended. "Same action? With one man, it is about 'saving,' the other, it's 'helping?' Explain this one to me."

"Uh . . . yeah." My mind is awhirl. "Well, it's just something you 'know.'"

"Correct!" Big D shouts his glee. "It's just like love—you know because your soul tells you!"

"Yeah . . . I see that now."

"And Green? What law was that about for you?"

I pause, remembering how we'd tried to change Green into someone fragrantly acceptable. "With him also, for me it was about saving him from himself. And then there is the law that states: *'It is only within my own mind that I can place correction—I have no control over another's.'*"

"You're getting it!" he responds. "Green simply would rather stink than have to take a shower. It's good you let go of changing him when he refused the lesson a GI shower provided. He got the lesson again from a much higher order." Big D's voice now carries an air of humor. "Even then, he did not accept it."

"What do you mean?"

"Ha!" He chuckles. "I mean, I gave him those grapefruits, and an army surgeon picked them. Green never procreated, and still, he prefers to stink. Six days from now, he will become a very smelly corpse. Now, what about Donner? The laws for him came as a double whammy."

"Ummm . . ." I gulp. Jangled a little at the thought that Donner had anything important to impart to my life, nothing comes immediately to mind.

From within the smoky swirl of Big D's hood, his glow seems to encourage. "Here, I'll toss you the first bone—*Law of Thought Energy: 'Thoughts are energy and exist in one of two forms: love or fear.'* From which energy did Donner generally operate?"

"From fear, of course."

"Why?"

Big D is nodding, and I'm beginning to feel like the dunce in the corner until I realize he has given me the answer in that simple, single word—*Why!* "That would be the *Law of Life's True Nature: 'Love is the natural way of being; we are always living in love, or crying for love.'*"

"Yes! Exactly so. Donner, too, just wanted to be loved." The heat lamp is now on, and I know the machine-gun perfection of my answers is about to be jammed. "Did you give him any love?"

"Uh . . . no, not really."

"Why not?"

"I just thought he was an obnoxious prick."

"Ah! So"—the heat is now intense—"similar to the way you felt about Private Critch, then? In what energy did you respond to him?"

"Uh . . . yeah . . . it wasn't love."

"Yeah, it wasn't." Big D pauses for a long time, and I begin to wonder if he awaits some further answer of me. He addresses my unspoken question. "No, I merely wondered if you would think to ask what the cost was that you paid by not responding in love?"

"Ugh! You got me." I grunt, suddenly seeing the smallness of my mind. "Tell me. I . . . uh . . . I do want to know."

"With Donner, the cost was the best friend you would have ever known!" Again, a long pause. "And Critch? Critch would have never been your friend. Yet, with your acceptance, he would have looked at whites differently. He would not have pulled the trigger three years later or died on someone's shiv in prison, only a month ago."

"There's more?" I finally ask, still reeling as if mentally kicked in the balls.

"Yes . . . much more." His words are low, and there are tears in his tone. "You cheated your soul out of truly making a difference in the world. With your influence, both Donner and Critch had the potential to change all human life on Earth, as you know it."

"My God! I don't see how that could be . . . ," then rush to add, "and I believe you. Big D, I didn't know!" I, too, feel his sorrow and it hurts, somewhere even past my core. I ask him the question, now burning on my mind. "Why does this hurt so? What is it here that is somehow beyond my grasp to know?"

"Yes, there's more. It is something that cannot be known within the puny confines of your conscious mind. You see . . . there is that potential with every person who ever cries to you for love." Big D studies me silently, one infinite minute more before continuing. "Sergeant Curtis felt it. Neither of you knew I was there that day, waiting. And when his heart touched that potential but one brief instant? When he deliberately chose love and ordered that bag of grub?" He falls silent, his statements but questions, the fruit of which require my own question to ferment.

"And if he hadn't?" I ask, my throat tight, as if wanting to swallow something painful.

"Then I would have taken 47 souls. And 53 more would have remained here, crippled for life—some mentally, others physically.

There would have been 23 fatherless children, 15 widows, 83 grieving parents, 136 anguishing grandparents, 188 mourning siblings, some 12,657 people attending funerals. And then there were the 3,968,021 who would have perished in the resulting conflict and the billions who would never be born." Big D pauses again, the tone of his last words having risen in pregnant expectation. "Need I go on?"

"No, you've delivered your point." My mind gasps in the rarefied air of such possibilities.

"Oh no! Like most, you've failed to carry my point home. In fact, you miss my point entirely. It wasn't just about Sergeant Curtis." Beyond the expressive glow in his eye sockets, his whole personage now burns with intensity. "You! In fact, any one of you there could have nudged his decision either way simply by touching the potential of love . . . or fear . . . sometimes even indifference."

"Huh?"

"Yeah, ever heard of *The Butterfly Effect*—how the flapping of a butterfly's wings in one part of the world can result in a hurricane in another? At some time in everyone's life, they will be that butterfly, and this is the third time you have been witness to it. Two would have affected the entire world—the last, only *your* entire world."

"Okay . . . please tell me. . . ." I know better than to show disbelief with something he tells me.

"Okay, smart-ass. This time, that mess sergeant made a loving choice, and it worked out in avoiding a second Korean War—one, by the way, you would not have survived." Big D's gaze now drills me with reproach. "And then there was the time you chose indifference, back then with that South Korean ranger who shot that infiltrator at the bridge into Tongduchon."

My ears now flaming, I duck my head, then reluctantly ask, "And the third time?"

"Oh, that was the time in that Uijongbu cop shop. For a second time that day, I intervened to save your life."

"I don't understand."

"You were correct about the tin-god stink on those MPs—a stink that went all the way up their command structure. They could have, would have, danced those batons across your skull and ended you, but for my intervention. Your platoon sergeant had nothing to do with protecting you. He couldn't; tin gods always have one another's backs."

"But—"

"Oh, don't do your Greek *butt shit* thing here again. Your shitty choice of choosing the energy of fear once more almost ended *your* whole world, and it would not have stopped with yours. Love was the correct choice—even indifference would have worked." Big D stops, and I hear disappointment in his next words. "You now know so much more than most ever will . . . ," he pauses a moment in silent emphasis, "and I am about done with saving you from your poor choice of feelings."

There are many things that obstruct our ability to know and give love. Shame is only one. Shames and shoulds—such are as the feces of other people's minds that they would heap upon us. To accept it does not mean we will be fertilized and grow; it just means our viewpoint of life will be obstructed and stink.

Redneck Spirituality—Book Two

Chapter Twenty-Four

My Soul for a Dream

My banishment to A Company meant moving to the Battalion Administration compound located about one klick north and across the river from the B Company compound. Meg searched around, found a nicer hootch close by, moved in, and set up house. An L-shaped fourplex, it had its own fenced courtyard with an outhouse and hand-pumped well. Not only roomier, we had considerably more privacy and quiet. No longer did we contend with the noise of partying coming from the Miss Kim Club, which had been our neighbor, just two feet to our rear.

A woman in her early forties, Sue rented the hootch to our left. Her Yobo was an older Spec Five from my unit. They were both tranquil and nice. The walls were very thin, yet the most noise we heard from them occurred only occasionally when the old man ate beans. We had a regular thing going—he'd fart and we'd laugh.

The hootch on our right was empty, but the one farthest was occupied by a woman named Lee. She was married and was waiting on the paperwork necessary to join him back in "the world."

We hadn't lived there long when, one evening, I arrived to find no sign of Meg. I thought it a little unusual, as I knew she was expecting me. When she still hadn't come home after half an hour, I asked Sue and Miss Lee. When neither seemed to know where she was, I decided to drop over to B Company for a beer.

The EM Club there had not changed. It still sported the same two slot machines, the same few girls in the same crowd. I visited with the acquaintances I knew; none were such as I'd ever called "friend." Talking to them, drinking my beer, I realized, for me it had always been so. The only person in this country with whom I shared anything more was not here, and I missed her.

I was just leaving the compound when three business girls—strangers—accosted me. Stranger still, one seemed to know something about me. She'd been standing near the gate with the other two as I came out. It seemed almost as if all three jumped in front of me, purposefully blocking my way, while the first began asking questions in a weirdly anxious manner.

"Hi, you na-mee Cheff, light? You Miss Pak Yobo, light?"

I said a cautious, "Yeah?" noting the nervousness in her voice.

"Oh . . . ahh . . . where you go now?" she continued, her tone belying casual interest.

Just then deciding, I replied, "I think maybe I'll go to the Miss Kim Club."

The other two immediately split, hurrying off in the general direction of the Miss Kim Club. The warning flags were now up, the whole thing feeling freakier with every second. I started to follow when the first girl stepped into my path and again asked another—this time transparently stupid—question.

"You thinkee I pritty? I likee you! Mebee we go my hootchee, leetul while . . . no?"

Taking her by the upper arms, I lifted her off her feet and set her down out of my way, then hurrying after the others, arrived at the Miss Kim Club within seconds of them. The entryway had an L-shaped, chest-high windbreak just inside. Walking in, I paused to rest my arms on the gritty stucco along its top while peering over at the scene.

It was some sort of private party—Koreans only. My arrival happened just in time to see the girls anxiously dragging Meg away from a Korean man she'd been dancing with, and out the back door. Turning back, I walked around to the side entrance of the back courtyard. As I stepped through the gate, I saw Meg sitting in a chair while the girls were pulling on her arms, urging her to go somewhere. For some reason, she didn't seem to want to go along.

"What's going on here, Meg?" I asked.

Meg didn't answer. I could see she was well on the way to inebriation. The girls chimed in together. "Ees no pro-blem. Oly leetul pa-ty. You know . . . leetul dreekee, leetul daanz. Na-ting wong."

I am not a jealous person and I trusted Meg—or felt I did—even in the face of the row of wood-framed paper doors on my right, one of which had once been Meg's. These were the rooms where the prostitutes lived and did their 'business.' But trust or not, these women were beginning to annoy me. "Go!" I said, forcefully thrusting a finger toward the doorway.

They went. I looked at Meg and repeated, my voice a little edgy, although not angry. "What's going on here, Meg?"

Again, she chose not to answer. Now I was becoming a little irritated with her also. "Look . . . let's go home and talk about this." Still no answer. She just sat there, looking at the ground. "Meg, I don't want to talk here. Let's go home." Reaching out, I gave her hand a tug. She jerked it away and remained sitting in the chair.

"Why are you here? You knew I was coming tonight. Are you mad at me? Why don't you answer?"

Silence. Meg just sat there, staring at the ground, and there was a sulkiness about her I found confusing and a little distasteful. After several moments, I said sadly, but decisively, "Look, five seconds"—I held out five fingers—"five seconds more, I go out that gate. I love you. I want you go with me. You no go, I never see you again!" I took her by the shoulders, attempting to look into her eyes. Hers did not look back. "You, me . . . *Oopso. Ah rhee so*? No more. Understand?"

No answer. I let go and silently waited the count of five, then held out my hand. She ignored it.

The moment stretched into an eternity, my hand out to her almost as a plea, regretting my ultimatum. Then, realizing my honor hung on it, I turned and left.

Stumbling down the uneven dirt path through the tightly packed hootches, it was becoming increasingly hard to see through the blur. Every step taken meant that much less meaning in my life. How could I do it—leave Meg like this? Yes, my word was on the line, but somehow that held little compensation. I returned to the courtyard.

Meg was there, still sitting in that chair. Again, I held out my hand. "Come on, you're going with me."

Again, no answer. Bending down, I quickly took her arm and flipped her onto my back in a fireman's carry. She struggled silently on our way down the hill, but was still by the time we reached the bottom. Setting her on her feet, I took her hand. She resisted.

"If you don't come, I'll just carry you—might look silly to the other girls."

She came, but wouldn't speak.

Back at our hootch, I tried to talk to her. She just sat there on her bed and remained silent. Time was running out. I had to be back by midnight. Finally, I said, "Do you have a Korean boyfriend?" A lot of the girls did. "Was that him you were dancing with?"

She came to life. "No! I do na-ting wong! Is oly pa-ty . . . danzing. Na-ting wong."

* * *

That was all she ever said about it—even to this day. A few times over the years of our marriage, it would cross my mind, this strange, weird little event I came to think of as insignificant. A few times I asked, "What was that all about?" Her answer has remained the same—only spoken with better and better English: "It was nothing—just a party. Forget it."

* * *

Hurrying on my way back to the compound that night, I raged inside. Loving Meg, wanting to marry her—hell, intending to marry her—required trust, despite the disturbing circumstances. I knew that without it, we could have nothing together. And still, I raged.

Why? Clearly, it was not jealousy; dancing was nothing to feel jealous about. I stopped briefly to karate kick a cinder block wall. The wall didn't seem to mind, but my big toe—almost healed from a previous injury—did, and in a big way. Now, I was really mad. Squealing through clenched teeth, I slammed my fist into the same block wall. Again, it did not mind. It almost seemed to mock, "Come on! Do me again. You can't hurt me." I no longer wanted to—at least not enough. I let it beat me. Isn't it funny how we can put sentient purpose behind an inanimate object by simply blaming it for our own pain?

* * *

One Saturday not long after, PFC Kerney came by our hootch for a little beer and bullshit. He was unhappy about his recurring cycles of VD and restriction to the compound. The captain down at the Med was threatening to tell his folks the next time.

Maybe it was the questions he asked, or it might have been the way his eyes followed Meg around, or perhaps it was just the way he drooled on his socks. Somehow I got the feeling he wanted to find a Yobo, and he wanted one like Meg.

We were there on the porch, drinking beer and talking, when Lee came out of her hootch on our right to use the well. When she bent over in front of us to pump the well, Kerney's drooling got worse. Then, after she'd disappeared inside, he asked, "Who was that, Sarge?"

"Oh her? Name's Miss Lee."

"Damn! She's got a great ass."

"Yeah? Guess she does at that. But forget it. She's married to some guy from the Med. He rotated out, and she's just waiting for her visa to join him stateside."

Two evenings later, I arrived to find Kerney sitting there, grinning. He was my new neighbor. I said nothing to him—just ducked my head, teeth gritted. But like most men, my feelings were directed toward the woman, Lee.

The summer turned and, with fall, there came a nip to the air. The leaves on the few trees and bushes along the hillside above our hootch had all turned. My time was more than short. It was October, and I was rotating out. Meg and I had been saving—or so she said—knowing it would be a month or so before I could find a job and get her some living expense money.

Our plans were for her to live with her folks near Seoul while the security check was being done. I believed our pending marriage would lend legitimacy to our relationship, making it almost okay in her daddy's mind. With my parents, I'd not mentioned it. Perhaps she hadn't, either. So many GIs rotated out, leaving so many promises—so many never kept. How would it sit with her family should I never come back? Ah, but then it was really *my* plan, and I did not see the gigantic cockroach jamming its gears. But Meg did.

* * *

Now the day was here. Meg was in my arms as we said our goodbyes, standing in the courtyard by the well crank overlooking Tongduchon. The town I saw now carried a beauty somewhere beyond its muddy streets and brothels—even its seedy characters, street girls, and horny GIs. All were actively clogging the streets in this unseasonably warm weather, but my mind wasn't on them or the weather.

Seeing through her tears, it was frustratingly apparent that Meg didn't believe she would ever see me again. Something seemed to click in place between my mind and my heart. I knew with a certainty, there was no way I would let this woman leave my life forever. My mind was set. So long as she, too, wanted it, nothing would stop my making her my wife. Yet, we were both aware of the words. These exact words had so often been said by others with the same burning in their hearts. Were ours really any different? Would my flame go out? Would Meg's? I knew Meg's fear . . .

~ *In the Present with Mati* ~

I cannot forget that night of the party at the Miss Kim Club. Clearly, there is something about it that I am missing. Is it about some insecurity within me concerning the possibility of her cheating, or is it something much more—something, well . . . different? Now, with Meg in my past, in writing this accounting in honesty and learning, I am finally willing to see the truth and to know what it is for me—willing, but still blind. And so I poke around with it here.

I made it my choice to love her. Did that scare her? Though I've never felt mine was a clinging love, certainly, it was intense and honest, both things Meg seemed unwilling to face—or return.

It is still hard to accept that something in Meg didn't want me, not truly. Was it just some part of her that feared, knowing unconsciously what loving me would require of her? Perhaps she just didn't want to be held within the fire of such an intense love. Although, within her ability, she gave me her love—I know she did. With me, was she settling for less than she wanted or being given more than she felt worthy of accepting? What does it matter? In her heart, she must have known. But in her mind? Hell, if we all consciously knew what we truly wanted, we'd have it.

Big D does not come at the ending of this chapter, leaving me again to ramble. Like me, does he feel it incomplete? Does it matter? I've come to accept his coming in his own way. Just now, I have an appointment with a rather special man named Mati.

* * *

Mati—pronounced "Muh-tay"—is an Elder of the Chumash Indians of California. Here in Las Vegas, he stands as a spiritual leader, linking the Native American spirituality and the whites who would experience it. He holds his sweats on the bleak, desert scrubland near the Paiute Reservation north of town. I am about to enter his sweat lodge for my first time.

He is near my own age, shorter than my six feet four but about average for a Native American. Rather slender, his rawhide appearance commands an air of dignity and kindness. I knew instantly upon meeting him that he was a man of great inner spirituality—a man to be trusted. I look into his wizened eyes, as with a note of humor, he ends his strict ceremonial instructions.

"Many whites have left here firmly believing that I purposefully was taking revenge for my ancestors by broiling their white hides." He chuckles. "It is not so. This is about touching spirit. You will be free to leave at any time between the rounds. Many have done so, and it is no dishonor. This is not a macho contest. We thank you for coming to pray with us in the Native American tradition. Just remember: I've done a lot of sweats. A few participants have passed out"—again the chuckle— "but I haven't killed anybody . . . yet."

Briefly, it crosses my mind how intense sweating thickens the blood, and after all, I am on blood thinners. Will I be his first? A strange breeze touches the back of my neck, and I shake off an uneasy feeling. It is not yet my time. My work is not finished, and I certainly don't see that I've given it up. Still, Big D has not come to me yet on this chapter. As if on cue, Mati steps over and interrupts my reverie.

"Jeff, come over and talk with me." Mati takes my arm, and together we step off several yards from the group. "I understand there are some medical concerns with you. Tell me."

"Yeah . . . well, I'm diabetic and I'm on blood thinners."

"Ho! Blood thinners? What kind and why?"

"Coumadin . . . injured a leg a few years back." I shrug. "Ended up in the hospital with blood clots on the lungs—nearly killed me." I feel uncomfortable speaking of it, almost as if I'm admitting some weakness or inner defect, though from what I know of Mati, he doesn't look at it in this way. "Doctors tell me I'll be taking it for the rest of my life. Tried to quit twice, but the clots came back . . . still haven't yet accepted it." I shake my head, aware that I've told him more than he needed to know, and knowing why, I stop. His is not a respect that requires anyone's asking.

"Jeff, just listen to your body. If it tells you to go, then at the end of the round, you leave." His eyes search mine, and I'm sure he sees my fear; it's not hidden. "Take it each moment, and when you don't think you can, go to your God. Just say to yourself, over and over: *God!—or Buddha, or whatever word you choose—help me.* He will. This is about prayer. In the black womb of Mother Earth, you may well meet your God. Have no fear"—the maze of laugh lines at the corner of his eyes crinkle—"you will live to tell of it."

* * *

The ceremony begins with what is a huge bonfire, but now is mostly coals and ashes, underneath which are many large boulders of lava. Lava rock does not explode when water is poured over it.

Circling clockwise around the fire, Mati stops at each of the four directions, then to Father Sky and Mother Earth, and lastly to the Great Spirit within. As each of the seven directions are acknowledged, a pinch of tobacco from a pouch is then offered with reverence into the fire.

The five women enter the lodge first. One after another, each person kneels at the entrance in ceremony, asking permission to enter. Then, welcomed by Mati, they crawl forward. Out of thirteen people attending, I am last.

I kneel, a middle-aged man clad only in a pair of blue, cotton swim trunks and carrying a towel. Like those before, I place my forehead to the earth and say the sacred words meaning *all my relations,* *"Mitakuye Oyasi,"* pronounced mah-tock–ee–ah-say, then ask "permission to enter?" Saying this with my ass pointing to the sky, I am struck with the profoundly ridiculous spectacle I must be exhibiting, yet "ridiculous" is not what I feel. Inside myself, is a sense of deep spirituality; outside, it doesn't matter. Then welcomed, I crawl gingerly over the small pebbles and dirt. Moving clockwise, I spread my towel at a spot just inside, behind and beyond Mati's helper, on the left of the door.

With everyone seated, rocks are then brought in. Each boulder is welcomed with ceremonial words and put into the low, central pit. Great bowling-ball-size chunks of lava, they are carried in on a pitchfork. Taken from the fire, each has been placed on the flat of a log and swept clean of ash. None have touched the earth between the fire and the firepit inside the lodge, the sacred Womb of the Mother.

Different herbs—sage, cinnamon, sweet grasses, and cedar—are dropped on the glowing rocks in prayer. As the pungent smoke rises, each participant urges it toward themselves by the waving of hands, smudging our bodies for the purpose of purifying our spirits. Then the flaps are dropped and there is total darkness, except for the glowing of hot lava.

I begin my battle. With the heat of the stones come flashes of a five-year-old, broiling under the hot summer sun of a cemetery of so long ago. The darkness now confines me, like the vine-encrusted graves of the orphans entombed there—both things I thought long buried in my past. Teeth clenched, I focus my mind on the true picture of this lodge, remembering its bent branch frame tied with rawhide straps. It sits twenty feet in diameter by maybe five feet high, all of it covered by huge blankets of earth-tone hue. I remind myself of the midmorning winter's sun, shining mildly down on the outside of the blanket, only a foot above where I sit. I visualize the relatively flat desert all around, how its gray dirt and rock expanse is cut by shallow, undulating, dry water courses and a low speckling of scrub brush, cacti, and yucca.

The gurgle of the dipper touching water is replaced by the hiss of steam off glowing lava. Mati begins his prayers. He speaks of how the Native Americans are opening their ceremonies to all the peoples of the Earth, so that all might touch Spirit; and how that necessitates the need for those who would take on the responsibilities and work in making it happen. He talks of his efforts in a sacred place at Twin Falls, Hawaii and asks that the needs of his own personal work there be fulfilled.

The air has become alive, with heat now reaching a level I have never before experienced. I struggle with myself to remain sitting, but am soon lying flat out against the still, cool earth. Yet, it seems there is no relief from the suffocating heat. I press my face into a hand towel, passing the time, second by second, while the Native American chants begin. There come four of them, each weaving their sacred, simple melodies around the beating of the drums. When it seems I can take no more, they end, and the blanket covering the opening is thrown back.

Struggling to a sitting position, my body feels unusually weak with the simple act of sitting up. Across the lodge, Mati's voice calls to me. "Jeff, are you okay?"

"I don't know—"

"Yes, you do! Are you okay?"

Taking a moment, searching myself—knowing better than most that I, alone, am the sole expert on me—that fact cannot be disputed. Looking down, I see that my skin runs with rivulets of sweat, and though there is a slight, uncontrolled tremor in the arm propping my body, I know I am all right.

"Yes," I answer. Then, realizing that I have not answered in a strong enough voice, I chide myself, only to discover it is my ego guilting me. Weak-willed as it may have seemed to me, my answer was truthful.

Mati talks and jokes with the others, arranging who will sing the next round and what the songs will be. The air slowly cools to an almost comfortable temperature, and the next load of boulders is brought in—seven more of them. After the water bucket is refilled, the flap is dropped. Again, the near total darkness is punctured only slightly by a baleful, orange glow coming off the hot lava. And again, I push back my fear. The water is dipped, the hissing begins, and in seemingly no time, I am flat on my back, skin burning, lungs suffocating—and my thoughts, for a time, know only the agony of futile resistance. I am amazed that those around me still sit upright. And more so, that there is breath enough in them to sing and pound the drums. Then, toward the end, voice placement has some of them also lying down.

This time when the entrance is uncovered, it takes me longer to sit. Grabbing myself behind the knee, I finally wedge myself up. There is no speaking out in the lodge, except with permission from Mati. Now several ask.

"Permission to speak."

"Yes," he answers, "what is it?"

Most then ask permission to go relieve themselves. One says she will end her sweat here. All, in turn, are given permission, and passing their hands over the fire stones in a clockwise movement, they bid their respects and exit, again bowing to the Mother at the entrance saying, "*Mitakuye Oyasi.*"

From across the lodge, Mati is studying me. Leaning on shaking arms and head swimming, I watch the others leave. He must know my thoughts, for he calls out, "Jeff, are you okay?" I cannot deny myself, nor do I wish to lie, so instead stay silent for a time. He continues, "Jeff, this is not a macho contest. If you are not okay, it is honorable to leave." With no answer forthcoming, he scrutinizes me silently a moment longer, then repeats, "Are you okay?"

By now, I am beginning to feel revived. Across the lodge from me silently sits a woman, her beauty radiant, although with a delicate, lobster hue. I want to finish this with her—not because of a wish to impress her, nor that she would require it—but rather, I see something special in her. She, too, came to this sweat to get healing and movement in her life, together with mine. Briefly, I wonder if she will be as the others: coming into my life, leaving something special of herself, then melting off into the night. *How many more will it take, or am I ready now? Is she my soul mate?*

"Jeff?" Mati's voice breaks my reverie.

"Yes," my response comes more firmly than expected, "I'm okay."

This third round now carries 21 boulders of lava, all hot, the new ones glowing. Again, I suffer through it, hugging the bosom of Mother, feeling her cool nurturing and grateful for it. The hand towel now continuously shields my mouth. Where it does not touch bare skin, my face feels scalded. Rolling over on my side, I turn my back toward the heat and suffer the scalding, steamy humidity, only to become aware that I no longer sweat. The drums beat, the melodies weave, while my mind screams—*Big D, where are you? Help me . . . oh God, help me!*

Suddenly, there is light. The round is over. I struggle to sit and, after several tries, make it. Looking directly into the eyes of Mati, I say strongly, "Permission to speak."

"Yes, Jeff, what is it?"

"I no longer sweat. I will leave now." I say this, feeling no hint of shame.

"Yes, go with our love, Jeff," Mati answers. "We are grateful you have come and prayed with us." From around the circle of the lodge comes the acknowledgment of all.

"Ah-Ho."

I do not feel judged, as passing my hand clockwise over the rocks, I then crawl on unsteady limbs to the entrance. Bowing to Mother Earth, I say my own acknowledgment: "*Mitakuye Oyasi.*" Outside, I am helped to a chair by the fire tender. He is African American. His weathered face shines with smiling goodwill as he wraps my shoulders with a dry towel and then hands me a cup of water.

"Just sip it. Don't try to take it fast."

Sitting there, I feel strangely light. My head feels numb and oddly hard inside, like a hard-boiled egg. Rubbing it with one hand, the other begins to shake, spilling the water in icy drips across my legs. Quickly, I grab for it with the other. From inside comes Mati's now familiar line, "Are you okay, Jeff?"

"Yes," I answer truthfully. "I'm okay."

For many moments I sit, slowly sipping and cooling, listening to Mati again setting up for who would sing what. I know it is over and I'm not feeling shame. I have done well, yet there is something that does not feel so over—or well. It is only when the fire tender begins bringing the rocks that I realize what it is: My book is yet unfinished. My coaching practice has suffered with my writing. In fact, it has been neglected to the point of near extinction, and I have done little silverwork of late. Bottom line: I am not sustaining myself. *Goddammit! I am stuck.*

~ *In the Present with Big D* ~

I hear him then in my mind—hear his familiar chuckle and somehow feel the way his bony fingers glide their way across my shoulders. *Big D! You're here?*

"Ha! Yes, exactly. The real questions are: Why are you here? Are you not still stuck? Whoa! Have you quit?"

What do you mean? I feel I have done my part. My body told me clearly to leave.

"Yes, that is so . . . and you may well have died in there had you stayed this time!" I feel the tip of cold, sharp metal measure its way across my neck. "The questions remain: Have you quit? What was it you came here to do?"

How do I answer? I know what it means when one's body is overheated and no longer sweats. Has my life so changed that, this time, I would willingly accept my death?

I sit here, watching the fire tender's ebony muscles knot, as with the pitchfork, he fishes for one of the few remaining stones. I see the scars—two sets of bacon strips, one across each breast. They are Lakota Sun Dance scars! I know what he endured in receiving them, though I have no experience of the pain required, or the spirituality. Somehow now, it is clear what I must do. But will Mati take such a chance on me? Throwing myself to my knees in front of the entrance, I say the words.

"Permission to speak."

"Yes, what is it Jeff?" comes Mati's familiar voice.

"I would like to finish."

"Are you sure you are okay?" Mati knows I am not, and I will not lie to him.

"Mati, you may well broil my white hide red." My lips turn up in a grimace. "I will survive—I have that on higher authority." I bow to the Mother. "*Mitakuye Oyasi*—permission to enter?"

He pauses but the briefest moment. "Enter."

In the lodge, I again set my towel in the same spot as before. The heat from the pile of stones—twenty-eight, big-assed chunks of lava— is intense even without the steam. The entrance blanket drops to black eternity. The drums, the songs, the hissing begins . . ..

As before, I lie there on my side, face down, mouth covered— enduring. Suddenly, I feel the simple tune. Its strange, unknown words weave their way through my consciousness, and I surrender to them. Everyone is singing, including me. What was it they called it? *The Bigfoot Song?* It ends and Mati begins one alone. I listen to the unfathomable words and let the drums sustain my heartbeat and the melody caress it as it slides by. Then, once again, there is light. The participants file out, beginning at the entrance, all moving clockwise around the lodge. Though last in line, I am unhurried, for I no longer feel oppressed by the heat. Outside, I spread my muddy towel and sit upon it with the others, drinking in the coolness and sipping water.

Big D? I call out in my mind. *It is finished. I will now move in my life.*

"Yes, you will," comes his admission, almost silently, riding as it often does on the whispering desert breeze. "And again, do your lessons always have to be so painful? Even when they are merely about, what for others, is just a little discomfort?"

You have a point?

"Yes . . . absolutely . . . and more." Though I feel his caress run tender with the gentle, desert winter's air across my skin, I am wary of what next he will say. "Perhaps here, you experienced a little of what Meg's experience was of you. You know me and, in the knowing, had the courage in the end to open yourself to the healing of the lodge. Meg does not."

What? I don't understand . . .

His subtle amusement now comes like a cooling breath, comforting my overheated body. "You said it yourself, remember? 'Perhaps she just didn't want to be held within the fire of such an intense love. . . .'"

My God!

"Yes. But praises aside, didn't you also say that through it all, maybe she was '. . . being given more than she felt worthy of accepting?'" The flow of his words stops, and when I do not respond, prompts with a sharp gust: "Perhaps, truth was . . . she was being given to by someone she saw only as shameful."

What?

"Uh-hum." He chuckles. "Look, you often wondered why so many GI Yobos had Korean boyfriends. Truth was, it was only a pretense, a sick, fucking illusion of innocent love." There is now a harsh grittiness contaminating Big D's murmuring breath.

I'm not following . . .

"Meg's resentment of you that night at the Miss Kim Club? She, too, wanted to know that innocent purity of love. And that *was* her Korean boyfriend. But then you showed up. . . ." More dust, and a certain chill, now rides on the surge of his words. "That only served to point out to her, in front of him, that she was only a GI whore—nothing more."

"Huh-uhhh . . ." The understanding hits me below the belt, driving brutally into the crotch of everything Meg meant to me, leaving me wordless.

"Ah, the difficulty of seeing through one's most private shame." The wind now dies with Big D's final whispers. "Don't blame her that she could not see the purity and innocence of your opened heart—or open herself to the healing of it. She was loved and cherished in *your* reality. But one doesn't live in another's reality. And in hers, there is a demon, remember? The one that tells her she is still . . . just a rented cunt."

I look about now at the spiny, gray silence of the desert. In the vast, aching, solitude of it, there is a presence. The Native Americans know it well. I, too, feel a certain reverence, knowing it is by no accident I am here just now—also knowing.

When a man doesn't feel he is enough—believe himself man enough—he sometimes seeks out a woman, any woman, who will affirm he is a man. He seeks to conquer her body to prove it to himself. And she allows him. For she is playing the same game.

Redneck Spirituality—Book Four

Chapter Twenty-Five

Back in "The World"

'The sun was not quite clear of the mountain, and fall now bit through the charcoal haze in the air as my bus rolled out of Tongduchon, headed for Kimpo Air Base. So different from the balmy day before when I said goodbye to Meg, it was as if Nature, herself, was declaring our relationship over. I sat on the back seat alone, watching the town waking around me for my last time, its denizens walking in hunched bundles, their breath trailing misty on the gray air. The lump in my throat refused to be swallowed.

Meg left for Seoul the night before. She was gone, and now I, too, was gone from what we had together here. Yet, life here would go on. For Meg and me, it would never again be the same. My sadness was that this now was the past, and I could not yet visualize how in my future reality, it would ever be this good. As much as I wanted it, I could not envision what our lives would look like together in my world. Would Meg still love me there? Was I strong enough to do what would be needed to even have her there? Just now, I was not feeling so strong. In my heart was a chill, filling an empty space not felt since the death of my brother. As with him, my mind would always hold the memory of loving Meg, but would my arms ever hold her again? Or would she, too, become the ghost of a loved one in my past?

The flight back to "The World" was uneventful. Landing in a drizzle at Sea-Tac Airport, we short-timers were bussed through a foggy pine forest to Fort Lewis to be processed out of the army. Just one among about two hundred, I spent a very dank week in that endeavor. Mostly, we policed the grounds in conscripted, soggy groups, picking up an unending supply of equally soggy cigarette butts. It was no wonder that the wheels of bureaucracy here seemed especially rusty.

In order to elude Sergeant Shanghai's butt patrol, I, too, soon learned to walk around in a purposeful manner, pretending I had some place to be while staying close enough to hear my name, should it ever be called over the speakers. Keeping that one, sunny thought foremost in my mind—that this was the last time the army would be able to fuck with me—I was oblivious to the major clusterfuck waiting just over the horizon.

Once processed and released, I counted my measly couple hundred bucks of final pay. The lightness of my wallet was nothing compared to that in my heart with the return of my freedom. As if to celebrate it with me, the clouds parted to release of the sun and the day bloomed. My heart warmed as I hopped a plane for San Francisco. There was someone there I wanted to visit and perhaps get to know. I'd not seen her much over the years, except for a couple of quick stopovers: one on my way to Australia, the other to Korea. Having been granted a yearly visit, she'd rarely managed to use it. My adoptive mother saw to that.

These days, she liked to be called Rhonda, for some reason preferring it to the name she was known by at the time she gave birth to me. At first glance, Rhonda seemed to be one of those people who just naturally loved life. But her life was not the perpetual-motion happy machine she pretended. Hers was fueled by booze. Once a beautiful woman—now pickled into middle-aged plumpness with tiny spider veins her makeup couldn't keep covered—alcohol's presence was pervasive on her breath.

Inside, hers was a life of loneliness and searching, like a nympho who'd never known an orgasm—or so it seemed. It was as if she'd been there, traveled all those carnal roads, but never the one that would lead her to fulfillment. Beneath it all, I now heard her cry her silent, lonely scream. Yes, her outgoing personality was only a cover, her mask to the world, and I felt her pain. She lived in Redwood City with her husband, Len. I served as best man at their wedding during my stopover on the way to Korea.

This time, the evening found us—me, her, and Len—at their favorite bar downtown on Broadway. We were hoisting a few, talking in the midweek quiet of the bar, when the door opened to admit one lone, shapely figure. Rhonda called to her, "Ann! C'mon over. I'd like you to meet my son Jeff."

Climbing a little awkwardly from my stool, I formally reached for her hand. My eyes first took in her blonde curls, which just managed to caress the cleavage of her shapely breasts, then rose to the regular features of a rather pretty face. Her eyes touched mine with a glint of deep blue, suddenly sparking a memory.

"Hi . . . I remember you! You sat at the end of the bar"—I pointed to the far stools, now occupied by three sailors—"the last time I was here, about a year ago." I felt a rising of my pulse remembering her, and an immediate stiffening of my member, even though hers was the face of someone at least ten, maybe even fifteen years my senior.

That attraction was the same back then, although at the time, I was too shy to take it anywhere. This time she joined us, even though the three sailors kept buying her drinks, each obviously vying for her attention. I don't know how well she knew Rhonda, only that her interest appeared to be centered on me, even after I'd told her about Meg and our plans together. Plainly, she could see I was not available for a serious relationship. Sex she could have with any one—or all three—of the sailors. So why me?

Perhaps Ann felt I somehow fit her purpose in life. Saving lonely loves from their loneliness for some is a full-time occupation. Though with Ann, she took no money for it—at least not from me. Or perhaps she unconsciously wanted to keep herself alone, free of the dangers of love and commitment. I've since known women to do just that, just so, by hanging around only with unavailable men. Perhaps she saw the love I held for Meg and somehow wanted to be close to it, somehow share in something she, too, had once known, but lost.

I spent that night, and several others, with Ann, and she was loved—or certainly, needed. Between the crisp, white linen fragrance of her sheets, I tasted the woman essence of her throughout those long hours of desperate release. With my fear masquerading as passion, I unleashed myself within Ann's body seven times during that first night.

Then the sky turned light, shining truth, questioning my reality again. Was I clutching to her out of despair for a love I feared I'd never know again? Was I needing to feel the man in me, needing to feel him as being man enough? Was this the truth of my reality just then?

Yet, one thing seemed sure: I was betraying Meg. Certainly it would be so in her mind, were she to ever hear of it. In mine was only confusion and need—a need that, for all its apparent passion, was not sexual. Still, my fearful need was stronger than my sense of betrayal. Oh, I'd not promised to abstain from sex, except in that it was my expectation of Meg. But like me in my space of appalling loss just then, I think Ann, too, was needy—and lost. Were we two weaklings, cripples, just trying to help one another stagger along this road in life?

The week's vacation I'd allowed myself with Rhonda was soon over, and I bid goodbye to her and to the bars—and to the taste of the salty sea air of windy San Francisco, alongside the taste and smell and feel of Ann. I traveled on to Salt Lake City. What was I to Ann? I'll never know. Certainly there was a clutching also for her toward me.

"Ha! Jeff, where did you get those scratches on your back?" remarked Rhonda that day as I changed into my new civvies. "Looks like you wrestled a cougar."

She bought me those clothes so I wouldn't have to deal with those who might spit on me for wearing an army Class A uniform—happened a lot in airports as we were all taken for "baby killers" coming back from Vietnam. I'd seen the dirty looks but was not fully aware of how liberally fucked-up public sentiment was becoming toward the military.

My parents were on a job in Chile, and their house was still rented out. I stayed with Aunt Annie while the renters were given time to move. Cousin Red, who had been drafted a year after me, was still in 'Nam. And Dick Newman—by then, we knew Dick was not coming back.

I started an urgent job search. No time was I going to waste in getting back with Meg or in taking care of her. I took the first available job and found myself working in a tire retread plant, chucking molds for a dollar-sixty an hour—a real killer of a job. I worked sixty to seventy hours a week on shifts varying around the clock. The plant rarely closed, except for New Year's and Christmas.

After shift, I would drag home to Aunt Annie's with concentric, white rings of sweat stains targeting my chest, underarms, and back. My forearms always bore a Zebra's branding of scars and blisters from the molds. I dropped from a weight of two hundred thirty down to one hundred seventy—damned skinny for a man standing six feet four.

The job consisted of rolling a bagger machine between two rows of clamshell tire molds, exchanging old tire carcasses with raw rubber coverings for newly cured, retreaded tires—an arduous, pain-filled nightmare of a process.

So it went for mindless months on end, this ordeal of sweat and branded arms while immersed in a pungent, odorous cloud of curing rubber and steaming silicone mold lube. Asbestos gloves served to keep my hands from getting burned, but did nothing to keep them from cooking—or from peeling between each scalded digit like a duck with a bad case of athlete's foot. Popping salt pills like a true addict, I endured—and dreamt of Meg.

The first month saw a ten-cent raise to a dollar-seventy an hour, and then again, a few months later, to a dollar-ninety. By this time, I was living alone in my parents' house in Sandy. My spare time was often spent rabbit hunting. Sometimes, I'd stop by for a few beers in a bar with the guys from work, although usually I begged off, preferring to save the money. Even with averaging a sixty-five-hour week, that amounted to one hundred twenty dollars at best. I was living below the poverty level. It seemed nearly impossible to save the fifteen hundred dollars I figured it would take to go back and marry Meg.

The lady with the balls, Janet, was still around. Janet no longer bought rubbers; she now preferred pills. And I saw her a time or two—well, maybe ten.

Then there was Gail, the woman who grew from the girl who once took my virginity—or do I have that backward? I began seeing her sometimes . . . well, okay, regularly. She was special. How often does anyone get to go back and do their first sexual partner up right?

Of course, all this was happening in-between the times with a woman, Maggie, from the retread plant. She had a son just six months my junior, and she was also dating the plant foreman. She called him "Peter Rabbit." Rabbits have a lot of sexual stamina, but they're extremely quick on the trigger. Obviously, she didn't see him as much of a man.

Perhaps this was why I'd taken the challenge and seduced her into my growing harem—this attractive, older woman who could well have been my mother. Aside from a normal hormonal flow was my insatiable need to see myself as a *real man*. I needed women in my life just then—women who found me irresistible, women who saw me as desirable. Besides slaking my sexual thirst, it gave me hope that Meg, too, also desired me and would be there when I returned.

A man? Hell, I had no idea what that really was. Except for my time in the army, my life was always suspended somewhere between my adoptive mother's raging blame and her subsequent guilty babying.

As for my father? The arctic winds of his disapproval always whispered of how he did not see me as capable—whispered because the distance between was too great for me to define what "capable" was by his example. From both my parents, the message was the same: A man was something I was not.

Oh, and what about the army? The army's requirements for being a man seemed to be: a) having a tolerance for pain; b) having the ability to kill; and c) having a dick hard enough to drill its way back to Korea. No—the army, too, said I wasn't a man, though on at least that last count, it seemed I was trying.

* * *

The vision of Meg was vibrant only in my dreams. In my reality, a fog of fearful futility often combined with the steamy fumes off the freshly cured retreads. Sweat ran especially salty at those times, stinging and blurring the vision of Meg in my mind's eye.

It was then I'd sometimes answer my call of dire need—go sit on the pot and look at her picture. Gazing into the eyes of her image, it seemed I could almost touch her soul. From within that special space she held within me, I'd gather courage. It didn't matter what I had to go through to be with her then—even hell itself.

Writing to Meg at least twice a week became almost a ritual. My letters had to be translated, and although her translator could also read Chinese, my chicken scratches eluded him. So I bought a used typewriter and learned to peck it like a famished chicken.

Several months passed, then for some reason, Meg's letter was several weeks overdue. The postmarks were in English, and in looking at the date, I noticed a curious thing: the name of the town was off the side of the letter—unreadable. Picking through the stack, I suddenly realized, so were they all. I thought it a little strange but chose to ignore it. Then one came that was readable—Tongduchon. Why was Meg in TDC? Why wasn't she with her parents? I refused to believe she would butterfly. She wasn't like Miss Lee, was she? No, of course not.

Now I was ready to do anything to get back there—and quickly. When I first got out of the army, I wrote my parents for help. Dad was now a big mucky-muck in an American gold/silver/copper mine in Chile, and for once, my parents had plenty of money. They refused, saying flatly they didn't think Meg was the right girl to marry: she wasn't a Mormon, wasn't American, came from a foreign culture, and wasn't even of the same race.

Between their *oh-so-logical* words, the message fairly shouted: just another foreign slut digging for American gold. Almost funny, coming from Americans digging for Chilean precious metals. Throwing that logic back into their faces, I wrote that none of it mattered. She was my woman—beautiful inside and out—and the one I wanted.

Bottom line, there was that army chaplain's religious shit stinking up my life again. What good Mormon would step into that shit and track it home by inviting a prostitute to the family table. To them, I was fouling the family for all generations to come. Pompous chaplains, Mormon parents, or hardheaded Korean fathers—was there any difference? To them all, falling in love with an American GI always said the woman was an unworthy slut—and the man, not much better. In marrying Meg, I was on my own.

Crumpling up their letter, I slammed it into the trash. Five hundred dollars was all I'd managed to save. Laboring under the expediency of desperate necessity, I cooked up a lie of how Meg was pregnant and that I was responsible. Meg didn't want to go along, but I insisted—even to having her take a fake picture. Responsibility was the only thing to which my parents would relate, still relate. If a man knocks up a woman, he marries her and lives happily—or unhappily—ever after. He must be responsible. It is the only acceptable way, the *Mormon* way, the *right* way.

* * *

Given we are now divorced, that recourse now bites me in the ass, as does the semantics of the word *responsibility*. It's funny. The true meaning of the word "responsible" is to be in a state of being able to respond. But I'd always been assigned responsibility for the way my parents felt about me. My mother's rages, my father's disdain—those were most often the behaviors they directed toward me. But were their feelings truly my albatross to bear? It would seem so, but were they ever of my own choosing? Why was it that to be acceptable, it would only be by doing my life as they would have me do it? That didn't feel like my having any ability to respond. Rather, it felt like control.

Yet, in their assigning me the power over their feelings, I did indeed have power, though I never liked to accept or use it. This one time, to my great shame, I deliberately played their game. Manipulating someone is something they have to give you the power to do. Wielding such power is the coward's way.

They sent the money, and Meg conveniently had a stillbirth. We lived with the guilt of that lie for the first twenty-six years of our marriage. But after meeting Big D, honesty became a requirement in my life. No longer could I live such a lie, pretending to grieve a stillborn son who never was. Against Meg's wishes, I told my parents the truth. They said they forgave us—they said.

~ *In the Present with Big D* ~

To finally acknowledge the truth and to live it—that is what matters to me now. Having judged myself wrong for so many years, I've forgiven myself. My being *wrong* then is okay with me now. Isn't this what forgiveness is all about? Whether forgiving ourselves or others, bottom line: Don't we forgive for the good of our own soul? Holding myself as unacceptable for so long took a great deal of energy. It was just not worth it.

My parents? I believe they did forgive Meg. But did they forgive me? It didn't appear so. That's about them. But their values and beliefs are no longer my own. I now see life from a different perspective. My own now centers around the Spiritual Laws—the truths of life. Sure, I tried to explain it to them. No sale.

Do my parents judge me as *wrong*? Do you? Doesn't matter. Fact is, I no longer spend time worrying about what others think; it's none of my business. Not judging others as wrong relieves me of the necessity of forgiving. Not knowing of their own judgments relieves me of the temptation to play my part in that game of control. I'd rather look to my own feelings and be responsible for their control. Life's so much simpler that way.

Typing these words now, I am unaware of the sweat until it stings my eyes. A pungent mist seems to surround me, and I know again the odor of silicone lube and curing rubber—and I feel the heat.

"It was a glorious time for you." Big D's voice is again close in my ear, and it is his breath that I now smell. It has cooled into the scent of new tires, reminding me of the dozen or so garages, warehouses, and tire stores in which I've worked throughout the years.

"How can that be, Big D?" I roll my eyes toward the sudden black swirl of him. "Self-respect was at a lifetime low for me then. My lack of integrity was such as I have never experienced—before or since. How can it possibly have been a glorious time for me?"

"Forget the lies, but remember the women—and the fucking. Each person passing through your life has taught you something. And as a man, everything you can learn about the enigma of a woman is worthwhile. Besides," his demeanor now silently screams of *intensity*, "didn't you say you have forgiven yourself?"

"Well, yes . . ."

"It would appear you lie!" Big D's breath now blows with scalding violence across my face, reminding me again of the retread molds—of the deadly violence of a curing bag that once blew as I reached across to release the pressure line. His finger stabs from the swirling blackness of his sleeve, jabbing forth his point with the same sizzle of a mold burn, searing quick agony once more across my arm.

"Shh.iiiittt!" I jump nearly out of my chair

"Well, do you or don't you forgive yourself?" he continues.

"*Owww, Shit!* Big D, I really want to. . . ."I blow frantic breaths at the rising blister. *Why is he dishing out such physical pain?* "Forgiveness or not, it's just hard to see any glory in it."

He withdraws from me to the distant side of the room. I swivel my chair from the computer, alarmed that he might be leaving, and watch him pace on silent, flickering feet that seem to glide as if on ice. Suddenly, he stops.

"You don't listen well when the subject conflicts with your 'good Mormon' conditioning. He grumbles, almost to himself, then turning back, he seems to have made a decision. "Don't want to deal with physical pain? Then forget the lies and, *for the moment*, disregard those women in your 'harem.' Now, what have you left of your memories of that time?"

I strive to think of it without the stain of guilt. "Well, it was a brutally hard time for me . . . agonizing, both mentally and physically. . . ." My voice trails off, not certain where to take it.

"Exactly! Don't you see the underlying glory in it?" He pauses, the glow of his sight unwaveringly upon me. "You have known something magnificent, such as few ever get to know. Do you not see it?"

"I . . ." My mouth works, but the words elude me.

"The pain . . . the sweat . . . the gloriously raw, indomitable choice to endure it all for love, not knowing the outcome—all of it on a promise, one *you* made *her*, and all of it dependent on *your* ability to love." He pauses a moment, letting his words sink in. "Did you ever even consider the fact that *she* never made any promise to wait for you? *She* just went along with *your* plan. You don't know how lucky you are. Those molds cured something far more important than a little raw rubber in your life!"

"I . . . uh . . ."

His gaze is now locked with intensity on me, and in it I sense something noble, like an eagle in flight. "You have known love for a woman such as few men are ever privileged to know. Most are given the opportunity, but few have the cojones to take it." He regards me silently for another moment. "This time in your life that you see as your lowest point—this was when your determination and love for Meg made you truly a man."

"But all those women—"

"Are of no real consequence to you." He chuckles. "You might well have been drilling your way back to Meg—just part of your process and, for you, nurturing. Such is only of *consequence* in the minds of others who are so small as to label it *wrong*. There is always *cause and effect*, but *consequences* are about them judging you *wrong and getting revenge.*"

"But the lie? I deliberately manipulated my parents. That can't be of *no consequence.*" I understand his words but am not ready to let go of the *wrongness* of it.

"Oh, and what is the consequence that you see there?"

"Well . . . at a minimum, it caused me to lose my parents' respect and acceptance!"

"You never had it." Big D says it calmly, as if it means nothing. "Wasn't even about you. When will you accept that?"

"But . . . shit!"

"Ha! Yes, 'Butt shit.' My sentiments exactly. 'If you'd only known.'"

I am speechless. The simplicity of it. . . .

Big D continues. "Your lie could have been your greatest gift to your parents. They didn't know, and you didn't have to tell them." He cocks his head, and his fixed grin seems to widen. "They might well have gained a great deal of respect for you in your coming clean. They might even have seen it happening throughout the rest of your life as well." He nods his head and pauses a moment. "They might even have come clean with you. . . ."

"What do you mean?"

"They never told you of how they had that non-existent baby blessed into their church, did they?" He continues without awaiting an answer. "They didn't tell you of how they went through the whole baptismal-for-the-dead scene in their temple, did they?" I am again without words, knowing well that they certainly must have blamed me for them having done something so sacrilegious in the sanctity of their most sacred place.

"Yes," he continues, "you gave them a great opportunity to learn." His flatly spoken words now carry a tinge of sad humor. "Too bad they refuse the lesson and will not learn from it on this side of eternity. They will only see smallness of their minds when they stand before their Lord in shame, having regulated themselves into less than the highest degree of glory."

"What? Big D, you mean all that hokey Mormon shit is true?" *Surely he's joking.*

"No joke, Jeff." His gaze now is painful, a white-hot glare which quickly ascends to the level of a judgmental God. It feels as if it will split my skin like a spit-roasted hog.

"Eeee-yiiiii . . . shit! Big D . . ." In a blink the heat is gone, but the light remains as if to help me see the realizations he is about to give—realizations difficult for me to even conceive.

"Jeff, don't make light of anyone's spiritual beliefs. They are all true."

"What? How can that be?"

"Spiritual Law . . . remember? *'I am the Creator.'* " As if it has done the job by pointing out this—the greatest of the Spiritual Laws—the light blinks off. Only Big D's grin now remains, like an afterimage from a flashbulb. His final words, too, come as an afterimage of the law. "If you can conceive of how you absolutely create your reality here on earth, why wouldn't you know that on the other side, you will be not only an absolute but an instant creator?"

I sit immobile, my jaw suddenly slack. All that faces me now is seemingly empty air and Big D's next words imprinted on my mind. "Oh yes. 26

After a further, undetermined time being zombied out, I respond, "Why, Bid D? Why do you lay this incomprehensible . . . *shit* off on me?"

As if as a fading echo from the great beyond comes his answer. "Because you asked . . . you asked . . . you. . . ."

Some people equate control with security. It is a fallacy. *There is no security in life. All things change.* It is the *Law of the Universe.* And although we may not agree, one has no control of how we expect it to be "out there"—"out there" in someone else's life or "out there" in the world. And yet, each person has full control of their own life "in here," for we are the creator. Ah, but when one recognizes their connection, their oneness to God, then all is of one's own domain. On that level, each is you—and me. On that level, we need no control.

Redneck Spirituality—Book Four

Chapter Twenty-Six

Victims, Dramas, and Control

Those last few minutes seemed to move with the speed of a drunken slug as they checked my bags through Kimpo customs. On the far side of the barrier stood my Meg, waiting. Then once again, she was in my arms. I held her long, for I did not want her to see my tears. Koreans don't admire uncontrolled feelings in a man. When at last she stood back, there was avoidance in her eyes, a slight, downward cast that spoke of her embarrassment. I took it to be because of my public display, then wondered at her first words.

"You have lost much weight."

Looking down at my old high school graduation suit, how it now seemed to hang off my frame, I had to agree. Rawhide and jerky—I was tough and fit, but hadn't shown this much bone since junior high. I grinned.

"I don't eat so well as when you feed me." Looking at the soft curvature of her, there was much I wanted to devour.

Outside we caught a taxi, and as we traveled north toward Seoul, our windows open, I breathed in a warm breath of things growing in this early May morning. The rice paddies we glided past sported the fuzzy green of healthy new life, as inside did I. Meg took us directly to a house she'd rented just over the mountain from Tongbu, the town her family lived in. Underneath her smile, her tone seemed somehow somber and strained, a gray rain cloud belying the sunshine of this day.

It all soon became clear that afternoon when I met Meg's family. No one but Meg spoke any English, and Meg was not predisposed to try to translate any conversations. That quickly became understandable as I observed what was not said between them—or me. All I have to remark on here is what I saw, and mostly felt.

Meg's father, Chae Dong, was of average Korean size, about shoulder high to me, although my vantage was mostly one of scraggly hairs across a balding head. That made no apparent difference as he carried a certain dignified surety that defied his physical stature.

His air was one of cold steel—and inflexibility. A few times, I caught his disapproving glance. I suppose we both viewed the other from a similar, though different, vantage, but from mine, I only looked down on him physically. While his judgmental thoughts as to his daughter's marriage to this ungainly, towering, stick of a man were on clear display, they did not matter to me.

Yet, I now saw the reason for the storm clouds of Meg's tension and knew her private shame had only to do with her father's views of her, not of me. Briefly, I wondered why he hadn't mellowed by this time. Somehow the feel of this moment seemed to be one of shocked surprise, and I was curious how long they'd known about me. I ignored his disdain, just as I hoped Meg would have the presence to do when, eventually, she would meet my own folks.

Chong Nan, Meg's step-mother, was a quiet, clean, plain-looking woman. She didn't appear to be especially quick of mind, but did impress me with her simple, folksier ways. She just seemed to be happy with who she was. There aren't many who can say that truthfully. Too, she did not seem so unhappy with who I was. I had a feeling I would come to like her.

The teenaged half-sister, Kyong Sil, was a slim, shy ghost who drifted about the gathering—too shy to make herself noticed, and too curious to go away and hide altogether. Catching her eye peeping around a corner, I winked and sent her scurrying.

Ok Buk was the younger half-brother. A serious and bright-eyed eight-year-old, with a closely mowed schoolboy haircut, he wore the black, military-style clothes worn by all Korean students his age. I didn't see him but a couple of times during my stay, as his time was taken up with the more sober stuff of life. In him were the hopes for the family's future; on him was the pressure of their expectations to succeed. Unlike Meg, he bore his albatross well, though perhaps nervously restless under his burden.

Lastly, there was Sun Yi. Shiny, black, almond eyes in a chubby face atop a sturdy, little body constantly acrawl, she was underfoot most of the time.

When we were finally alone that first night, I broached the question burning within my breast—one not of Meg's family or the tensions between her and her father; rather, my question concerned Tongduchon.

Meg explained how living with her father's hardheaded, controlling ways had become so unbearable, she had returned to Tongduchon to be near the only friends she knew. I trusted Meg, and having now met her father, and knowing from personal experience about hardheaded, controlling parents, it was easy to believe her.

Our wedding was scheduled for the twelfth, two days hence. It was generally considered shameful for any Korean to marry an American GI. I couldn't expect Meg's family to feel any differently. Hell, hadn't mine felt the same? Sitting in the courtyard of this rented hootch, I looked at the ancestral grave mounds sprinkled about the hillside above and pondered. Had I ever seen a hillside anywhere in Korea that didn't have grave mounds? They must mean a lot to the descendants still living here. No wonder Meg felt the need to separate our love from her family by this mountain. Obviously, they wanted no one to know of this ugly, round-eyed, scarecrow of a man who would pollute their bloodline for all posterity.

No problem. I was marrying Meg, not her family. *Narrowmindedness-eosis, such a sad, fucking disease.* I shrugged. It seemed that in their sanctimony, our parents all suffered from the same unholy affliction.

The day arrived—the date of our marriage. We'd been to the Embassy, and all our papers were signed and in order. Amidst the porcelain chatter and clink of silverware, Meg and I met with her interpreter at a coffee shop in downtown Seoul.

Now we had the choice of going before the mayor of Seoul and having the pomp and ceremony as he signed our marriage into effect—or just waiting here in the coffee shop while it was done for us. Either way, his palm got greased. Of course, no one from either of our families chose to be present. Had Meg even invited hers? I hadn't invited my parents over from Chile. Hell, hadn't even thought they'd consider such a trip. Besides, Meg was supposed to be pregnant. Briefly, I regretted starting this out with such a lie.

"What do you think, Meg?"

"Makee no matter, me . . .."

I looked around at the smattering of other foreigners and shrugged. "I like it fine right here." It just seemed right to stay there sipping coffee and talking. For me, it was simply about being in Meg's presence again—and enjoying the thought of being there for the rest of my life. Perhaps it was a mistake to skip the archaic splendor.

Thus, we were married. I loved her from across that table with every bit as much intention as with any damn official hoopla. Perhaps that was only a guy thing. It wasn't until later that night, as we lie on the floor in our sleeping blankets, embraced in one another's nakedness, that I made her my vows.

"Meg, our marriage today was only a legal formality—just signing papers. I want to tell you what it means to me, okay?"

Meg looked back at me, her eyes questioning and voice uncertain. "Yes . . . okay?"

"Meg, marriage means to me that I want to be with you for the rest of my life. I will take care of you and do my very best to see that you get everything in life you want. I will love you with all my heart, and during our life together, will be faithful."

Always the practical one, Meg saw the tears of feeling in my eyes and looked at me with concern. "What you mean—'faidt-pul?'"

I chuckled a little in self-conscious realization. Was my waxing a little too eloquent, and perhaps also, a little too melodramatic? "It just means, I no butterfly."

"Oh, no pro-blem. I no butterfry you, too."

"And Meg," my eyes drilled hers, "I'll make you happy!"

Meg kissed my cheek and snuggled cheerfully against my side. "Yes. I belly happy—now!"

Our next three days were spent mostly alone, together at that rented hootch. I could not seem to get enough of her. We did stop long enough to visit Tongduchon and to see some of my old "F Troop" who were still there. Then it was goodbyes at the Kimpo Airport, and for me, back home to await Meg's visa. Her new "immediate family" status would then allow her entry into my life.

She didn't arrive in the States until September. It was a long four months for both of us. She spent a month recovering from an operation. They'd removed an ovary due to a cyst. It was rough on her. I didn't find out until well after the fact. To me, when those last two months passed by without any answers to my letters, I was frantic. Then came a letter mentioning the hospital and giving the information on her flight—nothing more.

I couldn't wait or trust anyone to help her change flights in San Francisco. Rhonda and I were there as she passed through customs. The sight of Meg brought a surge of relief to my worried heart. She looked tired and sick—or so I took it—for though her greeting was eager, it held a note of reserve. Not exactly what I'd expected, but then, it was her first flight. Who wouldn't expect a little airsickness?

Our reunion for me was joyous. I felt as if I ruled the world—a king now, with this magnificent queen by my side. I'd slain every dragon that challenged my way and won her love. Yes, rather "King Arthur" of me, but then, I was blinded by the flashbulb of fresh love.

And while the picture now developing seemed real enough, I didn't yet see that the background still looked a little like Camelot.

We visited with Rhonda and Len for a few days and showed Meg around San Francisco. Then we flew to Utah, and I showed her Salt Lake City and the majestic Wasatch Front, the land of my birth. I was full of pride and love for Meg as I took her around to meet all my friends and family.

But the euphoria didn't last long. In only a matter of weeks, it came crashing down with the realization that Meg didn't like America, nor was she as thrilled as I just to be together.

Her stilted, broken words told me of her loneliness, how she felt cut off from all that was familiar. An alien on a strange planet, nothing was normal or comfortable for her—not the food, the customs, the clothing, or the language. She often spoke of how the people seemed so different to her, all large and clumsy looking, with big noses, light-colored hair, and large, round eyes. It came as a shock for me to see; Meg shared a little of her father's prejudices. Was she like a single ovum now swimming in my sea of spermy, weird-looking tadpoles—and drowning? Or did she just feel smothered by the love of this crybaby of a man who couldn't hide his feelings— inconceivable to me . . . then.

Seeing her unhappiness, I accepted the responsibility, assuming it to be my failure to make her happy. She, too, seemed to take this same view. And more, it appeared Meg now had a need to control. She began to exercise her power over me—that same power I'd given her on that crazy, weird-assed night of the Miss Kim Club dance.

Of course, I gave her dominion—gave it with all the natural ease of snow falling and never noticed how it accumulated. It was what I'd always been taught, conditioned, even programmed to do. My adoptive grandmothers on both sides were the matriarchs of their families, as was my mother in ours. When the men didn't shoulder all responsibility for their women's feelings, they felt the squeeze.

I didn't see how my thought system was fart-breath, backassward to what truly works. How my being responsible for Meg's feelings—and her mine—could have only one conclusion: We, neither one, had much control over our lives. I didn't see this, didn't smell the stench of our insecurities.

Of course, I handed my balls over to Meg. She held them and squeezed them often. Sometimes it seemed they were all she swung from, over the abyss of her darkest fears. And I, feeling responsible, allowed it. As my adoptive father before, I, too, had married the same woman and paid the same price of loving her.

Seeing her unhappiness, I tried all the harder to make her happy, and failing, the weight of it became my burden. Did my adoptive father also hate being a beast of burden? Meg had only been stateside a couple of months when the cycles began. Snapping rudely at her one day, I let some of my anger out in a crowded supermarket, not expecting her to take it personally.

"C'mon! Just pick out a can, and let's get the hell on outta here!" The store was thick with shoppers, and I felt like an ungainly grasshopper, constantly bumping and being bumped, holding my anger with every oblivious idiot standing in the middle of the way.

"I just looking at dees prices, Cheff . . . effyting so muchy!"

Just then, there came a bite of metal against my ankle. My breath hissed of pain as I whirled around to face Baby Huey's mother, a scowl upon her face.

"Sh . . . t!"

Mrs. Huey's baleful eyes never left my face. Hers, in fact, seemed to smile triumphantly as I hobbled our basket aside, letting her waddle past. Meg hadn't noticed. Her eyes were still shifting back and forth between the two cans in her hands.

Grabbing one, I stuffed it in among our meager horde. "Just pick one, goddammit!" My growl was low, though not so much that it did not cause a ripple of unease to roll down our aisle.

Glancing around, her face a frozen mask, Meg paused in silence, eyeing me. Her words, when they came, matched the chill of her face. "We go home now."

At home, the ice was still there, as was the silence. We each set our one bag on the table together and I turned to her. "Look, Meg. I'm sorry I spoke so harshly to you. I didn't mean it, honey."

"You buy me ticket . . . I go back Korea now." The ice was now a glacier, a great, frozen, immovable barrier with only the frigid crackling of her words threatening that any movement to come would be when that mass of ice would fall, crushing me. "No one neffer treats me that way!"

"Aw, honey, I'm so sorry! Please forgive me . . . it won't happen again." The silence had returned. "Honey, my life isn't worth living without you. Please!"

No matter what I said, only the occasional crackle of ice was heard for the next three days. "No one neffer treats me that way. I want divorce!"

Oh, sweet Jesus!

Realizing then how Meg held all meaning or real importance, how she was the driving force by which my life now ran, I could not, would not, face life without her. Caving in, I begged—pleaded—and with tears streaming, swore my love and devotion.

I don't know what stopped her from leaving that first time, nor the hundreds of times over the twenty-five years that followed. Possibly then, it was only that I had no money to buy her ticket, and she knew it. But giving her that control and the tears of my fear—those were a high price to keep her in my life. Respectable Korean men don't allow their feelings to show, nor their women to rule. With every repeat of the cycle, I felt Meg's grip tighten even more. When I met Big D in that hospital ICU, there was little vestige of my manhood left.

It was never a deliberately conscious thing for either of us. Like a slow rising anchor chain of divorce, each link would clank up to break the surface in the sea of our lives, over and over, often. I'd get angry, throw, or slam something. And while my words were never demeaning or my actions abusive, she'd deem them unforgivable and demand a divorce. I'd beg her to stay, then after she'd finally agree, I'd get angry inside and, within a matter of weeks, do something unforgivable all over again, all the while blinding myself to the truth: Begging for her love was just never acceptable. And confusing love with need was more than fucked up.

~ *In the Present with Big D* ~

"Sounds like maybe you did marry a little of Meg's daddy."

"Big D!" For a moment, his blackness swirls around me like a miniature dust devil before taking form next to my chair. "Yes, I suppose I did marry at least the hardheaded side of him."

"If you had it to do again, what would you change?"

"Oh, no doubt . . . the vows."

"You mean all that '. . . I'll make you happy' crap?"

"Exactly."

"Yeah, that was kinda like a drunken skydiver without a chute saying, 'C'mon, Baby, forget all that shit about gravity. I won't let you fall.'"

"Yeah," I shake my head, acknowledging his jab, "given Spiritual Law, we were definitely headed for a fall. Love . . . lust . . . needs. . . ." I chuckle. "My senses certainly were muddled."

"Stayed that way for about twenty-seven years, hey?" His grin widens. "I take it your vows would sound a little different were you to ever say them again?"

"True. Now they would be simply a promise that the creation of my joy will always remain my own responsibility."

"And the 'faithful' part?"

"I was always faithful to Meg."

"Oh?"

"Well . . . while we were actually together, anyway. I never cheated—not in Korea or here."

"Keep talking, and the term *'by the skin of your teeth'* is going to have a whole new meaning. Might need to grow a mustache just to disguise the truth, y'know."

"Okay, Big D, I admit it: I am skinning the truth a little close here."

"You both did. There's cheating in your head, cheating in your heart, and then there's cheating in actual deed. And for you, your only truth lies in that you didn't cheat in actual deed and, like you said, only while you were living together. You don't know how it was for her."

There is a focusing of his ruby gaze. "And seeing how, in the end, she let you go and now loves another"—he pauses with my quick intake of breath, then goes on—"now you wonder: Did she love you then, or was it all just a lie, one she told for the security you afforded her? And if not love, then is it a lie you're still telling yourself?"

"Yes."

"More . . . ," he continues. His words murmur soft and tender. "You wonder how she could have had other men in her life back then—and you know there were a few."

"Yes . . . it's true." I sigh with all the feelings of a flat tire.

"Then perhaps the question you need to ask is this: Why does it bother you? So what if, at times, you were not the only one Meg loved—or who loved her? Did you ever ask yourself, or her, just who it was took care of her back then in that hospital? You knew you didn't pay the bill."

"Oh, God, it's true." I duck my head, aware of the sudden burning of my face and ears. "After all my big words, I'm feeling jealousy—"

"Just fear." Big D's bony knuckle chucks my chin and lifts my head, again level with soft understanding. "Shame—jealousy—anger? They are of the same energy. Much easier when you know it is only fear and face it." He chuckles softly. "Easier still to just accept truth."

"What are you getting at?"

"You, Jeff, the truth about you." His gaze holds me in the stillness of the moment before he unleashes that truth. "Did you love any of those women you were fucking back then?"

"I thought I. . . ." Then, swallowing hard, I stop and begin again with the truth. "No, not really. I only fucked them out of my own fearful need to feel . . . well, wanted."

"Truth is: Meg loved him and didn't want to leave. It's the difference between women and men. Most women need at least the pretense of love when they fuck. And Meg? She wasn't into pretense—not since you broke her up with her Korean boyfriend."

"I . . . uhhh . . . see that now."

"Do you also see that you started your relationship with Meg in the same courageous space as you can leave its ending? Meg loved you; above all others, she chose you. Now that she chooses another, it doesn't mean she doesn't love you still."

"I hear you, Big D, but somehow it gives little comfort."

"Do you still love her?"

"Yes." There's a sudden intensity in his gaze.

"Then why did you divorce her?"

"Our marriage no longer worked."

"Why?"

"Because I met you and made an agreement. You know all that."

"Yes, and you need to acknowledge that you did your best for her all those years. In the end, your choice was between making her a widow or living without her. Was there really any choice—for you?" He stops for a moment, studying me, then demands, "Say it, Jeff. What was required of you to go on living?"

"Honesty and courage, Big D, and I couldn't live those two requirements—not while giving her control over my life. How could I honestly respect myself? Besides, I needed to believe she was there because she loved me."

"And . . ."

"And she couldn't live without the illusion of security that control over me gave. It was something she just . . . ," I shrug, "*needed.*"

"That's correct. *'The meeting of needs is the glue that holds a relationship together. Needs are the driving force behind every relationship. Love cannot suffice without meeting one another's fearful needs.'*"

My jaw hangs, the simplicity of it. . . .

He continues. "I've repeated it three times in three different ways; remember it. It is a *Law of Life*—one few people know, and fewer observe."

"Yes. And I see how she now keeps his balls in her pocket—"

"Oh, quit whining about your hairy little balls. *The real essence of this law is simply that in relationships, you both are giving the other the opportunity to grow beyond those fearful needs.*" There, that's four times I said it, his piano-key grin seems to hold a hint of irony. "You had the courage to grow, Meg didn't."

I cannot reply through the sudden logjam in my throat, nor do I want to. He continues.

"*'Change is the constant of the universe.'* Remember that law?" The irony is definitely there. "If you don't grow together, you can only grow apart." He pauses a moment, as if to add weight to his next words. "Besides her, you had me—*The Angel of Death*—to point out the bottom line of life and to help you grow. Meg didn't. She had only you and the imminence of your death . . . *your* death, not hers."

My head is bowed, tears dropping, no longer regulated to rivulets gathering in a soggy beard.

"Oh, and by the way, Jeff. There is a big difference between the characters of men between a man who shows his feelings openly—especially to those he loves—and the one who sheds tears only to feel victim or elicit sympathy from others."

How can I fault you for having the same weaknesses as I? Take a step forward, listen up, and know: I will deal with *my* weaknesses. *Yours* are not my rightful concern.

Redneck Spirituality—Book One

Chapter Twenty-Seven

A Goosed Gander

The army has a way of reaching out to touch someone—getting them to be the most pissed that they can be. The first summer after Meg's arrival, I was informed my skills as a 64B20 heavy truck driver were needed by the Utah Army Reserve at their annual, two-week summer camp and marshmallow roast. What bullshit! Hadn't I already done my duty to my country?

"Not so," I was told. There was a six-year military obligation to perform. Normally, it was two years active duty and then four in the inactive reserves. Utah, at the height of the Vietnam War, was one of only a few states that sometimes required active reserve duty from draftees. Perhaps it stemmed from the heritage of Utah's governing forefathers—control freaks all. Did the present ones, those at the draft board, still have a hard-on for me? It seemed so unfair. But the truth was, life really is perfect, just as it is.

When Meg heard this meant spending two weeks away from her, playing weekend warrior way up in Washington State, she panicked. She was in desperate fear of spending all those nights in a strange country, alone and without my protection—or so she said. And I believed it. Clearly, something about it for her held great fear. Seeing the dismay in her eyes, I tried everything possible to get out of it, starting with a hardship plea to the Army Reserve. They weren't buying.

Next, I went to my doctor, explained the situation, and asked him to find something medically wrong. A medical waiver would do the trick—piles perhaps. He did everything the doctor at the 7th Division Med had back there in Korea, well, except for the archery practice with my prostrate. And as his fat finger dipped to uncomfortable depths, he said, "Oh, did I tell you that I'm a lieutenant colonel in the Army Reserves?"

Back in the car, squirming in the uncomfortable slime, I mulled the situation over. Like my butt, it felt like hot saltwater taffy in my mind. At first it burned of gall, yet, the more I pulled and twisted, the colder it seemed and the harder it became. Short of fleeing the country, I had no choice but to suck it up.

It was Aunt Annie who came up with a solution. She arranged for her daughter, my cousin Judy, to stay over at the house with Meg. Whoa! Life is always perfect.

* * *

And so it was that I again found myself at Fort Lewis, Washington. The Utah Army Reserves really didn't need me as a driver. They never even arranged to renew my license. I was merely a slot on the roster they needed filled. All day, every day spent there with those Vietnam- dodging rich kids, I just did what they did—stupid, senseless, worthless work.

The unit I found myself attached to was a POL—Petroleum Oils and Lubricants—unit. Their duty assignment was to practice running a temporary field fuel oil storage facility, which consisted of several huge bladders of diesel fuel. Dirt had been bermed up around the bladders and lined with plastic in order to contain any leakage or accidents. Our job was raking the rocks off the berms and then putting them back again, only to rake them off again, ad nauseam. In-between, sometimes we got a smoke break. We'd use it to sit around, bullshitting and scratching ourselves. Even the smoke breaks were senseless. Can't smoke in a fuel depot, y'know.

* * *

The first night there, I accompanied some of the guys into town. There's not much in downtown Tacoma for GIs to do. The highlight of our evening was a floor show in a bar. We'd all had a few drinks, and none of us realized the nature of the establishment. One of our guys, James, had an incredibly long tongue. He could imitate a panting dog perfectly. He'd flap it out, pant it up and down several times, flip it up to touch between his eyes, then suck it back into his mouth. It was awesome—until he made the mistake of doing it in that bar during the floor show.

In no time, two of the "girls" joined our table. I was quite attracted to one, until she asked, "And what's your name, soldier?" in a deep baritone. It was a mistake, her asking that question while I was in the middle of slurping my suds. My reply came in a spray of beer.

* * *

One night out on this town was enough for me. I spent the rest of my evenings at the EM Club on Post. It was there that first weekend where I ran into an old friend from Camp Casey, Korea.

Coincidence? No, there are no coincidences—especially not in the perfection of my life just then.

My friend's name was Strom. Now a Spec Five, he flagged me down as I passed the bar, and we sat together and started to chew over old times at Tongduchon. We'd talked for only a few minutes when I noticed he seemed to have become somehow, well, withdrawn?

"What's wrong, Strom? You ain't looking so good."

"Oh, goddamn!" He stared intently into his beer a moment, as if making up his mind, then looked me in the eye. "I was on my second tour . . . had a Yobo and was going to marry her. It was all so perfect. Then I got TB."

"TB?"

"Yeah, tuberculosis."

"Shit! Thought you were going to tell me you had something serious—like your balls fell off or something. But TB? Hell, the army'll have you cured up in no time." I said it cheerfully, and even believed it. He ducked his head slightly, looking at me in silence. I got the message.

"I thought so at first, too"—his voice, when it finally came, was without emotion—"but this's different. It's not responding to treatment. All the army can do is give me another goddamn stripe and put me up at the Med." His acceptance of it showed sullen on his face. "I'm dying."

I had no reply. What do you say to a man who is dead? He had a disease he believed was killing him. True or false, in his mind, he was already dead. This was his belief, and eventually, I expected, would be his reality, if not his creation. Intuitively, I knew it was not my place to call him wrong.

"Uh . . . look, Strom. How catchy is this TB you got?" I suddenly remembered that some strains of TB were pretty contagious.

"Dunno. The army don't seem to worry about me running around, and my Yobo never caught it. I dunno."

We sat in strained silence a moment. Strom seemed to be making a decision in his mind. Suddenly, I saw him nod slightly, as if to himself, then he turned to me and told me something—something I didn't want to know.

"Did ya know that after you left TDC, Meg, your Yobo, came back?"

Caught a little off guard, I replied, "Yes, I know." Then he said something which cut to the heart and could have been poison to my soul.

"Yeah? Well, did ya know that she fucked some Spec Four from B Company for a while?" His eyes glinted blue ice—hard against mine. "Just before they packed my ass stateside, she took up with an old sergeant from A Company. His name was Grouse. I don't think you knew him."

My jaw hung slack for a moment, and there was that feeling of being hit so fast and hard that, at first, it doesn't hurt. Then I noticed an ache in my gut, almost as if I'd been kicked in the balls. And perhaps I had. My voice quavered a little when I asked, "Are you sure it was my Meg?"

"Yes," he said quietly, and looking into the pools of hopeless death in his eyes, I knew it to be true. He had no reason to say anything but truth; facing death makes us honest that way. In the time he had left, he needed to say his truth. I know it now, for I am kin to his need. Back then, I did not need, or want, to ask who the Spec Four was. I knew.

* * *

The bus ride across base to my barracks is only a dim nightmare in my memory. My mind was tossed about by the bomb blast of his words; my very soul seemed shredded by its shrapnel. The rest of that last week, likewise, is but a dim recollection of a war on the battlefields of hell—my private hell. It raged through my mind, ravaging it with hate, jealousy, anger, regret, and wrathful rejection. For a time, I even considered speeding Strom on his way. Yes, valiantly I fought against a seemingly unbeatable foe, an army spawned of every fear of my ego. My only weapons of defense were the love, respect, and the acceptance I held in my heart for Meg. When the smoke in my mind cleared, I'd made my decision, my peace with myself.

It sucked being forced to look hard at some things about myself—ugly things. Had I passed up any opportunities to soak Willy?

Sure, there was the loneliness, the fear of never seeing Meg again, missing her, missing her arms around me, the woman scent of her. Yes, I'd been lonely, and I, too, had cheated. Could I not accept those same human weaknesses in her? I knew she loved me, knew her heart. It was beautiful and good. My world knew none better.

Yes, I fought that battle and, in the end, believed I'd won. To those who fight in such a war, does God give medals for surviving the carnage—surviving and still loving? Bruised and bleeding, mine gave new meaning to a Purple Heart. But mine still beat—and it still loved.

It was toward the end on the flight home that I finally decided my course of action. There was no need for Meg to know of this. I would say nothing . . . just pick up my life and go on loving her the best way I knew.

Aunt Annie brought Meg to meet me at the Salt Lake City Airport. Meg's greeting was strangely cool. For the next few weeks, we both seemed to drift aimlessly about our lives, silently apart, as if we lived in slightly different worlds. Every effort my heart made to reach hers seemed to slip to the side. Finally, in the darkness one night, we touched.

"Meg, I won't go on like this!" I switched on the light and faced her from the far side of our bed. "We have to talk about whatever this is between us."

"No, Cheff, you no want talk to me—this right now!" Her eyes blazed a warning.

"Yes, Meg, I do." Facing it head-on, my eyes locked on hers. From hers, the tears began suddenly to well.

"Why you butterfry me wit Janet?" Her tears now ran rivers, as if given permission by the raising of her voice in indignation. "You tink you cousin Judy no tell me?"

My eyes dropped from hers. "Meg . . ."

"Why hor, Cheff . . . she so ah-golly . . . she havva ah-golly yellow hair, big nose. . . ." Her voice drifted off into silence, except for her sobs. I didn't know what to say. Obviously, my cousin Judy had been equally as ungraciously informative as my old friend Strom.

Meg continued. "Why, Cheff . . . you tinky she prettier than me?"

"No, Meg, she is not. Beside you, she is ugly." My eyes again held hers. "Look, Honey, let's just start all over again together. We have both made mistakes." I stopped to take a breath and swallow the knot in my throat. "They're past! Let's just go on from here."

"Why you still no forget!" Meg's voice spoke her indignation as she hitched herself up onto her elbow. "Was olly one ruitennant . . . rong time ago!"

Looking at her lie, I knew we must stop it right now. Starting fresh and clean was our only chance. Withholding what I now knew would only compound her lie with one of mine.

"Meg, at Fort Louis, I met an old friend . . . Strom. You remember Spec Five Strom?" My mention of his name and new rank might have cut through it all, as her face suddenly lost its color.

"Meg, I know about him . . . and about Sergeant Grouse after him."

Meg collapsed, back prone, her hands covering her face. She rolled away, weeping bitterly. I continued. "Meg, I love you. Let's put it all behind us and start again fresh . . . no more lies between you and me, ever. *Ah-rhee so*?" (understand?) Her sobs continued without acknowledgment. For a few minutes, I tried to get through, but when she took her blanket to the living room couch, I let her go. For me, the night was one of brief, fitful sleep.

When I got up for work, my breakfast was ready. Looking at her reddened eyes, I kept my silence, giving Meg her space. Finally, as I was finishing my coffee, she sat down, and with hesitant fingers, touched my hand.

"Yes, Cheff. We start again . . . no more lies, you, me . . . nebber."

I reached for her then, drawing her onto my lap and holding her close, rocking her in my fierce embrace. *"Ah-rhea-sumnida"* (I understand).

Later that evening, we discussed it honestly and openly. I didn't ask for the intimate details. They weren't important. It simply happened.

We put Specialist Strom behind us. Nor did my mind dwell any longer upon Sergeant Grouse. Perhaps, in some ways, I owe him my gratitude. He looked after my Meg while she lay sick and helpless in the hospital. He was there for her, keeping her company when I could not. And he wanted her. But she chose me. As Big D so aptly reminded me— she chose me! For most women, sex seems to be regarded as her love given. With men, it is his love accepted. Need either be called wrong? Perhaps sex is best regarded only in the view of one's own integrity.

~ *In the Present with Big D* ~

This chapter finished, I watch the sun rise. From a first violet lightening, it now flames the clouds in scarlet, soon to blossom golden into a new day. Once more, I feel its gift in the privilege of my life. A familiar voice speaks from beyond my shoulder.

"It is well. You have grown much, courageously accepting in your mind those things you cannot change."

"Big D! I wondered if you would show." Feeling as I do that this chapter is complete, his coming is a surprise. "Is there something I've missed?"

"Just one small thing."

"Yes . . ." *Uh-oh.* "What is it?"

"It's about Specialist Strom."

"Yes? What about him?"

"You acknowledge his connection with your present grace in life, and yet. . . ." I feel rather than see his speculation. The familiar ruby of his gaze seems lost in the matching flame of this sunrise. "You seem to regard his honesty as something ungracious."

"Yeah, it seems so . . . to me."

"Why?"

For a long moment, I am lost in that thought, then speak only my feelings, a process Big D has taught me. "Just as Cousin Judy was trying to save Meg from me, it feels almost as if he, despite his jealousy, was *saving* me from Meg . . . and I didn't appreciate it."

"No?" He chuckles. "Ha! Then you see both his message and the information being only for you?"

"Well, who else then?"

"Meg, of course. Although he didn't intend it, didn't it also touch her life?" The trees outside, now copper in this dawn, seem to rustle in the burst of his humor. "She had neither your courage nor inner connection. With her, it was only in the snare of a lie, which she could no longer deny; would she look within—and then, for only one brief moment."

Despite the apparent darkness of his subject, Big D's next words retain the bright freshness of this new day. "Life has been difficult for Meg, especially now. Such magnificence could be hers, would she only take her inward journey. Even with losing you, it has not been enough. For her, your leaving will always be seen as a bluff—one she has called."

"Why do your words now speak of Meg?" There is a lightness in his words, in his acceptance of it all, that somehow I feel is a stab resentment. "Don't you always counsel me to deal only with my own life?"

"This is of your life—of the last vestige of the chain binding you. And need I remind you to lose the attitude?" The red glare of his anger seems to blaze the Eastern sky, yet there is a kindness tinting his tone as he continues. "You are the one with the courage to break its shackle. It can be your gift. . . ."

I sit one long moment, contemplating his words before he continues. "No matter the turmoil, there is a complacency in the cocoon of her misery. That part of her that is tied to you waits for your rescue— for the clatter of hoofs and flash of your armor. And a like part of you still waits for her respect." The leaves outside now dance to the wind of his laughter. "This is the shackle. Look to it now in your hands!"

Surprised at the sudden power in his last words, I look down. Sure enough, it is there—an ugly, rusted manacle at the end of a heavy chain. While it is no longer around my wrist, my knuckles show white with the power of my grip.

"Let go." His words come softly now, and I know he is leaving me to the realities of my day. Looking up, I see the sun's brilliance begin breaking the line of the distant mountain. "It does not matter that she may never see her own magnificence, or know what it is like to have the courage of a butterfly. You do. You know that such an inner journey cannot abide any shackle." His words come now, almost indistinct, encased in the shifting pattern of the leaves. "She has nothing more to give you, save the knowledge of this. Let go, Jeff . . . let go. Set her free."

A birth is a gift to a mother by God—a soul given into her care and nurturing from the moment of conception. Her pain on birth is merely an indication, a reminder from God of its worth. It is a gift she can pass on to the world with her loving, responsible care, teaching her child what it takes to be her. The joys of her gift—and its awesome responsibility—sometimes she shares with her man. Through this child, they leave the world a legacy. It is a choice, our legacy thus given. Will it be our best or worst? With most, it is both. And for most, it is something that consciously doesn't much matter, until comes the time for dying—and for that child to carry on.

Redneck Spirituality—Book One

Chapter Twenty-Eight

Her Gift to Me

Oh, that Peter Rabbit—his was the memory of an elephant when it came to grudges. He'd been gunning since our coworker, Maggie, took up with me way back when. Perhaps, too, he wanted my life to be as miserable as his. It must have been so; he'd been riding me. Now his spurs had finally caught. Not even the fact the owner liked me, or that I'd survived the dust of carbon black for over three years now and could buff a tire carcass with the ease of an old frontier buffalo skinner—none of it would save my job. This coming Christmas would be skinny for Meg and me.

Maggie moved on to California in the summer, several months before Meg's arrival in the States, but now, over two years later, Peter Rabbit still remembered. And with me, he'd not been so quick on the trigger, nor was he shooting blanks.

The first big snowstorm always brought a flurry of business in winter retreads. In those days of bias-ply tires, it was necessary to have a more ruggedly designed traction tire during the winter than was used

326 Edmond E. Frank

during the summer, but few people bought new snow tires. Snow tires wore out relatively fast and were often too well worn in only one snow season to use again the next. Most people bought retreads every winter; they were more economical than new, costing about ten to fifteen dollars each.

* * *

That afternoon, I had a dental appointment to have a wisdom tooth pulled. It had to be cut out in pieces and, therefore, took longer than anticipated. I was late reporting to that night shift, sick and groggy from the anesthetic.

"Pete . . . look, I'm sick, man. Let me have this shift off."

"Sick? Shit!" Pete had his fists on his hips and was leaning forward onto the balls of his feet. Briefly, I wondered what kept him from pitching forward onto his pointed nose. "You sashay your prissy little ass in an hour late and give me this fucking shit?"

"Look . . . I'm sick—"

"Tough shit! You see those stock racks?" His position hadn't changed, except for an arm pointing toward the empty warehouse and outbound dock. Now he looked like a one-winged plane about to plow the ground. "You know we always get cleaned out on the first hard snow. Sorry as you are, we're depending on you."

"Hey, you got over twenty racks primed and ready now. That's more 'n the rubber extruder can do in a shift. And Mike's working the number two buffer . . . you don't need me!"

Pete's eyes narrowed, hard and mean, but refused to glance over at the proof of what I'd said. He swayed once, and there came a whiff of whiskey. "Just get your fucking ass busy on the buffer—or you're fired!"

"Fuckin' prick," I muttered as I turned to comply.

"What! What'd you say?"

"Fucking prime . . . Bugsey!" I deadpanned my answer, deliberately using the nickname he detested. "I said, '. . . just fucking *prime!*'"

* * *

A cold, efficient madman, through casing after casing, I worked that buffing machine—worked it in deadly silence, all the while surrounded with the roar of the exhaust fans and the rage of dual 200-pound electric motors. Viciously, I slapped the used tire carcasses onto the expanding inflation spool, then peeled them with blazing speed, the cruel rasps torturing the squealing rubber. Ultimately, in triumphant violence, I slammed each onto the tire trees to be spray prepped with glue. I was neither gentle nor careful, as I clenched the cotton wad between my thawing gums and tasted the iron of blood.

There were always a few casings that either started out too thin, were out of round, or through operator error were buffed into the cording and ruined. My percentage of such was a bit high this night. Still, after only four hours, my production was backed up into the receiving stockroom, clear up to the inspector, now frantically trying to provide sized stock to feed my greed. I had easily a full shift's work done—and then some.

In the smoke now drifting out of the cinder block maw of the buffing room, I stood, waiting for more casings to peel, and thought of Peter. I didn't really blame him for his feelings toward me, nor his pettiness. I was surprised he wasn't here riding me now. To put out more smoke than the fans could exhaust was a clear indication that my buffer's blades needed changing. It always seemed to happen on my shift, and Peter always seemed to catch it one moment before I intended to change them—and to take great pleasure in chewing on my butt.

"Shut down that machine and change those blades, ya lazy fuck!" He'd scream it in my ear over the roar. It was a tedious task to take apart that rasp—nothing but blades and spacers, over a hundred of each. Fuck if I'd do it this night. This time, I would leave it for the day crew. Ha! If the day shift buffer could even remember how to do it. My gums now completely thawed into a massive jaw ache. I went looking for Peter. Finding him gone, I went home.

It was my last shift there. My childish fit of temper was unacceptable. I was fired. In my heart, I knew it had to be so. Yet, in my mind, my ego would not accept seeing myself as in the wrong. After all, hadn't I stayed to put out a full shift's work even while being sick? Hadn't I kept up production—right up until it became bottlenecked by the inspector being unable to supply me with more work?

Yet, they fired me! Me, their best buffer—a valuable man who could do all phases of production. They were the ones who were fucked up. Ungrateful pricks! Well, weren't they? What did they mean, ". . . poor attitude . . . bad behavior?"

* * *

Right after New Year's, I loaded everything we owned into the back of our old Volkswagen Beetle. The early morning sun was bright, the snow deep. But its sparkling dazzle did not overwhelm the shadow of my fear as my Meg—my beautiful, pregnant Meg—and I headed for San Francisco.

My veteran's benefits had been footing the bill for a correspondence course on jet engine mechanics. The school was located in South San Francisco near the airport. I figured it would be a good place to be. Although I still had several months of correspondence work to complete, the course was to end with two weeks of in-shop training. I had hopes of then getting hired at the United Airlines repair facility there.

My breath puffing white, misting my view through the window, I paused one last time to survey the red brick home that had housed so much of my childhood. Then, when the gear stick dropped into first, I eased the clutch and heard the familiar early morning chill crackle under my tires on the hard-packed snow. Once again, I remembered the crunch of rock salt under my soles and caught a whiff of coal smoke where none now existed. And while the hairs in my nose once more felt that frozen pinch, this time I walked those Bingham steps with Meg—afraid, but no longer alone.

It all made perfect sense, this move. I blamed it happening now on the assholes at the plant who'd fired me, and on all the backwoods Mormon pricks who ran the Salt Lake Valley. I was convinced that was why I did not want to stay here in the only area on earth I considered home. An adult now, and responsible and capable of creating my life, I did not see that this was the first time of many I would run from, rather than face, my life's lies.

* * *

We stayed with my birth mother, Rhonda, in Redwood City while I located a job and an apartment. The job was at a tire shop in Palo Alto, the apartment nearby in Menlo Park. The tire shop owner was a crusty, old, ex-marine named Rich. It was a three-man operation. He and his son, Rich, Jr., ran the tire store up front. I handled his little 12-mold retread shop in the back, as well as his service truck. We fixed flats for two or three trucking outfits, and changed tires and sold retreads to several car lots. I hired on at $3.10 an hour, the same pay as they'd been paying me in Salt Lake City. Ten months later, I was still at $3.10, only now there were three of us: me, Meg, and our new son, Shane.

* * *

Shane's birth was hard on Meg. She was built small, and it was a tight squeeze. My first sight of him was one of red blotches and a head weirdly pointed out of shape. I thought he would be beautiful to me, being his father, but in reality, he looked plain ugly, and I wondered if there was something wrong with him. With his head all smashed up into a point like this, would there be brain damage? Would the other kids call him "Rocket Man"?

These were the thoughts in my mind as Meg held him that first time and beamed with pride. In the face of Meg's joy, I was ashamed of my concerns. There had not been time to ask the nurses, nor to see the doctor alone, to voice them.

Now speaking with little accent, her eyes sparkling, Meg said, "Isn't he just so beautiful—don't you think?"

I couldn't lie to her; there was our pact. Instead I said, "Ahh . . . ahh . . . he sure looks funny . . . ," and then stood there feeling helplessly foolish.

Wrong answer! I knew it right away. Certainly, that wasn't what I wanted to say. It felt almost as if it had slipped out the wrong end—embarrassing like that. Meg looked up at me with her nose kind of twisted out of shape, almost as if she was, indeed, smelling something bad. She gazed briefly back down at the baby in her arms. When her eyes again rose to meet mine, there was a glistening of unshed tears. I didn't know how to make it right for her, and so said nothing.

And later, when he was handed to me, I was afraid to touch him, and he seemed to know it. Screwing up his little face—including the one eye blackened by the birthing forceps—he wailed. Helpless, I watched as his little bullet head got all the blotchier. He flat scared the shit out of me!

In fact, my bowels felt weak from the first time I'd seen him through the viewing window. Was I ready for this responsibility, especially if there was something wrong with him? But then, what did I know about responsibility? Sure, I innately knew I was responsible for myself, and I'd been taught to think I was responsible for how others felt about me. Looking at this little, pointy-headed, blotchy bundle, I knew, without a doubt, that I was responsible for him until he, too, became an adult. It all seemed too much.

Still, no matter what Shane looked like, I could have acknowledged the beauty I saw in him by what was reflected in Meg's eyes. Instead, all I reflected was fear. Was it the same with my own birth mother when the time came for her to be my mother?

* * *

Busy with the baby, it seemed I was relegated to a ghost in the background of Meg's life. Over the next months, this feeling grew into a knowing I could not deny. Shane meant more to her than I did. Maybe that is the natural order of such things. Still, before Shane, it had always been me and Meg. I loved her, and there was nothing, nor anyone, allowed to stand between us. Now there was Shane, our cub. And Meg, like a she-bear, seemed almost to be protecting him from me—from me! God knew I'd never harm him, and yet, somehow there was shame in how I felt.

Whether making love or only talking, there was sure to come that cry—a cry to be answered immediately by Meg. I, too, could have attended him in the crib, changed his diapers, readied his bottle, fed him, held him, burped him, and loved him. I, too, could have fathered him, just as Meg was mothering him, and through him, could have cemented a bond between the three of us. It wasn't that I was unaware of my jealousy over Meg's bond with him. Hell, after a few years, I thought I'd worked through all that, until came the time when, after eighteen years, he went off to college. Meg grieved his absence but didn't turn to me. Perhaps I followed after my adoptive father, for I, too, buried myself in my work.

* * *

Two weeks before my shop training at the jet mechanic school, I told Rich about my dreams. "Rich, the in-shop training is only for two weeks. After that, I'll be happy to come back and work until I either find a job in the aviation industry, or you hire a replacement—whichever comes first." A look of shock passed over his face, immediately followed by anger.

"Forget about that hokey school, Jeff, you've got a good job here—a bright future. Haven't I turned the whole retread shop over to you?"

"Look, Rich, bias-ply recaps are almost a thing of the past." I shrugged. "With radials, even if they do ever figure out how to keep 'em glued, the casing can't hold up that long."

"Well . . . then there's the shop." Damn if his tone wasn't sounding desperate. "You're doing great brake and alignment work now, Jeff. In fact, I'll even give you a ten-cent raise!"

That brought a smile to my face, but I resisted the chuckle. "No thanks. My mind is made up." By then, I was aware he'd been paying me about half of what anyone as qualified was worth.

* * *

It was never clear exactly when it was that Rich fired me; he neglected to tell me. After I'd finished school and reported back, he said he'd found someone else. I knew from Junior, he hadn't.

Again, there were lean times. I couldn't get unemployment compensation right away, what with my two weeks of school, a week to apply, then another four as penalty for quitting my job without adequate reason. Add a couple more before I could receive my first check, and even then, there was a snafu. It was close to three months that we were without income, most of which time was spent looking everywhere for any work having anything to do with jet or turbine engines.

It was hopeless. I pulled on every local company's chain that had anything to do with turbines—rang all their chimes, sent flocks of resumes out all over the country. The airline industry was deep into their own version of *The Great Depression*, and I had no chance against all those who were unemployed with solid experience—not to mention those coming out of the Vietnam War, also experienced.

Food stamps fed us, but I had to pay the rent. I didn't wait for the first inadequate unemployment check to get straightened out. Instead, I took another job—again doing what I didn't like. It was with another tire company, working in their chain store on Stevens Creek in San Jose. Rich dropped by a time or three to offer me my old job back. 'Course, I thanked him nicely, then refused.

I worked at Stevens Creek only about a year when they asked me to manage their store across the bay in Newark. Then, a year later, they gave me a better one. It was nearby in Fremont. There, we bought our first home—a townhouse with a beautiful view and in a neighborhood that smelled of eucalyptus, up high off Mission Boulevard.

I worked long, hard hours soliciting business and running the store. For the most part, I did very well. My store was beginning to crank when one of those little unfair events happened along. But then, *fair* is not about foresight, nor hindsight, rather only the judgment of one's personal sight.

The man who'd managed the Fremont store before me wanted to come back—and he wanted my store. Never mind that he ran it into the ground just before they gave it to me. His brother, Chance, was the owner's right-hand man, a company supervisor. I was busted back to mechanic with a promise of another store when one became available, and if I ". . . straightened out my act." Seemed to me it was an inane reason, something to validate the stupidity of their own act. Unfair? Yeah, seemed to be so . . . in my mind.

I watched as the other man took over my store with me now working for him as an assistant—watched him sit back and suck up the benefits and glory of all my hard labor. I didn't see him busting his nuts, as I'd done, and I didn't see him as a good manager, one having anything to teach me.

A few months later, he was kicked upstairs to a much larger store, and I was again offered the Fremont store. My answer to the gods above? "Fuck that! Who needs it?"

Chance, the supervisor, paused then at my words, open mouthed. "Did I hear you correctly? You said—"

"Yes, Chance, you did . . . fuck it! Play your silly, fucking games with someone else." His mouth was again open when I added, "Fire me, or leave me alone."

For a long moment, he stared, then closing his mouth abruptly, turned and stomped into the office. The words he tossed over his shoulder seemed almost gleeful. "Wait right there!" Fifteen minutes later, he returned. Teeth gritted and in clipped tones, he relayed the message. "Boss says you're too good a man to lose, so here's what we're gonna do: You're going to transfer to Newark as assistant manager." Here, he paused and grimaced, as if from a bad taste. "Boss thinks that a little while working under a bonehead like Dave, you'll gladly take the job."

I grunted an acknowledgment and turned to leave.

He added, "I'm thinking I'll get you first!"

"You go for it, big brother!" I knew then that he held no power over my job—none that I gave a shit about.

An assistant manager was a glorified mechanic. I got to fix what the others screwed up. Still, as a mechanic, I actually made more per hour than the store manager, and without the headaches. What I refused to see was that as a manager, I was at the bottom of the corporate ladder.

Conversely, as a mechanic, I was at the top of the slop heap. Unwilling to climb that ladder made me a sweat hog, with nowhere to go except maybe becoming a better hog—a diagnostic tech. Some called us fender lizards.

But sweat hogs, or even fender lizards, are generally happy to be just that. They are comfortable wallowing around in the grease and grime. After a fashion, I was happy, too, or thought so for a long while—too long.

~ *Looking Back* ~

Turning those wrenches got us by for the twenty-seven years of my marriage and in raising our son, Shane. Back then, it bought the groceries. Yet, there is only dying in staying with a job that just gets one by. It takes such a big portion of one's life, while never allowing for any joy.

Later, working in the non-insulated sweatshops of sunny Las Vegas, it was never fun, nor was it fun having to feed my family by working on engines that burned and nicked my hands and arms until today they resemble healed hamburger patties. Yes, I've spent a lifetime of fishing around in the black, greasy slime underneath other people's hoods—people who did not respect me, and receiving for it, only a pittance.

Through all of this, I labored under the illusion of that next paycheck. It was so much easier than following my joy. I was blind to the fact that anything could happen. That check was never a surety. Yet, the mirage of it was more real than was the possibility of having my dreams come true. I have to admit that following my joy—writing, coaching, and working with silver, refusing to turn those wrenches—has been the absolute scariest thing I've ever done. And it has brought me the most joy.

Knowing Big D, having his presence so often in my face, has taught me to value myself above all else in life, except my son, Shane. Even with him, it is not really so much an exception. Isn't he that part of me that lives on in this world after I am dust? I've learned from Big D that we honor our souls when we leave behind the best of ourselves in our children, dishonoring when we leave anything less.

My adoptive mother, the woman who raised me, was a screamer, just as was her own mother. I am not. That part of her heritage was something I learned not to be. Big D is right: I learn best from my pain. But that was not the way I wanted my son to learn.

My son has married, and now, twice over, I am a grandfather. I see in my son the man I always wanted to be. He holds and caresses his children lovingly. And, too, I see the river of anger that flows within him, glimpse it in the occasional churning on the calm of his surface. I remember it well. Like my adoptive father was with me, over the years I've shown him little more than cold neglect. Where I could have uplifted and supported his belief in himself, I wasn't there. Is that why his anger stirs in him as once it stirred in me? Is it by my example that he works at a job that gives him little joy?

Yet, beyond it, I see the love and support he gives his own two boys, and have the greatest admiration for the relationship he has with them now—despite me. Just as I rejected carrying forward the worst traits of a screaming-meemie mother, my own son rejected the worst of the cold, distant, Lone Ranger in me.

Part of his heritage comes from Meg. She's given him the best of herself. And me? I question what part of me does he carry over with his own children? The fact that he is the only one in all my family who still loves and respects me says something. Having the ability to accept others exactly as they are—is that something he passes down from me?

Or did that part come from Meg? She surely did accept Shane unconditionally. But me? Meg loved me the very best she knew to do, but accept me—no. She never grew past the model she saw as being a man: her father. Regardless of who Meg was with me, as a mother, Meg is so much more than she seems to know.

~ *In the Present with Big D* ~

A cloud of tobacco smoke envelopes my face and stings my eyes. Wreathing about in ghostly lace, illuminated by the monitor's glare, it is bright against the darkest hour of this night. With it for me comes a hungering.

"Big D?"

"Yes . . . it's me." I turn now to face the glowing tip of his cigarette, nestled between invisible lips. "You and I, alone with your hungers."

"Why do you smoke? You were clear with me that I had to give it up."

"Didn't 'have to.' It was a choice." The glow at the end of his cigarette now wicks up, as does the glow of his eyes. Inside, between his xylophone ribs, there is a whiteness swirling. "It was always your choice: life or death. . . ." His words trail off, leading naturally into my question.

"But why do you now smoke? It seems somehow . . . well, hypocritical?"

"Doesn't matter about me. You look to yourself! You smoked out of your hungers—self-destructive, mindless cravings. . . ." Big D's grin seems to widen slightly with his next words. "The same as this craving you have for taking responsibility for other people's experiences in life."

"What? Whose?"

"Try: your son's and his sons'."

"What do you mean?" My head seems to swim in the smoke of his cigarette. "I don't see it."

"Try this, then." The smoke is now almost choking. "This chapter has little to do with your son and nothing to do with this. Yet, in these last rambling paragraphs, you have made it so. Ha!" He chuckles. "No wonder you are choking. I feel like choking back a little bile thinking about it, too."

"Look, Big D! Please make it clearer to me." My eyes now involuntarily shed stinging tears.

"Did you not do the very best you could in raising your child?"

"Yes."

"Then have you not fulfilled your responsibility to him?"

"Yes . . . I suppose so."

"Why, then, do you set yourself outside the law?" The glow of his eyes seems to narrow slightly, an indication of a crinkling of non-existent skin as he grins and continues. "Yes . . . the law. You know it well. Hell, you quoted this one twice just in the last chapter." The cigarette aligns in a jauntier angle. "*Everything is perfect, just as it is.*' We all get the lessons we need from our souls—and when we need them."

"Uh . . ."

"Let go of all this self-flagellation over your performance as a father." *Huuaaa-aak!* He hacks, exactly as a flesh-and-blood person would in clearing their throat. It appears as if there is something like magma rising from within. I begin to duck, but he seems to swallow, shaking his head as one would if swallowing bile, and continues.

"Besides, didn't you say your son is the only one in all your family who still loves and respects you? He sees who you are. Be okay with your part in his life, and be the best you can be in it right now."

As for his anger, Big D shrugs, then continues. "You've taught him well by the way you've dealt with your own. Given time, he will deal with his." Again, my jaw hangs slack with the simplicity of it all, while he fades, his form blending into the haze of tobacco smoke. "Accept the love he gives you. Let it nurture your soul as all such healthy hungers do."

"Wait! Big D, you haven't yet explained why you smoke."

His words drift on still air, as if from a great distance. "Tobacco is a sacred herb. Go back to the sweat lodge and learn how *not* to abuse it." His laughter floats softly to me now. "Along with Mother Earth, Father Sky, and all four sacred directions, was it not also an offering of tobacco to *The Great Spirit within you and me—the one inhabiting us all*?" Again, his soft laughter pulses the still air. "I smoke that offering in honor of who you are becoming."

One may change jobs, move to the far reaches of the universe, but one can never change one's life—not until one recognizes its lies. When life stands on the foundation of a lie, it cannot be joyful or functional.

Redneck Spirituality—Book Four

Chapter Twenty-Nine

The Freedom of the Country

After nearly eight years, I was sick of San Francisco and the tire company for which I worked. I was especially sick of the crowds, the waiting in line everywhere I went—in the supermarket, on the freeway. Even when fishing, there was a line completely around the lake. My heart longed for the freedom, the solitude of the country. I wanted a life outside the rat race. Sweat hog or fast rat, I was tired of it all.

Now, only three years after we'd bought our house, there was over $20,000 worth of equity. Meg didn't really want to leave, but I talked her into it. The deciding factor for her was, she didn't want to raise our son there in the city—a point well taken. The deciding factor for me? Chance was correct. I didn't like working for a bonehead, though personally, I liked Dave.

This time, it took the largest U-Haul van with our new Camaro in tow to move us back to Utah. We visited with my parents in American Fork, where they'd moved from Sandy. There, we bought a used Chevrolet pickup and a twenty-three-foot travel trailer.

Leaving six-year-old Shane with his grandparents, we hitched up the camper and headed for Moab, in the far southeast corner of Utah. I opened the windows and once more breathed in the scents of sage and cedar, and that extra something special that makes up the essence of the desert air. For Meg, there were no such nurturing memories. She only seemed to notice how the wind disturbed her hair and that it made the air conditioner no longer work.

It soothed my soul to be back in the canyon lands, Moab's majestic, sandstone abutments towering starkly naked above. Meg seemed a bit awed by it all—the cliffs, canyons, and endless, multi-hued red sands. I wondered if she would ever see the beauty of it here. Relaxing before our trailer at the Moab KOA, we sipped cold beers in the cool shadow of a cottonwood. How refreshing such times had always felt to me. There is nothing like a spot of shade from the afternoon heat of the desert sun.

"Meg, how do you like it here? Isn't it beautiful?"

"I . . . I don't know, Jeff." Her eyes were wide, like a confused deer. "Is nothing like I ever seen before."

"Do you think you'd mind living here?" Her eyes looked into mine and she shrugged, wordless. Something in them seemed to question my sanity. "Don't worry, Meg, it doesn't have to be here. We'll circle the area starting tomorrow—take our time and really see it all." I touched her hand and she smiled. "Like we agreed, we'll live somewhere in this area, and you get to decide just where."

Meg glanced up at the rim above, then down the main street of town with its fashionable little tourist shops and gas stations, mixed in with the occasional old sandstone buildings put up by the original settlers of this, the Wild West. At the far end, rimmed by cottonwoods, were the brown waters and sandbars of the Colorado.

"Is just so small, this town, Jeff; not so many peoples here."

The next morning found the shadows racing our truck and camper along the cliffs rimming the gorge as I drove the winding, two-lane road along the river toward the northeast. Though longer and slower, I could not resist traveling this scenic route to Grand Junction, Colorado.

There, we tarried a few days, getting to know the town. Although there were a lot more people, to me the town seemed somehow old in meaningless history—and flat. Meg, speaking from her traditional Korean neatness, said it was ". . . kind of dirty around the edges."

I had to agree. It seemed like a lot of folks here owned their own private junkyards.

Next, we went south over the high mountain passes through Silverton to Durango. Winter avalanches kept many of the mountainsides trimmed of timber. On one such, high above the little town of Ouray, we stopped to see what was drawing the attention of several motorists who were gathered at the roadside.

"What's going on?" I asked one gray-haired man standing there. He pointed down off the vertical face of the cliff.

"It was a motor home." His voice held an in-church hush, and his Adam's apple bobbed with his next words. "They just went over."

I looked down at the wreckage. It was so far down—about three thousand feet—that it took the glint of aluminum in the midmorning sun for me to spot it. It lay there on its side, a fragile, twisted toy.

"Why is everyone just looking? If they're alive, those people are hurt!" I said it, then cleared my throat, suddenly aware of the squeakiness in my voice. "Why isn't anyone helping?"

"There's several cars headed down to Ouray to get help. Other than that. . . ." He shrugged.

He was right. There was absolutely nothing more to do. I saw it in his eyes. He, too, felt this same overwhelming desire to help those people. I think he would have tried, had he my youth—and, of course, a three-thousand-foot rope. My feelings must have been painted across my face, for he placed a hand on my shoulder. "Look, Son . . . it's been about fifteen minutes, and nothing down there has moved. You might as well go on. . . ."

Back in the truck, Meg had her arms buried in the cooler, rummaging for Cokes. "You thirsty, Jeff?" she began. Then her eyes rose to meet mine and she stopped. "What is wrong?"

I didn't answer right away. My mind was busy considering how I could get turned around on this narrow dugway, not quite ready to accept the helplessness of the situation.

"Jeff?" Her expression said I was scaring her. "What is it?"

"It's just an accident, Hon . . . a motor home. It's taken care of; nothing we can do."

Meg's eyes traveled to the group still standing silent at the edge. When they again met mine, they were almost as round as my own.

I started the motor and resumed our climb. I did not speak of it to her again, nor did she ask. Death was not yet something with which either of us wished to deal. Death always asks for honesty in life. For me, I was not yet willing to acknowledge that it was not the crowds in California from which I was running.

* * *

As for those dead or dying people back there in that motor home? I did all I could in simply sending them my love and wishing them well. Back then, it felt like so little. And yet, now I wonder, what if it did not take a tragedy for us to come together with those we pass in life? Wouldn't it then be something great? Could I occasionally revisit this space with other strangers without the need of tragedy? Still, I wonder if there is yet more to the true message that those people's deaths spoke so clearly about life.

* * *

Silverton was a seasonal ski town. Very few really lived there year-round, nor did we consider it. Instead, we traveled on to Durango, a fair-size tourist town. Walking its main street was like walking through a craft fair. I rather liked that, but had to chuckle a time or two at the several old geezers hanging about. I wondered if some movie company might be having tryouts for the remake of one of those old-time Gabby Hayes movies.

A town of about ten thousand, Durango was situated in a mountain valley. The Animas River ambled peacefully through town, unlike its whitewater fall through the La Plata Mountains from up near Silverton. The town's main claim to fame—besides surviving its boomtown mining days—was also its biggest tourist attraction: a narrow-gauge train that made twice-daily trips up the gorge to Silverton and back. Its whistle was innately Durango.

From Durango, we traveled past Mesa Verde National Monument on the west to Cortez, where we spent a day. Situated in a green valley nestled under the Mesa Verde Cliffs on the south and at the foot of the sacred Sleeping Ute Mountain on the west, it was nothing short of spectacular.

Reminiscing casually to Meg, I said, "Y'know, back in my Fry Canyon days, this was once the end of a six-hour trip just to get our family's groceries." She rolled her eyes as in what, horror?

* * *

From Cortez, we traveled northwest down McElmo Canyon, past Montezuma Creek and Recapture Wash. At White Mesa, we turned north on Highway 191 toward Blanding, Utah. Stopping for sodas at Shirt Tail Corner just south of town, I pointed down Highway 95. "Fry Canyon's just down that-a-way—God how I loved living there as a kid!" My sudden pronouncement seemed to bring a certain terror into the familiar roll of Meg's eyes.

Blanding was once one of those last bastion outpost towns of the Mormon Empire. Now it was the jump-off point to the Navaho and Ute reservations—and, of course, to the Natural Bridges National Monument, Fry Canyon, and Lake Powell. That part I liked, but the "last bastion" part? Yeah, it was a very "Mormon" town, and a small one at that. Finding a job and fitting in; Meg did not have to say "no" to Blanding. We wasted no time there considering.

Next, it was northeast to Monticello, where we spent twenty minutes looking and forty-five minutes eating before heading north, traveling the fifty miles back to Moab. After setting up our trailer again in the KOA, we repeated the scene of four days before: the beers, the shade, the high sandstone rim above, and the main street of Moab before us.

"Meg, where, out of all the places we've been, would you like most to live?"

Meg splayed wide her hands and gave another familiar roll of her eyes. "I don-no, Jeff. Evvy place different, but I think the same. . . ." She paused to look around with the eyes of a trapped rabbit. "You choose."

I thought about it a long moment before continuing. Seoul, Salt Lake, San Francisco—all places from her past that teemed with people. Was it just the rawness, the miles and miles without people, the empty ruggedness of God's own country that put her in such fear? I decided it would just take some time for her. For now, even with her permission, I did not want to choose.

"Look, Meg . . . I like Moab best. Let's start looking for work here and just let the jobs I find make the choice for us. Okay?"

"Okay, Jeff." She shrugged.

The next day, I found two jobs; only one was of interest. It was with a local oil company. The owner had a front-end shop and needed a manager. I had a lot of experience both as a front-end mechanic and a tire shop manager, and it looked like a pretty sweet job. I talked to some of his employees in the two gas stations he owned in town. None seemed all that happy to be working for him. They may have been malcontents, but during this period in my life, I, too, found it easy to feel like a victim. Would I find myself later, whining along with them? During my interview with the owner, I hadn't felt comfortable. He seemed very excited to have found a new man; I just couldn't get excited about being that man.

However, it did look like a pretty juicy deal. Meg and I were sitting in the Canyonlands Restaurant/souvenir shop/gas station, discussing it over burgers. Hanging over the booth across from ours was a picture of one of the natural sandstone arches from nearby Arches National Park. Perhaps the man in the cowboy hat, sitting under it, thought I was looking at him. I don't know. Suddenly, he unexpectedly piped in.

"Say, Partner, I couldn't hep overhearin' . . . you a mechanic lookin' fer work here 'bouts?"

My eyes swept over him, traveling from his perfectly styled and creased black Stetson cowboy hat, with its brim sweeping down low over his eyes and neck, down past the red plaid western shirt and belted blue jeans with a big, shiny, oval buckle, on down to his lizard-skin, gray cowboy boots. He wore the clothes, but somehow I didn't think he was a real cowboy, although he did have a lot of weather wrinkles on his face and neck, and he looked more "Marlboro" than the Marlboro cowboy. Still, while the accent did seem to fit, something told me he wasn't into wrestling steers and stomping through cow puckies.

I replied a guarded, "Yeah . . ."

"Wal, I bin haulin' gas 'round hereabouts, an I knows a man has a shop over 'n Duranga, Cola-raddy . . . lookin' fer some 'un ta tarn sum wrenchis—ree-al nice fella."

I felt the urge to shiver, as a weird feeling crawled up my neck. Strange, but not unpleasant, it was as if something safe and nurturing inside me was stirring and expressing itself.

"Well . . . yes, I might be interested. Who is this guy you're talking about?"

"Name's Ga-reen . . . owns the Mo-bile stations over thet-a-way—fact, he owns 'em all in these parts. Lemme giv ya 'is number. Jist tell 'um Charlie said ta caul."

Twenty minutes later, I was hanging up the phone with an appointment to see Mr. Green in Durango the next afternoon. I liked him from the moment we met. His job offer was for a mechanic, working at the Mobil station there in town. The pay was fair, the employees seemed happy, and I felt comfortable around him. Feeling that stirring again, I quickly accepted.

* * *

We spent a week looking for a house with some land near town. There wasn't much available—certainly nothing we liked. Setting up our trailer temporarily in a camp park there by the Animas River, we had no way of knowing it would be there for the next five months. Finally, we bought ten acres of raw land just outside the little town of Breen, twenty miles to the southwest. Then we ordered a new 14 X 70-foot mobile home from the small-town, fashion- combined auto and mobile home dealership.

It took several more months to get everything set up. We cleared the land, poured concrete footings, had a septic system installed, and drilled a well. It was October before we finally moved in. I was doing things—building sheds and pump houses, wiring, and plumbing well-water systems—things I sometimes, hell, often, had little idea about how to do. But I learned.

Yes, as I hammered and built, I also nailed Meg down to this place where we'd spend many years. I didn't know how she felt. My perspective was too close to the joys of my own heart to see the cross she bore and how it had always darkened our marriage, how those nails I now drove again placed her there, only immensely higher. She'd always set herself up to be martyred by never telling me what *she* wanted. It was written there across the top of her cross—that sign I'd neglected to read back there in Moab when she'd left the decisions of this move up to me. *Suffering* . . . all Korean love stories had to involve suffering.

I loved life there: my job, our new home, living in the country. I've always loved outdoor stuff. The local motorcycle shop had some factory unsold stock of Honda 350XL Enduro Motorcycles. Though two years old, the bikes were brand new and the price was right. I bought one.

God how I loved riding—the wind in my hair, the ground flashing by underneath, even the bugs in my teeth. Yes, the bugs. They just naturally came along with the grin. And the ground? There was even joy in taking the challenge of sailing along so close to the ground and keeping the skin attached to my butt. There is nothing like the feel of power thundering between one's legs, and the clench of butt cheeks in the saddle when farting into the wind, letting the buffering of the wind erase the crude realities of my humanity. And maybe it was just about cherishing the wild freedom in each such moment of the ride, knowing it is all worth paying for, at any price.

I hadn't ridden since those years while working at the retread shop in Salt Lake City. That bike, too, had been an on and off-road Enduro—a 250cc Yamaha two-stroke. Now, as then, I often rode to work, but mostly, I loved riding the backroads and trails. There was so much country to see . . . so many stolen moments, just me and the bike, alone. Moments stolen from Meg—moments she did not want to share with me.

* * *

In our move to Durango, again, we'd just picked up and created a new life elsewhere, only thinking of it as being new, for we were the same people. Much as I loved living there, sadly, the real reason for our move was the same one as from our Salt Lake City days. Embraced throughout it all were Meg and I, twirling to the dance of our angers.

Like a record player stuck on repeat, the tune played itself out, only to restart over and over. I'd do something, say something out of my anger. Then Meg, in hers, would reject me and threaten divorce. Of course, I'd beg her, promise her I'd change—anything to get her to stay. And she always did. Then, out of disgust for my part in it all, I'd stuff it down inside. The poison of our angers infected our new lives, as it had before.

Was there ever a place in Meg's world where happiness and love had ever coexisted? It had in mine. Was that why I clung so tightly to this unhappy woman, why I tried so hard to bring her into my world? Would she—could she—have been happy being with someone else?

And, in my clinging, what part of my own purpose in life was I ignoring? What was the cost? Why was this bond so needy? The questions were obvious; the answers, not so much. Yet, of them both, I maintained a studied oblivion for so many years.

~ *In the Present with Big D* ~

"Why indeed? These questions you now know well—and their answers." Big D's words once more whisper into my ear, as they have so often during this writing. "Let go of your fixation on Meg. Beyond it is something altogether different in this chapter, something you feel is profoundly unfinished. What is it?"

His intrusion into the flow of my thoughts is followed immediately by a mockingbird from the tree outside my window. It punctuates Big D's words with the call of a meadowlark—something one would expect to hear in the light of day, never from the blackness of night. I think to speak once more of Meg, then reconsider, for the sounds of the mockingbird now are of an entirely different nature. It apparently has discovered the cat and now scolds with a cluck, followed by a raven-like squawk.

Is it coincidence that I pause to listen to its repeated, inanely monotonous complaint? I wonder if this is its own true voice, and I wonder if mine is something of the same. Haven't I, in this writing, been making this same cluck and squawk concerning Meg? I reach down inside myself for something different.

Could it have something to do with those poor bastards in that motor home? Were they still alive—was there some way I could have helped them . . . some way I couldn't see?

Big D answers my unspoken thought. "The road was steep and narrow—not much more than a paved, two-lane goat path. Remember?"

"Yes . . ."

"And you could not have climbed down those three thousand, near-vertical feet. Do you think you could have flown?"

"No." I know he mocks me, and too, I know I didn't even try. "But I could have turned around at the overlook at the top of the mountain. Hell . . ." I shrug. "Maybe even gotten back down in time to take part in the rescue attempt—"

"Stop!" His voice cracks, deafening like a close-by lightning strike. I jerk around, expecting to be burned, but am only surprised. There is no searing anger there. With his next words comes a prolonged flash of illumination. "Were you sincere in your concern for them?"

"Yes."

"Then accept that your intuition was correct. It was I who rescued those people . . . some to life and some to death."

"I don't understand."

"Sure you do; we've discussed this before." He chuckles as my mouth makes the same motions as a carp's when out of the water. "One had completed his purpose in life, one had given up on hers . . . the other two are still alive. Why do you have so much resistance to other people's deaths? Is it not perfect that death comes as a completion of life—or as a soul's choice?"

I do not answer and he continues. "Ah, Jeff, this is one you know intimately in your own life. And now you empathize the perfection of it as being painful for you. Don't you think those who have given up in life also had the chance to change their minds? Who is it that you think of now?"

"My parents."

"Why? Have you not come to an understanding concerning your relationship with them? You did write them that letter. . . ."

"Yes, and their lack of answer says, clearly, they want no more to do with me in life."

"Just so . . ." Big D's eye sockets now seem to focus their familiar ruby glow. "Then what is it about your relationship with them that is incomplete?"

"Obviously, it is about their deaths."

"Yes? And . . ."

"Oh God, Big D! It has been heavy on my mind. When one of them eventually dies, what am I to do? Will the other want me to turn around, as if to come down off that mountain—the one above Ouray? Should I?"

"You know where they go in their viewpoint of you." Big D winks his familiar flicker. "Where is that?"

"Well, these last years, it has always been to resentment."

"And when you come down to the one's funeral, how do you think it will be viewed by the other?"

"Likely, they will see it as me, the perpetrator of the one's death, trying to appease the other, as if coming to the rescue."

"Yes, you are the excuse they use for giving up in life. In their minds, you are, indeed, killing them, aren't you?" We both know the answer requires no reply. Big D continues with barely a pause. "How could you possibly show up any worse?"

I pause a long moment, remembering how other Mormon funerals have been. "They could view me as a vulture, circling in on the spoils."

"Do you want anything material of them?"

"No."

"What does it matter how the other vultures view you? And the survivor? As always, the surviving one will allow the relatives to pick the corpse clean of most of their possessions." His naked grin gapes even more widely. "Might tell them something, as you won't be among those doing the picking."

"Funerals are for the living, Big D. I want it to be the best it can be for the one who remains."

"And you?" There is that laser again in his stare. "Are you not a survivor?"

"Not to them." Aaaargh, I groan—*fuck!* "Look . . . I love them both, and I just want to share my energy with them, y'know. I want to express my love."

"That they will not accept love from you is not about you." Big D pauses. I feel rather than see his grip on my shoulder through the blur. "But this you know—just as you know that as it stands, you will not be welcomed at the funeral. Just so, you have no intention of going; we will see. Meanwhile, the game your parents seek to play with you is simply not healthy. And"—he stops as if to prepare me for some special insight— "games often end where reality begins."

What does he mean by that?

"So . . . ," he continues without answering my unspoken question, "what is it you really need here—now?"

My mind falters, still questioning the meaning of his words. A great sigh escapes as I answer. "I need to give my love and to know there is no mistaking its offering—now, while they still live. And yes . . . ssshit!" My words hiss with the futility of it. "I know that even in that, I am not welcome."

"Then perhaps now is the time for *real* love."

"What?"

The glow of his sight has softened and seems to sparkle strangely with glints in diffused light. "Sounds like another letter expressing your concerns—*and* asking *them* what *they* want— might be in order."

"Ah, Big D, they'd just take my letter, my concerns, as me laying some kind of guilt trip."

"Sure, maybe so . . . and too, it may well be tossed away unopened—like the last one. But then, it might be opened and read, maybe even cherished. If it is a gift from you of *real* love, none of that matters. A *true gift* carries no demand, no expectation—not even that it be accepted." He pauses, regarding me in silence; the sparkle now intensifies. "Need I remind you that *real* love . . . *is* a *true gift*?"

For a love to flourish, each must communicate, each must nourish. Each must be willing to look at, understand, and fulfill the needs of the other. Yes, everyone has a belief system about love. Mine is not the same as yours. The trick is for me to tell you mine and to hear yours, then to give my love to you in the way you want it.

Redneck Spirituality—Book Two

Chapter Thirty

Lessons of the Heart

The land about our ten acres was mostly rolling plateau, some planted in dryland wheat, some in pinto beans. The rest was sagebrush and a mix of cedar and pinon forests. Ours was about half open sagebrush and wildflower meadow and half trees, with a great view of the La Plata Mountains to the north. Right on the side of the mountain, a natural patch of pine forest grew in the shape of a perfect Indian head, feathers and all. Near it, like an exclamation point, was the tailings dump of an old gold mine. It seemed almost as if God were saying, "Yes, this is the West—land of cowboys, Indians, and gold miners, even back to the days of the Old Spanish Trail, then farther still. Throughout this land still wafts the spirits of the ancients."

And so it was that the craggy magnificence of the heights before us bore the name of a famous, old, Spanish gold mine—the La Plata. On the ridge above Cortez, thirty miles to the northwest, lay the ruins of Father Escalante's mission. Closer, a few ridges west, were the Mesa Verde cliffs, once home to the ancient Anasazi.

We set up our own home in a clearing just inside the tree line near the northeast corner of our property. Our front view was out across the meadow, with that Indian head on the La Platas framed through a few pinion pines—beautiful!

* * *

The Navajo, Southern Ute, and Hopi Indian reserves took up most of the land for hundreds of miles to the south and west. There were a lot of Native Americans to be found around the off-reservation towns of Farmington, New Mexico, Blanding, Utah, and Cortez, Colorado. They went there to do their shopping. But few were to be seen in the mountain towns of Durango, Colorado or Monticello, Utah—that is, not in the wintertime. I think it had a lot to do with the simple fact that a sad percentage of them spent time in the white man's towns only to do their drinking, and it gets cold in the rarified heights of the Rockies.

My friend Jimmy Begay was a Navajo. We worked together, though he only waited on full-service customers and collected money. I spent my time turning wrenches in the shop. Like many Native Americans, he didn't talk a lot. With most of the other employees being high school kids, when he did, it was with me.

Someone in Jimmy's family died, and when he returned from the reserve, I watched as he drifted about doing his job, his stocky body and wide face stiff and more unresponsive than usual. Usually I could coax a lopsided grin from his scarred countenance with its broken, flattened nose and crooked teeth. This day, I didn't even try. Instead, I just said, "Jimmy, if you feel like talking to someone about it, I'm here." He'd nodded and grunted in that "injun" way, and I let him be. It was on the third day when he came and sat next to me while I was taking lunch in the rare warmth of the winter sun, streaming through the service bay windows.

"Hey, Jimmy, how're you doing?" I handed him my extra sandwich. He nodded and took it without answering. Silently, we munched for a time. Then he began.

"Was my brother's wife, Mary . . . she died up in Monticello." More than usual now, his voice carried that queer, monotone, Navajo accent with words chopped off abruptly and pauses that left me hanging before his words began again.

"I'm sorry, Jimmy," I began, then broke off, not knowing what else to say. We chewed a few moments more in silence, then he continued.

"Mary was older . . . she married my only brother, Benny." He stopped talking and I remained quiet, knowing he'd continue in his own time—*injun time* as we whites called it. "I always liked Mary. Used to watch her dance at the powwows. She went all over, dancing at those powwows. Reminded me of a mountain stream . . . and leaves floating on the wind. She was graceful like that. Won lots of money, too. Mary was a beautiful woman back then." Jimmy stopped eating and was still for a long moment. I was tempted to break in, but didn't. His voice was somehow resigned when he finally went on. "That was before Benny was killed. Happened maybe ten years ago . . . Vietnam. Mary stopped living, too. Just took the government's money every month. Didn't dance no more after that. Stayed drunk all the time." Jimmy's voice caught then, and he looked up along the snow-caked ridge of the mountain. There were tears in his eyes; I felt privileged to be seeing them. "They found Mary frozen to the ground . . . out behind the liquor store in Monticello." He paused a long moment to swallow and clear his throat. "Had to pry her loose with a shovel. She was no longer beautiful. Smelled pretty bad, too, when they thawed her out." With that, Jimmy rose to go.

"I'm sorry, Jimmy. . . ."

"Yeah . . ." Even more so, Jimmy's voice held that flat, Navajo tone. "Thanks, Jeff."

* * *

Mary Begay was not so unusual. Alcohol was a problem—one not allowed on the reserves. The reservation cops went hard on Indians caught with it. While the police were hard, Highway 666 was deadly. Much of it ran through reservation lands. From Gallup, New Mexico in the south, it passed through Cortez, Colorado and on to Monticello, Utah in the north. Those Native Americans who came to town to drink would hurry to finish anything left over before they got back on the reserve.

A great deal of the commuting was over Highway 666. It had a reputation of being the "Devil's Highway," both for the amount of blood spilled and the number designating it. The roads in the area could be quite an obstacle course—especially to a man riding a motorcycle. I preferred to ride the trails. Nevertheless, with Meg, riding was something she required I do alone.

* * *

After buying the motorcycle, I soon added an old 1959 Mitchell outboard boat, and for just a few hundred, completely rebuilt it. Lake Powell, in the southeast corner of Utah, was one of the loves of my life. Seen by boat, it was an orgasmic experience.

Of special interest to me were the areas around the Hite Ferry Crossing, where I once fished the Colorado River for catfish during my

Fry Canyon days. Looking at the lake there, I felt like one of the privileged few. I knew what lay beneath its waves. We spent a lot of weekends boating, exploring, fishing, playing, and camping in the side canyons of Lake Powell. Meg couldn't swim, yet to my surprise, she found she liked boating. Finally, we had this to share.

* * *

For me, this country life was perfection, and like whipped cream over strawberries, there were other hobbies and interests that I enjoyed. Besides riding, there was lapidary, silversmithing, and shooting black powder rifles.

One rifle I even built myself. It took about five years, on and off. I got the parts from several different suppliers: a curly maple Fagen stock, Green River barrel, an L&R lock, and double-set triggers—all of the trappings—and fitted them all together, insetting the parts painstakingly, one sliver at a time. The finished gun was a .32 caliber half-stock, mountain style squirrel rifle. Beautiful! Well, to me at least.

I joined the Durango Muzzleloaders Club. Some of the members would dress up in mountain man attire—buckskins, moccasins, and all of it. I never did. It was optional in our club. But with Meg, perhaps it was the curl at one corner of her mouth that stopped me from fully joining in. With her, even the sulfur and saltpeter smell of freshly spent black powder brought on distain. Guess it did smell a little like a country boy's fart.

All the members brought their families, and the shoots always included a cookout—a family affair for all the members except me. After that first time, Meg wouldn't come or allow Shane to, either. Big boys and their toys. . . .

"Why do you have to go shooting today?" Meg spoke, her brow awash with wrinkled displeasure. "I thought we could go shopping down at Farmington. Soo Ki called yesterday and invited us to dinner."

"Can't . . . gave my word. They're expecting me to bring my target." I'd welded an old axe head, blade out, to a steel plate. If struck just right, a bullet would split, sending each half through two paper targets bracketed on either side at the rear of the plate. "I want to see how well my new .58 caliber Zouave will shoot. It ain't easy to split a round ball. Why not come and watch; I'm one of the few who can, y'know?"

"No! I'm going to Farmington . . . and Shane's going with me!" Her voice now carried a certain very familiar energy. I knew she wasn't finished. "If it's not your damned smelly guns, it's that noisy bike. Or else you're locked up in your shop, grinding on your rocks and playing with your damned silver. When are you going to weed the garden? I want it done . . . today!"

Sometimes I wished Meg still spoke in limited broken English. Now, looking at her scowl, I knew it was a choice between the garden or a divorce. Yet, even with this ugliness, there was something of Meg's beauty still there, something I didn't think I could live without. Where would I ever find another beauty such as this—one who would be willing to put up with me? "I'll take care of it after the shoot, dear."

My voice held steady, though something in my gut now churned. I thought I understood her begrudging the time I spent with the club or on the bike. Although those things took me away, she knew she was always welcome to come along. But the silver work? That I did at home. Why did she begrudge it, too?

I'd become quite good at it. Most of the jewelry I crafted was made for Meg. I'd spend hours perfecting a ring or necklace, and when finished, I would look at the shiny sparkle of the solid silver and the mellow reflection from within the glass-clean surface of the agate and know that this was one to cherish! I'd take it to her with pride. Surely this time she, too, would see its beauty.

Meg would usually glance at it and say something like, "That's nice . . . a little big though, isn't it?" Meg preferred dainty jewelry, and in gold—24 karat gold. Or perhaps it was simply her own way of saying, ". . . sure looks funny, doesn't it?"

* * *

We'd lived near Durango about two years when Meg decided to bring her family over from Korea. In the infinite wisdom of our government, we soon discovered how Meg's parents were considered as immediate relatives. They could get visas with almost no waiting, yet her teenage brother, Ok Buk, and youngest sister, Sun Yi, would have to wait on a list for about five years.

Our solution was to bring her parents over first on immediate relative status visas. Once here, they themselves applied as immediate relatives for the two youngest children. This worked because the sister, Kyong Sil, just younger than Meg, was married and elected to stay in Korea.

With the family coming, we needed more room. I designed and, with the help of Meg's father, built a complete roof over our mobile home, with an addition in the back for most of its length. I used rough-cut beams for the support structure, cheaply bought from a local lumber company forty miles away over in Dolores, Colorado. I'd never built a house before—didn't even think I had the ability—but then, Meg wanted it done.

Meg had a way of getting me to do things she wanted, when she wanted. Usually, she coupled this with the knack for picking a time I least wanted to do it. With the hugeness of the task, this sometimes led to some minor temper tantrums on my part, sometimes even a hammer or some other item zinging its way across the property.

Chae Dong would shake his head and sometimes grunt at Meg in Korean, "Why does he act this way?"—or so Meg would translate. Of course, such unacceptable behavior usually escalated into Meg's demand for a divorce. What did her father think afterward? He must have heard me prostrating my self-respect before her. There was nothing I would not do for Meg. Seeing his occasional looks of disgust didn't much bother me—not until there came a time when I saw them directed toward Meg.

* * *

Eventually, the whole family was there. The people of Durango were very kind and generous to them, some perhaps overly so. Mr. Green gave Chae Dong a job cleaning and helping at his truck shop at night. Her brother, Ok Buk, worked at the station with me. In school, Ok Buk and Sun Yi got all the extra help and attention they needed. Through it all, they were treated wonderfully.

So it was when, about a year later, Ok Buk put it out to the community that they were unhappy living in our home. A minor disagreement between them and Meg got blown out of proportion. The townspeople were again right there, providing subsidized housing, public assistance, and food stamps.

It was "saving" in the real sense of the word. All their well-meaning help cheated Meg's family, and Meg and me, out of facing and dealing with our issues. Just as such help always does, it provided a way out for them from being responsible for their own lives—the same kind of saving as had poisoned Mary Begay's life.

I didn't mind so much when most of the townspeople seemed to think I was abusing my in-laws. My heart knew it wasn't so. Those who didn't know me would think what they wanted. It wasn't something I could, or wanted to, control. Small-town gossip is an unbeatable bully best ignored.

The fact was, Meg simply objected to Sun Yi spending fifty dollars for designer jeans, as opposed to fifteen for regular ones. Such a simple thing. It should have—and could have—easily been solved within our family. I was, however, outraged when I saw the pain in Meg's eyes when her family laid the problem on her. Saying to her that they didn't want to live with a "GI whore," they promptly accepted all those "saving liberal" handouts and left without dealing with it. It was a battlefield, and both armies died—victims of war. As usual, the American government footed the bill.

Meg paced and fumed and vented her rage. The injustice of it all! We both held down full-time jobs: she, a waitress at a local restaurant, and I, of course, was a mechanic. Sure, the money they made part-time was theirs, but how dare they waste it on such vanity. *Worse*, how dare they treat her with such disrespect for objecting. I wondered how much of her family's disrespect was aimed at me? Meg never said. Besides, I kind of knew. Wasn't I the GI?

Still, Meg couldn't stay mad long. A few months went by without any interaction between our families, but slowly, through furtive meetings between our son, Shane, and his grandfather, we, too, were drawn back in. The anger and hurt began to subside. Sitting in their cheap, prefab, government-supplied apartment on their government-issued couch, drinking food-stamp tea, we forgave one another our perceived wrongs amidst the awkward rattle of cheap china.

~ *Looking Back* ~

For me, the lesson was learned. I no longer went about trying to save them from their lives. In bringing them over, we'd only meant to help Meg's folks—and did—but Meg's brother and sister? They'd liked it fine in Korea. There they could afford designer jeans.

Helping? Saving? There is such a fine distinction. I've since just been a spectator while they lived their lives, their way. I've glorified in their triumphs and empathized in their sorrows, and tried not to judge their continued dependence on the saving arm of government.

Perhaps the leaders of government will someday come to understand that it is not welfare that people need, but rather, self-reliance. If they would but spend their energies keeping the rich from oppressing the poor, and instead, provide education and training to those in need with a one-shot opportunity to help themselves.

Welfare? No, welfare is like giving people Milk of Magnesia in place of simply milk. Instead of adding anything to their lives, all of that self-reliance just gets wasted. Like explosive diarrhea, it gets all over themselves and everyone around. And generally, the shit keeps running for as long as they are alive—welfare is addictive that way.

There will always be those who will not take care of themselves. Why is it so hard to accept that everyone has the right to decide to live or to die, and to make that choice with dignity—or not. But no one has the right to take advantage of the weak, to make the choice for them by taking away that dignity.

Meg's family didn't stay in Durango much longer. When Ok Buk graduated from Durango High, they moved on to Junior College at Helper, Utah, then on to Salt Lake City and the University of Utah, where he graduated with honors, majoring in business. With his master's degree, he became an executive for a well-known financial institution.

His next oldest sister, Kyong Sil, the one who stayed in Korea, came over for a time but went back. It seems the standard of living there in Korea is better—in her opinion. When I left Korea in 1968, the average per capita income was about one hundred fifty dollars per person, per year—this according to one of my CO's indoctrination lectures. I saw nothing that disputed it.

Now, some thirty years later, money flows freely there. The Korean middle class is now joining that of the Japanese in spending their vacations touring the states. Prices here are much cheaper than in most other countries. I am awed by how fast America is slipping into the third world. Thanks go to our country's finest leaders and lawmakers—and traitors.

Ok Buk is now married. Bucking his family's prejudices, he married an American woman fifteen years his senior. She was his friend and chief supporter during his college years. They now have two little children, a boy and a girl.

Sun Yi graduated from high school in Price, Utah. She was a member of the elite girls drill team there—only the best looking and most popular. She has since married a returned Mormon missionary and joined the LDS Church. They have three beautiful little girls.

Meg's brother and sister did escape welfare, leaving only the stink of it behind on Meg and me. As for Meg's parents, Chae Dong and Chong Nan? They still live near their children in Salt Lake City—and still collect public assistance. Every few months, Chong Nan gets pissed at the old man's hardheaded, superior attitude and leaves him to stay with one of the children for a time. They always talk her into returning. Yeah, take away someone's dignity and it leaves nothing but anger.

* * *

Meg, Shane, and I lived on in Durango for several more years, where I continued to become more and more disillusioned with my life. Mr. Green was killed in an accident, and things changed. His blood seeped into the blacktop of Highway 666, his flesh shredded in the bar ditch alongside, among the shards of broken whiskey and beer bottles. I no longer felt appreciated or treated fairly. Funny how his death made so much difference in my life.

Being a mechanic, I made my living by the commission I earned from work performed in the shop. Yet, now I was constantly having to run out front to wait on customers or to take in UPS packages; we were a shipping point for UPS as well. The new manager hired high school kids—family friends—and their work reflected it. Often when a package would come in or a full-service customer, they would temporarily be missing or otherwise indisposed. I would have to take myself away from whatever commission work I was doing to handle business. When I complained, there would always be a plausible excuse, and I was always blown off as a whiner, as indeed I was, constantly.

Durango, being such a small town, there was no other place I cared to work, or that would pay me as well. Several times during the last few years there, I went looking elsewhere: St. George and Cedar City, Utah and even Page, Arizona and Grand Junction, Colorado. Page would have been my favorite, except it was no larger than Durango. It was, however, the only town on Lake Powell.

Perhaps it was really all about flies. There was a fly in my thinking, one that buzzed around inside my mind, telling me how all my problems were merely there at work. Its buzzing masked the true facts. The bile of my life's lies was becoming increasingly hard to swallow back down. I didn't see it at the time and so went about whining loudly and asking validation from anyone who would listen. The stench of it was so unattractive. . . . Yes, perhaps it was the flies.

My first and biggest obstacle was in selling the place. No one was buying. That one I solved by borrowing enough money on it to re-establish fifty miles away in Farmington, New Mexico.

~ *In the Present with Big D* ~

"God!" Big D's snort of disgust is evident. "You've managed to capture the whine and moan of that period perfectly. Even threw in a little of that better-than-thou preaching, too." Big D's voice suddenly falls quiet, deadpanning into my ear as he adds, "But you left one thing out."

"What?" Momentarily distracted by his sudden appearance, my reaction is defense. "Of course! I left a lot out. This was a period of nearly ten years, and the wrap-up concerning Meg's family, another ten."

"Ah, yes . . . defense." Big D chuckles. "Humanity's first line of denial to the truth." He now inhabits the space before my chair, his gaze blazing in fiery intensity such that the rest of him is only a smoky blur between me and the monitor of my computer. The flesh on my face feels like the skin of a hot dog must, just before it bursts. Surrounding me now is the smell of a campfire and hot dogs roasting on a stick.

"Owww—shit!" I thrust back on the rollers of my chair, yet the distance gives no relief from the agony. "Okay . . . okay!" My outstretched hands are only ten more weenies added to the agony. "Look, Big D, help me out here. Just tell me—please!" *Owww . . . goddammit!*

"Mandy . . ."

"Mandy?" The pain has lessened to a tolerable level and I sigh in relief, taking a moment to shift my brain. "She was just an *almost* indiscretion. Nothing really happened between us."

"Oh? Didn't it?"

"Yiiiii . . . shit!" I yelp as the heat comes back into searing focus.

"What was Mandy to you . . . truly?"

Frantically, I apply myself to his questions and feel the removal of his energy. It settles into a kind of warmth, yet I am aware of how quickly it can be reapplied. "Mandy was a few stolen kisses in a warehouse—nothing serious." I feel the heat rising and hasten to continue. "It almost became an affair, but she had the good sense not to show."

"Exactly, though it was only from her fear that she did not show." Big D regards me a long moment, his form swirling black, and his toothy grin somehow now seems toothier. "You had no such fear, had you?"

"No."

"In fact, for you there was an open welcoming, a yearning!"

"Well . . ."—I duck my head, sighing—"y-yes."

"It wasn't about the churning hormones of your youth, nor any neediness for a substitute to fill the fearful void left in your life by a half-world-away Meg." I feel a momentary burst of heat. "Well, was it?"

"N-no . . . sss–shit!" *Jesus.* "Take it easy."

"Why did you welcome it?" Big D's voice has gone soft. "C'mon, Jeff . . . only truth, remember? What did Mandy really mean to you?"

As I contemplate his words, a sadness envelopes me, one tinged by shame. "Mandy was just an attractive woman—one who wanted me."

"And Meg?"

The sight of Big D has turned to a wet blur. "Meg?" I shrug. "I no longer felt that from her."

"Ah, the substitute thing again . . . only from want—that being your new fearful need. Hummm?" He chuckles. "Seems it *is* possible to be even farther than a half world away."

How do we lose our self-esteem? Simple: by living in self-dishonesty; by not being the same on the outside as on the inside; by doing or saying other than we really are. In our higher minds, we always know, and in our hearts, are angry.

Redneck Spirituality—Book Two

Thirty-One

Is This All There Is?

*Farmington, New Mexico—*since moving to the area, we'd done the bulk of our shopping there. About a half hour's drive down Highway 140 along the La Plata River from our Durango home, Farmington sat in a green valley hemmed by bluffs of naked clay conglomerates. On one end of town was the confluence of the La Plata, on the other, the Animas, and through town ran the San Juan River. Sitting at the border of the vast, dry, dusty deserts of the Navajo, Hopi, Apache, and Zuni Reservations, and the cool greenness of the Southern Rockies, Farmington was also at the threshold of two societies—that of the white man and of the red man. Nearly fifteen hundred feet lower, it was much warmer.

Since we shopped there, and Meg's Korean friends all lived there, it was the simplest, most natural place to go. We bought an old, ammonia-era home—a real fixer-upper. But first, it was a cleaner-upper.

The old man we'd bought it from was a widower with three small dogs. He held those dogs so closely, it's doubtful that he ever let them outside for anything. He seemed oblivious to their natural needs. The house was slowly moldering away around him. That we would buy such a house was a real metaphor for our marriage.

Disregarding the stink in our marriage, we began rebuilding that putrid house. One of the first things we did was to rip down the drapes and roll up the carpets and drag them all outside. Hoofing that carpet out the door, the mold and ammonia off the dog waste stung my eyes. Squinting back at Meg, who was holding the rear, I said, "Whoo-eee! That old bastard must of had a stronger stomach than a maggot."

"Why is Americans so filthy all the time?" Knowing she was referring to me, and also where the conversation was headed, I didn't answer. Compared to Koreans, there could be no defense. I was a slob.

Using an industrial-strength cleaner, we disinfected everything. The floors around the kitchen sink and the bathroom toilet were rotted and had to be replaced. Meg wanted an open, airier feeling to the house, so we tore out several walls, thus opening it up between the kitchen and the living room. The wall of the third bedroom was removed, exposing it to the living room area. Half of the new space we walled to make a large bath off the master bedroom.

Some of the walls to be removed were weight bearing, and that was a problem. I solved it by first building a twenty-four foot, six-by-eight-inch beam from which to hang the ceiling joists. I constructed it by dragging several eight-foot, two-by-eight boards up through the access hole to the attic and bolting them together in place.

All of the changes I designed and then built with Meg and Shane's help. The kitchen cabinets and counters we bought pre-made from Sears. The installation and tile counter surfaces we did ourselves in a beautiful, dark blue, one-inch glazed ceramic. All totaled, we sank $15,000 remodeling the place and four months of time.

We didn't mind working days at our jobs, and nights, until one or two, on the house. It was a small price, we figured, for a home that would outlast us both. Meg and I were becoming very comfortable with fixing the "things" in our lives. Far easier dealing with the shitty "things" than with the "shit" in our relationship as it swirled around in the crapper of our marriage.

Meg was now working as a waitress for a large restaurant chain. It wouldn't be long before she became the manager. I worked for an independent franchise auto repair shop of a national chain. Shane, who began school as a first-grader at Durango, was now in high school and a great help on the house, although we didn't allow him to work late.

Just as I'd done so many other times in my life, I had again taken my family and run away. The bills all followed—and I paid them—unaware of what else would follow. The old relationships, jobs, and situations that had somehow turned sour, they too followed—same people, just with different faces.

By putting all that at a distance, I believed the slate of my life could somehow be wiped clean. I'd simply start over. Yet, the lies that ran my life hadn't changed, or even been acknowledged, and the truth of who I was becoming was still reflected in it.

My new job started out pretty well. The owner was just beginning his business and sent me to school in Dallas, Texas to be his diagnostic tech. I was doing the job anyway, but sorely needed the training.

A diagnostic tech repairs cars with runability—engine running—problems. Since the beginning of computerized cars in 1981, fixing such problems was often a long-shot-to-the-pot. The other mechanics wanted to go for the green in it, but the boss didn't like catching the splatter when they let the smoke out of some customer's computer—especially when it was a new one they'd just sold. The old "hang it together with bailing wire" or "repair it with a bigger hammer" just didn't get it anymore, and there were a few fender lizards still dinosaur enough to think it did. I didn't want to be one.

For a time, the old manager from Durango haunted the shop, ghosting in now and then, asking—hell, even begging—me to return. I might have. Not being appreciated was the main reason I'd left, but it was too late. We were invested by then. And too, there was the stink of all that gossip left there by Meg's family.

Being new to the auto repair business, my boss was constantly changing things around during those first few years. The policies and procedures part of that was irritating enough, but the pay schedule changes always got me sizzling. Of course, I didn't look at it as an opportunity to work out an equitable system with a pliable employer. Instead, it looked to me like being bent over the counter every few months and eating pork without using my teeth.

The bitching and whining was back like a motor at full throttle, except now running higher octane. Once again, it became my mainstay of conversation with everyone I knew.

I had no friends of my own but was too busy complaining about the lousy way others treated me to wonder why. With my coworkers, I kept my bitching to a low rumble. Besides, our relationships ended at the door of the shop.

And Meg? There were three couples, three Korean wives, who were Meg's closest friends. Those I called my friends were simply the husbands, which sort of gave me a captive audience. For the women, Korean food seemed to be the excuse, if not the glue, that held them together. So different were they, that had they been in Korea, I doubted friendship would have crossed anyone's mind.

* * *

I glanced down at the big pan of Korean ribs sitting on the bench seat of our truck between Meg and me. *At least now that we all live in the same town, we don't have to travel so far just to go to these damned dinners.* "Did you manage to get the bone chips cleaned off the ribs, Meg?" I liked the taste but hated the bone chip that seemed inevitable by the way Korean ribs were cut perpendicular to the bones. Sitting at the red light, I glanced over at her sour expression.

"You know I did." Her answer was cut short by a disgusted huff. "You don't need to ask. I know how picky you are."

"Sorry," I grunt. "You're right. It's the others who don't take as much care. I guess I'm just not in the mood for another of these dinners so soon. . . ." I cut myself short. The look she flashed me said clearly I was about to take it too far.

"Soon? It's been two weeks since the last time." Her eyes flashed. "That's not too soon."

"You're right, dear . . . sorry. It's probably just that tonight it's at Less Bok Ju's house." I changed the subject.

"Why? She just like me—'nother Korean." Meg's accent was coming back, a clear indication that she was getting pissed.

"Well, it's really about her husband." I lied. "I'm kinda feeling beholden for the work he did on the house." Meg just grunted, and I felt relieved to have dodged that bullet once again.

Bok Ju Jensen was an average-size woman in a very un-average-shaped body. She moved with a sort of willowy grace, and I found myself very attracted to her—too much so. She came from a town on the East Coast of Korea. Some said that the people from that province were deceptive and manipulative. But they hadn't met shy, beautiful Bok Ju. It didn't matter that I'd never made advances toward her. I still felt the need to lie to Meg.

Les, her husband, was short and thin and anything but handsome. I think it was just his looks and the meticulous organization with which he ran his life that said "nerd." The truth was, he had a great deal of common sense and was one of the most intelligent men I've ever known. I liked and, at the same time, disliked him. His abilities in life gave rise to a certain air. I gave him the respect he craved. In return, he helped me rewire my homes—both Durango and now, here. Les was an electrician.

We were met at the door by Bok Ju and Kyong Soon. I stood behind, holding the pot of ribs, while the girls exchanged hugs amidst a chatter of Korean. Looking up past Meg, Bok Ju said, "Welcome, Jeff, good to see you."

Ducking my head to the ribs that Kyong Soon was just then taking from me, I replied, "Good to see you, too, JuJu." That was the name by which we called her.

Following Kyong Soon inside, I peeled off to shake hands with Dennis. He was her second husband and ran a motorcycle repair shop. What with motorcycles and mechanics, I felt an affinity for him, but knew it would always be at an arm's length. Like so many other men in my life, we pretended but knew we were never really friends.

Handing me a beer, Dennis said, "How's it going, Jeff?" Then he turned toward Bart Mickelson without awaiting my answer.

"Ah, well, shit. Boss is lowering the hourly pay but not raising the commissions. Don't know what he's thinking this time." I grit my teeth in frustration.

"Maybe he thinks you'll work faster," Bart Mickelson chimed in from where he sat, nursing his Coke. Bart didn't drink beer—against his religion.

I shook my head. "Can't; any faster and I'll start making mistakes."

"Well, guess that's understandable, what with you working with the computers and diagnostics and all that. But what about the others?"

I ducked my head and looked up with raised eyebrows. "The others will just get sloppier. Ever considered what a sloppy brake job can mean?"

"Why don't ya just quit?" I didn't like the tone in Dennis's voice and might have understood it if I'd known that he was friends with my boss.

"Naw." I frowned. "I'm scheduled for some more training down in Texas."

Just then, Les came over and passed out the plates. "Time to chow down, guys. Food's out on the counter."

After everyone had loaded their plates and sat down at the table, I glanced over at Kyong Soon. A mature, dependable, even pretty woman, I wondered what it was that attracted her to Dennis. She so outclassed him. She looked up, meeting my eyes, and I smiled. Of the three, I liked her best; nothing sexual.

Just then, Bart's wife, Soo Ki, belched, and an uncomfortable silence interrupted the conversations. I couldn't help chuckling. At least she hadn't farted—this time. A round peasant girl, loud and unsophisticated, I liked her for the honesty of her ways. I think she liked me, too.

Her husband, Bart, owned a wrecking yard. A tall, ungainly, dirty-fingered hulk of a man, he was only slightly smaller than myself. Besides the indelible grease under our nails and in the creases on our hands, we had a lot in common. Among the guys, I liked him best.

During our whole marriage, Meg's core of friends had always been Koreans. Where there were no Koreans, Meg had no friends until she found some. We husbands had no choice. Our wives spent so much time together that we had to become friends. Perhaps it was out of a sense of obligation; perhaps it was just making the best of a boring situation.

I didn't see it at the time how the guys would always cringe at my arrival. It never took me long to begin moaning, groaning, and bitching about all the problems of my life. Yes, on the husband end of our wives' little circle of friends, I was the most boring.

Forty years old. When did my life become such a perpetual peeve? How did I become such a flaming victim? Was I always this way? These were the questions I needed to be asking—but didn't.

My natural reaction to everything happening was to look for the problems that were—or might be—presented me, and to avoid them. Or was it just my life that I was avoiding? Even those times I dealt with my problems, it was always done by asking someone else to change to suit me, or by changing something about my environment. But to change something about me? No. Not a chance.

* * *

After moving to Farmington, we traded our old Mitchell boat for a new, eighteen-foot Tara with a 125-horse outboard. It became the new joy toy. We spent a lot of time at nearby Navajo Lake, and as before, there were occasional long weekends at Lake Powell.

The joy Meg, Shane, and I found in boating was perhaps what allowed us to ignore the emptiness of the rest of our lives. Our sex life had slowed to once every three or four weeks. It seemed to take more energy for me to ignite Meg's passion these days—more anyway than I wanted to spend. Yet, the urge was still strong in me, and the feelings I held for her still flared, hard and often.

For a while, I tried to kindle her passion with toys and batteries; a long line of vibrators, dildos, and other sexual aids paraded through our lives. For me, things did pick up. For Meg, it usually amounted to the same disinterested line: "Well, it's okay . . . if you like it. It just doesn't feel . . . you know . . . *natural*." Anything "not natural" for Meg carried the stigma of perversion. Out of desperation, I considered more natural alternatives.

The words came out of the dark one night, following a particularly remote encounter. I was lying beside her, aching to hold her in my post-lovemaking embrace, yet knowing that, as always, it would not be welcomed.

"Meg, have you ever thought about swinging?" The sheen of her quick glance was illuminated by the dim glow from her night lamp.

"Swinging?"

"Yeah, you know . . . finding another couple to share our bed?"

"Oh . . ." There followed a long moment in which Meg seemed to actually be considering. "Oh no, Jeff! I could never be okay with you making love to another woman."

I almost dropped the subject, and would have, except— something. Something felt amiss. Then I had it, *that silent moment.*

"Do you mean you would consider doing it if it were just with another man?"

I'd said it, but it felt weird to me, like it was something entirely different than what was initially proposed. But was it? I wondered if I could handle it—Meg with another man, and me not having the same freedom? Then, hearing the open consideration of it in her next word, "Maybe . . . ," I made my decision.

"Well, I guess I would be willing, if we both liked the guy as a person. Hell, it might be a real turn-on, the three of us together in one bed—"

"Oh no, Jeff!" Meg interrupted. The look now twisting her face was the one she used whenever I farted. "I could never do that together with you. How could you watch another man making love to me?"

"Watch?" The thought hadn't crossed my mind. "No, Meg. I meant make love together, at the same time, in the same bed . . . together. . . ." The disgust now had reached her eyes. Silence again descended— and lasted until I broke it. "Meg, it just wouldn't be okay with me for you to make it with another man if I was not a part of it, you know?"

The conversation was over. She turned to lie with her back toward me.

Me? I lie there unmoving, in awkward discomfort, mouth open with nothing to say in this most surreal of nights. An unexpected slickness surrounded my feelings now as I thought about her. Beyond our missing post-lovemaking embrace, I felt there was nothing left— nothing for me to hold.

* * *

My job at the tire shop steadily declined during the last two of the four years we were in Farmington. I'd threatened to quit enough times that the owner was reluctant to spend any more time or money sending me for training. In those days of the first computerized automotive systems, even the dealership mechanics were lost in the educational carnage of it all. As an independent, I had to have training, and on more than just one brand. Computer systems were changing at a brutal rate, and I had to be able to fix them all. Hell, even Meg's employer sent her and her assistant manager, Jerry, down to Albuquerque for training on their new restaurant computers—twice.

Often, I was forced to get out the manual and learn *how* the system worked before I could even begin to find out *why* it didn't. A good diagnostic tech knows the systems he works on. He uses books, of course, but mainly for reference in guiding him through the tests. But figuring out what part was where, just what it did, and how—that was the rest of the story. Self-training was time consuming and rather hit-and-miss. It was just not profitable for me or the shop. Finally, there came a time where, *once again*, I was promised training, and *once again*, it didn't happen.

It was late 1989, and the local economy sucked. The domestic oil exploration boom of the early eighties was over. The local oil fields, which supported much of Farmington's economy, were laying off heavily.

Once again, I did pretty much what I'd always done—gave my notice, hoping somehow they'd make it right and give me that training I so desperately needed. When my bluff was called, my life was so full of bile that I took the "chicken exit." Loading everything, I put my house on the market and blew that town—leaving nothing but a bad smell.

This time, I headed for Sin City, Nevada. The economy in Las Vegas was cooking, and I had a better job lined up with another major repair shop chain. Yes, one more time, I recycled my life. *Once again*,

I was running. Yet for me, everything I cared about in life was back there in Farmington—boating the lakes, riding the back trails, black powder shoots. . . .

And for Meg? There were our friends—well, hers anyway. And too, there was her prissy, newly rebuilt house with its ungodly expensive, super vortex equipped grill-top stove, surrounded by a sea of gleaming blue tile work. . . .

Me? I was one pissed-off hombre. But Meg? I never even stopped to wonder why Meg also was eager to go. From whom, or what, was she running? Or was she, too, just tired of my bitching?

It was only the two of us now. Shane went off to college that fall; our chick had left the nest. After all those years, Meg and I were finally alone. Though sorry to see him go, I'd been looking forward to being the only one in Meg's life, newlyweds once again—sex anywhere, anytime, anyhow.

Yet, somehow, it just wasn't happening. Meg was lost without Shane and didn't turn to me. And sex? She didn't seem to need it. Instead, we were farther apart than ever—well beyond the length of any dick. Well, mine anyway.

* * *

In Las Vegas, Meg found work as a waitress in a casino. She confided to me how she'd always wanted to be a masseuse and work for herself. She found a school, and I helped with her studies to the best of my ability. Muscle groups, tendons, and ligaments were pretty intense subjects—subjects about which I knew little and had even less interest. Although we'd grown apart, it wasn't that I didn't still cherish her or feel a need to support her.

I like to think that my belief in her made a difference, but Meg had to do the learning on her own. God, I was proud when she graduated and eventually settled into her new occupation, working with a Korean friend.

* * *

This was where our lives were in early September three years later, when we met Bart and Soo Ki for a few days, boating at Lake Powell. It was the first time any of us had been out on the south end of the lake. Such a long time it was since I'd enjoyed the slick-rock canyons, deep waters, and red sands of my most treasured of places.

The day still carried the bright smolder of summer, and the cherished aroma of sage and cedar hung tranquil on the still air as the Mickelsons and their two teenaged daughters met us in the parking lot of Wahweap Marina, near Page, Arizona. Getting out of our truck, I turned and slapped my grimy mechanic's hand into his own equally grime-infested one. As his free hand grasped my shoulder, I grinned. *Hell, at least this one husband actually likes me.* Then, catching sight of his hand still clasping mine, I felt a pang of jealousy. *His wife would never fault him, no matter how dirty his hands might appear to be.*

Looking out at the naked, raw beauty of Lake Powell spread before us, with its majestic, sandstone cliffs and occasional looming butte, I asked, "Well, where do you want to start?"

"Let's just wing it. . . ."

We spent most of the first day finding a suitable site to set up our camp, finally settling on a private little cove in Gunsight Canyon. Like the rest of the lake, it was a beautiful spot, flanked as it was on three sides by the magnificent, orange, sandstone cliffs of the Wingate formation—very effective for sheltering our cove from the wind.

Setting up our tents on the sandy beach, we fixed and ate dinner. Afterward, we sat around the campfire. Along with the nostalgic scent of cedar smoke, we chewed over old times before zonking out for the night in our sleeping bags.

The early morning air over the glass of the lake lent to the feeling that the whole world was paused in expectant wait, solely for our pleasure. It seemed to lend a certain fresh hunger to our bacon-and-egg breakfast. Then Bart, his two teenaged daughters, and I took their boat out to explore the local side canyons, while Meg and Soo Ki visited in camp.

We were rounding a bend between the narrow sandstone walls of West Canyon, when suddenly, we found ourselves facing two very attractive—and very naked—women sunning themselves on a houseboat anchored tightly in the crook of the next bend. I'd been sitting back just enjoying the scenery, and continued to do so without pause as we cruised slowly by, merely smiling and nodding to the ladies, who calmly smiled and nodded back.

Bart, who was busy steering the boat while at the same time averting his face, nearly ran us into the rock wall. I couldn't fault him. He was being true to his own beliefs, which said: A member of the bishopric in his ward of the Mormon Church didn't look at naked women—especially not in front of his daughters.

After lunch, we all piled into Bart's boat for a little ski tubing in the calm waters of our cove. That ski tube was my favorite "boat toy," favored well above skis or ski boards. It was just a big, rubber donut with two handles, measuring sixty inches across, and was filled with enough air to turn my face purple every time I blew it up. We tied it to the ski rope using a wide band of nylon strapping.

I liked to ride it best while up on both knees. Sometimes, getting it bouncing, I monkey-jumped it over the waves. Other times, I would pull up on the handles, raising the front until the tube was catching little but air.

As the boat would turn, it acted as a fulcrum. The tube, out at the far end, would slither to the side. If the boat turned into an ever-decreasing radius or—God forbid—swept quickly back in the other direction, the speeds that tube reached were breathtaking. At those times, with the wind and spray funneling through the donut hole directly into my face, I'd rear back on one handle and lean into the corners to keep from digging into the waves.

This day, it became a contest between Bart and me to see who could most spectacularly shake the other off the tube. Finally, with the tube crossing the wake at seventy plus, he won. Like a flat stone flung, I found myself skipping across the water on my back. Problem was, the last skip ended too quickly, almost as if the lake had reached up and snatched me into its depths. Something tore in my right calf, and there came a burning sensation. Then, buoyed by my life vest, I bobbed back to the surface.

Ah, but nothing so small could ever take a macho man like me out of the action, now could it? I ignored it—just belched out what water I could, cleared my suddenly soggy sinuses, and waved an "okay" to Bart. He circled the tube back, and I climbed on for another ride.

The trip back to Las Vegas two days later was painful. The leg, now noticeably swollen, hurt whenever I sat still for any period of time. We dropped off our boat and gear at home, then caught a sore night's sleep between the luxury of sheets. Daybreak found us off on a six-hour drive to visit my parents in American Fork, Utah.

The leg was worse. I could only drive for about an hour before stopping. Walking seemed to make the swelling and pain subside temporarily. We arrived at my parents' home, and I'd just set our bags down in the middle of the living room when it first happened. There was a sudden tightness in my chest, almost like something I'd swallowed was stuck about halfway down, and a strange, weak dizziness.

So what? I shrugged mentally. *It's been an eventful few days since we started our vacation. Besides, the elevation is higher here.*

There I stood, six feet four and weighing about two hundred fifty pounds of mostly work-hardened muscle—nearly invincible. Besides, I've rarely been sick. *Hell, whatever this is, it's nothing.* Catching the flicker of Meg's eyes, I smiled and finished my shrug physically.

* * *

At work, two weeks later—still in denial—I climbed from beneath a truck and stood up. Instantly, my vision blurred and filled with bright pinpricks of light. Staggering to the service manager's desk, I collapsed onto one of the customer stools.

"It's gotta cracked seam on the fuel tank," I reported, trying to stay focused on the job between gasps. "Not something I want to mess with." For some reason, my head wouldn't quit spinning, and the air seemed devoid of oxygen. "B-best send him to a welding shop. Needs to be empty . . . and f-filled with inert gas . . . b-before w-welding." It seemed so dark in the shop, and my arms felt like rubber as I leaned on the counter. The wheezing gasp in my voice was somehow embarrassing.

"Jeff . . ." The service manager's face swam before mine. "You don't look so good," Bob said. "You better come in and sit down." He wedged my arm over his shoulder, hustled me into the waiting room, and dropped me like a half-filled potato sack into a chair. I sat there a long moment, just blinking and squinting through the sea of tiny flashes swarming before my eyes. What was he saying?

"Jeff! Stay with me here. Do you need an ambulance?"

"What? No, I'm okay. Just stood up a little too fast . . . you know?"

"Look, I'm calling Dr. Laring. His office is just down the street. I want you to go and see him, okay?"

"Yeah, well . . ." I looked around, just now noticing how the others in the shop were circled around me, staring. "Okay, I guess that's best. I am feeling kinda weird. Look, call Meg and have her come and get me. And uh . . . thanks, Bob." Suddenly, it seemed important that I not be a bother.

A few minutes later, Bob pulled his car up to the front door. "I'm taking you now," he said, hoofing me into it. "Meg will meet you there later."

* * *

For over an hour, I sat in his doctor's waiting room. By then, I was feeling much better. Dr. Laring turned out to be a tall, thin man about my own age. His black hair was balding and resembled a freshly thinned sugar beet field on top. I wondered how long it would take for his transplants to fill in.

After a cursory once-over, he hooked me up for a treadmill EKG to check my heart. Fifteen seconds later, I was collapsed into a chair. Dr. Laring's skinny butt was all I could see through the swarm of tiny flashbulbs as he hung out the doorway.

"Nitroglycerin! Now . . . STAT!" Doctors do get a little overexcited about patients dying in their office; bad for business, you know.

He put the pills in my hand. I couldn't see how many, what with the swarming lights. I slapped them in my mouth and followed with a paper cup of water. Was it his hands or mine that sloshed it all over my leg? In only moments, my sight was clearing and the room no longer spun.

"I'm calling you an ambulance and admitting you to the hospital—"

"No, Doc; not paying for no ambulance," I interrupted.

"Oh, yes you—"

"Won't." I finished for him. "Look, my wife's here and the hospital's only a block away. She can get me there faster and for a lot less money."

That seemed to calm him, and maybe it was also because it would get me gone faster. Bad for business when patients who walk in get hauled off on a stretcher. An hour later, I was bunking out in intensive care at Sunrise Hospital.

It took them until the following afternoon to sort it out. There was a torn vein in my leg. Kneeling on it in cold water caused a blood clot to form. Now some of it had broken loose and was lodged in my lungs. The only treatment was total bed rest and blood thinners to dissolve the clots. Until then, I was in grave danger—indeed, in danger of needing a grave.

~ *Looking Back* ~

With all the jobs I've left, it's clear: I've always had a huge need to feel wanted. Most of this world has this same need, and there is nothing wrong with having "needs." Everyone has them. It's just that many of us go about filling them in ways that are not healthy. Some with this same need might beg for the approval of others—become "kiss-asses" and give of themselves with clear expectations. They play to the guilt of others: "I've been so good to you. Now you gotta be good to me."

Me? I did a great rendition of the Lone Ranger and his trusty sidekick, Meg—always in the hope someone would rescue me, tell me I was needed and wanted, and ask me to stay. I played to both the guilt and pity of others. Life doesn't work very well that way, unless you like finding yourself camping out in the cold.

There are much healthier ways of getting our needs met than playing those silly control games humanity so likes to play. If I'd known about, and followed, Spiritual Law, I'd simply have given what I wanted to have returned: I'd have appreciated others, I'd have been of service to them, and I'd have cared about them. And I'd have done it all honestly and without expectation. Now that it seemed I might be doing the ultimate Lone Ranger act on the *real* stage of life, suddenly I became aware of just how few would care. Worse, I was about to find, of those who would, how pitifully little it would be. As sure as gravity, the law is clear. You do get back what you put out, though not always when or from whom it is expected.

~ *In the Present with Big D* ~

"Mind if I break into the service?" Big D's interruption comes with a knobby tap on my shoulder. "Wouldn't want your congregation to fall asleep, y'know?"

"Yeah, Big D, I see what you mean." I reach toward my computer keyboard, thinking back over this last bit. "It does sound a little preachy . . . shhh-it!" I've long since learned to accept his gentle prods almost as quickly as those not-so-gentle ones.

"No, no—don't delete it. What you say is true enough, and if your readers don't accept the preacher in you by now, you know they're no longer reading."

I feel his bony hand on my shoulder, reminding me of one of those crane machines kids used to feed with quarters in hopes of grabbing the one truly great toy out of the pile of cheap junk. Such machines could be found at the entrances of nearly all supermarkets, way back before the days of computer games. *How many adults will hook this book and feel they got the one really great prize?*

Big D answers my unspoken thought. "They won't if you don't show that one *really great* gem of honesty here." His sudden, clutching claw emphasizes his words. "You left out the most important part."

"Whoa, hey!" My chair swivels around almost of its own accord to meet his smoky swirl. It is so familiar now, as are the twin fires of his eyes and fixed, piano-key grin. The rest flows seamlessly into the blackness of the night. "I've admitted to stuff here in this chapter that most couples have considered—at least in their minds—and some have even done. But few men would ever have the balls to admit it."

"I'm not talking about your great balls, but rather about your other gift—the one you've shined off acknowledging, except for once, in this writing."

"What 'other gift?'"

"I speak of the one others tend to label 'moose milk, magnets, and woo-woo.'" Big D's lower jaw drops slightly with his soft chuckle. "Even you discount it more often than not."

"What . . . you mean like metaphysics and intuitive stuff?"

"Exactly! Yours is the power to feel the energy of others."

"Yes, I'm aware of that." I shrug. "But what has that to do with this chapter?"

"For one, it has to do with Meg and her affair with her assistant, Jerry."

"What?"

"Yes, you knew about it from that first training trip they made together down to Albuquerque. You felt it, and you knew."

"Look, I made up my mind years ago to trust her. . . ."

"Yes, and you did." Big D's voice drops nearly to a whisper. "But the truth remains: You knew. Why else did you question her about it?"

"She said she didn't, and I trusted her."

"No! You accepted her lie." Big D's words now come evenly spaced and hard, like his knuckles, now gently thumping a cadence on my chest. "You didn't . . . want . . . to know."

"Why, Big D? Why would I hide from it?"

"Because he satisfied her. With him, she allowed herself to orgasm."

"But how can that be? Didn't you tell me how she could never be so vulnerable—"

"To you! With him, no matter what she did, there was no love, no respect to lose." His words and gaze now soften. "Too bad. Even her giving him the gift of her orgasm was something you had the courage to face . . . if she would have just somehow let you be a part of it."

"Ah, God, Big D! If she fucked around with him, how could I blame her? I almost did the same with Mandy."

"What you would not face was never about blame, or shame, or even cheating." Big D's voice now comes lovingly, though his words sear me to the core. "Again, it was about the distance between you." With his next words, again comes that gentle thumping cadence. "A distance you no longer wanted to—or even could—close." He pauses one long moment. I have no response. "Jeff, you grew away from her long before the hospital, where you thought you first met me. The events there served to show you who Meg was, and for the first time, you truly saw her. But it was *not* the first time for you and me."

"What? What do you mean?"

"I mean . . . your power extends well past the ability to feel the energy of others. You feel the energy of your higher self. Everyone has the ability to look outside themselves and use blame to keep themselves blind to it—and to their true responsibilities. But you? You feel it stronger than most. In your cycles here on earth, you've known me before. You are an 'older soul.' This cycle you've always felt, and heard, and sometimes you've even taken direction from me, though often, you mislabeled it as cowardice."

"Cowardice?"

"Why do you think you felt such shame when letting go—when divorcing Meg? And later, letting go of your parents after they disowned you for divorcing her? And then there was a child in Fry Canyon who, at the time, had not the physical strength to climb the cliffs like his older brother."

"W-what?"

"That's right, Jeff. You did none of it out of cowardice. In Fry Canyon, where you first came to believe yourself a coward—hell, that was just me, protecting you." He chuckles, and the glow from his empty eye sockets seems somehow misty. "Yes, you were afraid of heights. But that never stopped you when you knew you had to step through your fear. Cowards don't step through their fears, but then, you know that, Jeff. Don't you think that applies to you?"

I can only stare at him, my mouth agape. He continues.

"Jeff, look. *'Life is always perfect, just as it is.'* You know that law?"

"Well . . . yeah . . . sure. It's been mentioned several times here lately. Why do you keep reminding me?"

"Because you *don't* know it. If you did, then nothing in life would ever bother you—no regrets. You *do* have a lot of regrets. Well, don't you?"

"C'mon, Big D, doesn't everybody?"

Yes . . . and this can be called the *Law of Acceptance.* It's only those things in your past that happened—*the ones you don't accept*—that are the cause of all your mental pain. *'You are the Creator.'* I'm sure you know this law?"

"Course, it's the big one, the law most of the others are based on."

"That's right. It means: *'There is nothing in your life that didn't consciously, or unconsciously, require YOU for it to be there.'* The *unconscious* part is your *soul's* doing. Do you know that?"

"Well, yeah." My mouth hangs open. *Where is he going with this simple shit?*

"Then know this, Jeff: Even the whining, blubbering, flaming victim you became during these last chapters was never a coward." His jaw bones gape wide as he chortles in glee. "Hell, that was who you needed to see yourself as being . . . to be ready."

"Ready?" *What—the—fu-u-u-ck?* "Ready for what?"

"For that time in the hospital when I ripped away your blindfold of blame and self-deception. Yes, *that* was who you needed to be *then* to become who you are *now*. Dontcha see?" He stops to pin me with his gaze. "I am the Angel of Death. But Jeff, death is always your choice. And for most, it is an unconscious one. That's right"—he flashes an ivory grin—"it is *your soul's* choice." He pauses, the glow of his sight intent on mine. "It's nothing I haven't told you several times before. Maybe now you're ready to hear."

I am the Angel of Death only because—his voice, with its bottom-of-the-barrel tone, now moans with infinite intimacy inside my head—***I am also your soul, remember?***

When life squeezes you, don't expect orange juice. You get to see what's really inside you. Remember, *you are the creator*, and that's why you arranged to be squeezed. There is something you need to see—in you.

Redneck Spirituality—Book Two

Epilogue

The Ass End

~ *Once again, back full circle.* ~

"No! Definitely not!" Dr. Laring's orders were chillingly specific. "Not even for that. If you do, you might be found dead on the pot. You will stay in bed and use the bedpan."

A wrong move now, quite literally, would never be repeated. My legs were to be up on the bed, and not dangling off the side for any reason. Especially, I was not to walk around—not even those three steps to the commode.

Since the age of three, when I had my tonsils out, the use of a bedpan has been something I would do anything, risk anything, to avoid. I still remember the incident. I was little, the bedpan, awkward. I slipped; it spilled, overturning onto the bed. The nurse launched into a tirade of humiliation, which lasted all the while she was cleaning and changing the repugnant mess from all over me and the bed.

"You stupid . . . filthy . . . little beast! They should keep you in the basement. You don't deserve to be up here with the others." Most of the half dozen or so children in that hospital ward stayed silent throughout her rant. Only a few dared the glare of her glance to snicker, but once she'd gone? Well, I became the center of their attention. Kids can say the meanest things. Me? I wanted to curl up into a little ball and disappear.

I didn't want to be center stage in that play. And yet, aren't we all just actors on the stage of life, with only one way to get off? The incident resulted out of a natural function of life, something of which no one needed to be embarrassed. I stood there alongside my bed, hanging my head, bedclothes smeared and smelly with my excrement. I could have risen to the occasion, bowed to the audience, made faces at them, and clowned around until everyone—maybe even nurse Cruella—was laughing.

Still, the way it happened was perfect for me to become who I am right now. Yes, for my life to unfold the way it did, much hung on the humiliation of that very moment. For me, to find this joy now required it all.

A few years later, I found myself in a Salt Lake City hospital, facing this same nemesis. I did not survive the rigors of primitive, exquisitely rugged Fry Canyon completely unscathed. As Mike put it, I "busted a ball" and needed a hernia operation. There was some scar tissue, and the operation was more involved than expected. I awoke back in the ward, alone, except for the other inmates.

With the curiosity of an eight-year-old, I naturally had to peel the bandage for a look. What lay underneath came as a shock. The wound stretched across the left side of my abdomen, up and down for more than six inches. All puckered up and clamped with wicked-looking metal staples, it was nothing like the two inches they told me to expect. And I hurt badly. Worse, I had to go . . . real bad!

But to use that bedpan—and again, in an open ward? Somehow, I managed to release the side gate, crawl out of bed, and hobble over to the john, where I promptly locked myself in for the duration of a good, long, painfully constipated dump.

The nurse came in and, finding me missing, began flailing at the bathroom door. "Jeffrey. Jeffrey Williams! Are you in there?"

"Yes, I'm here. Lemme alone. I'm okay!"

Surprisingly, she did. For the rest of my time there, I managed to continue to do my business when the nurse wasn't around—and she allowed it. I guess she saw my level of commitment in the price I was willing to pay in pain and respected me.

Yet, here I was, nearly forty years later, a big boy now, and again facing the dreaded bedpan—only the price was no longer one of ridicule, nor even of pain. Rather, the price was now life itself. Would I use the damned thing? No way! Besides, using a toilet was the only way to wipe properly.

I was always a good wiper. Being married to a clean freak like Meg, any skid stains showing up in my shorts, I was sure to hear about. Somehow I kept it all zipped, never quite understanding the depth of my feelings about what she considered my more loutish characteristics, as illuminated by her disdain. Facing death on the pot was easy, *especially* when the dreaded bedpan was coupled with her contempt.

Meg came to visit that sixth evening and, as usual, took it as her duty to give me my sponge bath. We hadn't talked much since the diagnosis. Meg only came in for about an hour after work, and I did not ask her to forfeit sleep. Somehow, her work required longer hours these days—busy season. Well, that's what she said.

Death now permeated my life, and I was in a fervent, though outwardly calm, contemplation of the possibilities. Meg? I don't know. Perhaps it was the opposite for her. She'd not spoken of it. Was she in an equally fervent denial of it all? Neither of us spoke now. It seemed we were both lost in our own individual thoughts as Meg began my bath that day.

She worked slower than normal. Methodically, she soaped, rinsed, and wiped me dry. I watched her. Now over forty, her still-smooth, trim figure always brought delight to my senses, and her exotic Asian features now seem more beautiful than I could ever remember. *Big D, if you do take me now, this woman will be the most missed of all my life.* The monitor's sudden, few skipping beeps were as an agreement.

That the Angel had answered in that manner did not come now as any surprise. Although no one else knew of it, throughout the long hours alone, Big D and I conversed often. He now seemed almost as a friend. Still, agreement or no, he was the Angel of Death, and he was right there at my side. I was sure of it.

Wordlessly, Meg motioned for me to turn over. Like washing dishes, she continued her thorough job, lulling me with her warm, soapy massage. Then she moved down past my back.

"Ughhhh! Do you always have to be so filthy? Why can't you wipe your butt better?"

My whole world rocked with me as I rolled back and looked over my shoulder, first at her accusing scowl, then at the tiny, tattletale, yellowish streak across the white washcloth. The shame and embarrassment of that three-year-old—all of it—came flooding back. Dropping my eyes from hers, I replied automatically, "I'm sorry, dear . . . I will."

Yet, inside, there came a wrench, and what started as humiliation turned to sudden, resentful fury. It burned at my gut no less painfully than if I'd been impaled. For the first time in our marriage, I didn't want Meg touching, speaking to, or even being there with me. Though different, it was akin to one of those physical pains when one screams at those who would touch him, believing that the least bit more sensation would be too much.

In that moment, I died. The person I was, ended. Death is only a shift of consciousness. I shifted, only in this death, I kept my body. The person I became was no longer running, no longer telling himself lies.

The truth? God how it hurt! So much so that the person I became would have welcomed a quick, even painful, physical death. Yet not quite, for all those hours communing with Big D served to point out that I was not a person who could go easily into the grave. I simply did not like who I saw myself as being—*this cowardly liar.*

Now willing to face the truth, I realized Meg was not truly loving and accepting of me, and that was something this person I was becoming would require. In fact, I now saw it was the one great lie I'd always told myself every single day, just to get by. And I knew, too, without a doubt, that no matter how much I might want it to be so, Meg never loved me the way I wanted to be loved. Meg, as if given the vocal order, departed right after my bath. Not a single word more did she speak to me, and I, none to her. I was glad when she was gone and thought a lot about that. Clearly, she knew how serious the situation was. She knew tomorrow might not find me still living. The ICU is a deciding place between life and death.

I was her security. I'd always known it, but never before felt it. She was afraid of being without me. All those years together, she'd always been afraid of being alone. Why hadn't I seen it? She didn't want my love, only the security it afforded.

Now life was squeezing her. When you squeeze oranges, orange juice comes out. Hell, what else would be in them? Just so, I was now seeing what was in her, what she truly felt and thought about me. Now, with Big D squeezing me, I was also seeing what was in me.

She'd always acted like she was disgusted with me. Yet, it was I who chose to view it as an act, wanting to believe that, in reality, she respected and cherished me. Now, finally willing to accept the truth, I kept asking myself: How could she feel this way about me—disgusted? If I died tonight, was this how she wanted to say goodbye . . . forever? And me, feeling glad to see her gone, would this be me saying it to her?

No, my physical body did not die. And yet, we most surely had both, just so, said goodbye. The consciousness I once was, the one who had loved her so blindly all those years, had indeed died. Only just had I come to know Big D, and while he seemed inclined to give me a reprieve, my life was tentative. Nothing now but ***honesty and courage*** gave any possibility of a future. Of that, Big D was clear. Conversely, those lies no longer had reason; failing in honesty, there would be no future.

Life . . . honesty? For me now, they were the same word, only now spelled differently. The breath of it rippled through the fog of my love, giving me a glimpse of who Meg was in her reality.

And of me? Looking back at it all today? Try this—the real truth: ***I needed Meg with a passion that shook my world.*** For twenty-five years, I needed her to love me, then needed to experience Big D, before I finally began loving and accepting myself. Only then could my need know some satisfaction. Only then could I truly love her—honestly, without any fearful need.

Yet, for Meg, in the months to follow, it was not love that she seemed to see coming from me, but rather, what the world terms as selfishness. Self-love or selfishness—it didn't matter. I still found it impossible to satisfy her fearful needs; just as before, only my lies had satisfied mine.

My world is not out there—it's in here! Yes, the answer to everything is within! Yet, within is an individually personal journey. Some go, some don't. And some would rather die first. It is the journey to meet a hero who resides where few have the courage to go.

Of Meg and me now? For her, I cannot say. Though we live in the same city, we have not seen one another but twice in over three years—and then, only because Shane was in town. Meg wanted it that way. And still, I feel no animosity. If she does, it has never been seen by me. For me, it has been time enough to know a sorrow such as I never dreamed possible. For her? I don't know.

Hell, it doesn't matter if the reality of that love was once only my own medieval creation, complete with helpless maiden, flashing sword, white horse, and even a dragon or two to slay for my ego's sake.

It doesn't matter if hers was entirely different—or exactly the same. It only matters that for a time here on Earth, our souls traveled together, and our hearts touched one another's and learned something of love. Certainly, mine did.

Oh God, Big D! I thank you for these last moments of truth. In the end, when the beliefs upon which I based my life proved to be the lies of others too cowardly to face the truth of their own, there was you. When my life was nothing but ashes and pain, I had my motorcycle and the desert—and I had you, showing me the truth.

My mourning has run its race, two wheels thundering across the blacktop, eighty-seven horses unleashing their fury to the twist of my grip. Exactly so, at an insane pace, I screamed challenge to the lightning, and my tears ran, drop for drop, with the passing desert monsoons. Then howling on into the parched desert air, I shed my agony into its eternal wastes, like the diamondback of its skin. The lump in my throat eventually cracked and crumbled away. Now my memory of Meg is of love—my love.

~ *In the Present with Big D* ~

It is done. My search through my past for the "who" I am is finished. Is it now time to create the "who" I want to be? Somehow, I feel it's no longer necessary.

Certainly, through all this, I've changed—realized things about me that amaze and thrill. Yet, sitting here now in the darkest hours of a new morning, there is only the dim radiance of my computer monitor, and I am somehow empty. I call out once more to the depths of my being: "Big D! Where are you now?"

His voice comes with a richness of tone I have never heard from him before, and a gentle reassurance. "I'm here . . . I'm with you." Amidst the glow of my screen there is a gathering of light, which condenses into a vague form that quickly expands to fill the space in front of me. My desk, keyboard, and screen—all of it—seem to have been replaced with Big D and me, alone in the desert. Yet, the figure that focuses into sharp relief has not the familiar blackness and grinning white bones of Big D. This one's flowing robes look like they are woven of spun spider silk, each strand of which carries a slightly different hue of neon glow.

"Big D?"

"Yes. I'm here . . ."

"But you're glowing, and you look just like the 'Jesus' in the picture that hung on the wall of the chapel of the Mormon Church where I grew up. You share that same courageous, calm nobility—only with my own face."

"Perhaps your reality of me has changed."

"How can that be?"

"Sure, Jeff. Each man creates seeing me in the reality of which they view their life. You? You've always seen your life as spartan, meager, hard, bare bones, stripped of nearly all joy." He chuckles, regarding me with eyes that sparkle as he shrugs. "Don't sweat it. Some see me as monstrous, dripping with puss and decay—the incarnate of all that is fearful and evil. Not many ever grow to a space where, in the end, they will see me as you now do. Indeed, few alive have ever seen their soul."

I do not answer; his statement requires none. Instead, I bask in the peaceful radiance of it. Yet still, there is that strange emptiness that cries to be filled. . . .

Big D continues, "Why is it, do you think, you now feel emptied?"

"I'm not sure. It's almost as if the glass from which I've been drinking is now drained, and I don't know how or where to fill it." I pause a moment, reflecting deeply, then add, "And I feel my thirst building."

"Of course." His tone continues low and understanding. "You have emptied yourself of nearly all the baggage from your past. You no longer feel the energy of it driving you." He chuckles softly now. "And you no longer bear its weighty burden."

"But what do I do about this emptiness?"

"Look into your life now . . . imagine it in your mind just so: as a glass."

I feel his strong hand on my shoulder and am aware of a comforting brightness swirling around me. Before me materializes a glass, held steady in his fleshy grasp.

"Now, what do you see?" he continues.

Looking into the glass, I see a liquid that shines with its own luminescent, multicolored glow. "I don't know . . . it is so beautiful! What is it?"

From beyond the glass, there is a twinkling in the blue depths of Big D's eyes, so different, yet no less familiar than the glow of ruby before. I hear unrestrained joy with his next words.

"It is your life—our life! This is what you've filled it with since you met me there in that hospital." His gaze has locked onto mine, and I feel a comforting warmth. "Ah, yes! You have put so much beauty into your life since then. And with the completion of your past now, there is so much room for more!"

"But how do I do that?"

Big D's grin explodes into laughter. "Well, you can begin with this book . . . your story!"

"What do you mean?"

Big D's face moves in close. "You must let go of it!"

"But I don't understand. You helped me write it." *Surely he doesn't mean for me to just throw it away.* "Goddammit . . . it's special!"

"Throw it out of your life—out to the universe. It will either live or die, according to what it may come to mean to those who will read it. Where it is concerned, you have done your part."

The swirling luminescence of him whirls merrily away, a glowing glass in one hand and a book in the other. Like a discus, he hurls the book outward into the night. Out it sails, to explode in the far distance like a thousand Fourth of July starbursts. Then, gliding back on unseen feet, he again stands before me. The un-spilled glass still held in one hand, he soberly holds it out toward me.

"This is what is important." He gestures with it toward the billion sparkles of the book, still drifting on the night sky. "That book . . . hell, that book will touch others where the truth of their own lives is similar to yours. Might even give them the opportunity to dump some of their own shitty burdens." He brings the glass back before me. "This next book is the one that will give others the ability to change something, to see the nuts and bolts of how it's done!" His blue-eyed gaze now flares brightly. "Will you write it? Will you show them how to flush that toilet—to unload their shitty burdens?"

"I don't know . . . I have so much I want to do!" My mind seems overwhelmed just contemplating it all. The thought of all the hours already spent writing . . . the driving need to get it all out. Yes, it was a source of satisfaction, my having accomplished it. But now I have to ask myself: would writing further, telling the rest of my story—would it be a "take" from the rest of my life? And after all, he is *asking* this of me, not *telling* me.

"Oh God, Big D, there is so much I want to do! I want to ride my motorcycle in the wind through the craggy heights of the mountains and the red rock sandstone canyons of the desert. I want to fish, and camp, and to know the love of women. Once I find that special one, I want to love her even more. And I still haven't discovered my purpose in life—"

"Whoa there!" Big D chuckles. "Look into the glass! It is all here. Have you not poured into it all your heart's passion, your joy, even this book? Are you not following your destiny? You may not yet see it clearly, but so long as what you put into this glass is of your passion and joy, you cannot help but fulfill your purpose in life." He falls silent, giving me a moment to contemplate his words.

"So will you write it?" His eyes bore into mine. "Will you acknowledge that these private thoughts do make a difference in this world?"

"I don't know if it's in me." I duck my head, avoiding. "I still feel emptied and incomplete."

"Here!" Big D passes me the glass. "Drink! This is from where true nourishment comes. Drink of the joys of your life!"

I take the glass from him and, raising it to my lips, pause. From it, I inhale an essence—heady, like the most intimate of womanhood. Drinking it down, the taste is like the nectar of sex with someone one could only call *soul mate*—erotically exquisite like that.

With it comes a rushing, as if once again, I am on the back of my motorcycle, banking along the rim above Zion Canyon with nothing between me and the precipice of life.

Pure joy blankets the back of my throat and tickles my nose, and I am filled with an energy—a fulfillment such as I've never known. For an unknown space of eternity, my life swirls in weightless bliss.

Then, when the whirl subsides, the room is as it was before. My computer screen still glares before me, and the clock in its corner says 2 a.m.—just as before. Softly, from the far reaches of my mind, comes Big D's parting whisper: ***This is your own true sacrament . . . drink of it often.***

Soul of an Eagle

of an

THE SEQUEL
NOVEL TO
The Courage of a Butterfly
by Edmond E. Frank

**The Sequel is Now Available
October 2021**

ABOUT THE AUTHOR

Astute people immediately turn to this section, wanting to know the author's credentials, those credentials being the determining factor for reading. You might ask yourself: Is it possible your soul put this book in your hands, knowing there is something here that you need? Because if that is so, then my credentials are impeccable—don't you think?

Or, maybe you don't think? Not everyone is spiritually aware, and this book fits into that venue. But what if your soul—that spiritual part of you—*is* trying to tell you something? Are you listening? When your life is in chaos, you need to become aware. Maybe this book is in your hands for that purpose. Your soul will only put up with so much of your shit before it hits the reset button. I've been there—and just maybe, that is all you need to know about me.

For those who may have found these words insulting, just know: If it's in your face, and stinks, that's when your soul is pointing out what you most need to see. Guaranteed.

Back then, when death was in my face, I'm convinced that's exactly what my soul was showing me. Big D may be a fictional character in this book—to you. But in the reality of my life, it was different. While I never saw him in person, nor heard him audibly, I assure you, I knew his presence—INTIMATELY. Crazy? Maybe.

When you're face-to-face with death, you have no time for lies. Then, the longer you may live, the more you begin to realize just how much of your life was premised on lies. Most are lies your parents, society, and even your religions have dumped on you. Lies coming from such respected sources are usually accepted as truth.

But it's the ones you tell to yourself—consciously or unconsciously—that allow you to get through the day without having to change your whole life. Those are the ones that stink so bad that you immediately get honest and knowingly accept whatever changes may come. Of course, none of this could happen for me without a reprieve from the Angel of Death.

If you read this book, you'll remember about my own fear of heights and understand how my lie concerned courage and my lack thereof. With Death's reprieve, the first thing I did was to go sky diving. Then there were the lies I told myself about my wife; those took a little more time.

Meanwhile, there were the lies of my forefathers, passed down through generations and meant only to conform me to their standards. Then there were lies of society, meant also to conform and control how I lived my life outside my family. Lastly, there were the lies of my Mormon faith. Theirs really were a stretch, and no less controlling— controlling my mind and pocketbook.

They all wanted control of me in their lives. But the truth for me lay only in controlling me in my own. The only thing others needed to be concerned with was: Do I control my life in the energy of love, or not? That is the one question about me that rightly concerns everyone.

Such a simple thing, it took me some time searching to realize its truth. I began by seeking for it among other people who no longer bought into those lies—people who saw life differently. Those people I found in The New Age.

Many of these folks believed in moose milk and magnets— things to which they attributed strange powers. And who's to say some of that shit wasn't nurturing, or even valid. Shit is that stuff that has nurtured you. If you accept it, it becomes YOUR shit and doesn't stink. But do moose milk and magnets work? I don't know.

For me, it was among such open-minded people that I discovered the Spiritual Laws—and New Thought. With that, there came experiential self-help seminars—those that were based on Spiritual Laws.

For the next twenty-five years, I studied those laws everywhere I could find them. I went to the seminars, and then went again, only on the support teams. I realized that my life could only make a difference in this world through serving others—others also searching for the truth.

After that came Coach University. I became a Certified Personal Life Coach and started a coaching practice. Problem was, I was not good at public speaking, and not even Toastmasters could fix that. Coaches need to do a lot of speaking engagements for the purpose of head-hunting clients—big turnoff.

So, for the last twelve years, I drove Para Transit buses serving the disabled while I wrote this and other books. Are these Spiritual Laws the truth of life? I believe so. They WORK; the lies don't.

In the beginning of this section, I got into your face about the soul thing. That was for a reason. IF this book is in your hand, and IF you are NOT searching for the truth—IF you don't yet even see the lies, then the only reason you are holding this book is because your soul picked it up while you weren't looking.

And remember: Your soul has control of the reset button. . . .

NOTE:

This book is written under my name, Edmond E. Frank—as will be its sequel. The narrative of this book in essence follows the true story of my life. If you read it for more than just what needs to be termed "its fictionalized story," you may be interested in the non-fiction books I've written. They are authored under the name—E. Egorhh Frank.

OTHER WORKS

Authored as Edmond E. Frank

The Soul of an Eagle—THE SEQUEL
A Butterfly's Transformation—IN POETRY
An Eagle's Flight—IN POETRY

Authored as E. Egorhh Frank

Redneck Spirituality—THE SERIES
Book One
Book Two
Book Three
Book Four
Book Five
Books One and Two Combined Edition
(In print form only)

NOTES_____

NOTES

NOTES_____

NOTES

www.ingramcontent.com/pod-product-compliance
Lightning Source LLC
Chambersburg PA
CBHW032001120726
47898CB00005BA/1447